The Author

Margaret Ricketts was an 85-year-old retired teacher when she wrote the main part of this book but it was completed over 2 years later. She has been a one- parent family for the past fifty years, bringing up four children and having a very successful teaching career. She has always been fascinated by what motivates people and the book reflects her interest in this.

Acknowledgements

I should like to record my grateful thanks to Sue Brewer my copyist, Caroline Mylon my editor and Karen Dowie my illustrator for their hard work and dedication to the success of my books.

OTHER MEMOIRS AND MAGINATIONS NOVELS

Summer Sunshine

Autumn Leaves

MEMOIRS AND MAGINATIONS NOVEL

Margaret Ricketts

Winter Frost

Michael Terence
Publishing

First published in paperback by
Michael Terence Publishing in 2021
www.mtp.agency

ISBN 9781800941694

Cover image
by Karen Dowie

Cover design
Copyright © 2021 Michael Terence Publishing

I dedicate this book to my son Philip for his constant encouragement and his ability to navigate the wonders of technology on my behalf.

The story so far:

Book One, "Summer Sunshine," tells the story of Adam Richards, returning to the family fold after an eleven-year absence. His wife, Leah takes him back after hearing how his shame at abandoning his wife and four young children weighed on him so heavily that he felt unable to contact them and lived a lonely existence, whilst working hard to make something of himself. He returns to Swanton, the market town in Oxfordshire, where he used to live with Leah and they are reunited. They soon realise that the love they felt for each other has not faded and they renew their relationship. Adam also reconnects with two of his four children: Peter who is married with two young children and Alice whom Adam steps up to save from an abusive marriage with William.

At the end of Book One, Alice is on the brink of a nervous breakdown and Adam and Leah deem it better that she moves in with them but this leaves Alice's two young children alone in the house with their father and although he bonds with the son, Jonathan, ten-year-old Jessica suffers isolation and fear at his hands.

Adam has found himself an apartment to live in whilst still seeing Leah regularly. But as matters unfold, it looks as if he and Leah are swiftly returning to married life, together in the family home. Meanwhile Adam's secretary, Sally has attracted the love of the millionaire son of a Lord and the Managing Director of Adam's company, Dominic West.

Book Two: "Autumn Leaves" shows Adam and Leah not only rekindling their love for each other but bonding in support of their daughter Alice, helping her to get the divorce she wants from her abusive husband and bringing her young daughter, Jessica to live with her in their house. Adam steps up as the head of the family and seems keen to make up for lost time with his wife, children and now grandchildren. All he wants is to focus on his family and lead a quiet life. That is not to be, as more and more responsibility is piled on his shoulders at work. He reluctantly accepts a directorship of the company and when he delivers his masterplan to develop the upper floor of his company's offices, he attracts even more attention as a man of vision. Meanwhile, Dominic West, the young, millionaire Managing Director confirms his love for Adam's secretary, Sally by proposing to her. Bill, a new employee at Adam's company falls for Alice and as Christmas approaches, all the characters come together with plans of how best to celebrate it. Adam finds himself at the centre of a vortex of very different lifestyles.

Chapter One

Winter 1985-1986, Swanton, an Oxfordshire Market Town

Christmas Day was fast approaching and Adam was more than ready for the beginning of the holiday. It had been a very busy few months and he was looking forward to a more relaxing time. He knew that Leah his wife was tired too and she had been very relieved when the school holidays had arrived. He thought about all the extra work that Leah was faced with over the Christmas period and he was determined to support her as much as he could. There was definitely a festive atmosphere in the house and he began to feel more cheerful.

He went to work the next day feeling refreshed. Barry saw him come in and followed him into the office.

"How are you this morning, Adam?"

"I'm feeling much better thank you. I've got all my wits about me today so you had better be on your toes."

"Oh, dear. Then you won't want to know that two of the computers are on the blink and Bill is trying to fix them?"

"These annoying little things happen," said Adam, sweetly. "I'm sure Bill will find the problem."

Barry looked at Adam and sighed.

"I never know what you will say next when you are in this mood."

"Well, how about this for starters?" Adam said with a mischievous smile, as he produced a gilt-edged card from his pocket.

He passed it over to Barry who read it in disbelief.

"When did this come?" he stammered.

"Yesterday morning. It was a total surprise and it knocked me for six."

"Is this why you were acting so strangely, yesterday?"

"There were other reasons," Adam said, "but this was the biggest shock."

"Have you told Leah? What did she say?"

"She said she would need a new dress, of course, that was after she managed to breathe again."

"Does anyone else know?" Barry enquired.

"Sally knows because she and Dominic will also be there and Alice knows because she saw the card last night, but I'd like you to keep the secret for now."

"Of course, I will," said Barry. "Mr Carr was right, wasn't he?"

"What has it to do with Mr Carr?" asked Adam, frowning.

Barry looked hard at Adam.

"Mr Carr always said that you were destined for higher things, didn't he? And that is coming true."

"But these things keep happening," Adam said helplessly. "I don't go looking for them."

"You still don't accept yourself, Adam, do you? You are a very charismatic man. People respect you and are ready to learn from you. You are a man of the people and you would be an excellent Member of Parliament," he added as an afterthought.

"I have no interest in politics," Adam said firmly. "You will never persuade me to enter that minefield."

"You could be an Independent M.P. Anyway, you said that you wouldn't want to go to Head Office with its fitted carpets and dinners at the club and look at you now: a director in the business with all that involves."

"You're not helping to make me feel better," Adam said crossly. "You'd better go and inspect your computers. You can bring me a coffee at eleven o'clock."

Barry stood up but before he left, he said:

"I'm sorry if I upset your good mood but someone had to tell you. You can't seem to see it for yourself." He went towards the door. "I shall probably get fired," he muttered as he went out.

Sally saw his face as he walked past her office. Oh dear, she thought. What has happened now? She picked up her diary and knocked on

2

Adam's door. He didn't answer so she opened the door and went in. He was sitting in his chair with a vacant look on his face. She closed the door with a bang, making him jump.

"You were miles away," she said. "What were you thinking about?"

"I was thinking of the best way to sack Barry," he said seriously.

"What for?" she said, horrified. "What has he done?"

"For insubordination," Adam said with a straight face. "For destroying the good mood of his superior."

"You are obviously feeling better," she said after looking at him closely.

"I was until Barry gave me a lecture on my charisma and told me that I should be a Member of Parliament. Why do people keep pushing me up the ladder?"

"They are only concerned you reach your potential. They are urging you to succeed, telling you what you don't know yourself."

"I have already succeeded beyond my wildest dreams and I don't just mean at work. But things keep happening and I don't have the time to enjoy what I have," Adam replied.

"It has been an exceptionally busy time and the tornado named Dominic has affected us all. Once you have your office upstairs you can begin to plan your area work more and that will help you to feel more in control," Sally said comfortingly. "Until then, you must take every day as it comes and not try to look too far ahead."

"Is that what you have decided to do?"

"I'm trying," she said. "But it is not always easy. For instance, at the moment I am concentrating on getting enough food for the Christmas holiday and trying to focus on Christmas dinner."

"Thank goodness I don't have to worry about the food shopping and I think most of the preparations are under control so I'm going to think about Christmas."

There was a knock at the door and Barry came in with two cups of coffee.

"I've brought some chocolate biscuits to sweeten the air," he said solemnly.

"I suppose that's a start," Adam said grudgingly, "but it will take more than a chocolate biscuit to put things right. It will take at least two or three."

"I'm going to leave him to you, Barry. When he is in this kind of mood, I can do nothing with him," and she left the office.

"Have another biscuit if it will help," said Barry offering the tin to Adam.

"No thank you, I don't want to make myself sick." He looked at Barry. "How are your computers?"

"Bill has managed to get them working thank goodness, although we are not as busy as we were yesterday."

"We close at noon tomorrow and it should be fairly quiet. We should all be out by two o'clock at the latest," Adam said.

He walked out into the main office with Barry. Bill saw Adam coming and he asked him quietly: "Can you spare a minute?"

"Come to my office in five minutes," Adam said. "I'll see you then."

Bill arrived promptly.

"It is a personal matter," he said. "Is it convenient to bring it up now?"

"Yes, of course," Adam said. "How can I help?"

"I want to buy Alice a Christmas present and I'd like to buy a silver bracelet. Will she like that?"

"I'm sure she will love it."

"And a watch for Jessica?" Bill added.

"That will be perfect. We have plenty of wrapping paper, you can have some of that."

"Has Alice heard any more about her divorce?" Bill asked.

"Yes, William has agreed to everything we asked for. Now we just have to wait for the house to be sold."

"I'm really looking forward to Christmas," Bill said. "It makes a big difference having children around. Thank you for inviting me."

"I know what Christmas is like spent alone," said Adam, looking at him. "I wouldn't wish it on anybody. We shall look forward to seeing you tomorrow evening."

Bill left the office and Adam sat back in his chair. He remembered what Bill said about children and a sudden thought struck him: this would be his first family Christmas for thirteen years and he knew it would be wonderful. He immediately felt better and he called Sally in.

She sat in the chair opposite and opened her diary.

"You can put that away," he said. "No more appointments until after Christmas."

She sat and waited for Adam to speak. Eventually, he said:

"I've decided not to fire Barry. I'll forgive him instead."

"A good decision," she said solemnly.

"It is better to forgive and forget."

"Much better," she said. "Have you anyone else in mind who you can forgive?"

"Not at the moment," Adam said with a straight face, "but I'll bear it in mind." He noticed that Sally's mouth was twitching. "You know me too well," he said and they both burst into laughter.

"You have a wicked sense of humour," she spluttered.

"Leah tells me that too. You women all think alike. Have there been any phone calls?"

"No, it's been very quiet. Dominic did phone me last night to say that he was staying at his club. He said that there were a few things he needed to do today and he will be here tomorrow before twelve o'clock."

"I hope he remembers that we finish at twelve tomorrow. We shall all be longing to get home."

"I'll remind him," she said. "He did say that his father was also staying at the club and would be there over Christmas. He sounded a bit worried about him."

"I had a feeling that all was not right between his parents," Adam said thoughtfully, "but I suppose they know how to put on a brave face at these society events."

"I don't know what Dominic has in mind but he did ask me about my spare bedroom and if I knew any good hotels in this area."

"He is obviously gearing up for another of his little surprises," Adam said with a touch of sarcasm.

"Sir Humphrey will be at the family lunch on Thursday, then we are coming back on Friday so I assume he will be at his club. I suppose he might come to Oxford on Saturday and Sunday. He could stay at the Randolph?"

"Don't forget you are coming to us on Saturday evening," Adam said. "If necessary, he could come as well?"

"That is very kind of you. I hope Dominic will let me know what is happening."

"I'm sure he will," Adam said gently. "He is bound to ask you first."

"There seems to be quite a lot of friction in his family," she said anxiously. "He hardly ever talks about his sons."

"I've noticed that. It is almost as if he has disowned them."

"One day I'll ask him but not just now."

"Every family has its skeletons in the cupboard, Sally. The more distinguished the family, the more skeletons there are."

"It frightens me sometimes when I think of what I am getting into."

"I think Dominic is trying to break the mould," Adam said sincerely. "He has no airs and graces although he still has great respect for his family values. He is trying to bring it into the twenty-first century. I think he will ultimately succeed with your help."

"I know I have a lot to learn but I will do my best to support him."

"I know you will," Adam reassured her. "But don't forget that Dominic has a lot to learn about the way to treat a woman. He has lived in a man's world for a long time."

She stood up to leave. "I must do some shopping in my lunch hour," she said. "I'd better get some extra food in."

Adam looked at his watch.

"If you get me a cup of coffee now then you can take an extended lunch hour. Julie can look after the office."

She thanked him and soon returned with the coffee. Adam sat in his chair thinking about the conversation they had just had and wondered why Dominic had so little interest in his sons. He'd never even shown a photograph of them and he never mentioned his ex-wife. Adam didn't even know her name or the grounds for his divorce. Dominic was the Managing Director, so Adam decided to check for details on the company computer. There was very little information, other than that his wife's name was Susanna and she was the daughter of Sir Toby Belvoir. It said that they were divorced and her new partner was a prominent politician. He was interrupted by his phone ringing.

"Mr West wishes to speak to you," said Julie.

"Thank you, Julie. Put him through."

"Hello, Dominic. How are you?"

"Hello, Adam. Actually, I am a bit fraught today. The cleaner arrived as arranged so that was good and I managed to get to Garrards to buy Sally's present. But then I had lunch with Father and he dropped a bombshell. He and Mother have parted and when he has left Parliament, they will get a divorce. I really wasn't expecting this," he sighed.

"It is not the sort of news you want to hear at Christmas," said Adam, trying to console him. "Sally said you were worried about Sir Humphrey?"

"Everything will appear normal during Christmas. They have had plenty of practice at pretence over the years."

"I think you need to talk to Sally about it. Women can sometimes find solutions which we don't see."

"I'll ring her this evening. Where is she now, Adam?"

"She's gone shopping."

"I put some money in her account yesterday."

"I don't think she will be touching that yet. She considers that to be for clothes, not day-to-day living expenses," said Adam. "She was wondering if your two boys will be at the dinner on Thursday?"

"I expect so, their mother likes to have them on display at these family functions," replied Dominic bitterly.

"And your ex-wife. Will she be there?"

"My mother will want to turn the screw. She'll be there," he sighed.

"You must warn Sally about these family tensions," Adam said firmly. "She needs to be forewarned."

"I'll tell her tomorrow night."

"Don't forget we close at twelve tomorrow. You need to be here earlier than that."

"I'll set off soon after breakfast. I expect the traffic will be quite heavy," said Dominic. "I need to go to the house this afternoon and collect the rest of the bottles out of the cellar. There is some vintage stuff there. I shall have to take it to Sally's house. Well, it is nearly all wrapped up here and I shall be glad to hand the keys over. I'll see you tomorrow."

Adam had hardly put the phone down before it rang again.

"Your daughter wishes to speak to you," Julie said.

"Put her through," he said quickly.

"Hello, Alice, are you alright?"

"I'm sorry to bother you at work, Dad," she said breathlessly, "but we can't move for boxes. There must be twenty of them."

"Don't worry, I'll come home early and take them down to the apartment."

"The sooner the better," Alice said. "Mum is going mad."

"Make her a nice cup of tea," he said, "and tell her I'll sort it out. I'll be home soon."

He went into the main office and found Bill.

"Tell Barry I shall be leaving soon after lunch," he said. "Alice is overrun by boxes and Leah is not very happy about it."

"Boxes," he repeated, looking at him in surprise. "What kind of boxes?"

"Full of Dominic's ancestral belongings," Adam answered. "Alice agreed to sort it out for him. Goodness knows what she will find."

"Let's hope she doesn't find any mouse droppings," Bill said with a smile.

"Leah will run a mile if she does," Adam grinned. "She can't stand mice."

He returned to his office and noticed that Sally was back. There were half a dozen M&S bags by her desk.

"How did you manage to carry all those?" he asked her.

"I had to borrow a trolley," she said, sounding tired. "I've sent Julie back with it."

"You can't carry it all on the bus tonight," Adam said with concern. "Why don't you take a taxi?"

"That never occurred to me. I suppose I could afford it."

"You could afford a thousand taxies," he said, firmly. "Make life a little easier for yourself. I shall be going home soon. Alice is swamped by Dominic's boxes and I need to move some of them."

"I'll be glad when he has finally got rid of that house," she said.

"I had a phone call while you were out," Adam said looking at her closely. "He said that he was going back there this afternoon to collect the last bottles from the cellar then he will be handing the keys to the estate agent."

"Thank goodness for that. What else did he say?" she said in a worried voice. "I know that look. It usually means bad news."

"He said that his parents would be divorcing when Sir Humphrey is no longer an M.P," he said quietly.

"I'm not surprised," Sally said in resignation. "The signs have been pretty obvious."

"They may have been obvious to you but I don't think that Dominic saw it coming."

"I hope he won't get involved," she said anxiously.

"I don't think he knows what to do. He is going to need your calming influence."

"Life gets more and more complicated," she sighed.

"You must remember your decision to take each day as it comes. That's what I'm going to do."

"Barry was right," she said. "You are full of sensible suggestions."

"Just be careful, Sally," he told her with a straight face. "If you go down that path, I may not forgive you."

She went up to him and kissed him on the cheek.

"You are a wily old rogue," she said affectionately.

"Not so much of the old," Adam muttered as he went out.

He left the office early in the afternoon to go home but on the way, he stopped at the toyshop. He bought half a dozen packs of cards including 'Snap' for the children. Then he chose several family games like Twister and finally, he found an attractive chess set. He paid and packed them in the car, satisfied that they would keep everyone amused over Christmas.

When he arrived home, he went to go in by the back door but the side entrance seemed to be jammed. He found his key and opened the front door. He went into the lounge and Alice greeted him.

"Thank goodness you have come," she said. "Mum is in a big strop."

Leah was sitting in her chair with her lips pressed firmly together. Adam went up to her and kissed her.

"Cheer up," he said. "I'll soon sort this out."

"That's all you seem to do," she said with feeling. "Sort out Dominic's mess."

Adam took a step back as he heard the anger in her voice.

"Dominic has been very generous to us," he said firmly. "The least we can do is help him out when he needs it," and he walked out of the room.

Alice followed him looking anxiously over her shoulder.

"Will Mum be alright?" she asked.

"Christmas may be a happy time but the run-up to it is very stressful. Mum is tired out. We'll get these boxes out of the way and then I'll talk to her, I promise," he said.

Between them, they loaded up the car with boxes and took them to the apartment. They stood them tidily in the hall and then went back for a second load.

"We'll leave two boxes here," said Alice. "So I can start looking at them after Christmas."

"I can manage this lot," he said. "You stay with Mum. By the way, where is Jessica?"

"Jen has been making biscuits and she asked Jessica if she would like to help. It is just as well that she didn't see how angry Mum was."

"I won't be long," he said. "We'll have a nice cup of tea when I get back."

Alice tidied up the utility area and swept the floor. She put the two boxes in the corner so that they were out of sight. Everything was back in its normal place and she went into the lounge. She found Leah asleep in her chair so she laid the table ready for tea. She went back to the kitchen and put the kettle on. She sat on the kitchen stool and thought about Christmas.

What a difference a year made. She remembered the last Christmas Day when they had gone to William's parents for dinner and how he had humiliated her in front of them. She knew she had drunk too much and he had slept on the sofa. The memories made her shudder and she was glad when Adam came back.

"Alice, are you alright?" he said as soon as he saw her.

"I was just remembering last Christmas and it was painful."

Adam looked at her with compassion.

"I did the same thing earlier today," he said. "And then I thanked God that this year would be so much better now that we are a family again."

"We have some good friends too, Dad. They are almost like family."

He thought for a minute then said:

"I think that is why I get on so well with Sally and with Dominic. We are the family they never had. I feel almost fatherly to both of them."

"Bill feels the same. He has great respect for you."

"I like him," Adam said simply. "He will be a great son-in-law."

She looked at him in surprise and blushed a little.

"Aren't you jumping the gun?" she said sternly.

"Sorry," he said and kissed her. "I thought you already knew."

He stood up and went into the lounge. Leah was just waking up. He took her hand and led her out to the utility area.

"All gone," he said. "Those pesky boxes have all gone."

"You missed two," she said accusingly as she noticed them in the corner.

"I might have missed two but I have moved eighteen," he said indignantly.

Leah turned to him and smiled.

"You always know what to do," she said. "I'm sorry I snapped," and she kissed his cheek.

They heard a car stop outside and Jen and Jessica came in.

"Look what I made," Jessica said full of excitement and she showed them the plate of biscuits.

"We were just about to have a cup of tea, Jen," Adam said. "Won't you join us?"

"I've got half an hour to spare," she replied. "Then I must go back and finish the Christmas cake which we always take to Barry's parents."

They all sat down and Alice brought in the tea. Jessica offered her biscuits to them and soon they were all gone.

"Did you make them all by yourself?" asked Leah.

"Yes, I did but Auntie Jen put them in the oven for me."

"I hope you will make lots more," Adam said as she curled up beside him. "They were delicious."

"I shan't be sorry when Christmas Day is over," Jen said. "Barry's mother never stops talking and his father always finds something to moan about."

"I've had days like that in the past when the elderly relations were alive," Leah said thoughtfully. "I used to dread going to see them."

"This year is going to be different," Adam said firmly. "I just know it is."

"I'd better go," Jen said standing up. "Barry will be home soon and he is so tired. He needs a lot of TLC."

"He will certainly need it this evening," Adam said. "He nearly got fired this morning."

Everyone looked at him in amazement.

"What do you mean?" Jen said in a shaky voice.

"It's alright," Adam assured her. "I changed my mind and forgave him."

"But what did he do?" Jen demanded.

"I am sure he will tell you about it," he said with a smile.

Suddenly Jen realised that Adam was being deliberately evasive.

"Is this one of your jokes?" she said.

"I didn't think it was a joke but it all turned out alright in the end. He still has his job, no worries."

Jen went off feeling very unsettled. Leah turned to Adam.

"You are up to your tricks again," she said. "Sometimes you have a cruel sense of humour. What did Barry do wrong?"

"He didn't do anything wrong. It was what he said that upset me," Adam said reluctantly.

Leah sat and waited but he said no more.

"Tell me what he said?" she eventually asked him.

"It doesn't matter," he said a little crossly. "It's not important."

"If it is not important then there is no need to keep it from me," Leah said clearly.

"Oh, alright then," he muttered. "He said that I was a very charismatic man and I would make a good MP."

"He is probably right so why did it upset you?"

"I don't want to be a charismatic person whatever that means and I certainly don't want to be an MP," he said peevishly.

"You are what you are," Leah said firmly. "So why don't you accept it and get on with your life?"

"That is the problem I have. Other people are telling me all the time what I am supposed to be and I have lost sight of the real me."

"Your success has come very rapidly but your character has been building up over years. You have gone through a lot of changes but the real you has been obvious to everyone. It is only since you admitted to your guilty feelings that you opened the door to your old self. Life does not offer opportunities for us to turn them down. They are there to be embraced and enjoyed not only for yourself but others will benefit too," Leah concluded.

Adam looked at her in amazement.

"Wherever did you learn wisdom like that?" he said incredulously.

"Perhaps I have been more accepting of what life has thrown at me than you have," she said calmly. "I can encompass the good things as well as the bad."

"My problem is deciding what the good things are," he said. "In my darkest hours, I had a dream of perfect happiness with you. It was just the two of us. I suppose that now seems very selfish. It never occurred to me that other people and events would intrude into our life together."

"Have you heard the expression 'Man is not an island'? Everybody is influenced by the action and thoughts of others. They can point to how successful you are as a complete person and their opinions should not be ignored."

"Well at least I have achieved the first part of my dream," he said as he took Leah into his arms. "I have my perfect life partner," and he kissed her tenderly. "I may have to rethink my future, but not until after Christmas."

That evening as they sat in the lounge Leah said:

"I wonder if Thomas will phone. He usually does on Christmas Day."

"It's their midsummer," said Alice. "It must be very strange to have Christmas on a boiling hot day. Have you told him that Dad is here?"

"No, I haven't spoken to him. I don't think he knows. I'll tell him when he phones."

"I wonder if Harriet will be with him? I should like to speak to her," said Alice.

"They will be at least twelve hours ahead of us," Adam said. "So, he

14

may phone this evening."

"Would you like to speak to him, Adam?" asked Leah.

"I think it might be better when he comes home," he replied after thinking for a moment. "I'm sure you can explain what has happened."

"He might say that he would like to speak to you?"

"In that case, of course, I will talk to him."

At one o'clock the phone rang. Leah went to answer it.

"Hello Mum," came a voice from twelve thousand miles away. "Happy Christmas."

"Thomas!" Leah exclaimed in a delighted voice. "We were just talking about you."

"You don't usually have company on Christmas Eve," he said cheerfully. "Who is there with you?"

"Your father and Alice."

There was silence at the other end of the phone until Thomas managed to say: "Did you say Dad was there?"

"Yes, I did. He is back home."

She heard Thomas telling Harriet what had just been said.

"Do you mean you are living together after what happened?" he said.

"Yes, we are a happily married couple again."

"But why is Alice with you?"

"Alice and William are divorcing and she and Jessica are living here at present."

"This is all a big surprise," said Thomas. "Can I speak to Dad?"

"Yes, of course, you can," Leah answered. "I'll just get him."

She went into the lounge and called Adam. He took the phone and he felt his stomach turn over.

"Hello Thomas," he said with a slight hesitation.

"Hello Dad," Thomas said coolly. "We seem to have missed out on some rather important family matters. How did it happen?"

"I got a promotion to an office in Oxford and we met again at a friend's house."

"What kind of office are you talking about?"

"I am area manager for the largest Building Society."

"That's nothing like the job you used to do. How did that come about?"

"It's a long story," Adam said. "It must wait until I see you. Can I speak to Harriet please?"

He heard Thomas pass the phone over.

"Hello Dad," Harriet said reluctantly. "Are you okay?"

"Yes, I'm fine. Perhaps this time next year we can have a real family Christmas?"

"That would be nice," Harriet said faintly. "Can I speak to Alice?"

"Yes, of course, you can," Adam said immediately, handing the phone to Alice.

She took it into the hall and had a long conversation with her sister. At the end of it, she called Leah.

"Harriet wants to speak to you!"

Leah took the phone.

"Alice has been telling me how happy you are with Dad. Are you sure that it is the right thing to do, Mum?" said Harriet.

"Yes, I'm sure," Leah answered firmly. "A lot of things have changed but we still love each other."

"In that case, I'm pleased for both of you," Harriet said sincerely. "I'm not sure how Thomas feels. He seems a bit upset."

"I hope he will accept it. I know it must be a shock to him," Leah said.

"Don't worry. I'll talk to him. I hope you have a happy Christmas. I'll phone again in the New Year."

"Thomas sounded rather stunned," Adam said when she returned.

"When you went away, he suddenly realised that he would be looked on as the man of the family. He never really came to terms with that and I have always felt that was why he went as far away as possible," Leah said thoughtfully.

"It was nice to speak to Harriet," said Alice. "Sometimes I forget that I have a sister. I'm off to bed, I hope I don't dream about boxes."

Adam and Leah sat on the settee quietly thinking their own thoughts. Adam got up and went for his jacket which was hanging in the hall. He took the little blue box out of his pocket and went back to Leah.

"We are not going to have much time to ourselves over the next two days," he said. "So, I want to give you your present now," and he handed her the box.

She opened it and gasped.

"It is a symbol of my love for you," Adam said simply.

He took the new wedding ring out of its box and slipped it on her finger. She stared at it and then looked at Adam as the tears began to trickle down her cheeks.

"I am so lucky," she sobbed. "I am married to the kindest, most thoughtful man in the world," and she clung on to him as she sobbed her heart out. He held her tightly until she stopped crying.

"That's better," he said as he comforted her. "You needed to get rid of all that pent-up emotion. Time for bed."

Chapter Two

The next morning, Adam was up early. There was something he wanted to do before going into the office. He parked the car and went to the covered market. He found a flower shop and chose two bouquets. One was for Leah and he chose pink roses; the other was for Sally and this time he chose cream roses. He took Leah's flowers back to the car and laid them carefully in the boot, then he went to work. He was pleased to see that Sally was not in her usual place and he went into his office. He took out his pen and wrote a message on the card then he stood the flowers up in his wastepaper basket.

There was a knock on the door and Barry walked in. He didn't look too pleased. He sat down opposite Adam and glowered at him.

"You really landed me in its last night," he said. Adam looked surprised but Barry continued, "Jen was in a right state when I got home. She really thought that I was to lose my job."

"But I told her that your job was safe," Adam said, trying to explain.

"How could she believe you after what you said to her? She was nearly hysterical," Barry said crossly. "I tried to ring you so that you could reassure her but your phone was engaged for ages."

"That was a phone call from New Zealand," he said lamely. "I'm sorry I upset you both. It won't happen again."

"I am used to your warped sense of humour but other people are not. Sometimes you come out with really hurtful comments," Barry said sternly.

"I know. I suppose it was one of the ways that I used to protect myself."

"Well, you don't need to protect yourself now," Barry stated. "Sometimes it's others who need protecting from you."

Adam thought for a minute or two then said:

"Do you remember what I asked you to do when I first came?"

Barry looked puzzled and shook his head.

"I asked you to promise you would tell me if I became too cocky and

I totally accept your criticism of what I did. It was completely out of order and I apologise. I would never deliberately upset Jen or you and I am very sorry."

Barry stood up.

"It takes a lot to upset Jen," he said, "and I know I have been a bit touchy lately but I am tired. I'll be glad of the break," and he left the office.

Adam sat in his chair contemplating what had just been said. I must get rid of that cruel streak, he said to himself. It's hurting me as much as others. He called Sally into the office.

"Fetch two cups of coffee and bring them back here," he said.

She soon returned and she sat in the chair opposite him.

"Did you get all your bags home last evening?" he asked.

"Yes, I took your advice and ordered a taxi. It was much easier."

"Dominic will be here soon," he said. "But I want to give you your Christmas present."

He picked up the roses and took them to her. She gazed at them in wonder.

"Adam, they are beautiful," she said as she read the card. "You are so kind," and she stood up and kissed him.

"You have been a wonderful support to me," he said emotionally. "If I wasn't a happily married man, I would be challenging Dominic."

She kissed him again on the cheek.

"That would be an interesting battle," she said and she took the flowers into her office.

Five minutes later, Dominic arrived. He noticed the roses on Sally's desk as he passed her office. He went in and kissed her.

"Who is your secret admirer?" he asked and he read the card.

"You must admit that they are beautiful," she said.

"Not as beautiful as you," Dominic whispered in her ear.

Dominic knocked on Adam's door and walked in. Adam was drinking his coffee.

"Would you like one?" he asked.

"No thank you," Dominic replied as he sat down. "I'm hoping Sally can leave a bit earlier. We have quite a lot to discuss before tomorrow."

"It is quite quiet. We shall all be ready to go home soon after twelve. Have you completed the sale of your house?"

"Yes, I handed the keys over and I've got a car full of vintage wine," Dominic said. "I'm hoping that Sally can look after it for a few weeks."

"Your boxes arrived yesterday," Adam said. "All twenty of them."

Dominic looked at him aghast.

"Twenty," he repeated. "I thought it was six the last time I looked. Gretchen must have found more things. Twenty is a lot," he said apologetically.

"Leah thought it was a lot," Adam smiled. "She went into a big sulk."

"I'm so sorry. What did you do?"

"I took them down to my apartment. There's plenty of storage space there."

"It has all been a bit of a nightmare, Adam. And now there is Father's news as well."

"You must have had a suspicion? You knew they weren't happy together."

"They have lived their own lives for years. It had just become their normal existence. I never dreamed that they would actually divorce."

"Who has started the ball rolling?"

"Mother, of course," Dominic said bitterly, "on the grounds of incompatibility."

"Is Sir Humphrey going to contest it?"

"He won't contest the divorce itself but I am pretty sure he won't agree to the money side," Dominic said wearily. "Sally and I were looking forward to a few days together but now that will all change."

"What is planned now?"

"We shall attend the Christmas lunch as arranged then Sally and I will go back to the Grosvenor for the night and we shall return here on

Boxing Day. Saturday, we hope to visit her mother in the morning and we are coming to you in the evening. But I am concerned about Father being on his own."

"I guess he is staying at his club?" asked Adam.

Dominic nodded his head.

"He could have dinner with you at the Grosvenor and you could see him for coffee before you leave on Boxing Day. He could book into the Randolph Hotel in Oxford after you have visited Sally's mother. You are very welcome to bring him with you on Saturday evening if he would like to come. On Sunday, I'm sure Sally can rustle up something for lunch."

Dominic was looking at Adam with his mouth open.

"I wish I had your organisational skills," he said admiringly. "You make it sound so easy."

There was a knock on the door and Sally came in with her coat on.

"It's eleven forty-five," she said, "and Barry is beginning to shut down the tills."

"I'll come out and say Happy Christmas to the staff as they leave," Adam said. "We shall look forward to seeing you on Saturday. Let me know about Sir Humphrey," and he went into the main office.

Sally collected her bag and the flowers and she and Dominic left. Adam spent the next ten minutes saying goodbye to the staff and Barry and Bill pulled the blinds down at the front window. They double-checked all the doors and windows and made sure that the alarm was switched on. When they were all happy that the place was secure, they went out through the main entrance.

"We shall eat at six, Bill," said Adam. "I'll see you then."

He said goodbye to Barry and walked up the street to the market. There was not a great choice left in the flower shop and he chose a large bunch of colourful tulips. He drove home and on the way, stopped at Barry's house. He found Jen in the kitchen and went and kissed her.

"I'm very sorry I upset you and I have been well and truly told off by your husband, do please accept my peace offering?" and he gave her the tulips.

"I forgive you," she said. "As long as you don't do it again."

"I'll try very hard not to," he promised. "Happy Christmas and we'll see you on Saturday."

He drove home and parked his car on the grass. He opened the boot and took out the roses. He went in through the front door and found Leah in the lounge. He went up to her and kissed her.

"Happy Christmas to my wife," he said and gave her the roses.

"Oh Adam," she said, "they are just like the ones you first gave me."

"I know," he said as he kissed her again. "You've no idea how nervous I was that evening."

"Have you had a good day?" she asked.

"Yes, a very good day. We may have an extra visitor on Saturday."

Chapter Three

On the way to the car, Sally went into M & S and bought a small Christmas cake to take to her mother. Dominic drove home to the sound of clanking bottles in the boot.

"I hope you can find a temporary home for all that wine, Sally," he said.

"How many bottles are you talking about?"

"About five dozen," he answered. "It includes some real vintage wines."

"I suppose it can go in the garage," she said.

When they arrived home, Dominic transferred it all into the empty garage and breathed a sigh of relief.

"That was the final thing from the house. I never thought I would finish it all before Christmas and I am mightily relieved."

"It has been a hectic few weeks for you," she said. "I hope life will be easier after Christmas."

"Not much chance of that. Now we have the added complication of Father."

"Sir Humphrey will make his own decisions," Sally said firmly. "Your role is just to be there when he needs support."

Dominic looked at her.

"What you are really saying is that I should mind my own business," he said in surprise.

"I suppose I am. You need to concentrate on your business role and your own needs. I'm sure your father has plenty of friends who will offer him advice."

"He has certainly supported me for the past month and we have spent a lot of time together. I just don't want him to feel lonely at Christmas."

"You know what Adam has suggested and I think his idea is a good one. Why don't you phone Sir Humphrey and see what he says? He may already have made his own arrangements."

"I'll do that this evening. I'm sure he will be at his club then. It's good to be here with you," he said, kissing her. "Are we going out to eat, I'm starving?"

"I've got plenty of food here," she said. "In fact, I bought so much that I brought it home in a taxi."

Dominic laughed.

"That's a first," he grinned.

"Actually, it was Adam's idea. He told me I could afford it."

"That man is full of good ideas which turn into practical solutions," Dominic said admiringly.

Sally didn't comment but she thought of what Barry had said.

"We will have some soup for now," she said, "and I will cook something this evening."

After dinner, they went back into the lounge and sat on the settee. Dominic put his arm around her.

"This is bliss to get away from all the noise and bustle of London," he said, lying back and closing his eyes.

Sally sat by him deep in thought. He was soon fast asleep and she quietly stood up and went upstairs. Her suitcase was on the bed in the spare room and she started to pack it ready for the next day. She knew she would be wearing the dress which Alice had given her but she wasn't sure if she would need the evening dress. She packed some trousers and a jumper for the return journey and put her shoes in her holdall. She hadn't known what to buy Dominic as a present so she had opted for a pale grey silk tie and a promise.

She was beginning to understand the style and couture of the clothes she would be expected to wear and she realised that she would have to do some serious shopping. She went back to the lounge and found Dominic still asleep, so she went into the kitchen and put the kettle on. She made the tea and put it on the coffee table then she kissed him on the forehead.

"Wake up, sleepyhead," she whispered.

Dominic stirred and opened his eyes to find Sally leaning over him. His arms went around her as he pulled her down on top of him.

"That is a dangerous place to be," he said with a glint in his eye.

"I don't mind being in a dangerous place with you," she said softly, stroking his face. "I know I shall be safe," and she kissed him and sat up. "I've made some tea," she said and pointed to the cups on the table. "And I need to ask you something. Do I need an evening dress with me tomorrow?"

"That is an easy one to answer," he said. "We shall be having dinner at the hotel but I'm not sure if it is anything special. I should pack it just in case. I've put my dress suit in the car."

"That is only my first question," she said. "There are plenty more."

He raised his hands as if in surrender.

"I confess to whatever I'm being accused of," he said jokingly. "Can I kiss you now please?"

"I'm being serious," Sally said sternly. "There really are some things I need to know before tomorrow. You promised me that you would tell me."

"Oh dear," he said, suddenly being serious. "I don't know where to begin."

"Tell me about your mother first?"

Dominic thought for a moment then he said:

"She is the only daughter of Sir Toby Belvoir and she married my father when she was twenty-two years old. It was really a marriage of convenience but it has lasted forty years. I don't think they ever really loved each other and she was only looking for someone with enough money to support her lifestyle. They have lived separate lives for years and Mother has had a number of different affairs."

"You said her father was Sir Toby but I understood it was Lord Kitson?"

"They are the same person. When my grandfather was raised to the peerage, he changed his name by deed poll. I think he wanted to remove all his previous French connections and be a true Englishman. My grandfather disapproved strongly of Mother's lifestyle and he practically disowned her. That is why she has stuck it out with Father. He has funded her all these years. Now I understand she has found a different source of income and I suppose he will be there tomorrow," he said

25

bitterly.

"Surely Sir Humphrey could contest the divorce on the grounds of her adultery?"

"Father likes a quiet life and he would rather not have her actions made public."

"Tell me about your father's family?" she asked.

"Father's parents both died after he got married and he was left with no family. It was then that Lord Kitson took him under his wing and helped him to develop a career in politics. My grandfather also gave him a major role in the company but he resigned that when he became a government minister. There was even talk of him becoming Prime Minister," Dominic said with a faraway look.

Once again Sally was reminded of Barry's words but she didn't say anything. As they sat in silence, Dominic was thinking about his grandfather and Sally was thinking about what she had heard.

"You told me that you had a brother and sister," she said.

"Edward was five years older than me and he was very much like Mother. He flitted from place to place and never really had a career other than being a social butterfly. He was killed in a skiing accident when I was ten years old."

"Would he have taken over the business instead of you?"

"I doubt it," he replied. "He was not a businessperson. He had no interest in money, other than having enough for his own needs."

"What about your sister?"

"She got fed up of mother parading her in front of all the eligible rich men, so she found herself a millionaire and went to live in America. She has no family loyalty and I haven't spoken to her for years."

He stopped talking with such a sad look on his face that Sally put her arms around him.

"I'm sorry if this is upsetting you, Dominic," she said softly, "but I really need to know so that I don't make any unintentional comments tomorrow."

"I understand," he said. "It is a different way of life for you to get used to. I really do want to help you," and he took her hands. "Is there anything else that is bothering you?" he said gently.

"Yes, there is one thing," Sally said with hesitation. "It's about your ex-wife."

"I don't want to talk about her," he said, looking at her in dismay.

Sally didn't say anything but just waited.

"Why do you ask?" he said eventually. "I didn't think you were the jealous type."

"That is an unkind thing to say," she said shortly. "I thought you knew me better than that."

"I'm sorry," he said sincerely. "What do you want to know?"

"I'd like to know her name and if she will be there tomorrow?" Sally said quietly.

"Her name is Susanna and yes I expect she will be there tomorrow."

"Can you describe her to me?"

"Do I have to?" Dominic answered flatly.

"Yes please."

"She is a younger version of my mother," Dominic said bitterly. "She will be dressed in the latest fashion and probably weighed down in jewellery. I'm so glad that I never mentioned Grandmother's box in the bank. She will drink too much champagne and try to flirt with all the men."

"You really aren't painting a very cheerful occasion," she said, with a shudder. "I'm getting more apprehensive by the minute."

"There will be some friendly people there too," he said, hugging her. "And I promise that we shall leave at the earliest possible time."

"Can I ask one more question?" she said. "Will your sons be there?"

"Almost definitely," Dominic answered. "Mother likes to give the impression of a happy family."

"What are their names? Do they look like you?"

"James is thirteen and will be going to Eton in September. His brother David is eleven and at a boarding school in Surrey."

He fell silent for a few minutes. Then he looked at Sally.

"You asked if they looked like me," he said slowly. "The answer is no; they don't look like me because they are not my children."

Sally was shocked and she didn't know what to say but Dominic went on.

"I told you that she was a younger version of my mother. Well, it was a bit more serious. My wife had an affair with her new partner when he was still married. It lasted for three years and that is when the boys were born. She is now living with him and I am pretty sure he is the boys' father. I agreed to bring them up as mine but we have never been close. I intend to have a DNA test and if my suspicions are true, their real father can take responsibility for them."

Sally felt so sorry for Dominic. She put her arms around him to try to comfort him.

"It's true isn't it?" she said. "Money can't buy happiness. That's why I am not bothered by all your money. My happiness is just being with you."

"I have always wanted to make my grandfather proud of me," he said. "That is why the business has been an essential part of my life up till now. Making money and keeping it solvent was important and it still is. But I am beginning to discover where true happiness can be found and that is all because of you." He kissed her on the cheek. "I want you to be my wife. I want everyone to share in my happiness."

"I will marry you soon," she replied, "but I would like to know where we shall live?"

"We will look for a house in the New Year. Let's get Christmas over then we will talk about it. May I phone father now?"

Sally handed him the phone and went to the kitchen to start cooking their evening meal while Dominic spoke to Sir Humphrey. A few minutes later, he followed her into the kitchen and sat on one of the stools.

"Father has agreed with our suggestion and he said he would like to go to Adam's house with us on Saturday evening. He isn't looking forward to tomorrow either but at least he will meet up with some old friends."

"You'd better ring Adam and let him know the latest arrangement," Sally said.

"I'll do that now."

He went back into the lounge and had a lengthy conversation with Adam.

"Dinner's ready," she called and they sat in the kitchen to eat it.

Afterwards, Sally cleared the dirty plates and Dominic offered to make the coffee. She went and sat down and waited for him to bring it in. Then, she looked at him and laughed.

"You didn't ask me if I wanted milk and one sugar. You wouldn't get a job as a secretary."

"I'll do better next time," he said, laughing with her.

"It's funny," Sally said. "Sir Humphrey said exactly the same as you when he was offered coffee at the office. How did he sound when you spoke to him?"

"He sounded quite chirpy. I think he had been having an early Christmas celebration."

"He was probably trying not to think about Christmas Day," Sally said as she cuddled up to Dominic.

Adam had been relaxing in the lounge when Dominic phoned. When he was told that Sir Humphrey would be joining them on Saturday evening, he had a slight panic. He was not sure how he would tell Leah and what her reaction would be. He decided to wait a couple of days.

By six o'clock Bill had arrived and they all sat down to their evening meal. Jessica was so excited that she couldn't sit still so Adam and Bill took her into the lounge and played a game of I Spy with her. At eight o'clock Alice took her up for a nice warm bath before going to bed. Leah went into the kitchen to finish the preparations for Christmas dinner, leaving Adam and Bill in the lounge. They chatted to each other for a while then Bill said:

"How would you feel if I asked Alice to marry me when her divorce comes through?"

"I'd be delighted," Adam said warmly. "That is assuming that you love each other and you are not already married?"

"We do love each other but we were a bit concerned about how Jessica would react. I think we are over that particular hurdle. Now."

"And what about the second question?" Adam said.

Bill looked at him and smiled. "I can assure you that I am not married and never have been. I have never before found anyone whom I could spend my life with. I'm afraid 'Love them and leave them' has been my motto."

"It's just as well to sow your wild oats before you settle down," Adam said wisely.

"Thank you," Bill said. "Your approval is important to me."

"Can you keep a secret?" Adam said quietly.

"Yes, I can."

"I've just heard from Dominic that his father will be joining us on Saturday evening. I haven't told Leah yet so please don't breathe a word to anyone," Adam said in a whisper.

Bill looked stunned.

"Do you mean Sir Humphrey who we met the other day?" he stuttered. "We shall all have to be on our best behaviour."

"I don't think so," Adam said. "I think he will probably enjoy the company."

#

Bill was still looking surprised when Leah walked in. She took one look at them and immediately said:

"What have you two been talking about?"

"This and that," Adam said airily.

She stared at Bill who was still looking a bit shaken.

"Be careful what he says to you," she warned him. "He is full of little surprises. I'm going to bed. I shall have to be up early to put the turkey in the oven." And she went upstairs.

Soon after, Alice returned to the lounge.

"I'm quite worn out," she said wearily. "Jessica is so excited."

"I think I'll have an early night," Adam said. "Tomorrow will be a long day."

Alice and Bill stayed on the settee quite content in their own company.

Sally and Dominic had a relaxing evening too until Dominic said:

"Time for bed, my love. We don't want to yawn our way through dinner however bored we will be," and he followed Sally up the stairs.

Chapter Four

Christmas day started early for many families and Adam's was no exception. Jessica was awake by seven-thirty and immediately saw the stocking at the foot of the bed. Leah had filled it with all the traditional bits and pieces and a tiny bear was peeping out of the top. Alice got out of bed and put her dressing gown on.

"Jessica, I'm going to make a cup of tea," she said. "Wait until I come back."

But Jessica could not wait. She tip-toed into Adam and Leah's bedroom and whispered to Adam:

"Granddad, wake up. Father Christmas has left me a surprise."

She slid under the duvet between Adam and Leah. He sat up and kissed her.

"Happy Christmas, Jessica! What is in your Christmas stocking?"

Alice came in with the tea.

"I've switched the oven on, Mum," she said. "I'll just take Bill his tea."

Adam and Leah looked at each other and smiled.

"We shan't see her for a while," Adam said.

Jessica started to take things out of the stocking. She kissed the teddy bear and gave it to Adam to hold. As each little present came out, she became more and more excited. At the bottom was the Christmas orange. The contents were scattered all over the duvet.

"Now I'm going to put it all back in," said Jessica. "Because I want to show Bill what was in my Christmas stocking."

"I must go and put the turkey in the oven," Leah said as she got out of bed. "Why don't you go and get dressed first, Jessica?"

Jessica went off and Leah went downstairs. Adam was left sitting in bed surrounded by paper and nuts and all sorts of other small things. He waited for Jessica to return and helped her to pack the stocking. She took it downstairs and waited for Bill to get up. Meanwhile, Adam lay down

32

and went back to sleep.

Dominic and Sally had an early start too. They were both feeling nervous about the day ahead.

"I promise I won't leave your side, Sally," he said, as they lay in bed.

"And I won't let you down," she said, kissing him. "But please don't let me drink too much champagne."

"I'll keep an eye on it," he said, laughing.

As they sat having breakfast Sally suddenly said:

"I've no idea where your mother lives. Where are we going?"

"It is actually Father's house. He never put it in joint names. It stands in its own grounds in Richmond Park."

Sally thought for a moment.

"If it is solely your father's house why has he allowed your mother to go on living there?"

"Convenience, I suppose," Dominic said, shrugging his shoulders. "His work in Parliament has kept him fully occupied and he has not bothered to change his domestic arrangements."

"It seems to me that a lot of issues have never been resolved in your family, Dominic," she said thoughtfully. "Many things have just been swept under the carpet."

"Perhaps that is one of the shortcomings of people who have plenty of money. They can't be bothered with solving any problems in their personal lives because they are under the impression that they can buy themselves out of any situation."

"That is a very profound statement," she said, "especially on Christmas morning."

He put his arm around her.

"Since I met you, I have begun to think in a different way," he said with feeling, "and having friends like Adam and Barry has opened my eyes to a different way of life. Being with you is now so important to me."

Sally went upstairs to finish packing her case. She took her dress off its hanger and slipped it over her head. She called Dominic and he came up the stairs.

"Can you zip me up, please?" she said.

"I'd rather unzip you," he said putting his arms around her waist.

"Maybe later," she said with a smile, "but for now I am trying to keep calm."

He carried her suitcase and holdall downstairs and she followed with her coat.

"Christmas present time," he said as they came into the lounge. He produced a rectangular box from his pocket and gave it to Sally. "This comes with all my love."

Sally opened it and found a necklace of cream pearls lying on a bed of blue velvet. She gazed at them in wonder.

"They are beautiful," she said looking at him. "Really beautiful."

He took them out of the box and fastened them around her neck.

"Perfect, just perfect," he said emotionally. "You will be the belle of the ball."

She put her hands around the back of his neck and kissed him.

"Thank you," she said. "I shall wear them with pride."

They loaded up the car and were soon on their way. The traffic was light and they made good time. At eleven forty-five they were driving through some big iron gates and along a tree-lined avenue. Sally could see deer grazing among the trees. The road followed a slight bend and they came in sight of the house. It was a large Georgian mansion surrounded by formal flower beds. A gravel drive led up to the front door which was reached by an impressive set of stone steps. There were already about a dozen cars parked in the drive and Dominic drove into a parking space near the front door. He helped Sally out of the car and they walked up the steps together.

A maid greeted them at the door and took their coats. There was a buzz of noise coming from the room on the left. Dominic looked at Sally and put his hand on her elbow.

"Ready?" he asked quietly.

Sally swallowed hard and nodded her head. They went through the door and entered the room. All eyes seemed to be turning towards them and Dominic kept a tight hold on Sally. The conversation had started again and Dominic steered Sally towards a large lady in a magenta dress with diamonds at her throat and on her fingers. As they approached her, she turned around and said in a booming voice:

"Dominic, how nice to see you."

He kissed her briefly on the cheek and, still holding on to Sally, he said:

"May I introduce my fiancée? This is Sally." Then he turned to Sally, "This is my mother, Lady Melissa West."

Sally held out her hand.

"I'm pleased to meet you, Lady Melissa," she said and deliberately kept her hand there until Lady Melissa had to take it.

She shook hands as if she was holding a wet fish. Sally's stand did not go unnoticed by Dominic. We may be in for some fireworks, he thought nervously.

"Is father here?" he asked briefly.

"He's over there somewhere," Melissa replied, still looking closely at Sally and in particular the pearl necklace.

"We'll go and say hello to him."

Dominic took Sally across to the other side of the room. On the way, they helped themselves to glasses of wine from a passing waiter. Sir Humphrey saw them coming and went forward to meet them.

"Sally," he said in a delighted voice and kissed her on both cheeks. "Dominic, my boy, it's good to see you," and shook his hand.

"Can you look after Sally for a few minutes?" he said. "There is something I need to do."

"I have to go and check that the lunch is nearly ready," Sir Humphrey said, "but I'm sure Lady Harrington will look after her."

Sally noticed an elderly lady with a silver-headed walking stick sitting on one of the chairs. She patted the chair next to her and Sally sat down. Dominic leaned over:

"I won't be long," he said.

He left the room and went across the hall into the dining room. He quickly looked at the place settings and found, as he suspected, that he was placed near the top of the table and Sally was sitting much further down. He removed Sally's name and moved all the others along until there was a space next to him where he replaced Sally's name. On the other side of Sally, there would be an elderly gentleman who had often visited Kitson Manor. Meanwhile, Sally had been having an interesting conversation with Lady Monica Harrington.

"I have known Dominic since he was a little boy and I know all about his mother's rejection of him. Lord Kitson never approved of his daughter's behaviour and that is why his grandparents virtually raised him. Melissa has tried to harness him all through his life and it is only quite recently that he has stood up to her and his ex-wife."

Sally was silent and Lady Harrington looked at her. Finally, Sally said:

"Are you saying that Dominic has changed since we have been together?"

"He has changed a great deal. He is a much happier man, more willing to be open about his problems and he is not so inward-looking as he was. It is obvious that he loves you very much and Melissa is absolutely livid that he has chosen you instead of one of her little rich offerings."

"That is one thing that I find quite difficult," Sally admitted. "I can't get my head around all that money so I have decided to ignore it as far as possible and let Dominic decide about it."

"A very wise decision," said Lady Harrington. "He is an excellent businessman. You can have complete trust in him." Lady Harrington looked around the room. "I can see him coming back but oh dear, look who is bearing down on him."

Sally looked up to see a pencil-slim, expensively dressed lady just about to stop Dominic. She knew at once who it was.

"I think he might need your support," Lady Harrington said. "Have you got the courage?"

"Yes, I have the courage. I will go to him now."

Lady Harrington watched her go. Humphrey was right, she thought. Dominic has chosen well.

Sally walked across the room to where Dominic was standing. It was

36

obvious that he didn't know what to do. Sally walked up to the woman with him and held out her hand.

"I'm Sally, Dominic's fiancée," she said in a friendly way. "And you are?"

"I am Susanna, Dominic's ex-wife," she stammered as if totally out of her depth.

"I'm pleased to meet you," Sally said in a formal way and with her hand still outstretched so that Susanna had no option but to give it a flabby shake.

"Are the boys here with you?" Sally asked sweetly.

"Yes, they are here somewhere," came a short reply as she turned to Dominic. "Nice to see you. You are looking very well," and she walked off.

Several other people had witnessed that exchange and they couldn't help admiring Sally. Dominic took her over to the side of the room.

"That was a masterstroke," he said adoringly.

"It was simple common straightforward manners," she said rather embarrassed.

Just then the gong sounded in the hall. They went into the dining room where everyone was searching for their place names. Melissa and Sir Humphrey sat at the head of the table and Melissa signalled to Dominic to sit by her but he went to the other side of the table. Sally sat between Sir Humphrey and Dominic. The result was that Susanna and the boys were now sitting at the middle of the table. Melissa was furious that her carefully laid plans had gone wrong. Her face was almost the same colour as her dress. Sir Humphrey sat serenely by her, seemingly unaffected by her discomfort. They had a delicious lunch and half-way through, Dominic and Sally changed places so that Sally could sit by Lady Harrington. The old lady chatted away about her past life and Sally was fascinated. Once or twice in the more risqué parts of the story, Sally couldn't stop herself from laughing out loud. Melissa looked at her in disgust but many of the other guests watched developments with interest.

Towards the end of the meal, Sir Humphrey stood up. He thanked everyone for coming and wished them all a Happy Christmas. Then he said:

"Most of you know that Melissa and I are getting divorced. It is a sad day but an inevitable one. I would like to drink a toast to the happy gatherings we have had in the past." Everyone then sat down but Sir Humphrey remained standing. "I would like to propose one last toast: to Dominic and Sally, the next generation. May they have a long and happy life together."

Everyone raised their glasses but Melissa said nothing.

When the meal was over, everyone returned to the drawing-room. The men were served with port and the ladies with champagne but Sally stuck to the wine. They mingled with the guests and many old friends came up to congratulate Dominic. It was noticeable that Melissa and Susanna kept their distance. Out of the corner of her eye, Sally saw the two boys come into the room followed by a well-dressed man whose face seemed vaguely familiar. They came up to Dominic and said:

"Hello, father."

Dominic shook hands with the boys and commented on how much they had grown, then he greeted the man accompanying them and introduced them all to Sally. The man kissed her hand and the two boys shook hands with her and said in a very formal way:

"How do you do?"

She stepped back as Dominic continued his conversation with the man. She looked closely at the boys and studied their faces. She could see little resemblance to Dominic. They had piercing blue eyes and very light hair with a hint of ginger in it. Dominic's eyes were brown and he had dark hair which curled up in the rain. She looked at the man who was with the boys and noticed that his blue eyes were darker and his goatee beard and eyebrows were tinged with auburn.

As she stood there, Sally was aware of a commotion at the door and Susanna stormed into the room. She walked straight up to the boys and said in an affected voice:

"There you are. I've been looking everywhere for you."

She looked accusingly at the man who was standing there in embarrassment and then she noticed Sally. She gave her the most disdainful look which would have made most people curl up. But Sally was made of sterner stuff. She looked back with a slight smile on her face. Then her eyes moved to the boys and the man standing with them. She then looked straight back at Susanna with a cold stare. Dominic was frozen to the spot as Susanna turned on her heel and left the room in a cold fury. The man put a hand on each of the boys and ushered them through the guests, most of whom were lost for words.

"I think it is time for us to go, Sally," said Dominic quietly, putting an arm around her.

They walked through the drawing-room to the sound of whispers. As they reached the door, Sally noticed Lady Harrington sitting there with Sir Humphrey. She went over to say goodbye to her and leant over to kiss her on the cheek. Lady Harrington squeezed Sally's hand.

"Well done, my dear. You have passed with flying colours."

Sally stood up and smiled.

"I hope we shall meet again," she said sincerely.

Sir Humphrey had risen to his feet to say goodbye to Dominic.

"I'll see you later," he said and then turned to Sally. "I am very proud of you," he said quietly. "You are a breath of fresh air," and he kissed her.

As they went into the hall to get their coats, Dominic said:

"I suppose I ought to say goodbye to Mother. You wait here."

He went back into the drawing-room but couldn't see her anywhere. He spoke to his father and Sir Humphrey promised to do it for him. He hurried back to Sally and they walked down the steps. They said very little on their journey into London and it was only when they were in their hotel room that they relaxed. Dominic took Sally in his arms and held her closely.

"You were marvellous," he said. "You charmed everyone."

"Except your mother and ex-wife," replied Sally, drily.

"They didn't need to be charmed, they needed to be put in their place and you did that beautifully."

"All I did was to approach it on the basis of good manners. I didn't plan anything. I behaved as I felt," she insisted.

"That very approach takes them out of their comfort zone. They have no idea how to react naturally. Everything is dramatized."

She looked at him in astonishment.

#

"How long have you had that opinion, Dominic?"

"Since I met you," he said simply. "I was part of that way of behaving but you have been so thoughtful and down-to-earth and it is beginning to rub off on me."

"I love you the way you are," she said, kissing him. "I don't want to change you but I might try charming you."

They sat on the settee holding hands.

"What did you think of my two boys?"

"They were too uptight for my liking," Sally said honestly. "They seemed to have no spirit. In any case," she added, "I don't believe they are your boys."

He looked at her in amazement.

"Are you saying that I am not their father?"

"They are not a bit like you. Their eyes, their hair, their general demeanour is not you. It is much more like the man who was with them. I assume that he is Susanna's new partner?"

"Not exactly new. She left me for him about fourteen years ago but he already had a wife and after a couple of years, she begged me to take her back. That was when I bought the house in Hampstead."

"For someone who deals in millions of pounds," she said. "Your maths is very poor."

He looked at her in disbelief.

"What do you mean?" he stammered.

"You said she left you fourteen years ago, well James is thirteen and David is eleven. They must have been toddlers when she came back to you with two children and yet you hadn't slept with her for two years. Of course, they are not your flesh and blood."

"I suppose I am like my father. I used to like to hush things up; some warped sense of duty but looking back on it I guess it was an easy way out."

"Has her new partner still got a wife?"

"Unfortunately, she died of cancer last year and that was the trigger for divorce."

"Who is he?" she asked. "I've seen his face before."

"He is often on the front pages of the newspapers. He is the Home Secretary in the present government. He has done a lot of work with Father."

"I don't suppose that he would admit to being the boys' father but if he is back with Susanna, they can always say that they are her sons."

"I have never felt close to them," he said. "There were always tensions between us. I shall seriously think about that DNA test now."

"What is happening this evening?" Sally asked. "Shall I need to change?"

"You are fine as you are, no evening dress required."

She breathed a sigh of relief.

"I might try the champagne this evening. Be reckless," she said glibly.

"Just make sure you don't go to sleep before your head touches the pillow. I'm looking forward to your charm offensive," Dominic reminded her. He looked at his watch. "It is five forty-five," he said. "We will meet father at seven-thirty."

Sally kicked off her shoes and hung up her dress. She wrapped herself in the fluffy bathrobe and lay on the bed.

"Come and lie with me," she said as she patted the bed.

Dominic took his shoes off and hung up his jacket on the back of the chair. He lay down by Sally and they both went to sleep. He was woken by the phone in the room.

"Sir Humphrey has left a message for you. It says that he has been delayed and will meet you in the bar at eight o'clock."

"That's good," Dominic said. "It gives us time to freshen up."

Sally took a small Christmas parcel out of her case and gave it to

Dominic.

"Happy Christmas," she said as she handed it to him.

He opened it up and inside was a lovely silk, dove grey tie.

"Thank you," he said. "I shall wear it this evening."

They went down to meet Sir Humphrey and all three went into the dining room. They sat and chatted and ordered a comparatively light meal. Dominic ordered champagne and Sir Humphrey looked at Sally.

"I noticed you stayed off the champagne at lunchtime?" he said.

"I didn't want to find myself in the soup," she grinned.

"It was other people who ended up with egg on their faces," he said seriously, "and they deserve every bit of it."

"I do hope I didn't offend anyone," Sally said contritely.

"There were two people who were already offended before they even met you," Sir Humphrey said with a smile, "but there were many others who admired the way you managed a difficult encounter."

Dominic took Sally's hand and looked at her.

"I know how nervous you were and I am very proud of you," he said. "You supported me when I was in a tricky situation. It made all the difference to me to have you by my side."

"It's been a long and tiring day," Sir Humphrey said as he stood up. "I'm glad it's over." He kissed Sally goodnight and said goodbye to Dominic. "I shall come to Oxford tomorrow morning," he said. "I'll let you know when I have arrived."

Dominic and Sally watched him go and Sally said:

"He seemed very tired this evening."

"It must have been a stressful day for him too," Dominic said thoughtfully. He put an arm around Sally. "Let's go upstairs. I'll get the waiter to bring the champagne up."

They went up to their apartment and five minutes later the champagne arrived. Dominic turned to Sally and took her in his arms.

"I've had to share you with so many people today," he said quietly. "Now I want you for myself."

"I'm all yours," she whispered and she stroked the back of his neck.

He shivered and held her close.

"You promised me this morning that I could unzip you," he said breathing heavily.

"I always keep my promises," Sally said softly and she turned her back to him.

He undid the pearls and laid them on the table. Then he slowly pulled the zip down until the dress slipped off Sally's shoulders and she stepped out of it.

"Wait a minute," he gasped and went and fetched one of the fluffy robes which were hanging in the bathroom.

He tossed it on the settee then he picked Sally up and laid her on top of it. He could hardly contain his desire for her as his clothes ended up in an untidy heap on the floor. They lay together on the settee until their heartbeats returned to normal and even then, neither of them wanted to move.

Eventually, Dominic stood up and picked his clothes up from the floor. He took them into the bedroom and hung them up. He went into the bathroom and took the other robe off the peg, then he returned to the lounge. Sally had pulled the robe around her and was sitting up. He poured two glasses of champagne and gave one to Sally. His hand was shaking as he passed her the glass. She drank half of it straight away. Dominic looked at her in surprise.

"Are you alright?" he said anxiously.

"Yes, I think so. I'm still recovering from a passionate experience."

She drained her glass and Dominic refilled it, then sat down beside her.

"It's been a difficult day with so many conflicting emotions which I couldn't control. I'm sorry, my love I don't know what came over me," and he looked at her with tears in his eyes.

"I really am okay," she said, putting her arms around him. "It was just so unexpected."

"My life is full of unexpected things at present," he said with feeling. "The only sure thing is my love for you."

"I know you have been worrying about today but it is over now. We have three more days to spend together and you can forget about your problems. I'm going to have a shower and then you can have the rest of your Christmas present."

She went into the bathroom and ten minutes later she came out ready for bed. Dominic was sitting on the settee looking sad. She went up to him and took his hand as he stood up.

"Come on," she said encouragingly, "a nice hot shower will do you good and then it will be bedtime."

She led him into the bathroom and left him. She went back into the lounge and turned off the lights. In the bedroom, she switched on the bedside lamps and laid Dominic's pyjamas on the bed. He emerged from the bathroom wrapped in a towel. Sally went up to him and kissed him.

"You smell nice," she said and handed him his pyjamas then she pulled back the duvet. "Time for bed."

They lay down side by side and she leaned over and kissed him lightly on the lips. She stroked his face with soft fingers and then gently massaged his head. She heard him sigh and she knew that he was beginning to relax. She continued to run her hands gently over his body until he responded to her touch. He looked into her eyes.

"Sally," he said with a hint of desperation. "Sally," he gasped. "I love you."

"I love you too," she whispered, moving closer to him.

He put his arms around her and showed her once again how much she meant to him.

They were both overcome with exhaustion and they lay back on the pillows. Dominic held Sally's hand and soon they were both fast asleep.

The next morning, they ordered breakfast in their apartment and by ten o'clock were on the way home. They spent the rest of the day relaxing and at four o'clock Sir Humphrey phoned to say that he had arrived in Oxford.

"We are going to visit Sally's mother in the morning," Dominic told him. "We will join you for lunch at twelve o'clock."

Dominic looked at Sally and said:

"How would you feel if we invited father back here after lunch, then he can come with us to Adam's house?"

"That seems like a good idea," she replied. "We shall need to order him a taxi to take him back to the hotel at the end of the evening."

"I'll do that in the morning," he said.

On Saturday morning, Sally wrapped up the Christmas cake and the bottle of sherry. They drove to Witney and parked the car.

"I wonder what sort of mood she will be in?"

"The sherry will soon put her right," Dominic assured her.

They knocked on Mary's door and went in.

"Happy Christmas mother," Sally said sweetly.

"A bit late to say that," Mary muttered. "I didn't see you at Christmas."

"Better late than never," Dominic said as he stepped forward.

"I see you've brought Nick with you," Mary said grumpily. "You'd better make him a cup of tea."

Sally went to put the kettle on.

"We've brought you some presents, Mary," said Dominic, handing her the two presents wrapped in Christmas wrapping paper.

Mary took them and started to poke at the smaller one.

"What is it?" she demanded.

"Why don't you open it and see?" he replied, patiently.

She ripped the paper.

"That's a small one," she said in a disgusted voice.

Sally came back with the tea.

"Why don't we each have some cake with our tea," she suggested.

"Might as well," Mary said in a resigned voice. "It won't last very long anyway."

Dominic had taken the paper off the bottle of sherry and now he showed it to Mary.

"That's better," she said looking at him. "When are you going to make an honest woman of my daughter?"

Dominic was smiling and Sally said:

"Mother, that was a rude question!"

"Soon, very soon," he answered which seemed to satisfy Mary and she lapsed into silence.

Sally collected the cups and the plates and washed them up. Suddenly Mary said:

"You'd better go. You don't want to miss the bus."

Sally kissed her mother and Dominic patted Mary's hand.

"We'll come and see you another day," he said.

As they went towards the door, they heard Mary say to herself:

"I suppose I shall have to buy a new dress."

"She's hard work, isn't she?" said Sally, as they sat in the car.

"She's old and she only has her memories to keep her going," replied Dominic. "She doesn't really mean half of what she says."

They drove back to Oxford and met Sir Humphrey in the bar of the Randolph Hotel. He ordered a bottle of wine and they sat in the comfortable lounge area.

"I've booked a table for one o'clock," he told them. "How was your mother, Sally?"

"As miserable as ever," she replied. "Do you know she calls Dominic, Nick?"

"She sounds quite a character," said Sir Humphrey, laughing.

"She wanted to know when I was going to make her daughter an honest woman. She was worried that she would have to buy a new dress," Dominic said solemnly.

"It will be purple polyester with green and yellow flowers on it," Sally said in a serious voice and all three of them burst out laughing.

A waiter came up to Sir Humphrey.

"Your table is ready, sir."

They followed him into the dining room and Sir Humphrey ordered another bottle of wine. They ordered their meals and they sat and talked about the previous day.

"I said goodbye to your mother on your behalf," said Sir Humphrey. "And I received some pithy expletives for my troubles."

"I'm so sorry father," Dominic replied seriously. "I should never have put you in that position."

"Don't worry about it, my boy. I've been there many times before."

They enjoyed their lunch and returned to the lounge for coffee.

"Would you like to come home with us this afternoon?" Dominic asked. "Then we can all go to Adam's together."

"Are you sure he doesn't mind my joining you?" Sir Humphrey asked anxiously.

"You have already met many of the people who will be there," Sally said. "Adam will be most welcoming."

"I'll just go and get my coat," Sir Humphrey said and went up to his bedroom. He took a parcel out of his case and carried it downstairs. He gave it to Sally to hold. "Be careful with it," he said. "It is quite fragile."

They got into Dominic's car and drove to Sally's house with her sitting in the back seat.

"This is a very pleasant part of the country," said Sir Humphrey. "There must be some nice houses around."

"We haven't had time to look yet," said Dominic. "We shall start looking seriously in the New Year."

They were soon back at Sally's house and they went in. It was quite warm and cosy and Dominic led the way into the lounge. Sally put the parcel on the table but then Sir Humphrey said:

"That is your Christmas present. You can open it now."

She carefully removed the wrapping paper and opened the box. Inside was an exquisite Lalique fruit bowl.

"It's beautiful," she said. "It will take pride of place in our house."

"It's the genuine article," Dominic said. "You chose well."

"I have to admit that I am not solely responsible for the choice. I took Lady Harrington with me when I went shopping. She knows more about antiques than I. Her house is full of treasures."

"I'll keep it safely in its box until we have a house," said Sally as she replaced the lid.

Sir Humphrey sat in the fireside chair and Dominic sat on the settee by Sally. Sir Humphrey stretched out his legs.

"This is a most comfortable chair," he said and went to sleep.

Chapter Five

While Sally and Dominic were having a stressful time on Christmas Day it was all very different at Leah's house. Jessica had woken everyone up and after breakfast, she said to Bill:

"I want to show you what I had in my Father Christmas stocking. Come with me."

Bill followed her into the lounge and started to unpack the stocking. She gave Bill the small teddy to hold and she talked about each tiny present as she pulled it out. Bill was very patient with her. Alice and Leah had been in the kitchen preparing the Christmas lunch and they came into the lounge for a rest. Adam had enjoyed a lie-in that morning but he too was now dressed.

"Happy Christmas everyone!" he said, coming in to join them. "I wonder if Father Christmas left any presents last night?"

"He left me my stocking," said Jessica.

"I think I can see more parcels under the tree," Adam said as he looked towards the conservatory.

Jessica stood up and went to look through the double doors.

"There are loads more presents out there!" she said excitedly. "I wonder who they are for?"

Leah stood up and opened the doors.

"See if any of them have names on," she suggested.

Jessica went out and picked up a parcel.

"This one says Alice and here's one that says Jessica. Look," she said, "they all have names on them. There's one here for Lucy and one for Benjie." She was jumping up and down with excitement.

Alice went out to her.

"Calm down," she said. "You'll make yourself sick. Why don't you find the ones with your name and bring them into the lounge? I'll help you."

Soon there was a pile of presents on the lounge carpet.

"My goodness," said Adam. "What a lot of Father Christmas surprises."

Each present had a tag on it to say who it was from. Jessica picked up the largest one and read the label.

"This says from Grandma and Grandad," she said and ripped the paper off. She looked at the teddy bear with its blue bow and cuddled it up to her. "I love my teddy. Thank you, thank you," and she kissed Leah and hugged Adam.

She was thrilled with all her presents. The last one was quite small and it said: 'To Jessica with love from Bill.' Jessica opened it carefully and inside was a proper girl's watch with a leather strap. She looked at it and then looked at Bill.

"It's a real watch," she said, "a proper grown-up watch." She went up to him and put her arms around him. "Thank you, Bill," she said. "Will you put it on for me please?"

He took the watch out of its box and fastened it around her wrist.

"Is it lunchtime yet?" Adam asked her.

"Not yet," she said, looking at her watch. "It's only a quarter to twelve."

"That means it is coffee time," Adam decided but he didn't move off the settee.

Leah looked at him.

"I get the message," she said and she went into the kitchen.

Jessica had curled up by Bill with one of her books. Alice looked at the mess on the carpet.

"You need a black bag for all that paper," said Adam.

Alice looked at him expectantly but he still didn't move.

"Are you stuck to that settee?" she said crossly as she left the room.

"I would have offered," Bill said in an innocent voice, "but I can't move."

Adam looked at him and grinned.

"You're learning fast," he said and the two of them shared the joke.

Alice came back with a bin liner and filled it with all the old wrapping paper. When she had left the room, Adam collected together all the presents and stacked them neatly by the fireplace. Leah came in with the coffee.

"This is a nice tidy room," she said as she sat down.

Alice glared at her father and Adam just smiled back.

Alice and Leah served up the dinner and Adam carved the turkey. Everything was cooked beautifully and this time Adam and Bill cleared the table and did the washing up, leaving the pots and pans for Leah and Alice. They retired to the lounge and flopped down on the settees. Before long they were all asleep.

The rest of the day passed quietly and by eight o'clock Jessica was ready for bed. She said goodnight to Adam and Leah and then she said to Alice:

"I want Bill to come and say goodnight when I'm in bed."

She picked up her teddy bear and went upstairs. Bill felt in his pocket to make sure he had Alice's present and followed her. Jessica was soon in bed and Bill kissed her goodnight.

As they left the room, he took Alice by the hand and led her into his room and kissed her.

"I haven't had a chance to give you your Christmas present," he said, handing it to her. "With all my love."

Alice opened it and inside was a shiny silver bangle.

"It's beautiful," she said as she put it on. "It's really lovely," and she kissed him. "I love you so much. Thank you, Bill."

He put his arms around her and they fell back on the bed. He stroked her face and murmured:

"I love you, Alice. I need you."

"Not now," Alice gasped, "but soon, very soon."

Bill raised himself and looked at her.

"It can't be soon enough for me," he said tenderly and kissed her.

Downstairs in the lounge, Leah took an envelope off the mantlepiece and gave it to Adam.

"This is your Christmas present," she said as she kissed him.

"I've never had a white envelope as a present before," he said slowly, looking at it.

"Well, why don't you open it?" she said impatiently.

Adam looked closely at the writing on the front, he smelled it and held it up to the light, then he carefully opened it. He took out the printed card, read it and then turned to Leah in disbelief.

"A whole weekend together. Just the two of us?" he said.

"Yes, that's right," she replied firmly. "It's for next weekend and is all paid for so there is no backing out."

He put his arms around her.

"I wouldn't dream of backing out of a whole weekend with my lovely wife," he said sincerely. "That is a great Father Christmas surprise."

He gave the envelope back to Leah and she went and put it safely in a drawer. Then she came back and sat next to him.

"Another busy day tomorrow," he said. "Two more excited children."

"I wonder if I shall have my usual box of chocolates?" Leah said dreamily.

"All this excitement has quite worn me out," he said wearily. "I think an early night is called for."

Alice and Bill came back into the lounge. Alice was looking flushed as she showed them her Christmas present. They both admired it and Adam gave a thumbs-up to Bill. They chatted a little longer until Leah stood up and said:

"Pete and his family should be here by eleven-thirty and we must eat at one o'clock sharp. Janet will be wanting to go to her mother's in the afternoon." She said goodnight and went up the stairs.

"You can put the lights out," Adam said to Alice and he followed Leah.

"It's been a lovely day," Leah said contently as they lay in bed.

"Yes, it has," Adam agreed. "A proper family Christmas."

He decided not to torture himself thinking about past Christmas's, there was no need. He put his arm across Leah as if protecting her. They both relaxed and were soon asleep. They didn't hear Bill and Alice come upstairs and they never knew that Jessica slept alone that night.

Alice was first up on Boxing Day morning and she took her parents a cup of tea. They lay there contemplating the day ahead before they decided to get dressed. Leah hoped that it would all go smoothly and Adam tried to reassure her. They went downstairs and Leah tidied up the lounge. Adam went into the conservatory and rearranged the presents under the tree. They extended the dining table so that it could accommodate nine people and Leah found the large tablecloth. She took the cutlery out of the drawer and laid the table. Alice brought in the clean wine glasses.

Adam carved up the rest of the turkey and put the slices on a large meat dish. Then he sliced up the cold ham which had been in the fridge. Alice prepared the vegetables and by eleven o'clock everything was ready. They all sat down at coffee time but Jessica kept looking out of the window. She saw Peter's car stop outside the house.

"They're here!" she cried.

Leah went to open the door and Adam followed her. Peter undid their seat belts and Benjie and Lucy came running up the path.

"Granny Leah! Granny Leah!" shouted Benjie as Leah opened her arms to hug him.

Lucy went straight to Adam and he picked her up and kissed her.

"Grandad Adam," she said. "I've got a present for you."

"Let's go inside," Adam said. "It's cold out here."

Peter collected some bags out of the boot and Janet was slowly getting out of the front seat. By the time they reached the front door, the others were in the lounge. Peter dropped the bags in the hall and joined them.

"Happy Christmas," he said to his parents and Alice.

Then he turned to Bill. Adam introduced the two men and they shook hands. Janet was standing behind him so Peter took her arm and brought her towards Bill.

"This is Janet, my wife," he said and Bill held out his hand; she looked at it and then decided to shake it.

Benjie and Lucy had been listening to all this with interest. Bill looked at Benjie and said:

"I'm Bill, what's your name?"

Benjie stood in front of him.

"I'm Benjamin, Adam Richards but I am called Benjie. I'm nearly seven years old and this is my sister Lucy Ann. She is only three and a half."

"I'm very pleased to meet you," said Bill, shaking hands with him.

Lucy looked carefully at Bill then she looked at Adam.

"This is my Grandad Adam," she said. "Do you know him?"

"Yes, I know him," Bill replied.

"That's good," Lucy said. "He is my bestest grandad," and she took hold of Adam's hands.

Janet left the room and went into the hall.

"Benjie, Lucy," she called sharply. "Come here."

They left the room and came back with their arms full of presents. Benjie looked at the names and he said:

"That is for Jessica and that is for Alice." He took one of the presents Lucy was holding to go with the one he still had in his hand. "That's for Granny Leah and that is for Grandad," he said. "I chose them myself, and I paid for them," he added as an afterthought.

Janet went to speak but Peter stopped her. Lucy was still holding her two presents.

"Do you need some help?" Peter said quietly.

"No thank you," Lucy said and she gave one of the presents to Leah.

"Thank you, Lucy," Leah said.

Lucy looked at Bill then she said to Leah:

"I haven't got a present for Bill. Can you share?"

"Yes, of course, I will," Leah said at once.

"It's nice to share," Lucy said dreamily. "Sometimes I share with my brother."

Benjie was about to argue but again Peter stopped him.

"You are holding one more present," he reminded her.

She looked at the box she was holding in her hand.

"This is for you Grandad Adam," she said as she gave it to him. "You must open it now."

Adam took the wrapping paper off and opened the box. He took out a coffee mug with 'I love you Grandad,' written on the side. Adam bent down and kissed her.

"Thank you, Lucy," he said. "That is a lovely present," and a tear rolled down his cheek.

"You're not s'posed to cry at Christmas. You're s'posed to be happy," she said to him.

"These are happy tears," Adam assured her as he wiped his eyes.

Janet looked enquiringly at Peter.

"It was entirely her choice," he said.

Jessica had been silent but now she said:

"Father Christmas left some presents here for you." She looked at her mother. "Shall we go and get them?"

The grownups all sat down and Alice and Jessica went into the conservatory. They came back with their arms full of presents which they piled up on the carpet.

"Take it in turns," Peter said. "Benjie can go first."

Benjie looked at the largest parcel and began to rip the paper off. When he saw the Lego Ferris Wheel, he let out a whoop of pleasure.

"That's cool, that's really cool," he said. "Thank you," and he got up and kissed Leah and Adam.

"Lucy's turn," Peter said and she unwrapped the little penguin which Leah had chosen.

"I love him," she said and showed it to Jessica.

They took turns to open the other presents and Benjie was thrilled with his water gun. Peter looked at his father in despair.

"You know that will cause trouble," he said.

"It's just a bit of fun," Adam said soothingly. "You can leave it here. I'll buy another one and then they can have water fights in the summer." He glanced at Janet who was sitting stony-faced.

"There is one more present for Lucy in the conservatory," Jessica said and she took Lucy's hand and led her through the double doors. The pram was standing by the wall with the doll inside it.

Lucy couldn't believe it.

"Is that for me?" she cried. "Now I'll be able to take my dolls for a walk." She picked up the doll and it said, 'Ma-ma.' "It can talk to me," Lucy said in wonder.

"Shall we take it into the lounge?" Jessica said. "I'm sure they would all like to see it."

Jessica lifted it over the door frame and Lucy pushed it into the lounge. They all admired it but Janet said:

"How on earth are we going to get it into the car?"

"It will fold up like a pushchair," Adam said. "It won't be a problem."

Leah and Alice left the room and went into the kitchen to dish up the lunch. The children stayed in the lounge playing with their toys. Benjie was longing to try out his water gun.

"Come with me," said Adam.

They went into the utility area and Adam filled the gun with water.

"Not in here," he warned Benjie. "You can stand in the doorway and point it outside." He opened the outside door and Benjie began shooting out the water.

"This is great!" he shouted and let out a whoop of delight.

Peter came out to see what all the noise was about. He looked at his father and said affectionately:

"You're just a big kid, aren't you?"

Janet appeared at the kitchen door to tell them that dinner was ready. She took one look at what Benjie was doing and shrieked at him.

"What do you think you are doing?"

Adam looked at her.

"He's having fun. That's what you are supposed to do at Christmas time," he said coolly. "Why don't you loosen up and have fun too?"

Janet gave him a disdainful look and turned round to go back inside. Peter went up to Benjie and put a comforting arm around him.

"I think we'll leave this with grandad," he said quietly as he took the gun from him. "You can use it whenever we come to visit," and he took Benjie off to wash his hands.

Adam collected two bottles of wine and a bottle of coke for the children. He went into the dining room where everyone was seated and filled the glasses which were on the table. Janet immediately drank half her glass. Leah poured the coke for the children and then Adam stood up.

"I want to propose a toast to our family Christmas and to remember two of the family who are far away from us," and he raised his glass. They all stood up and clinked their glasses.

"Can anybody propose a toast?" Benjie asked.

"Yes, of course, they can," Adam smiled.

"Right," Benjie said decisively and he stood on his chair.

Janet was about to tell him to get his feet off the chair but Peter gave her a look which distinctly said 'keep quiet.' Benjie held up his glass and said:

"I want to propose a toast to my sister Lucy and to Alice and to Jessica," and he continued until he had said the names of everyone around the table, "and to me," he finished up. They all raised their glasses to him.

"Now we must eat," Adam said. "Then we can have another toast to the cooks."

Lucy was sitting between her mother and Bill. She looked at him and said:

"Do you like toast, Bill?"

Adam heard Lucy's question and he looked at him and grinned. Bill was not sure how to answer so he said:

"Yes, I like toast for my breakfast."

"Do you have it in a glass?" Lucy added.

Bill looked helplessly at Adam who was trying not to laugh.

"No, I have it on a plate," he said.

"But you've just had it out of a glass," she said, looking puzzled.

"That's a special kind of toast you have at parties," Bill replied.

"I like marmite on toast," she said. "Anyway, I usually eat soldiers," and that was her final word.

Bill was relieved that the conversation didn't get more complicated. He looked at Adam who was laughing quietly to himself and he smiled.

At the end of the meal, Adam refilled all the glasses and stood up.

"That was delicious," he said. "We must drink a toast to the cooks. Alice and Leah," and they raised their glasses. "One last toast to the clearer-uppers," he said and turned to Peter and Bill.

Everyone laughed and left the table. The children went back to playing with their toys and the ladies sat down and relaxed. Lucy found one of her picture books and took it to Leah.

"I'm going to tell you a story," she said and cuddled up. She started to describe the pictures but soon her eyes closed and she was fast asleep.

The men soon had the table cleared. Adam took the cloth off the table and put it in the washing machine. They left the pots and pans till later. Adam looked at Bill and laughed.

"You had a grilling at the dinner table," he said.

"She is quite a little cutie," said Bill, grinning at Peter.

"They are good kids," Peter said proudly. "I just wish their mother wouldn't nag them so much." He looked at Adam and said, "How is Alice's divorce coming on?"

"William has agreed to everything and now we are waiting for the house to be sold. Bill is most interested in the outcome," Adam said.

"Is it serious between you two, Bill?" he asked.

"Yes, it is," Bill replied. "We are only waiting until the divorce is finalised."

"Well, good luck to both of you," Peter said shaking his hand. "Alice has had a rough time and I hope you will be very happy together."

Bill thanked him and they returned to the lounge. Janet was getting restless and kept looking at her watch.

"We must be going soon," she said shortly. "Mother will be expecting us. Put the presents in the car, Peter."

"We will take Lucy's pram and Benjie's Lego and leave the rest here for them to play with when we visit," Peter said firmly.

Adam showed him how to fold the pram and they put the contents into a large bag.

"Keep the doll out so that she can have it when she wakes up," Leah said.

Benjie was reluctant to move.

"Come along," Janet said sharply. "You know there will be more presents for you."

Benjie pulled a face but he put his coat on. Peter carried Lucy to the car and strapped her in. Adam took Benjie's hand and walked out to the car with him.

"Don't forget," he whispered to him. "I will get another water pistol ready for when you come down next time."

He kissed him goodbye as Peter fastened his seat belt. Janet had said a hasty goodbye to everyone and was already sitting in the front seat. Peter went back indoors and kissed Alice and Jessica. He shook hands with Bill, then he went up to Leah.

"Thanks for everything, Mum," he said. "I'm sorry we have to rush off," and he hugged her.

"It's alright, Peter," she said quietly. "I quite understand."

He turned to Adam.

"It was so nearly a proper family Christmas. Perhaps next year we will be a complete family."

"That would be nice," Adam said seriously, "but it has been good to see you. Look after yourself and remember that I am here if ever you want to talk." And he put his arm around Peter.

"Thanks, Dad," Peter said in a choked voice and went down the path to the car. As soon as he sat in the driver's seat Janet looked at him and said:

"Where on earth have you been? We shall be late."

"Oh, shut up," he replied, not even bothering to look at her. "We shall only be late for tea and biscuits."

Adam closed the front door and they all sat in the lounge.

"I think there is trouble ahead," Leah said quietly.

"Unfortunately, I think you are right," Adam said. "It all depends on which one cracks first."

"Janet was not a friendly person," Bill said. "I tried to talk to her but she spent most of the time sending text messages."

"All we can do is watch and wait," Adam said with resignation.

Jessica had been looking through her box of games and she took out a pack of cards.

"Who wants to play snap with me?" she asked hopefully.

"I'll play with you," said Adam. "So long as I can go to sleep afterwards. We'll play the best of three."

He dealt the cards and they won one each of the first two games.

"Now for the decider," Adam said in a determined voice.

The play was fast and furious and in the end, it was just won by Jessica. Adam lay back on the settee.

"That's enough excitement for me," he said. "Now it is someone else's turn."

"It's your turn now, Bill," said Jessica, looking at him.

"Our reputation stands on your shoulders, Bill," said Adam.

"No pressure then," he replied, laughing.

Again, they each won a game but Bill easily won the decider.

"Well done," Adam said. "You should get a promotion on the back of that. You are now the chief wine-fetcher and your duties start right now."

Bill went out to find a bottle of wine and Alice followed him into the kitchen. He took her in his arms and stroked her face.

"Are you happy, Alice?"

"Yes, I am very happy," she replied and kissed him.

She found four clean glasses and Bill opened the wine. They took it back into the lounge.

"What time is it, please Jessica?" asked Leah.

"It's almost half-past three," Jessica said as she looked at her new watch.

"It's a bit early to start drinking," Leah said.

"Nonsense, my love," said Adam. "It is just the right time on Boxing day."

"You've got an answer for everything or an excuse," she said wearily, "and you can make people believe you."

"It's just one of my many talents," Adam said graciously. "I've got others as well," and he kissed her.

"I think I will play snakes and ladders next," Jessica decided. "It's your turn mummy."

"We'll play on the dining room table," Alice said.

"I'll come and give you moral support," Bill said, and they disappeared into the dining room and shut the door behind them.

Adam and Leah were left in the lounge. He put his arm around her.

"It seems a long time since we had the room to ourselves."

"I'm really looking forward to next weekend," she said, sighing. "I need to slow down. I'm running out of energy."

"You're not feeling ill, are you?" he asked, anxiously.

"No, I'm not feeling ill," she replied. "For years my life was pretty predictable, home alone, school, shopping. I knew what the pattern was and it just happened. Now I hardly know from day-to-day. So many new faces and new experiences. I'm not used to it and it bothers me sometimes."

Adam was silent for a few minutes.

"I suppose I am to blame for the way you are feeling. I am very aware of the effect the last five months have had on me but I hadn't realised how it had affected you. You really are always so calm and sensible and I love you for that. I have felt so happy to be with you again. You are my whole life. Everything else is only part of it."

"I don't think I fully understand the new you," Leah said slowly. "It is so different, almost opposite to what you once were. You are confident, successful, socially aware. Everyone respects you and your opinions and yet you still love me and I love you. I don't understand it," she sighed.

"Does it bother you that much?" Adam said with real concern in his voice.

"Many people have come to me with their problems and I have been able to help them," Leah told him, "but I don't seem to be able to help myself."

He put his arms around her.

"The first thing you must do is not to use the word problem. It is a reaction to all the shocks and surprises of the past five months. Let me ask you a question. Do you regret that I came back into your life?"

She looked at him in dismay.

"Of course, I don't regret it," she said firmly. "It was the best thing that ever happened to me. What about you?"

"It was what I had dreamed about for thirteen years," he said, "and I couldn't quite believe it when it actually happened. The past five months have been the happiest of my life because you were there. So many other things have been happening at work. I haven't consciously sought any of them but they have just come my way. I am not an ambitious man and would prefer a quiet life, but if I don't take the opportunities when they come then I know I would regret it."

"I'm very proud of you. Of course, you must do that. I know I have told you to let go of the past but I wonder if I am finding that difficult too."

"What do you mean?" he asked, looking puzzled.

"Perhaps I have been making unnecessary comparisons," she said thoughtfully, "and not totally accepting the new you."

"The new me loves you as much as the old one," Adam said seriously. "It is just a deeper love than before."

He leant over and kissed her and she put her hands around the back of his neck.

"Don't do that," he said as a shiver ran down his spine. "You know what that does to me."

The dining-room door opened and Jessica came in.

"Mummy won the game," she said and sat on Leah's chair. She picked up her book from the coffee table and said, "Mum's gone to make a cup of tea and Bill is helping her."

Adam looked at Leah and smiled.

"Time for a nap," he said.

Bill had his arms around Alice.

"I think I'd better go and check that everything is okay at my house tomorrow morning," he said.

"And I think it might be a good idea to take Jessica out tomorrow. It will give Mum and Dad a bit of space before the evening. The local garden centre has a temporary ice rink. We could let her try ice skating?"

"That's a great idea," he said. "It's years since I went ice skating."

"Is that another of your many sporting activities?" Alice teased him.

"Not all my activities are sporting," he said as he kissed her.

They took tea into the lounge and told Jessica what they had planned for the next day.

"That's really cool," Jessica said excitedly. "I can't wait."

"We will be out most of the day, Mum," said Alice. "Is there anything I can do before we go?"

"No, I can manage," Leah answered. "It is just a question of cleaning glasses and plates. I've no doubt the wine will flow." And she looked at Adam.

"Well, it is a party," Adam said innocently, "and we still have that other magnum of champagne which Dominic brought."

"I'm glad I shan't be driving," said Bill.

"I expect Jen will drive Barry home and Dominic can soak it up with a sponge," said Adam.

"What about Sir Humphrey, Adam?" Bill asked. "How will he get back to Oxford?"

"Taxi I expect. Dominic will have ordered a taxi for him."

"I've only met him briefly," Bill said sounding a bit concerned. "He seemed pleasant enough."

"He won't expect any special treatment," Adam assured him. "I'm sure he will enjoy the company." He turned to Leah and said, "I wonder how Sally survived Christmas Day?"

"She certainly looked the part," said Alice.

"I have a feeling that she will be wanting time off to go shopping," Adam sighed.

"Well, you can't refuse the MD's wife-to-be," Alice said. "Have they fixed a date yet?"

"Not as far I know," Adam said looking at Leah. "I suppose that will mean another new dress."

"Don't sound so mean, Dad," Alice said crossly. "You will probably have a new suit too."

"I've already got three suits," he said. "I don't need another one."

"You can't give her away in one of your old suits," Alice said sternly. "You must have a new one."

"Who said anything about giving her away?" Adam demanded. "She's not mine to give. Now I could quite happily give you away because you are my daughter, and I could do it in an old suit," he added.

Bill was quietly laughing but Leah said:

"Stop it you two. You are upsetting Jessica."

Jessica had stopped reading her book and was looking at Alice.

"What's all this talk about giving people away?" she asked fearfully.

Bill put his arm around her.

"Nobody is being given away. It is just grown-up talk for something that happens at weddings."

"Who gets given away?" Jessica persisted.

"The bride," Bill answered.

"Who gives her away?"

"Usually it's her father," Bill answered.

Jessica considered this all very carefully.

"Does that mean that Grandad will give you my mummy because he doesn't want her anymore?"

"No, no," Bill said quickly. "Grandad will always love your mummy because she is his daughter. But I love her too and he is passing her over to me so that I can look after both of you."

"That's alright then," Jessica said thankfully. She went back to her book. "Grownups say such silly things," she muttered.

Adam filled Bill's glass and raised his own.

"Very well done," he acknowledged. "That was tricky."

"I've always found it best to answer children's questions honestly but in a language they understand," he said. "That's why I enjoy coaching junior rugby best."

"Time for your bath in ten minutes, Jessica," Alice said. "It's nearly eight o'clock."

Jessica put her book down and kissed everyone goodnight.

"I've never been ice skating," she said. "It will be exciting."

Leah picked Lucy's present up from the coffee table. She unwrapped it and laughed.

"I knew what it would be," she said as she looked at the box of Milk Tray. "Last year it was Black Magic." She opened the box and offered it to Bill. "I was told to share," she smiled, "so help yourself. Did you know that Alice was very good at sport when she was at school? She could easily have become a P.E. teacher but I couldn't afford to send her to college."

"I didn't know that," Adam said. "Has she told you, Bill?"

"No, she hasn't mentioned it."

"She played badminton for the county and hockey. She represented them in athletics but it was in badminton that she had her greatest success."

"Did she play tennis and netball as well?" Bill asked in amazement.

"Yes, she could play all kinds of sports and I just wonder if Jessica has inherited any of her talents," Leah said.

"I'll take Alice down to the local leisure centre and let her try out different sports," Bill said. "I should like to get fit again."

"I'm thinking of buying her a small car so that she is mobile," Adam said. "I think it would make a big difference to her. She would be able to take Jessica to join various clubs."

"Perhaps I could persuade her to join a badminton club?" Bill said. "Then we can all go together."

"Don't rush her," Leah warned him. "There might still be some bad memories lurking in her mind."

Alice came back into the lounge.

"Thank goodness, she went straight to sleep tonight. There's not much room in the bed with the teddy bear."

"Perhaps you will have to look for alternative accommodation," Adam said with a straight face.

"She needn't look very far," Bill said with a grin.

"Will you two please stop embarrassing me?" she said crossly.

"We're only trying to help," Adam said innocently. "Come on Leah, let's go and find our little nest."

Chapter Six

Adam and Leah didn't rush to get up the next morning but Jessica was up early. Alice went downstairs and made the tea which she took up to her parents.

"We are just going to have some breakfast then we will be off," she said.

"How do you feel about spending the whole morning in bed, Leah?" asked Adam.

"I would feel that I had wasted half a day," she replied.

"We wouldn't waste the time," Adam said persuasively. "We would use it for some meaningful activity."

Leah looked at him and laughed.

"You are an old rogue," she said as she kissed him.

"We're off!" shouted Alice up the stairs. "See you later," and they heard the front door shut with a bang.

The house was still and quiet as Adam put his arms around Leah.

"Alone at last," he said, softly. "Just the two of us."

They lay there for a few minutes gazing into each other's eyes. Neither of them wanted to break the spell. Adam leaned over Leah and slowly kissed her. He moved closer to her and she felt a thrill of passion throughout her whole body. He held her close still until the two of them seemed fused into one.

"I love you so much," Leah whispered. "I can't find the words to tell you."

"I know how much you love me," Adam said. "I know it every day. Sometimes I don't know how to show you that I feel exactly the same. You mean everything to me."

"We must both try harder to let go of the past," Leah said quietly. "Let's love each other as we are today."

"We can start right now," Adam said as he stroked her face until they were soon lost in their own little world. They lay there in perfect contentment.

"I must get dressed," she said, eventually. "There are things to do."

He reluctantly agreed with her and they were soon downstairs. Leah looked at the clock.

"Good heavens. It's eleven o'clock. It's coffee time."

She put the kettle on and made the coffee. Adam carried it into the lounge together with the biscuit tin.

"Have we got everything we need for this evening?" he asked.

"I need to go and get some fresh nibbles," she said, "and you had better check the wine."

Adam went out to the utility area and when he returned, he said:

"I think I'll get another half dozen bottles just to be sure. I'll come with you to the supermarket. I'll get some more wine glasses while we're there."

They drank their coffee and then went off to the shop. They filled a trolley with food and wine and Adam paid for it at the checkout. It was nearly lunchtime so Leah bought some sandwiches and they returned home. They unloaded the car and went into the lounge to eat.

"I'm not cooking anything for tea," Leah said. "There's plenty of things in the fridge which need eating up."

They remained seated on the settee just enjoying each other's company until Leah said:

"I suppose we'd better do something about this evening. I'll put some plates and glasses on the dining room table and you can bring the wine in."

"We forgot to get any ice," Adam said suddenly. "I need to put the champagne in an ice bucket."

"You will have to go back to the shop and get some," she said.

So, Adam put his coat on and went off. While he was away, Bill arrived back with Alice and Jessica. They went into the lounge and Jessica flopped down on the settee.

"I'm tired out," she gasped.

"Well don't go to sleep yet," Alice said. "You need something to eat," and she sat down by Jessica. She looked at Bill who was holding something behind his back.

"I don't know where he gets his energy from," she exclaimed. "We only sat down once and that was to eat our lunch."

Bill went up to Leah and gave her what he had been hiding. It was a beautiful creamy white orchid in a pot.

"This is to say thank you for a wonderful Christmas," he said and he kissed her.

At the same moment, Adam walked in.

"What's this?" he said in a severe voice. "A strange man kissing my wife?"

"He brought me a lovely present," Leah said. "Look," and she pointed to the orchid.

"It's a thank you for your hospitality," Bill said sincerely, "and for allowing me to share your family Christmas."

"You are part of the family now. You will always be welcomed," said Adam, putting a hand on Bill's shoulder. "How did the skating go, Jessica?"

"I kept falling over," she complained. "I'm black and blue all over."

"A nice hot bath will soon sort that out," Alice said.

"Did you have a go, Alice?"

"No, I didn't, Dad. It looked too dangerous for me and Bill was doing all sorts of twirls and turns. I would never have kept up with him."

"I learned to skate as a child," he said, trying to look modest. "It just came back to me."

"He didn't fall over once," Jessica said. "Everyone stood back and watched him."

"You never said you could skate," said Alice.

"You never said you'd won prizes at badminton," he retorted. "So now we are quits." He put an arm around her and gave her a quick kiss.

"I'll go and make you some sandwiches," said Leah. "You rest after

69

your busy day," and she went into the kitchen.

"Did you have a nice quiet day, Dad?"

"We had a lovely lay day, Alice. I only went shopping twice."

Bill looked at him and laughed.

"Why didn't you get it all the first time?" he asked.

"Because I forgot something important. I forgot the ice for the champagne," Adam said.

"Well, that is important," Alice said with a hint of sarcasm.

Adam looked at her reproachfully.

"A good host never serves warm champagne," he said firmly.

"I'll remember that," said Bill as Alice remained silent.

Leah came back with some sandwiches and mugs of tea.

"The bathroom is going to be a busy place," she said to Adam. "I think we should go up and get ready."

They left the lounge and went upstairs. Adam found a clean shirt and Leah chose a dress.

"I really must update my wardrobe," she sighed. "It is ages since I bought anything new."

"Alice is right you know," he said. "You are going to have to go shopping."

"I really dislike clothes shopping. Will you come with me?"

"Of course, I will," he said at once. "When do you want to go?"

"Sometime during the school holiday but I can't think about it now."

They went back to the lounge.

"The bathroom is free," Leah said. "Who is going next?"

Bill looked at Alice.

"I'd like to have a shower," he said. "Shall I go next?"

"Yes, that's fine," Alice said. "Then it will be time for Jessica's bath and I'll get ready after that."

Bill left the lounge but Alice stayed on the settee.

"He has worn me out today," she said wearily. "He has so much energy."

"He is a sportsman," said Adam. "He is very fit but recently he hasn't had the opportunity to use up his energy. He must be feeling frustrated."

"I know he likes to go running and he wants to find a gym," Alice said, "but he says he has been so busy at work that he hasn't had time to think about it."

"We have all been under pressure," Adam said seriously, "but that will change in the New Year. I am going to recruit more staff and work out a new rota system."

"He is quite nervous about this evening," Alice said. "He is not used to meeting these important people like you are."

"I think he will be pleasantly surprised," said Adam reassuringly. "I hope he will be able to relax and enjoy it."

"None of your tricks and little surprises this evening please Dad?"

"I'll be on my best behaviour," he said sweetly. "At least to begin with."

Alice looked at him in despair.

"You are impossible," she said and kissed him.

Jessica was half asleep on the settee.

"Come on," Alice said taking her hand. "Time for your bath."

"My legs hurt and my arm," said Jessica as they went upstairs.

"A nice hot bath will do that good," Alice assured her. "You might feel a bit stiff in the morning but it will soon wear off."

Jessica was so tired that she went straight to sleep. Bill came across the landing to say goodnight to her but Alice stopped him at the door.

"You smell nice," she said.

"I'll see you downstairs," he said, kissing her.

There was a shout from the back door and Jen came in carrying a tray of canapes. Barry followed her with three bottles of wine. Bill met them in the hall and kissed Jen. He took the wine from Barry and put it on the sideboard in the dining room with the other bottles. Leah and Adam came out to greet them and Adam took Barry into the lounge.

"How has your Christmas been?"

"Christmas Day was pretty awful at my parent's house but the rest of the time has been relaxing thank goodness."

"We were all exhausted," said Adam. "Next week we will begin to recruit more staff and we will find time to organize a new rota."

"You're looking pleased with yourself, Bill," said Barry. "What have you been up to?"

"Oh, this and that," he answered nonchalantly.

"A little bit of this and a lot of that," Adam said wisely.

"You're a dark horse," laughed Barry.

"I'll go and get the drinks," he said blushing slightly.

Leah came in with Jen who went and kissed Adam.

"You're looking well," she said. "Have you had a good holiday?"

"It's been a family Christmas," Adam said. "Not quite a holiday. That comes next weekend, courtesy of my wife," and he put his arm around Leah.

Bill made sure that everyone had a drink and they settled down to chat.

"I've never met Dominic's father," Jen said. "I understand he is a Member of Parliament?"

"Not for much longer," said Adam. "He retires at the end of January."

"I've never met him either," Leah added. "Adam thinks he's quite the lady's man."

"Sally gets on with him very well and I would always trust her judgement," Adam said firmly.

There was a knock on the front door and Adam went to open it. Dominic was standing there with his arms full of bottles. He staggered into the hall and Adam was quick to take several from him. He led the way into the kitchen and Dominic gratefully put the bottles down. He looked around.

"Where's Father?" he said.

Sally had shepherded Sir Humphrey into the hall and he was carrying a large magnum of champagne.

"Bring it in here," Dominic called from the kitchen and he came out and took it from him.

Leah had come to the lounge door and she kissed Sally.

"You look a bit harassed," she said.

"It's been just like having to deal with two naughty schoolboys when those two get together," she sighed. "You know what a tornado Dominic can be, well his father can go one better."

"Let me take your coat," said Leah. "Then you can come and sit down."

Leah took Sally into the lounge and the men both kissed her.

"Sally needs a drink," she said to Bill.

He went and poured her one.

"Where's Alice?" she said, looking around.

"She will be down in a minute," he said. "She is just checking that Jessica is asleep."

In the kitchen, Sir Humphrey was rubbing his arm.

"You're lucky I didn't drop that," he said to Dominic. "It was jolly heavy."

"Well, you won't have to carry it back," Dominic said. "We'll soon demolish that."

"Let's go and meet the others," Adam said smoothly and he led the way into the lounge.

Dominic shook hands with Barry and Bill and said:

"I think you have already met my father?"

"Very briefly," Sir Humphrey said. "I'm looking forward to knowing them better."

Dominic then moved on to the ladies. He kissed Jen's hand and said:

"This is Barry's wife, Jen."

Sir Humphrey took Jen's hand and kissed it. Dominic moved on to Leah and he kissed her on both cheeks.

"This is Adam's wife Leah."

Sir Humphrey kissed Leah's hand and said:

"I have heard some very complimentary things about you. I am delighted to meet you."

Sally was sitting next to Leah and Dominic stood in front of her.

"And this is Sally, my long-suffering, soon-to-be wife," and he put his arms around her and kissed her.

"I know my eyesight is not as good as it used to be," Sir Humphrey said jokingly, "but she looks vaguely familiar."

Sally looked at Leah in despair.

"See what I mean?" she said. "I've had a whole afternoon of this."

"Behave yourself father," said Dominic. "You are not in London now. You are among friends."

Sir Humphrey sat down in Leah's chair.

"This is very comfortable," he said, stretching his legs out.

Bill poured the drinks and they all sat around and chatted. Alice came in and greeted everyone then she came to Sir Humphrey and he stood up.

"This is my daughter, Alice," said Adam.

Sir Humphrey kissed her hand and said:

"How lovely to meet you."

She went and sat by Bill and he put an arm around her. Sir Humphrey sat in his chair observing the four happy couples in front of him. He drained his glass and Bill got up to refill it.

"Thank you, Bill," Sir Humphrey said as he looked at him. "Are you married?"

"Not yet," Bill replied. "We are waiting for Alice's divorce to come through."

"I shall be getting divorced soon," Sir Humphrey said sorrowfully.

"Then my troubles will really begin."

Sally gave Dominic a warning look but Sir Humphrey carried on.

"Do you know what will happen? I'll tell you," and he took a long drink of wine. "I shall be hounded by wealthy widows. They hunt like a pack of lionesses and one by one they attack their prey, that's me. If one fails there's always another one waiting to pounce."

"What would you do, Adam? You are the font of all knowledge."

Adam laughed.

"I should say 'Not tonight Josephine, Emmeline, Margarine or whatever your name is,' and walk away."

"I'll try that," said Sir Humphrey, visibly cheered and he drained his glass.

"I'm sure it won't be that bad," Sally said quickly.

"Father is right," Dominic said. "I have had personal experience of it."

"When were you chased by wealthy widows?" Sally demanded.

"The wealthy widows were not the problem," he replied. "It was their wealthy daughters."

"I think you had better get that ring on your finger pretty quickly," Adam said to Sally with a twinkle in his eye.

"Don't worry," said Domini. "Sally can deal with any troublemakers, can't you, my love?" and he kissed her.

"I think it is time to lift our spirits," said Dominic, standing up. "Let's open the champagne."

"Excellent idea," said Sir Humphrey, not moving out of his chair.

Adam and Dominic went into the kitchen.

"Your father is going to have to make some major decisions," Adam said. "It is not going to be easy for him."

"He has some good friends and one in particular," Dominic said. "Lady Harrington is the widow of Lord Harrington. Father has known her for years. Sally met her on Christmas Day and they got on very well."

"I was wondering how you both enjoyed it," Adam said. "How did

Sally get on with your mother?"

"Sally was magnificent. She didn't flinch in front of my mother or my ex-wife."

"I knew she wouldn't let you down. She will get more comfortable as time passes."

"She charmed everyone," Dominic said proudly. "Everyone except my mother and ex-wife who were their usual unpleasant selves. Father thinks she's wonderful."

"You don't know how lucky you are. When are you going to make an honest woman of her?"

"Soon, very soon. I'll let you know next week."

Adam put the glasses on a tray and Dominic carried the champagne.

"I'm sorry about the glasses," Adam said. "Tesco doesn't do cut-glass."

"I'll speak to my secretary," Dominic said as they went into the lounge.

He went and stood in front of Sally and said in his best business voice:

"Miss Moneypenny please note a dozen cut-glass champagne glasses for my friend Adam. Put them on my Harrods account."

"Yes, sir," she said. "Any other orders?"

"Yes," he replied and bent down and kissed her.

He went back to the coffee table and started to open the champagne. The cork popped out and shot across the room.

"Bravo!" Sir Humphrey called out as Dominic quickly filled the glasses.

When everyone was served, Sir Humphrey raised his glass.

"A toast to good friends and to the success of the company."

They all raised their glasses and immediately had them refilled by Dominic. Barry and Bill started to reminisce about their time at university and Sir Humphrey joined in with comments about things that had happened in Parliament.

"Time for us to retire, I think," Leah said and the ladies went into the dining room.

"I dare not drink too much champagne," said Sally, as they sat around the table. "It makes me so sleepy. I think I'll stick to wine."

"What was Christmas really like?" Alice asked her.

"I was dreading it and so was Dominic but, in the end, I quite enjoyed it."

"How did you get on with his mother?" Leah asked. "What's her name?"

"Her name is Melissa and his ex-wife is Susanna. I was very polite and that seemed to throw them. I think they intended almost to be rude to me but I didn't give them a chance."

"So, what did they do?" Alice persisted.

"His mother was in a right strop because Dominic changed the place names on the lunch table so that I could sit between him and his father," Sally said, smiling. The others all laughed and Sally continued: "Susanna tried to get Dominic's attention but I stepped in between them and she turned on her heel and stalked off."

"Well done," Jen said clapping her hands. "I like your spirit."

Leah refilled their wine glasses and they picked at the nibbles on the table.

"I'm taking Adam away next weekend," she said. "It is his Christmas present."

"That's a lovely idea," Sally said. "He could do with a break. He has been working too hard."

"We are going to a hotel on the Hampshire border. I think it is quite near Kitson Manor. Do you think Dominic would mind if we went and looked at it?"

"Of course, he won't mind," Sally said firmly. "You won't be able to go inside but you can explore the grounds."

"When are you hoping to move into it?" Jen asked.

"Not for two or three years. It has to have a complete refurbishment. We shall be looking for a house in this area until it is ready."

"It would be great to have you nearby," said Alice, excitedly. "We could go shopping every week."

There were sounds of great hilarity coming from the lounge.

"I wonder what they are up to?" Leah said fearfully.

She opened the dining-room door and looked at a scene of utter chaos. There were paper aeroplanes flying around but no-one was to be seen. There was plenty of noise coming from behind the furniture and Leah said in a very loud voice:

"What's all this?"

One by one, faces began to appear above the backs of the settees. The champagne bottle on the coffee table was empty and there was no doubt who had been drinking. Each man got unsteadily to his feet and tried to pick up the paper which was on the carpet. Several of them fell over as they bent down and eventually, they all gave up and sat down.

Alice, Jen and Sally were standing behind Leah and they were trying to contain their laughter.

"I warned you what they were like, Leah," said Sally. "And I bet I know who the ringleader was." She marched up to Sir Humphrey and pointed her finger at him. "Father," she said, "you are a disgrace."

Sir Humphrey looked at her with bleary eyes.

"I know I am," he hiccupped and pulled her down and kissed her thoroughly.

Dominic suddenly came to life.

"You are out of order," he said sternly as he pulled Sally up. "That's my job," and he kissed her.

Leah felt sorry for Sally and she said:

"We are going to put the kettle on. Alice and Jen will make sure that you clear up this mess."

She took Sally into the kitchen and sat her on a stool. She switched on the kettle and found enough clean mugs for everyone.

"You see what I mean," Sally sighed.

"It is only banter, typical man ego," Leah said, "but I can understand how annoying it can be. They will both be back to their prim and proper selves tomorrow."

"We have ordered a taxi to take Sir Humphrey back to Oxford at midnight but there is no way that I would let Dominic drive me home," Sally said in a worried voice.

"Adam will ask the driver to make sure he takes Sir Humphrey right into the hotel and a porter will see him to his room," Leah said firmly. "And then we'll ask the taxi to come back and take you home. You may have to pay him a bit extra."

"I don't care how much it costs," Sally said wearily. "I just want to get home safely."

They made coffee and returned to the lounge. The paper had been cleared from the floor and the furniture put back in its proper place. The men were all sitting down looking like naughty children who had just had a good telling off. Alice and Jen looked pleased with themselves.

"That was fun," Alice said as she gave Bill his coffee.

Sally took a mug of coffee over to Sir Humphrey.

"Drink this," she ordered him. "It has milk and one sugar just as you like it." She stepped back smartly and went to Dominic. "This will help to sober you up," she said firmly. He went to grab her but she moved away. She sat down next to him and said: "I need some cash to pay the taxi driver."

Dominic pulled out his wallet.

"Help yourself, my love," he said lurching towards her.

She opened the wallet and found it full of fifty-pound notes.

"Haven't you got anything less?" she asked.

"Who wants less?" he said in a disgusted voice. "Less is more, or should that be more is less? Anyway, ask Father. He's got more than me."

Sally turned to Sir Humphrey who was half asleep.

"Have you got anything less than a fifty-pound note?" she asked him.

"I've no idea," he answered. "Have a look," and he took out his wallet.

She opened it up and again found it full of high-value notes. She looked at Adam for help.

"Why don't you take one note out of each wallet?" he said. "That will make it feel fair."

So that is what Sally did.

Leah called Adam into the dining room and explained what he had to do when the taxi arrived.

"Make sure that you ask him to see Sir Humphrey safely into the hotel and ask him to come back here to take Sally and Dominic home. He will earn a good bonus tonight."

It was nearly midnight and Leah looked out of the front window.

"The taxi is here," she said and Adam and Bill helped Sir Humphrey out of his chair.

"Best party ever," he said and he turned to Dominic "I'll see you on Monday. Lots to do," he said.

He kissed all the ladies and shook hands with the men. Adam and Bill helped him out to the taxi and he patted Adam's arm.

"Great time. Will be in touch."

Adam spoke to the driver and gave him one of the notes and he drove off.

The cold night air had refreshed Adam and Bill and they took some deep breaths. Jen and Barry came through the door and she was holding the car keys.

"Thanks for a lovely evening. It will be remembered for a long time," she said with a laugh.

"I'll see you on Monday, Adam," said Barry. "If I'm in a fit state."

"You'll be fine," Adam said slapping him on the back.

"I've seen you in a worse state many a time," Bill said helpfully.

"Ditto, ditto," Barry replied and they both laughed.

Jen drove off and Bill and Adam went back indoors.

Sally was standing in front of Dominic.

"You are not driving home," she said firmly. "Give me the car keys."

"I'm perfectly capable of driving my car," he said definitely and he went to stand up.

"You're not even capable of standing up or putting yourself to bed," she said.

"I can stand up long enough for you to put me to bed," he said grinning at her.

"We are going home by taxi and that's the end of it," Sally said decisively. "I'm going to get my coat."

"Women are such bossy creatures," Dominic said sorrowfully. "They need to be kept in their place."

"Be careful what you say," Adam warned him as he noticed Alice beginning to bristle.

"And what place should they be kept in?" Alice asked indignantly.

"In the kitchen, in the house, in the shop, in the bedroom," Dominic said. "Definitely in the bedroom."

"Do you think that women are just puppets and the men should pull all their strings," Alice said crossly. "You've got a lot to learn about the opposite sex."

"Calm down Alice," Adam said quietly. "You should know that it is the drink talking."

Sally came back in.

"The taxi is here," she said. "Hand over your car keys."

Dominic gave them to her and stood up. He kissed Leah and Alice goodbye and shook Bill's hand.

"You've got a fiery one there," he said and Bill smiled at him.

Adam went out to the taxi with Dominic and he kissed Sally goodnight. He paid the taxi driver the other fifty-pound note and he drove off.

He went in and locked the front door. He checked the back door and the windows and said to Leah:

"We'll clear up in the morning, it is time for bed."

They said goodnight to Alice and Bill and were soon in bed under their double duvet.

"That was a good party," Adam said, "but I am not planning another one. It was certainly interesting. I think everyone enjoyed themselves."

"There will be a few hangovers in the morning," Leah said. "What did you use to make those paper aeroplanes?"

"We ripped the pages out of a book that was on the coffee table."

Leah looked horrified.

"That was Jessica's book," she said. "The one she was reading."

"I'll take her to choose a replacement tomorrow," he said and turned over and went to sleep.

It took the taxi fifteen minutes to get to Sally's house. She helped Dominic out of the taxi and took him into the house. She walked up the stairs behind him and helped him undress and put his pyjamas on. She went back downstairs and locked the front door. She extinguished the lights and was soon in bed beside him. He was already asleep so she kissed him lightly and said:

"I'll get you an aspirin in the morning."

Jen drove Barry home and took him into the house.

"Good party," he said as he stumbled up the stairs.

"It may not feel so good in the morning," she warned him as she put him to bed.

Meanwhile, a porter had helped Sir Humphrey into the lift. They went up to the first floor and the porter unlocked Sir Humphrey's door.

"Thank you, my man," Sir Humphrey said and gave him a fifty-pound note.

The porter left him and Sir Humphrey didn't bother to undress. He lay on top of the bed gazing up at the ceiling. "Top hole party," he said. "Nice people, good friends," and he closed his eyes.

Bill and Alice were left in the lounge. He put his arms around her and kissed her.

"What a night," he said. "I've been to some pretty raucous parties in my time but this was something else."

"How is it that you are reasonably sober while the others were all pretty comatose?" she asked him.

"Experience, my love. I didn't actually drink that much."

"How did you manage that?" she asked incredulously.

"I made sure my glass was always half full so it wasn't often topped up. Dominic kept filling up the empty glasses."

"Sometimes I feel really sorry for Sally," Alice said. "She has her hands full with him."

"I thought she managed him very well," Bill replied. "He is putty in her hands."

"She would never take advantage of him," she said firmly. "I know that she really loves him and she isn't bothered by all his money."

"Dominic is first and foremost a businessman. He can be ruthless when necessary. I wouldn't like to have to negotiate with him."

"He is also a very generous man to his friends," Alice said. "I don't think anyone fully understands him."

"I think Sally does," he said as he stood up. "Come on, it's time for bed."

Chapter Seven

The next morning Alice was up first as usual. She went downstairs and put the kettle on. She went into the lounge and noticed Jessica's ripped-up book on the coffee table. Bill had followed her downstairs and she showed him the book.

"I'm afraid it got turned into aeroplanes," he said.

"What are we going to tell Jessica?" Alice demanded.

Bill thought for a minute.

"We are going to have to tell her a little white lie."

"You had better make it up quickly," she said crossly. "I can hear her getting up."

Bill took the book and put it in the rubbish bag which was in the utility area. He went back into the kitchen just as Jessica came through the door.

"I've just been into the lounge," she said. "What a mess! It must have been a good party."

"Yes, it was," Alice said kissing her but looking at Bill.

"I couldn't find my book which I left on the coffee table," Jessica said. "Do you know where it is?"

Bill put his arm around her.

"Someone got a bit too excited last night and spilt a whole glass of wine all over your book. They were very sorry and want to buy you another copy to replace it."

"Oh well, I'd nearly finished it so I'll get a different one. Can we go after breakfast?"

"We'll go later this morning," Bill promised with a sigh of relief.

Alice made the tea and took it up to Adam and Leah.

"Time to get up," she said loudly. "There is work to be done."

Leah opened her eyes and sat up but Adam just groaned.

"Fetch your father a couple of aspirins," she said to Alice. "He's not

84

feeling so good."

Alice went to the bathroom and came back with a glass of water and two aspirins. She went to open the curtains but Adam stopped her.

"I can't face the day yet," he mumbled as he took the aspirin.

"How is Bill this morning?" Leah asked.

"He's fine. He's having breakfast with Jessica."

"He must have a constitution of an ox," Adam said faintly.

"He's got more sense than some others I know," Alice said firmly. "Are you alright Mum?"

"Yes, I'm fine. I'll get up now."

Alice went back to the kitchen and found Bill alone.

"Where's Jessica?" she said.

"She's gone to tidy her room. How's your father this morning?"

"A couple of aspirins will soon put him right," she said and at that moment the phone rang.

"Hello, Sally," Alice said. "How's things this morning?"

"He's seventy-five per cent sober and should be okay by twelve o'clock," Sally said with a sigh. "He is going to need his car; can someone come and collect him?"

"Dad is not fit but Bill could come. I'll just ask him."

Alice called Bill and passed the phone over to him.

"Hello Sally," he said. "How can I help?"

Sally explained what was needed.

"I'll pick him up at eleven-thirty but I don't know where you live. You'd better give me some directions."

Sally told him how to get there.

"See you later," he said and went back into the kitchen. "I must go back to my house this afternoon. There are things to get ready for work. I need to do some grocery shopping so I'll take Jessica with me to the supermarket then we will go straight to pick up Dominic."

"That sounds fine," Alice said. "It will get Jessica out of the way while

Mum and I clear up."

Leah came down the stairs.

"Who was that on the phone?" she asked.

Alice told her what had been arranged.

"That's good. Your father is in no fit state to drive. Best to let him sleep."

After Sally had spoken to Alice she went back upstairs with a cup of tea for Dominic.

"My mouth is like a back-door mat," he complained.

"Is there any wonder?" she said. "Drink this and I'll get you some aspirins."

She went to the bathroom and came back with two aspirins. He took them as he drank his tea and lay back on the pillow. He put up his arms to Sally.

"Come and lie by me," he pleaded. "I'm not well."

"I know you're not well," she said firmly. "It's your own fault," and she lay beside him.

"Don't shout at me, please. I need some TLC."

She relented a little and turned to stroke his face. He didn't move and she kissed him lightly on his lips. He moved slightly so that he was facing her.

"When shall we get married?" was his next direct question. His eyes were drawing her ever closer to him and she couldn't resist him.

"Tomorrow, next week, as soon as possible," she gasped as his hands stroked her body.

She was utterly caught in his spell and she couldn't escape. She surrendered completely to him and they were locked together as one. They lay there, not wanting to move.

"I must love you and leave you this afternoon," he said. "It is back to the real world tomorrow. I want you to come to London next weekend so that we can go shopping."

"How shall I come? Adam will be leaving work early on Friday. I can't leave the office too early."

"I don't think I will be down this Friday," Dominic said. "There are business matters I have to catch up with. If you come up by train, I will arrange for someone to meet you at the station. We can stay at my apartment."

"I'm happy to do that. What about coming back?"

"I'll bring you back home," he said. "When I'm dressed, I must phone Father."

"I hope he is alright," she said anxiously. "He was not too steady on his feet last night."

"He'll be fine," Dominic said as he kissed her. "He's an old hand at party-going."

They went downstairs and he picked up the phone. He dialled Sir Humphrey's number and waited.

"Hello?" said a booming voice.

Dominic held the receiver away from his ear.

"Don't shout, father," he said. "I'm a bit fragile this morning."

"You're out of practice," Sir Humphrey said. "Must do something about that."

"You have obviously fully recovered. What are you doing today?"

"I'm just packing my bags. Then I'm heading back to my club."

"I'll see you tomorrow morning at ten o'clock sharp at Head Office," said Dominic and put the phone down.

"You sound better already," said Sally.

"I have been neglecting the business lately. I can't afford to do that for too long."

"I shall start looking at possible properties in the area," she said. "I could get the details and we could look at them together."

"That would be a good start," Dominic said. "We can't spend our married lives apart."

Sally put the car keys on the coffee table.

"Bill will be here soon," she said. "I hope he doesn't get lost."

"Adam has a good team but he needs more lower managerial staff. I understand that Bill is going to take charge of the educational side upstairs and I think Adam needs to recruit two new under managers to help Barry. In a few months, he could promote Bill to manage upstairs."

"Do you want me to suggest this to him?"

"Yes, you could do that. Let me know what he decides?"

There was a knock on the door and Bill stood there.

"Come in," said Sally.

"Jessica is in the car. We have been shopping."

"I'm just coming," Dominic said as he picked up his car keys. He kissed Sally and said, "I'll see you later."

Jessica moved into the back of the car and Dominic sat next to Bill.

"Thanks for the lift," he said. "I certainly had a skinful last night. You don't seem to be suffering."

"Rugby players have regular blowouts," Bill laughed. "You find your own way to control your excesses."

"What's a blowout?" Jessica asked.

"It's when a man has too much to drink and he ends up with a fat beer belly," said Bill.

"You haven't got one of those," she said, sounding grateful.

"That's because I regularly go running and I like to go to the gym."

"I quite like running," she said. "I used to come first in the cross country at school."

"We'll go for a run together soon," Bill said. "That would be fun."

"It would be fun for me but it may not be fun for you."

"Why do you say that?"

"Well, because I would beat you," Jessica said sweetly.

Dominic looked at Bill and laughed.

"Now you have a real challenge against a ten-year-old girl."

"I shall soon be eleven," Jessica announced.

"And what would you like for your eleventh birthday?" Dominic asked.

"I'd really like a new bike and a baby sister."

"I'll tell you what," Dominic said seriously. "I can't do anything about the baby sister but if you beat Bill, I'll buy you a new bike."

Bill was grinning from ear to ear.

"Don't worry," he said. "You won't have to get your wallet out."

They reached Leah's house and Dominic went in. Bill left his groceries in the car but Jessica got out clutching her two new books. Adam came downstairs and was sitting in the lounge drinking a strong cup of coffee.

"Would you like one?" he asked Dominic.

"No thanks. I must get back to London today. I've got a lot of catching up to do this week. By the way, did you get the invite to father's retirement do?"

"Yes, thank you," Adam said. "I shall be replying to it tomorrow. Is it a very formal affair, Leah wants to know what to wear?"

"It's not a sit-down meal, just a buffet. So, it will be afternoon dresses for the ladies and usual suits for men. I can book you in for the night at the Grosvenor Hotel. The week after next will be the farewell party for the old Board of Governors and the day after that the new Board will be sworn in. This is a male-only event so no wives have to attend. I'll send you the details."

"How is Sally this morning?" Adam asked.

"She's fine. She's coming to London by train on Friday and we shall be going shopping on Saturday." He took his car keys out of his pocket. "I have a busy week ahead. I need to catch up on any developments on the business front and I need to arrange a wedding."

"Have you discussed that with Sally?" Adam said urgently.

"We haven't talked about any details but I intend to get a special licence so that we can do it soon."

"Sally needs to know what you are doing," Adam said firmly. "She will be upset if you start doing things without her knowledge."

"I'll make sure I tell her first. I'll be in touch with you during the week."

He said goodbye to Leah and drove off. On the way back to Sally's house he thought about what Adam had said and he realised that he had nearly made a dreadful mistake. He hadn't even asked Sally where she would like to get married or who she would like to invite. He was about to go ahead and just arrange it all himself. He mentally thanked Adam for making him think.

He parked the car and went into the house. She was washing up in the kitchen and he went up to her.

"Dry your hands and come with me. We need to talk."

She followed him into the lounge and they sat together on the settee. Dominic took her hand and looked into her eyes.

"Sally," he said tenderly. "I want you to be my wife as soon as possible. How do you feel about our marriage?"

"I'm ready whenever you want me," Sally answered. "You know how much I love you."

He kissed her.

"I'd marry you tomorrow if I could but you know there are certain formalities which we can't avoid."

"I don't want a big fuss," she said. "I'd be happy with just the two of us."

"We have to have witnesses and it would be nice to share the day with our friends."

"What do you suggest then?"

He thought for a minute.

"I will have to get a special licence because we want to do it without having to give six weeks' notice. Then I suppose we arrange a date at a registry office."

"I'd rather be married in a church," she said. "And I know which church."

He looked at her in surprise.

"Which church are you talking about?"

"The little church near Kitson Manor," she said dreamily.

Dominic was lost for words.

"I don't even know if the vicar would be willing to marry us. Some vicars won't marry divorced people."

"I just feel that it would reassure the villagers that we really intend to live there one day."

"I hadn't thought of it that way," he said, kissing her cheek. "The idea is growing on me."

"There won't be room for many guests," Sally said. "Just a few friends."

"Are you thinking of the friends we were with last night?" he said with a smile.

"Yes, I was. The only other person I would want is my mother plus her carer. What about your mother?"

"I would have to ask her," he said, "but I don't think she would come. I would like to ask Matthew Dunn and his wife and of course, Father would be there."

"That would be fifteen people altogether. That would be just right. What date have you in mind?"

"It will have to be a Saturday," he replied. "Otherwise, there will be no-one left to run the office. I'll try for Saturday week."

"I think I can wait that long," she said putting her arms around him and kissing him.

"I'll do my best to make it our very special day," he said, holding her close.

"I'll put the kettle on and make you a coffee before you have to leave," she said.

Dominic went upstairs to pack his bag and collect his belongings. Sally made the coffee and they sat on the settee.

"I'll try to phone you every day, Sally and I'll let you know as soon as I have any news."

She went to the front door with him and he held her tightly.

"I shall miss you," he said. "I can't wait until I can come home to you every night."

"I shall miss you too," she said tearfully. "The house will seem empty without you."

He kissed her goodbye and she stood and watched him drive off. Then she went back indoors and sat on the settee as the tears began to flow. She suddenly felt exhausted and she lay back and closed her eyes.

Leah and Alice had managed to tidy up the house before Bill and Jessica returned. Adam was feeling better and was sitting in the lounge.

"I'll make some sandwiches for lunch," Leah said and went into the kitchen.

Bill went upstairs to collect his things. He packed his bag and took it down into the hall. Then he went back into the lounge to talk to Adam.

"Will you be getting an update on Alice's divorce this week?" he asked.

"I expect Matthew Dunn will contact me but if I haven't heard by the middle of the week, I'll phone him," Adam promised.

"Do you think we shall be as busy at work as we were in the run-up to Christmas?"

"It should quieten down," Adam said, "but we still have the building work to contend with. That should be finished in three weeks, then the carpet goes down and the furniture arrives. It should be ready for the grand spring opening in about six weeks."

"Will all the new computers be in by then?"

"I hope so," Adam said, "but there are bound to be teething problems."

"It would be helpful if I could have some expert advice on the new system," Bill said thoughtfully. "I need to understand how it works."

"I'm sure that can be arranged. I'm also going to take on more staff and organise a rota. I shall be looking for people who have already had some experience. I shall name them 'under managers' and I would expect to call on them at very busy times. You will still be the assistant manager for now but when the education side is up and running you could be promoted to manager."

"Thank you for letting me know," Bill said gratefully. "That means I can think ahead." He sat in silence for a minute or two then he said: "Alice and I would like to get married but I need to ask your permission."

"You don't need my permission," Adam said cheerfully, "but I give you my blessing."

"That's good enough for me. Thank you," he said, smiling.

Leah came in with the sandwiches and Alice brought the plates. They sat around in a rather subdued atmosphere.

"I shall miss having you around, Bill," said Leah.

"Not half as much as I will miss him," Alice said close to tears.

Bill put his arm around her.

"I shan't be a million miles away," he said lightly, "and there's always the phone." He stood up and kissed Jessica. "Be a good girl," he said. "I am going to do some serious training." He went to Leah and kissed her. "Thanks for having me, I've had a wonderful Christmas," and he hugged her. Adam stood up and they shook hands. "I'll see you tomorrow," Bill said emotionally. "Thanks for everything."

Alice went with him to the front door. He held her tightly.

"One day I won't have to love and leave you. I hope that day comes soon."

She was choked with tears and held on to him.

"I'll phone you later," he said and kissed her.

She watched him get in the car and drive away. She closed the door and went upstairs to his bedroom. She flung herself on the bed and sobbed. She didn't hear Jessica come in.

"Mummy," she said quietly. "Mummy, please don't cry," and she put her arms around Alice and lay down beside her.

Alice looked at Jessica through tears.

"I miss him," she sobbed. "I love him so much."

"I love him too," Jessica said. "One day we will be a proper family."

Chapter Eight

When Adam arrived at work the next morning the builders were already in. There was a lot of hammering going on and he went to find Mr Carter.

"Three more days of banging and then the various offices will all be built. The lift people are coming next Monday and I hope the electricians will be here by the end of the week."

"It's all going according to plan," Adam said. "Well done."

He went back downstairs and into his office. He called Sally in and she came with her diary which she placed on the desk.

"Dominic and I talked about the wedding yesterday," she said.

Thank goodness for that he thought.

"Did you make any decisions?"

"Not exactly. I told him what I would like and he said he would try his best to do it."

"So, what does he have to do now?"

"He has to get a special licence and ask the vicar if he will marry us," Sally said simply.

"Which church and which vicar?" he asked, puzzled.

"There is a little church right on the edge of the Kitson Estate. It only holds about twenty people. It would be ideal for us," she said enthusiastically. "Leah said you might go and look around the grounds of the Manor, if you do, you will see it on the road out of the village."

"Have you fixed a date yet?"

"Dominic is going to try for a week on Saturday."

"That doesn't leave you much time for all the other things that need to be done, like flowers, dresses, invitations."

"I'm hoping we can have the reception up here somewhere. There will only be fifteen of us so it shouldn't take too much organising."

"Who are your guests going to be?" Adam asked although he had already worked it out.

"Everyone from last evening," Sally said, "plus my mother and her carer and Dominic wants to invite Matthew Dunn and his wife."

"What about his mother?"

"He will have to invite her, but he is pretty sure she won't come," Sally said. "There's not much I can do until we have a definite date."

"There's plenty to do here," he said, drily. "I want to recruit more staff and discuss a new rota. We have to decide on the furniture and carpets for upstairs and I think it is time to pay some more visits to various branches."

"What would you like to do first?" she asked, opening her diary.

"When Bill was appointed, I asked Barry to keep the information on the other shortlisted candidates. See if you can get it from him. I'd like to look through it."

Sally went to find Barry but he was busy in the main office, so she spoke to Laura, his secretary.

"I've got it here in the filing cabinet," said Laura. "But I ought to let him know I am giving it to Mr Richards."

"Ask him as soon as he is free."

"He hasn't got a lot of free time this week. He has clients every day," Laura told her.

"Try to share them out with Mr Birch. Make sure they each have their own clients."

"It gets very busy here, Sally when there are so many appointments. I have to deal with all the paperwork."

"You need some help," Sally told her. "I'll see what I can do."

She left Laura and went back to Adam's office.

"Barry will bring the file when he is free. I had a chat with Laura and she is finding it difficult to cope with being secretary to Barry and Bill. I think she needs some help."

"It is obvious that we need to target certain areas for the extra help," he said. "Make a note of where we should look. It might be possible to promote some of the present staff. Have we got profiles on all of them?"

"Yes, they are in my filing cabinet. I'll get them out."

Adam was looking thoughtful.

"It will probably be easier to recruit people to work on the tills and we could train them up to suit our way of working," he said.

There was a knock at the door and Barry walked in.

"I've brought the file," he said. "What have you in mind?"

Adam explained to him.

"That sounds good," he said. "We could do with the extra help."

"Give me a day or two to look at the files," Adam said. "Then I'll come back to you."

Barry left the office and Adam opened the file. Sally returned with the other details and they sat there discussing the different possibilities. They were interrupted by the phone ringing.

"Mr West wishes to speak to you," Julie said. "He said it is confidential."

"Put him through," Adam said. "Hello, Adam Richards speaking."

"I don't want Sally to hear this," Dominic said quietly.

Adam turned to Sally.

"This might be a long call," he said. "Why don't you take your coffee break?"

She got up and left the room.

"Hello Dominic," Adam said after she had left. "Sally was standing right by me, but I have sent her off for her coffee break."

"This is a secret I didn't want her to hear," Dominic said mysteriously. "Do you remember I wanted to buy her a car? Well, I've just been talking business with one of the big manufacturing companies we deal with and they happened to mention that they wanted to get rid of a fleet of small cars which they own. They have offered me a deal, two for the price of one. Are you still wanting a car for Alice?"

Adam took a deep breath.

"Yes, I am," he said, "but I wasn't thinking of a new one."

"It would only cost you insurance and road tax, the car would be free."

"But you still have to pay for the other car. I couldn't allow that."

"The other car will be for my wife and it can therefore go through company funds," Dominic said. "The second car is totally free."

"I really feel I should be making a contribution," Adam said uncertainly. "It is such a wonderful surprise."

"I assure you it is a genuine offer, Adam. I wouldn't have anything to do with it if there was a hint of anything illegal."

"What can I say, but thank you," Adam stammered. "I really am lost for words."

"Don't say anything to Sally, I want it to be a surprise. If you tell Alice make sure she keeps it a secret. I'll let you know which day they will be delivered but it will certainly be before the end of the week."

Adam put the phone down and sat back in his chair. He needed a few minutes to collect his thoughts about what he had just heard. That man never ceases to amaze, he thought and wondered what on earth he would do next. He needed to clear his head and went down to the main office to speak to some of the staff. He was getting to know them quite well and as he talked, he was discovering their suitability for promotion. He made a mental note of one or two names and then went to the staff room to make himself a coffee. When he saw the waste-bin full of plastic coffee beakers, he was determined to do something about it. They were not exactly helping the environment. He took the coffee back to his office, called Sally in and told her what he had seen.

"Things have to change," he said.

"What do you suggest?"

"Coffee tastes better out of a proper mug," he said. "We order three dozen coffee mugs, medium-size and get rid of all the plastic ones in the recycling bin."

"What about the washing up?"

"Every member of staff should wash their own mug but in addition, they must sign a rota for making sure all the mugs are clean by the end of the day. You see to ordering the mugs and I will get the rules printed out and I'll sign them."

Sally left the office and Adam opened the file which Barry had brought in. It contained the details of six of the unsuccessful applicants for Bill's job. He studied them carefully and made a note of their particular strengths. He called Sally back in.

"I need to know which part of the office requires additional staff. Ask Barry to see me at two o'clock. I'm going to take my lunch break now."

He went to his favourite bistro. It was cold and damp outside and he ordered a bowl of hot soup. The Christmas lights were still on in the shops and many of them had sale notices in the window. Adam remembered that he had promised to go shopping with Leah during the school holidays. He decided they had to do that one afternoon this week and made a mental note to talk to her this evening. He walked briskly back to the office and saw Bill checking the computers.

"Is everything okay?" he asked.

"I shall be glad when we have our reliable system," Bill said. "These machines are wearing out."

"We may have to close the office for a couple of days when the new system is put in place. It is a major job," Adam said. "Is Barry around?"

"He's having a quick break, then we shall swap over. I understand you are seeing him at two o'clock?"

"I want to talk to him about additional staff," Adam said. "I'll keep you informed."

Adam went towards his own office and called to Sally as he passed:

"Any phone calls?"

"Just one," she said, following him into his office. "Dominic rang to say that he has been in contact with someone about the special licence and he has an appointment tomorrow morning."

"That's a start," Adam said. "I'm sure the pace will increase over the next few days." He pointed to the file on the desk. "When Barry comes, I want you to join us and take notes."

She returned to her office and Adam continued to study the file. At two o'clock, Barry came as arranged and the three of them discussed the problem. By the end of the discussion, Sally had written down six areas where extra help would be needed.

"We must have more supervisory staff," Adam said. "Bill will still be assistant manager and I shall call the newcomers under managers."

"How will you define their job?" Barry asked.

"Because this is such a large and busy office, we need responsible people who can support you and Bill. Our work is expanding all the time and sometimes you two will be busy with interviews and business applications. That is when you will need a responsible person in the main office. When upstairs is completed, we shall need extra staff up there in the offices."

Barry nodded his head in agreement.

"So, what do you want me to do?" he asked.

"I think you have enough to do at present. I'll deal with this but I will keep both of you fully informed."

Barry returned to the main office and Sally collected up her notes.

"I'll get these printed out and they will be ready in the morning," she said.

"There will some phoning around to do tomorrow," Adam said, "and there are a couple of our present staff I would like to talk to."

"It looks like I'm going to be busy," she said. "Thank goodness I have Julie to help."

"I shan't be in the office on Wednesday afternoon. Leah needs a new dress and I've promised to go shopping with her."

"I've got that to look forward to on Saturday," she said with a sigh. "It sounds as if I shall need half a dozen new dresses and now, I shall have to get something to get married in."

"You can have whatever you want. I'm sure you will choose well," Adam said soothingly.

He sat back in his chair as Sally went out. Take one day at a time, he reminded himself. He opened the file on his desk and started to compare the applications with the list of jobs available. He matched two of them as possible under managers and made a note to discuss them with Barry the next day. Then he took the furniture catalogue out of his drawer and had a quick look through it. There was a very wide choice and he realised that he would need help choosing the right pieces. He called Sally and told her to bring her notebook with her.

"I want you to come upstairs with me and make a note of the

furniture we shall need for the upstairs offices."

They left Julie in charge of the phone and went out into the main office. Adam was pleased to see that there were no queues at any of the tills as they went upstairs. The builders were still working and the various rooms were beginning to take shape.

"It's much easier to think about furniture now that we can actually see the dimensions of the rooms," Adam said thankfully as they walked into what would be his office.

"It's quite big," Sally said, impressed. "Much bigger than the one downstairs." She went into a smaller adjacent room. "I assume this will be my place?"

"I made sure it would be big enough for two desks so that Julie is also available but I think she could also double up as receptionist, at least to start with."

"That should be fine," Sally said. "What about these other two offices?"

"Bill might need one when the education side is up and running. He could also use it as his assistant manager's office. He is fit enough to run up and down stairs."

"What about the staff room?" she asked.

"The reception desk will be at the top of the stairs with the lecture room behind it and beyond that will be the staff room. The spare office will be a storeroom."

"You will need to get carpets and flooring down before any furniture is delivered."

"Yes," he said, "but next are the electrics, then carpets, then furniture and finally computers. I just need to get an idea of the office equipment first so that we can order the desks. The technical department will need something to stand the computers on."

Sally made a list as they looked around. It included desks, chairs, filing cabinets and shelving. Adam decided not to think about the seating in the lecture room until later. He looked at his watch.

"That's enough for today, Sally. We have made a good start. We'll carry on tomorrow."

They went back to his office.

"Have there been any phone calls, Julie?" he asked.

"Just one from Mr West. He said he will ring you this evening."

It was nearly closing time and Adam cleared his desk and put the furniture catalogues in his briefcase. He called Sally in.

"I need to reply to Sir Humphrey's invitation. Remind me to do it tomorrow?"

He left the office and drove home. He went into the lounge where Leah was sitting.

"Have you had a good day?" she asked.

"Yes, Sally and I have worked hard," he replied as he kissed her. "I've taken Wednesday afternoon off so that we can go shopping."

"I shall have to decide exactly what I need," she said. "I must ask Jen if she knows any smaller boutiques in Oxford. I can't just go into M&S and buy something off the peg."

"I'd better send my best suit to be cleaned I suppose. Can you or Alice take it to the cleaners for me?"

"I'll do that tomorrow," she said. "I shall need two new dresses, one for the reception for the new Board and one for Sir Humphrey's retirement party."

"What about Dominic and Sally's wedding? You'll need a new outfit for that."

"Have they fixed a date yet?"

"Not as far as I know," he replied, "but it will be in the next two to three weeks."

"As soon as that?" she gasped. "How on earth can they organise a wedding in two or three weeks?"

"You know Dominic only has to click his fingers and the deed is done," Adam said in a resigned voice. "He is going to ring me this evening. Maybe he'll have some news then."

He took his shoes off and lay down on the settee.

"Alice is cooking the meal," she said. "I'll go and make you a cup of tea."

"Where's Jessica?"

"She is doing some homework in the dining room. I shall make sure she does two hours each day so that she won't find it too hard when she goes to her new school."

Adam stretched out and closed his eyes. When Leah came in with his tea, he was fast asleep, so she drank it herself. She sat and thought about all the events of the coming month. She wasn't looking forward to any of it but she knew she would have to make an effort for Adam's sake.

Jessica came into the lounge to show Leah the maths which she had been busy doing.

"I'll look at it later," Leah said, "when you are in bed."

She stood up and went to lay the table ready for tea.

"Five minutes!" Alice called out from the kitchen.

"Can you wake Grandad up please, Jessica?" asked Leah.

She went up to Adam and shook his arm.

"Wake up, tea's ready."

He grunted and opened his eyes.

"Okay, okay," he said. "There's no need to shout." He stood up and joined the others at the table. "I'm very hungry," he said. "I could eat a horse."

Jessica gave him a horrified look.

"Nobody eats horses. What a thing to say."

"It's just one of those odd expressions from a long time ago," said Alice.

Adam smiled at her.

"Children sometimes do stupid things. What have you done today?"

"I haven't done anything stupid," Jessica said indignantly. "I've been busy all day putting my soft toys in their right place in my bedroom."

"I've been busy all day too," he said. "What about you Alice?"

"I took my application form into the library, then I bought some fresh vegetables from the market."

"I did my bit towards preserving the planet this morning," said Adam and told them about the plastic cups.

They chatted around the table until Leah said:

"I'll tidy the kitchen."

Adam helped to clear the table and then joined Alice in the lounge.

"When do you think we could take the Christmas tree down?" Alice asked. "I should like to make a start on those boxes."

"I don't see why you can't take it down tomorrow but I wouldn't empty too many boxes at present."

"Why do you say that?" she asked.

"I think January is going to be a busy month for all of us. I can feel it in my bones. I'm waiting to hear from Dominic about his wedding plans."

"It takes time to organise a wedding, Dad."

"Not when Dominic is doing it," he said firmly. "I shouldn't make any plans for Saturday week if I were you."

"You must be joking! Even he couldn't do it in less than two weeks. What does Sally say about it?"

"She has decided to go along with his plans. It is going to be a simple affair and that is what she wants."

"You will definitely need to get a new suit," Alice said. "You can wear it at some of the other functions you have to go to."

Adam gave her a hard stare.

"Do you know what I am really looking forward to?" he demanded. Alice shook her head. "I can't wait for Friday afternoon when your mother and I can forget about all these intrigues and just think about each other."

"Would you mind if Bill came to keep me company?"

"I had already assumed that he would," he answered with a grin.

"Jessica will sleep in her own room tonight," Alice said. "She has spent a lot of time up there today rearranging it to her liking."

"We must get her a desk up there so that she always has somewhere to do her homework," Adam said. "I've been looking for new office furniture today and there might be something suitable in the catalogue."

"I'm going to try and persuade her to have a shower instead of a bath so that she will get used to it," she said and went upstairs to find Jessica.

Adam thought about taking the furniture details out of his briefcase but decided against it, thinking it would be better to look at it with Sally. It needed a woman's touch. He laid his head on the back of the settee and closed his eyes. Leah came in and sat beside him.

"Are you alright?" she asked, holding his hand.

"Yes, I'm fine. Sally and I were busy all day with one thing and another."

"There is something troubling you, I can tell."

"How can you tell?" Adam said in astonishment.

"You have that look in your eyes and you go quiet," she said. "Is it something I can help with?"

"It is something which you will find hard to believe," he said slowly.

"Then it must be something to do with Dominic."

"Got it in one," he muttered and told her about his offer of a car for Alice.

Leah sat with her mouth open but no words came out. She was totally stunned.

"What are you going to do?" she gasped.

"There's not much I can do," Adam said in a matter-of-fact voice. "You know that when he decides to do something, he is immovable."

"Have you told Alice?"

"Not yet, I was waiting to hear when it might be delivered."

"What make is it?"

"All I know is that it is a small car," he said. "I don't know any more than that."

At that moment the phone rang.

"Is it a convenient time to talk?" asked Dominic.

"Yes, go ahead," said Adam.

"I've got a whole lot of things here which I need to tell you. It would have been difficult to do it at the office. The first thing is regarding the car. It will be delivered to you on Wednesday afternoon between two and two-thirty. Alice needs to be there to sign for it. I've given her name as Richards because I didn't know her married name. Sally's car will be delivered to her house at six o'clock on Wednesday."

"Are you going to tell her about it?"

"No, I shall tell her to be sure to be home and to expect a parcel. Now about the wedding arrangements; I shall be going to Somerset House tomorrow to apply for a special licence and Matthew says that there shouldn't be a problem. I've spoken to the vicar of the church in the village and he is quite willing to marry us on Saturday week, that is assuming the special licence is in order. Sally reckons that there will be fifteen of us at the reception and that is too many for her house. What do you suggest?"

Adam guessed what Dominic wanted him to reply.

"I suggest you tell me what you have in mind," he said.

"You are putting me on the spot, aren't you?" he grumbled.

"If you don't ask you don't get. Have you never heard that saying?" Adam said pointedly.

"Alright," Dominic said. "I'll tell you my idea. Most of the guests will be coming from your area so I thought it would be a good idea to have the reception there and your house is ideal. We have a fleet of limousines at Head Office and I would use them to take the guests to the church and bring them back to your house. We have a catering department at Head Office and they would provide all the food and drink, plus waiters. It would mean Leah giving up her kitchen, but I don't think she will mind that will she?"

"Have you discussed this with Sally?"

"Yes, I spoke to her before I spoke to you," Dominic said. "She liked the idea but felt it was taking advantage of you."

"I'll have to talk to Leah," Adam said. "I'll let you know by Wednesday. There is one other thing. This invitation to the Houses of

Parliament. Can I ring his secretary and accept or should I send a written acceptance?"

"Since this is the first one, I think a written note would be best. She will remember your name and any further contact could be by telephone. I'll speak to you tomorrow."

Adam stayed in his seat. That familiar knot was rumbling in his stomach. What did Dominic mean by 'any further contact'? He went back into Leah and told her everything that had been said.

"We owe him a favour," Adam said. "We must think carefully about it."

"I think we could manage fifteen quite comfortably," she said. "We could open up the conservatory."

"I suppose we should just have to make space available," he agreed. "We wouldn't have to provide any food or drink and Dominic said the catering department would include waiters."

"No washing up," Leah said brightly. "It really wouldn't be much trouble. The one thing we might need to get are flowers for the house. I wonder who will put any flowers in the church?"

"Maybe we could visit it and talk to the vicar when we are down there this weekend?"

"There is one thing which is troubling me," she said. "Who will give the bride away? She has no relations except her mother."

"That is up to Sally," Adam said tiredly. "We shall soon find out."

Alice came downstairs and into the lounge.

"Jessica was not very keen on her shower," she said. "She much prefers a bath." She stopped talking and took a closer look at her parents. "What's the matter?" she asked anxiously. "What has happened?"

"You had better sit down before I tell you," Adam said.

"Is it bad news?" she asked fearfully.

"No, it's not bad news," said Leah, hastening to reassure her. "I suppose it could be called exciting news."

Alice breathed a sigh of relief.

"It must be to do with Sally and Dominic then," she said gratefully.

Adam told her what had been suggested and she was quite taken aback.

"Dominic is the limit," she said. "How does Sally feel about this?"

"Apparently he has already spoken to Sally about this and she is willing to go along with it," he said resignedly.

"What do you think Mum?"

"I think it could work quite well," Leah said. "We shan't need to worry about shopping and cooking, and we can just enjoy it."

Alice looked at Adam.

"Are you going to agree to it then?"

"Yes, I'll tell Sally tomorrow. By the way, can you make sure you are here on Wednesday afternoon? Your mother and I are going to be shopping and we are expecting a delivery between two and two-thirty."

"I'll make sure I am here," she said and kissed him. "I said you would need a new suit, now you've got to get one."

"I don't see why," he said grumpily.

"You can't give Sally away in an old suit," Alice said firmly, "and you'll need a buttonhole."

"I'm going to bed," he said shortly. "I've made enough decisions for one day," and he left the room.

"Will he be alright, Mum?"

"He'll be fine after a good night's sleep," Leah replied. "The trouble with men is that they can't multi-task as well as we can."

"It's really quite exciting isn't it?" Alice said. "I wonder if we shall meet Dominic's mother."

"I don't think she will come," Leah said, sounding grateful. "She would put a damper on the whole day."

"I assume that the guests will be everyone who was here last Saturday, plus Sally's mother?" said Alice.

"That doesn't make fifteen," Leah counted up. "I wonder who the other two will be?"

"Dominic has never mentioned any other particular friends, has he?

And Sally has no other family."

"I'm sure we shall find out more details soon," Leah said as she stood up. "I'm off to bed."

Chapter Nine

Adam slept all night and woke up feeling refreshed in the morning. He kept reminding himself to take each day as it comes as he walked into work. The builders were already busy upstairs and he went up to speak to Mr Carter.

"Nearly finished the noisy part," he said. "The electricians should be here tomorrow."

"How long will they take?" Adam asked.

"The basic wiring should be in by Friday. Then the technicians can start next week."

"I'll inform the relevant department," Adam said. "Thank you, Mr Carter."

He went down to his office and opened his briefcase. He took out the furniture catalogue and called Sally in. He looked at her closely.

"You look tired," he said. "What's the matter?"

"It's Dominic," she said wearily. "He kept ringing me last night like an excited schoolboy. Every time I closed my eyes the phone rang."

"What on earth was he so excited about?"

"He was saying something about me being home at six o'clock on Wednesday evening and that I should expect a package. I'm always home by six o'clock, he knows that. I don't know why he had to remind me three times," she sighed.

Adam smiled to himself.

"It must be an important package," he said in a serious voice.

"Do you know anything about it?" she asked accusingly.

"I don't know what he puts in his important packages," he said with a straight face.

"I know that look," she said grumpily. "You're hiding something."

"Let's forget about Dominic and his little surprises and get down to some work?"

Sally was still not satisfied with his answer but she opened her diary. Adam produced Sir Humphrey's invitation from his pocket.

"I need to reply to this on company notepaper," he said. "Can you print something out and I'll sign it?"

Fifteen minutes later she came back with a piece of paper in her hand. She put it on the desk in front of Adam.

"Is that alright?" she asked.

He read it carefully and then he signed it.

"Make sure it is posted today," he said. "First class."

Sally went back to her office and Adam sat back in his chair. He could tell that Sally was putting on a brave face and beginning to feel the strain. He knew Dominic had an appointment that morning and he decided to speak to him immediately after. He went down to the staff room and made two coffees. He returned to his office and called Sally in.

"Sit down," he said. "I've made you a coffee. I've been thinking about the next two weeks. If things go as planned you will have plenty of other things to keep you busy. If you need any time off you only have to ask but I think it is important for you to stick to your work schedule as much as possible. I have decided to put all branch visits on hold until upstairs is finished but in the meantime, I would like you to explain the procedure to Julie so that she can take over if necessary."

She looked at him with tears in her eyes.

"Thank you," she said. "I really appreciate what you have just said. I don't want to let you down."

"I know that," he said gently, "but your circumstances are going to change and you mustn't be afraid of the future. If you can pass your skills on to someone else you would be doing them and me a great favour." He waited while she wiped her eyes. "Now, there is something else I need to talk about."

At that moment the phone rang.

"Mr West wishes to speak to you," Julie said.

"Tell him I'll phone him in half an hour and hold any more calls."

Sally looked at him in surprise.

"You don't normally put Dominic on hold," she said.

"What I want to say to you is more important right now. I had a long conversation with Dominic yesterday evening and he told me some of the details about the wedding. He said that he had talked to you about them but I want to know how you really feel?"

He told Sally about the proposed arrangements for the reception.

"He explained all that to me," she said. "But I thought he was taking advantage of you and Leah."

"I don't think Dominic would know how to take advantage of anyone," he said firmly. "It's more likely to be the other way around. Anyway, Leah and I talked it over and we are more than pleased to do it for you."

She stood up and kissed him on the cheek.

"Thank you, please thank Leah from me. I have been really worried about it."

"Leah is quite happy to hand over her kitchen to someone else. She is looking forward to being waited on."

She returned to her chair and she was looking hard at Adam. Eventually, she said:

"There is one other favour that I want to ask you. Will you give me away?"

"You women all think in the same way," he laughed. "Alice said I should need a new suit. I shall be delighted to walk you down the aisle."

She stood up and kissed him on the other cheek.

"Thank you," she said. "Thank you," and the tears ran down her cheeks.

Adam put his arms around her.

"It will be hard to let you go. You are like a daughter to me," he said quietly.

"You are special to me too," she said as she wiped her eyes.

"I'd better phone Dominic with my apologies before he fires me," Adam said.

He pressed the number on his phone and Dominic answered.

"Hello Adam," he said in a cross voice. "What do you mean by putting me on hold?"

"I'm sorry," Adam replied in a contrite voice, "but I was busy comforting your wife to be."

"That's a firing offence," Dominic said sternly. "What have you been doing to her?"

"Trying to explain why you kept ringing her last night. She needs her beauty sleep."

"Ah, yes I'm sorry about that. I was at the club with Father and he was drowning his sorrows. I had to keep up with him."

"So, my job is safe?" Adam asked innocently.

"It certainly is. I couldn't let you loose in any other organisation."

"In that case business first then matters arising," Adam said. "The building work upstairs is nearing completion and the electricians will be in tomorrow. I need to order the desks for the offices before the computer team come next week. I need the number of the technical department."

"I'll get my secretary to phone it through. Now let me tell you what I've been doing. I've filled in the necessary forms for the special licence and sent them to Matthew for him to deal with. He says it is all in order and shouldn't be a problem. Sally will have to sign something when she comes up at the weekend. I've spoken to the vicar and he is okay for Saturday week. I'll organise the cars and …"

"Just slow up a minute," Adam said firmly. "You really must think of the effect all this activity is having on other people, particularly Sally. I know there are certain things which only you can do but other people can help too. I talked to Leah about your suggestion for the reception and we will be pleased to put our house at your disposal. With regard to the catering, you must talk it over with Sally. Obviously, you deal with the drinks but she might have preferences for the food. It would be helpful if you could arrange for someone from the catering department to come and meet Leah so that she knows exactly what is involved. Now, what about invitations? Are you getting official ones, or do you want me to mention it?"

"You'd better ask Sally about that," Dominic said. "It is just the people who were at your place at Christmas, plus Jessica of course and possibly Sally's mother. Can I leave you to deal with that?"

"Yes, I can do that. There is one more thing you should know. Sally has asked me if I will give her away and I have agreed to do it."

"That's wonderful news! Father has agreed to be my best man. I hope he doesn't drop the ring."

"Sally is going to need a lot of help with her shopping at the weekend. Just concentrate on that, but there will be one outfit she will want to choose entirely on her own, so make sure that you are elsewhere at that time," warned Adam.

"I promise I'll remember that. When I was with Father last night, he mentioned that he would like to bring someone with him to the wedding. Sally has already met her and she is a charming old lady and a particular friend of Father's. Her name is Lady Harrington and she is the widow of Lord Harrington who died last year. Would you mind if she came?"

"No, of course not, but don't forget to mention it to Sally."

"I'll tell her this evening. I'm off to the bank vault to see what other treasures I can find in Grandma's jewellery box."

Adam put the phone down and looked at his watch. It was nearly lunchtime and he decided he needed some fresh air. He went into Sally's office and told her that he was taking his lunch break then went out through the main door. He decided to walk down some of the side streets, in the hope of finding some exclusive dress shops. He found himself in front of the museum and noticed that they had a coffee shop in the basement. He went in and bought a coffee and a roll. As he went to find a table, he saw a stand with a variety of magazines on it. He picked out an Oxfordshire one and started thumbing through it. He noticed that there were plenty of small and exclusive dress shops but not many in Oxford itself, so it looked as if they would have to take a trip further afield. He made a note of the magazine and called in at the bookshop and bought one on the way back to the office.

It was comparatively quiet in the main office and he went to find Barry and Bill. They were drinking their coffee in Barry's office.

"We were just talking about the new staff," Barry said. "Have you made any decisions?"

"I haven't had a chance," Adam said. "I'll look at it this afternoon. Actually, I came in to give you both an invitation to a wedding."

"A wedding!" Bill exclaimed. "Whose wedding?"

"Dominic and Sally are getting married on Saturday week. Service at the church near Kitson Manor, Reception at my house."

"At your house," said Barry. "That's going to be a lot of work and a crowd of people."

"It's all arranged," Adam assured him. "I doubt if Leah will be allowed in her own kitchen."

"I don't understand," Bill said. "What about the food?"

"It's all been taken care of by the catering staff at Head Office. Chauffeurs provided for the journey to the church and back."

"I'd better get a decent suit," said Bill, "and a tie and shoes and a smart shirt."

"It might be money well spent," Adam said with a grin. "You never know when you might need it again. I'm supposed to get a new suit too since I am giving the bride away."

"It's quite a small number of people for a wedding, especially for someone like Dominic," Barry said.

"They just wanted their friends there. It will be about fifteen people altogether."

"I never thought I'd be called a friend of the Managing Director," Bill said in wonder.

"You should always be prepared for surprises in this office," Barry said wisely. "Things can happen very quickly," and he looked at Adam.

"Things happen too fast for me," Adam said firmly. "They pile up like a wobbly tower which could come crashing down at any time."

"That's a defeatist attitude," Barry said severely. "We always try to look on the bright side."

"I'll pencil you in on the guest list," Adam said. "I'm sure you won't want to miss this experience."

He left them and returned to his own office. He called Sally in.

"I'd like to spend some time looking at these job applications but first of all I need to ask you about your mother."

She looked at him in surprise.

"What about her?"

"Will she be coming to the wedding?"

"That's a tricky one," Sally answered. "Of course, I shall ask her, but I don't know what she will say. If she came, she would need to have a carer with her."

"Is she that infirm?" he asked, surprised.

"My mother is a very difficult woman. She has a very sharp tongue and can be embarrassing in company. If she came, I would be constantly worrying about what she would do next. This is why she needs someone with her who can keep her under control."

"Has Dominic met her?"

"Yes, he has and he is very patient with her but that is in her own environment with no-one else around."

"What are you going to do about it?"

"I'll talk to Dominic and then decide," she said.

They settled down to the task in hand and by the end of the afternoon they had matched up possible applicants with the various job vacancies.

"We'll start with the under managers," said Adam. "I'll speak to each of them tomorrow morning and if they are still interested you can arrange an interview for early next week. Be sure Julie learns how to do it in case you are not around."

Sally made a note of Adam's instruction and at the same time, the phone rang.

"Hello Adam," said Dominic. "I thought I would let you know that father is really pleased that you and Leah are coming to his retirement party. He is looking forward to introducing you to some of his friends. Can I speak to Sally?"

"She is standing right next to me," Adam said and passed the phone over.

He left the office and went next door to speak with Julie. When he knew that Sally had finished the call he returned to his own office.

"Dominic said that Sir Humphrey would like to bring Lady Harrington to the wedding. I met her on Christmas Day and it was obvious that they have a sort of special relationship. She was very kind to me and I got on well with her. Would you mind if she came?"

"No, of course, I won't mind," Adam said. "It will be nice for Sir Humphrey to have a companion."

"I'll tell Dominic this evening," she said as she left the office.

Adam sat back in his chair. Something Dominic had said was bothering him. Why would Sir Humphrey want to introduce him to some of his friends? That familiar knot came into his stomach. Should he keep it to himself or should he share his worry with Leah? He decided to go home and talk to her. He reminded Sally that he would not be in his office on Wednesday afternoon, then he picked up his briefcase and left. He went straight home and found Leah in the lounge.

"You're home early," she said as he kissed her. "Are you okay?"

He told her about his discussions with Sally and the extra guest expected at the wedding, then he sat back and closed his eyes. She looked at him carefully and moved over to sit by him on the settee.

"There's something bothering you," she said softly. "What is it?"

He opened his eyes and looked at her.

"Why do you ask?"

"I know you well enough," she replied. "Are you going to share it with me?"

"It's just something Dominic said. It probably doesn't mean anything."

"Can I be the judge of that?" Leah said firmly and Adam repeated what Dominic had said.

"I think you are being oversensitive," she said. "I'm sure Sir Humphrey wouldn't do anything to embarrass you."

"You are probably right," he sighed, "but these little hints keep coming and I can't help feeling there is a purpose behind them."

"Well, there are more important priorities right now, like going shopping tomorrow afternoon."

"You're right," he said putting an arm around her. "We have a lot of shopping to do. How many outfits do you need?"

"I need a long dress for the new Board of Directors' dinner and something for Sir Humphrey's party and now I need an extra outfit for a wedding."

"I'd better get a new suit for the wedding since I am in loco parentis as the bride's father. Did you remember to take my other best suit to the cleaners?"

"Alice took it down this morning. It will be ready on Thursday."

"I told Barry and Bill about the wedding this morning. Bill said that he would have to buy a new suit and I told him it would be money well spent," Adam said with a grin.

"You just need to speak to Alice and Jessica then we shall all know about it," she said.

"There is one other couple," Adam said thoughtfully. "I must remind Dominic to tell them about the arrangements."

"I'd better go and get the tea ready," she said. "It's oven chips and sausages tonight," and she went off to the kitchen.

He stretched out on the settee. He was sure Leah was right, he should get his priorities sorted out and he closed his eyes. He was woken by the sound of the front door closing with a bang. Jessica came in carrying a large carrier bag.

"Look!" she cried excitedly, "I got my new school uniform today," and she took it out of the bag. "I can throw my old one away now."

Alice followed her into the lounge and Leah came to see what all the noise was about.

"It cost me a small fortune," said Alice, sitting down heavily on the settee. "I shall be glad when I start to get some maintenance money."

"I'll ask Matthew Dunn about it next time I speak to him," said Adam.

Jessica took the bag up to her bedroom and hung the new skirts in her wardrobe.

"Alice, I'm afraid you are going to have some more expense," said

Adam and he told her about the wedding arrangements.

"That doesn't give us much time," she said. "And what about Sally? How is she going to get everything done?"

"Fortunately, most things are being done for her," Adam said soothingly. "Catering, cars, church, Dominic has organised it. Sally will only have to think about herself and her own outfit."

"If the reception is being held here that is going to mean extra work for Mum and me."

"All we have to do is clear the surfaces," said Leah. "And I don't mind handing my kitchen over to someone else."

"I'll have to get a new dress for Jessica," Alice said, "but I might be able to use one of the dresses I have already for myself. I said you would need a new suit, Dad and I was right, wasn't I?" She stood up to leave the room but she suddenly stopped at the door. "What about photographs? Has Dominic arranged for a photographer?"

"He hasn't mentioned it," he said. "I'll have to ask him about that."

Adam was glad to have a quiet evening at home. Alice spent some time upstairs going through her wardrobe. Jessica joined her and they talked about the wedding. Alice explained who the guests were and Jessica looked apprehensively at her mother.

"I don't know any Sirs or Ladies," she said. "Are they real people?"

"Of course, they are," she said, smiling. "Sir Humphrey is quite a jolly old gentleman."

"Can I have a new dress?"

Alice agreed and she put her arms around her daughter and kissed her.

Downstairs, Adam and Leah were talking about their shopping trip the next day.

"If you take the bus into Oxford and come to the office by one o'clock, I shall be ready," he said. "I'll tell Barry to look out for you."

"You must remind Alice to be here tomorrow afternoon," she said. "I don't know what her reaction is going to be."

After a while, Alice joined them in the lounge.

"Sally is going to London on Friday," said Adam. "She and Dominic are going shopping on Saturday."

"It's going to be tricky for her to choose a wedding outfit when he is with her," said Leah.

"I've already warned him about that," he said.

"You think of everything, don't you?" Alice said. "What else have you told him?"

"Just to remember to consult Sally before he makes any decisions. Don't forget you need to be at home tomorrow afternoon."

"I won't forget," she said and kissed them goodnight.

Chapter Ten

Adam was up early on Wednesday morning. He had a quick shower and was in his office by nine o'clock. He went upstairs to speak with Mr Carter and to ask him if the electricians would be arriving.

"They will be unloading their equipment this morning and hope to make a start today," replied Mr Carter. "We shall be removing as much rubbish as possible so there will be a lot of coming and going."

"I'll tell Mr Wilson," said Adam. "We'll manage without two of the tills."

He went off to tell Barry before going to his own office. He called Sally in.

"Did you have a more peaceful evening?"

"Yes, thank you," she replied. "I only had two phone calls."

"I'm pleased to hear it. Let's get down to some work." He opened the file in front of him. "I want you to phone these two people and ask them if they are still interested in a job here. If they say no, then I don't want to speak with them but if they say yes, then I would like to have a word."

Sally went back to her office and explained to Julie what she was about to do. Adam took the furniture catalogue out of his briefcase and began to study it. Ten minutes later, Sally was on the phone.

"I've got Kenneth Rogers on the line," she said, "he would like to speak with you."

"Put him through," Adam said and she switched the call to him.

"Good morning Mr Rogers," Adam said. "I understand from my secretary that you are still interested in working in this office. Have you applied for any other positions since you wrote to us?"

"No, I haven't. I'm only interested in a position in Oxford."

"What is the particular reason for that?" Adam asked with interest.

"My wife works for the NHS and she has been offered a consultancy at the Nuffield Hospital. We are looking to live in the Oxford area."

"I would like to meet you," Adam said. "My secretary will discuss a date with you for early next week. I'll put you through to her."

He passed the call back to Sally for her to arrange an interview.

He thought the man had sounded promising. He went back to looking at desks and chairs. He called Sally in.

"I think it is coffee time and ask Bill to come and see me."

"I've arranged an interview for next Monday at eleven o'clock," she said.

"Make sure Julie knows about it, Sally."

Five minutes later, Bill arrived carrying two cups of coffee. He sat down opposite Adam and waited for him to speak. After a few moments Adam said:

"What I am going to tell you is in the strictest confidence, do you understand?"

Bill nodded his head wondering what was coming.

"I am going shopping with Leah this afternoon and Alice has been told that she must be at home at two o'clock."

"But why?" Bill stammered.

"She has been told to expect a package but it is a lot bigger than a package. It is actually a new car."

Bill's mouth opened but no words came out. He took out his handkerchief and mopped his brow. Adam watched him with amusement while he drank his coffee.

"Barry was right," Bill gasped. "You should always be prepared for surprises in this office."

"That's not quite everything," Adam announced with a grin. "Sally will get one too this evening."

"Does she know about it?" Bill said incredulously.

"No, it will be a surprise."

"This has got Dominic's name written all over it," Bill said firmly. "I feel really sorry for Sally."

"Apparently he was offered two for the price of one, just like you can get at Tesco."

"A bit more upmarket than that. Did you realise that all these surprises can be mentally draining?"

"I know that," said Adam. "It happens to me all the time."

Bill drank his coffee and stood up to go but Adam stopped him.

"There is one other thing I want to run past you. I've just been on the phone to Mr Kenneth Rogers. Do you know him?"

"Kenny Rogers!" Bill exclaimed. "Yes, I know him. We played in the same England team but I've lost touch with him."

"Well, he is coming in for an interview on Monday, so you will be able to catch up with him," Adam said. "You can show him around."

"He's a good chap," Bill said as he went towards the door. "His wife is a physiotherapist."

Adam sat back in his chair and looked at his watch. He needed to stretch his legs. He told Sally that he would be out for half an hour and walked to M&S to buy some sandwiches and a bottle of water. He returned to his office and noticed Sally was on the phone. She saw him walk by and a minute or two later his phone rang.

"Dominic wants to speak to you," she said and transferred the call.

"Hello, Adam. Matthew has got the special licence; it just needs Sally's signature. I'm coming down this evening for her to sign it. I might see you in the morning before I go back to London."

"I've told everyone about the wedding arrangements but I think it would be better if you asked Matthew and his wife," said Adam.

"I'll do that and arrange for a car to collect them," Dominic said. "Is there anything else?"

"One other thing. What about photographs?"

"I know someone who will do that," Dominic said. "I'll sort that out. Make sure that Sally isn't late leaving work this evening. I should be there by eight o'clock."

"I'm glad you are coming tonight," Adam said. "She might need some help to get over the shock. I'll see you tomorrow."

He looked at his watch and saw that it was nearly twelve-thirty. He sat in his chair and ate his sandwiches, then he called Sally in.

"Leah will be here soon. Can you go and watch out for her?"

Sally went off to the main office and Adam cleared his desk. He locked away his briefcase and put his coat on. There was a knock at the door and Leah walked in. Adam kissed her and said thank you to Sally. Leah looked around.

"It's not exactly a hive of activity," she commented looking at the clean desk top. "I must get you one of those executive toys to play with."

"I always tidy it up when I am expecting visitors. A tidy desk mirrors a tidy mind."

He put his hand on Leah's elbow and steered her into the main office. Barry saw them and came over to say hello.

"Have you come to see what Adam does all day?" he asked.

Leah smiled at him.

"Everyone seems to be very busy," she said.

"This is a quiet time," Barry answered. "You should have been here the week before Christmas."

"We're going shopping," Adam said. "I'll see you in the morning," and he guided Leah out into the street.

They went into M&S and looked around but there was nothing that Leah liked.

"Alice told me that the biggest department store has a number of different franchises for designer clothes. Let's go and look in there?"

They walked down the street until they came to the store and went up to the first floor.

"This looks more promising," Adam said as they noticed the dresses on the display models.

Leah chose a dress from the rail and showed it to Adam. The material was a soft stretch jersey with a crossover front and long sleeves. The fitted skirt flared out at the hem. The colour was navy with an all-over pattern of small emerald and pink leaf shapes.

"I like it," he said, enthusiastically. "Try it on."

An assistant came up and took Leah into a changing room. Five minutes later she came out wearing the dress. Adam looked at her in admiration.

"That's perfect," he said. "Do you like it?"

"It feels very comfortable," Leah said, looking at herself in a long mirror. "I've already got shoes to go with it but I shall need a clutch bag."

Adam paid for the dress and they went to the accessory area. Leah found a navy bag and then Adam took her to the jewellery counter. He found a delicate gold chain with an emerald pendant attached to it.

"There are some matching earrings, would you like those too?" he asked.

"No thank you, I don't wear earrings. What I would like is a cup of tea."

They went up to the café and ordered a pot of tea and a fruit scone.

"That dress will do for the wedding and Sir Humphrey's party," Leah said, "but it will be cold in January and I haven't a coat to wear over it. I don't want a thick heavy coat, more of a 'going to the theatre' lightweight one."

"We'll go back and have another look around," he said. "Don't forget you still need an evening dress for the New Directors' dinner."

They returned to the fashion department and looked at the evening dresses. Leah found a navy 'theatre' coat which was exactly what she wanted. There was not a big selection of evening dresses but there was one that she quite liked. It was a fully-lined navy lace dress with an intricately embroidered design on it. It was a straight style with a round neck and three-quarter length sleeves. Adam encouraged her to try it on and she found that it fitted her perfectly. She was unsure about it until she looked at the price tag and saw that it was not too expensive. She decided to have it together with the coat and Adam paid for it.

"I suppose I ought to have a hat for the wedding, then I shall be all set up."

They went to the hat department and Leah bought a navy hat with a trimmed brim. By now they both had their hands full of bags.

"That's enough for one day," she said. "Let's go home."

They returned to the car and soon they were driving out of Oxford.

"I wonder how Alice is?" Leah said. "I hope it wasn't too much of a shock."

They drove up to the garage and saw a brand-new Mini Cooper parked on the grass.

"Nice motor," Adam muttered as they collected up all the parcels.

They went to the front door and Adam rang the bell. The door was opened by Jessica.

"Thank goodness you've come," she said. "Mummy has been crying all afternoon."

Adam dropped the parcels on the hall floor and went into the lounge. Alice was sitting on the settee. Her face was streaked with tears. When she saw Adam, she burst into sobs.

"She's been like this all afternoon," Jessica said in a worried voice.

Adam sat down by Alice and took out his handkerchief and gave it to her.

"Now stop this crying and dry your eyes," he said firmly.

She looked at him in surprise but stopped sobbing.

"That's better," he said, putting an arm around her.

"Let's go and make a cup of tea," Leah whispered to Jessica, "then you can tell me what's been happening."

In the lounge, Alice was sitting quietly but she said nothing. It was obvious that she was in a state of shock and Adam waited patiently until she was ready to talk.

"A man knocked on the door and said he had a delivery for me and I expected a parcel and he said 'where shall I park it?' and he pointed to the car, and I didn't believe him." She stopped for a minute to get her breath back and then went on. "I said he must have the wrong house and he showed me the paper he was holding in his hand and my name was on it and he said 'sign here', so I signed it and he parked it on the grass and then he went. What does it mean?"

"It means that you are now the proud owner of a brand-new Mini Cooper," he said.

"But where did it come from?"

"From the factory I expect," he said vaguely.

She looked at him closely.

"You are being deliberately evasive Dad. Tell me the truth."

"If you go and wash your face first then I'll tell you," he said.

Alice went upstairs and had a good wash and she brushed her hair. Then she went back to the lounge. Leah had made tea and they all sat down. Adam explained about the car and finished by saying:

"Sally has got one too."

"I still can't believe it, Dad. How did you find a friend like Dominic?"

"It's as much a mystery to me as it is to you. My existence is one big mystery."

Leah looked at him sternly.

"That's enough of that kind of talk," she said firmly. "You know you have worked hard and you are now reaping some rewards as a result of your efforts."

He didn't answer her but his mind went back to the past ten years and admitted to himself that he had made some sacrifices but that still didn't automatically entitle him to rewards now. He looked across at Leah who was watching him intently.

"I can't explain our friendship," he said quietly. "All I know is that I would trust him with my life."

Alice stood up and left the room but she was soon back carrying the bags which had been left in the hall.

"It looks like you had a successful shopping day," she said in an excited voice. "Show us what you bought."

Leah got up and opened the bags. She held the dresses in front of her and put the hat on her head. Alice and Jessica clapped their hands in appreciation.

"I'd better go and hang them up," she said.

She left the room and Alice and Jessica followed her. Adam stayed on the settee and rested his head on the back. He was pleased Leah had bought her dresses and knew that they would help her feel more confident. He thought about Alice's reaction to the car and wondered how Sally was feeling. No doubt he would find out in the morning. He made a mental note to order the furniture tomorrow and he needed to contact Matthew Dunn to see if there had been any progress on Alice's divorce. He closed his eyes. One day at a time, he thought as he fell asleep.

Chapter Eleven

Sally arrived home at her usual time and was busy in the kitchen when there was a knock at the door. A smartly dressed man stood there with some papers in his hand.

"Mrs Sally Browne?"

"Yes."

"I have a delivery for you. Please sign here."

She signed her name.

"Where would you like me to park it?" asked the man, pointing to the gleaming white Mini Cooper parked on the road.

"Are you sure that is for me?" she gasped.

"Right name, right house," he said looking at the number on the door. "I'm sure it's for you."

"You'd better park it in front of the garage," she said faintly.

The man moved the car and then came back and gave Sally the keys and the paperwork. Sally thanked him and closed the door. She staggered to the lounge and flopped onto the settee. This had Dominic's name written all over it; she couldn't even imagine what he might do next. She lay full length on the settee and closed her eyes. Once her heart had stopped pounding, she relaxed and went to sleep.

She didn't hear Dominic come into the house. He kissed her lightly on the forehead.

"Wake up Sleeping Beauty," he said, softly. "Your Prince has come."

She opened her eyes and looked at him. She struggled to sit up and he put his arms around her and kissed her properly. She pushed him away and stood up.

"Something happened two hours ago which I don't understand at all. I'm not even sure that I didn't imagine it."

"I've only been here for ten minutes. I was miles away two hours ago. What are you talking about?"

She gave him a hard look.

"You know very well what I'm talking about. You must have noticed that you couldn't park your car on my drive this evening?"

"I noticed a white Mini there. I thought you might have a visitor," he said as he kissed her.

"You are my only visitor," she said patiently. "So, please explain yourself."

"Father Christmas doesn't only deliver presents on Christmas Day. Sometimes he has to work overtime. It is a late Christmas present," he said kissing her again.

She looked at him in despair.

"But Dominic, you can't just give me a new car."

"Oh yes I can, my love," he said, taking her in his arms. "I can give you anything you want. You need a car; I give you a car. It is as simple as that."

She knew it was useless to argue with him so she sat down. He sat beside her and waited for her to speak. It was some time before she could say anything but finally, she blurted out:

"I don't know what to say. Thank you is not enough. How can I ever thank you? I don't know how to do it," and she burst into tears.

He put his arms around her until her sobs subsided. He was concerned at the intensity of her reaction. As he sat there, he began to realise that his pleasure at being able to give Sally what he thought she needed was very selfish. She was beginning to feel the pressure of their situation and was struggling to respond. He desperately wanted to talk to her, but he wasn't sure how to begin.

She stood up and said:

"I'm going to wash my face." She went into the kitchen and washed it under the cold-water tap, then she switched the kettle on.

Dominic had followed her.

"I'll make the tea," he said. "You go and sit down."

He took the tea into the lounge and they sat on the settee holding hands.

"Sally," he said quietly. "Do you think you could honestly tell me why you are upset?"

She thought for a moment.

"I have to tell you something else first."

Dominic's heart missed a beat. He was suddenly very afraid.

She turned to him and held both his hands. She looked straight into his eyes and saw the fear in them.

"Dominic," she said softly, "don't be afraid. I would never do anything to hurt you, I love you too much and that will never change."

He put his hands on her shoulders but his eyes never left her face.

"Sally, my Sally," his voice quivered with emotion as he spoke her name. "You mean everything in the world to me," and he rested his head on her shoulder. They sat back side by side in silence, each one trying to collect their thoughts. It was Sally who spoke first.

"Dominic, I have to be honest with you. I don't feel as if I am in control of my own life. Everything is happening too quickly and I am not making my own decisions. I don't even have time to get used to one thing before another one is piled on top of it. I never know what you are going to do next and I really can't cope with any more of your surprises."

He listened to what she said and he thought long and hard before replying.

"Sally," he said. "I have never in my life experienced emotion like the love I have for you. I have never met anyone who returns that love to me in such a pure and unconditional way. Before I met you, it was an accepted fact that feelings were mirrored in expensive gifts."

She looked at him with sadness in her eyes.

"Dominic," she said. "Please don't think that I am not grateful for your gift of a car. It will certainly be most useful to me but to be able to look forward to it instead of it being a fait-accompli would have given me a lot of pleasure."

"I was afraid that if I told you we would have an argument about it."

"We wouldn't have had an argument. We might have had a discussion. You sometimes think of me as a business partner and not as a life partner. Our love is a new experience for both of us. I have never before met such a complex character as you and you say that you have never met a woman who loves you in a true and sincere way. We have many challenges ahead which we are both going to have to face."

They sat in silence for a few minutes.

"Do you remember the very first evening you spent here?" she asked.

He nodded his head.

"I remember it very well," he said. "I found it so easy to talk to you that I couldn't stop myself opening up my most innermost thoughts."

She looked at him.

"I learned more about the real Dominic that evening because you freed him from all of the conventions and social restraints with which you were living. You felt vulnerable and yet relieved. I fell in love with you that evening and I wanted to take you in my arms and comfort you like this," and she put her arms around him.

He rested his head on her shoulder.

"Why didn't you do that?" he asked.

"Because you were the big boss and I didn't want to lose my job," she replied with a smile.

He looked at her intently.

"How do you feel about the fact that I have found you a better job as my wife?" he asked.

"That's not a job, that's a pleasure," she said as she kissed him. She stood up and went into the kitchen. She came back with a bottle of wine and two glasses. Dominic opened the bottle and poured the wine.

"Shall we have a discussion about the toast?" he said with a twinkle in his eye.

"No," said Sally. "I know my place."

He raised his glass.

"May we face up to life's challenges together and have a long and happy life." They drank their wine and sat down. Dominic opened up his briefcase and took out an envelope. "This is the special licence for our marriage," he said. "I have already signed it but you need to do the same. It needs a witness to the signature so I will come to the office with you in the morning and ask Adam to witness it."

He gave it to her and she looked at it then gave it back to him.

"Tell me what your thoughts are about next Saturday?" she asked.

"We can use the company car and drivers," he said, "and I know an excellent catering company which will provide the food and drinks. Does that sound alright to you?"

"Yes, it sounds fine but we will have to look at the organisation of it. You need to put the catering company in touch with Leah so that she knows what to expect. I hope the cars won't be too big and you must get one of them to collect Matthew Dunn and his wife; another car will take you, your father and Lady Harrington to Adam's house before you go to the church. You will need to collect your buttonholes. I will deal with the flowers and what about a cake?"

"I thought it was going to be a quiet wedding," he said putting an arm around her. "But there seems to be a lot to think about."

"It's really a question of organisation and letting other people help," she said. "I'll have a word with Adam, you just concentrate on what you have to do."

"Where would you like to go after the reception? We'll have to have a delayed honeymoon," Dominic asked.

"I'd really like to come back here because I'd like to visit Mother the next day."

"Then that's what we'll do," Dominic said as he clasped her to him. "I must remember to get some sherry."

They sat quietly talking about arrangements for the coming weekend until Sally yawned and said:

"This has been quite a day. I'm ready for bed."

"You go on up," he said. "I'll put the lights out."

She went upstairs and by the time Dominic joined her, she was fast asleep.

Chapter Twelve

The next morning, they travelled into Oxford together and because of the traffic, Sally was late for work. She hurried into her office and was relieved to find Julie already there. Dominic went straight into Adam's office and took the special licence out of his briefcase. Adam called Sally and she came in and signed it and he witnessed it.

"Now I have to send it to the vicar and he will arrange for a registrar to be at the wedding," said Dominic.

He put the envelope back in his briefcase and stood up. He shook hands with Adam and kissed Sally.

"Let me know what time you will be arriving and I will meet you at the station," he said as he left the office.

Adam looked at Sally and smiled.

"There goes a busy man," he said. "Now we must get busy."

"I'll go and check with Julie to see if there have been any phone calls," she said as she left the room.

Adam put the furniture catalogues on his desk and sat back waiting for Sally to return. He knew he had to concentrate on ordering furniture but there were so many other things on his mind. It was not long before there was a knock at the door and Sally came in.

"It has been a quiet morning so far," she said. "Julie is coping very well."

"What is in the diary for today?" he asked.

"Just one appointment; Mr Kenneth Rogers is coming at eleven o'clock."

#

"I had forgotten about that interview," he said, looking at his watch. "I had better have a word with Barry and see if he can do it."

Sally went to find Barry and ten minutes later he arrived in Adam's office.

"I'm sorry to spring this on you," Adam said, "but I really need to get this furniture ordered. Mr Rogers will be arriving in half an hour. Bill knows him very well so he can show him around and give you some background information. You can report back to me at twelve-thirty and I'll see him at two o'clock."

Barry agreed to organise it and left the office to look for Bill. Adam called Sally and sent her for two cups of coffee before they started to look at the catalogues. They worked hard for the next two hours making a list of furniture for the new offices. Adam stood up to stretch his legs.

"We won't order it today," he said. "We'll check the list tomorrow and order it then. Let's have a break."

Sally collected up the papers and put them in a file.

"I'll take my lunch break now," he said, "but first I need to speak to Matthew Dunn. Can you see if he is available?"

Five minutes later Adam's phone rang.

"I have Mr Dunn on the phone," Sally said. "I'll put him through."

"Good morning, Adam," said Matthew. "How are you?"

"Good morning, Matthew. I'm very well and very busy with marital affairs."

Matthew burst out laughing.

"Our mutual friend is certainly hyperactive at present," he said. "I understand we shall all be meeting on Saturday. Bit of a panic here too on the lady's dress outfit."

Adam laughed.

"Thank goodness that's sorted for Leah. There are many other things needing attention. I'm really ringing about the divorce. I promised Alice I would find out how it was progressing. She is wondering when she might start getting the maintenance money for Jessica."

"Everything is moving along nicely," Matthew assured him. "I am just waiting for the completion of the sale of the house but there is one thing I need to check and that is the pension arrangements. I am enquiring if Alice can opt out of his pension and take her current share in cash. It should all be finalised in two to three weeks."

"That is very good news," Adam said. "Alice will be pleased. I look forward to seeing you on Saturday."

134

"It should be a most interesting day," Matthew said as he put the phone down.

Adam called Sally.

"I shall be seeing Barry soon after his interview with Mr Rogers then I will take my lunch break. I'll meet Mr Rogers at two o'clock and when we have finished, I need to talk to you about Saturday's arrangements. We shall need a relief manager in on Saturday morning since we shall all be at the wedding."

"I don't think that Dominic realises what has to be organised," Sally said. "He just clicks his fingers and everyone stands to attention. I've told him to concentrate on what he has to do and to trust other people to help."

There was a knock on the door and Barry came in.

"I've sent Bill out with Kenny Rogers for a lunch break," he said. "We've had the most interesting chat."

"I'll go and print out these lists," Sally said as she returned to her office.

Barry sat down and took out his notes.

"I think Kenny Rogers will fit in well in this office. He has a degree in Sports Development and a secondary degree in Business Studies. His wife is a physiotherapist and has recently been appointed Head of Research at the Nuffield Hospital. They have no children but Kenny has worked a lot with teenagers in the local youth and rugby clubs. He has been in his present post for three years but I get the impression that he is not overly ambitious. His real love is sport, particularly rugby."

Adam had been listening carefully to Barry.

"Do you think he would be fully committed to the way we work here?"

Barry thought for a moment.

"I think it would be quite a challenge for him but I am pretty sure he would rise to it. I would be interested in your opinion."

"I'm going to take my lunch break now," Adam said as he stood up. "I'll see him after. Just one other thing I need to know. Would you offer him the job?"

"Yes, I would," Barry answered. "I think he would fit in well."

He collected up his papers and left. Adam put on his coat and went out through the main door. It was very cold with a hint of snow in the air. He hurried up to the bistro and was glad of the bowl of hot soup Bridget brought him. On the way back to the office, he called in at the Covered Market. He wanted to check what services the various flower shops offered. He found one which was exactly what he was looking for and made an appointment to talk to the owner the next morning.

As he passed her office, he asked Sally if there had been any phone calls.

"It's been very quiet," she said. "Shall I go and find Mr Rogers now?"

"Yes, it is a few minutes early but I don't suppose that matters."

Five minutes later, Sally returned with Mr Rogers. The two men shook hands and then faced each other across the desk. Adam spoke first.

"How does this office compare with your current working environment?"

Kenny Rogers was not expecting that question and he had to think about his answer. Eventually, he said:

"This office is much bigger and obviously much busier. Everyone seems to know exactly what is expected of them but all the staff appear to be very happy working here."

"We work as a team," said Adam. "I understand that you have experience of teamwork?"

Kenny Rogers relaxed a little.

"I certainly have. You can't play rugby for your country without being a dedicated team player."

"How do you think your rugby experience would help if you were working in this office?" Adam asked.

This question really stumped Kenny. He had no idea how to answer it. Adam smiled to himself realising that had punctured the young man's ego somewhat.

"Let me re-phrase the question," he said. "What contribution do you think you could make to the smooth running of this office?"

Kenny found this straightforward question easier to answer.

"I have had three years' experience working in a small office and I would hope that I can build on that. I have done a lot of work with young people and I understand that you are hoping to develop something similar here."

"What ambitions do you have?" Adam asked bluntly.

"My ambitions are modest," Kenny replied. "My main concern is that my wife finds fulfilment in her job. Of course, I want to make a proper contribution to our marriage but I am happy to play second fiddle to her career."

"Just one more question," Adam said. "If you were offered the post, when could you start?"

"My wife has already moved to Oxford in rented accommodation. We do not have a house to sell up North and I am staying with my parents at present. I would have to give the office a week's notice so I could start on Tuesday or Wednesday next week."

"Thank you," Adam said. "My secretary will escort you back to Mr Birch and I will let you know my decision later this afternoon."

He called Sally and asked her to tell Barry he would like to speak to him. He sat back to consider the conversation with Kenny Rogers. It was not too long before Barry came in.

"What do you think?" he asked eagerly.

"I got the impression that he thinks his past sporting achievements give him some sort of divine right to get anything he wants," Adam said. "He has an enormous ego which I shall delight in tackling."

Barry looked at him in astonishment.

"Whatever made you think that?" he gasped.

"He obviously doesn't see himself as the main breadwinner in the marriage but as a useful accessory to his wife's career. He has very little work ambition and I am not sure about his actual level of intelligence."

"But he has a degree in Sports Development," Barry said. "He must have intelligence for that."

"Not necessarily," Adam said thoughtfully. "If you are an exceptional athlete or sports star, a university will automatically award you a first."

"How do you want to proceed then?" Barry asked.

"I see it as a challenge. I'll offer him the job but with a review at the end of six months. He will be answerable to you and I shall explain his duties very clearly to him. It will be interesting to see his reaction. Send him back to me."

Barry left the room and soon after Kenny Rogers returned. He sat opposite Adam and waited.

"I would like to offer you the post of under manager in this office," Adam said, "but before you make your decision, there are some facts you need to know. The appointment will be subject to a review at the end of six months. When we are working in the office, we address each other in a formal way. You will be answerable to the manager Mr Wilson and he will explain your everyday duties to you. These will vary from manning a till to making him a cup of coffee if requested. Now have you any questions?"

Kenny Rogers was staring at Adam with his mouth slightly open.

"Thank you for your explanation," he finally stuttered. "I understand what you have said and I would be pleased to accept the post on those terms."

"Good," Adam said as he stood up. "Let my secretary know when you can start." And they shook hands.

Kenny was visibly shaken as he went to find Bill.

"That was an experience like none other," he said.

Bill smiled at him.

"You can't pull the wool over Mr Richard's eyes," he said. "He can read you like a book."

"He offered me the job and I accepted," Kenny gasped. "He spelt out the conditions very clearly with a review in six months."

"He is offering you a great opportunity," Bill said seriously. "It is up to you to make the best of it."

"I know," Kenny answered, "but it is quite a daunting prospect. I'd better go and tell my wife the good news."

Bill accompanied him to the door and wished him good luck. Meanwhile back in his office, Adam called Sally in.

"How did you get on with Mr Rogers?" she asked.

"I've given him the job," Adam said, "but with a review in six months."

"It sounds as if he did not make a good impression on you."

"He is full of his own importance," Adam said shortly. "We'll see how he develops. I need to speak to the manager in the Bicester office to ask him to be in charge of this office on Saturday morning. Can you get him on the phone and send Julie for two cups of coffee?"

It did not take long to make the necessary arrangement and Julie soon came in with the coffee.

"Now, let us get down to more personal business," Adam said as he looked at Sally. "First of all, I want to talk to you about flowers. Have you thought about a bouquet or posy and buttonholes?"

"Not really," Sally said in surprise. "What have you in mind?"

"We would like to order a couple of flower arrangements for the house but Leah wants to make sure that they will be what you would like."

"I don't want a bouquet but a small posy might be nice. I think I'd like pink rosebuds and cream orchids."

"That sounds lovely. So, the men can have buttonholes of pink rosebuds. What about the ladies?"

"They would need a small spray instead of a buttonhole," she replied. "And Jessica could carry a miniature version of my posy."

"That is a wonderful idea," Adam said happily. "That will make her feel a bit special. That's settled then. We will deal with all the flowers and they will be delivered to our house on Saturday morning. I assume Dominic will spend Friday night in London but he will have to call at our house before travelling to the church. I wondered if you would like Bill to bring Alice over to keep you company on Saturday morning?"

"That's a wonderful idea," she said. "I will be so nervous that I shall be glad of someone to talk to. I just hope that Dominic will not take it into his head to phone me that morning."

"Don't worry. I'll have a word. Leah and I will go and look at the church this weekend and maybe have a word with the vicar."

"If you want any information you need to go and see Mrs Watson at the village shop. She knows all the gossip."

At that moment the phone rang.

"I have Mr West on the line," Julie said. "He wishes to speak to you."

"Thank you, Julie," Adam said as he greeted Dominic.

"I've arranged for our catering manager to visit Leah on Monday morning at eleven o'clock. I hope this is convenient?" Dominic said.

"I'm sure that is fine," Adam answered but Dominic hadn't finished. "I've booked two photographers, one at your house and one at the church. The cars are all booked too."

"I've just been talking to Sally and you will all have to come to our house on your way to the church in order to collect your buttonholes," Adam said. "Sally has chosen the flowers she wants."

"We shall have to leave a bit earlier," Dominic said, "but that's not a problem. I'd like to speak to Sally but first I want to know how the building work is going?"

"Most of the construction is complete and the electricians should be in next week. Sally and I have chosen some of the furniture and we shall be ordering it tomorrow morning."

"I'm glad to hear that everything is on schedule," Dominic said. "Next week I'll come and have a look with you and no doubt father will want to pay another visit. We are looking after things at this end between us since it is such a busy time. Now can I have a quick word with Sally?"

"Yes, of course," Adam said. "I'll pass you over to her."

He gave the phone to Sally and left the office. Dominic asked Sally what time she would be arriving the next day.

"It is going to be a busy weekend," he said. "On Sunday I want to take you to the bank to look at grandmother's jewellery box. You may find something old which you would like to wear."

Their conversation continued for a few minutes and when it was over Sally went to find Adam. She told him what Dominic had said about the jewellery.

"I think he would like me to wear something which belonged to his grandmother," she said. "He was very fond of her."

140

"You will be shopping on Saturday so by Sunday you should know what your wedding outfit will be. That fits in very nicely. The bank doesn't usually open on a Sunday so Dominic must be a very valued customer."

"Yes, I suppose so," she sighed. "It all gets a bit over-powering sometimes but at least he told me about it and didn't suddenly spring it on me."

"What time will you be leaving tomorrow?"

"I'm catching the two-forty train from Oxford."

"Leah and I are going away for the weekend so I shall be in the office until twelve o'clock. We will make it a priority to order the furniture but no other appointments. Now, I think it is time to go home and update Leah on some details."

He collected up his papers and went to find his car. As he drove home, he thought about the weekend ahead. He was really looking forward to spending the time with Leah, just the two of them. He parked the car and went into the house. Alice was busy in the kitchen but Leah was in the lounge. He went in and kissed her.

"Have you packed your case?" he asked.

"I'll do that tomorrow morning. I shall be glad to get away from the phone."

"Who has been phoning you?"

"Dominic phoned twice and then the catering manager rang and Jen has been wondering what to wear on Saturday. I was just having a rest."

"I'll go and make the tea," he said. "Then I'll tell you all about my day."

He went to the kitchen and spoke to Alice.

"I had a word with Matthew Dunn today and he said that everything should be settled in two or three weeks. He is just sorting out the pension and waiting for completion on the house."

Alice kissed him.

"That is good news. Bill and I can start thinking about our plans now."

"I've also talked to Sally about flowers for the wedding and I suggested that she might like you to go over and keep her company during the morning. I don't know how you feel about that?"

"I think that would be a lovely idea," Alice exclaimed. "Otherwise, she would be on her own and that's not very nice."

"I'll confirm that with Sally tomorrow morning. I know you are going to have some expenses so I am going to help you out," and he took one hundred pounds out of his wallet and gave it to Alice.

"Thank you, Dad," she said gratefully. "I will pay you back."

"Never mind that," he said quickly. "Just make a nice cup of tea for your mother and me."

He returned to the lounge and Alice followed with the tea. Adam told Leah about the divorce and how Alice would stay with Sally on the wedding morning. Then he told them about the flowers.

"Sally has chosen pink rosebuds and cream orchids," he said. "I shall order two large displays for the house. We shall need six buttonholes for the men and five sprays for the ladies. Sally wants a small posy and a miniature one for Jessica. The flowers will be delivered here by ten o'clock in the morning."

"The catering manager is coming to see me on Monday morning," said Leah. "I must remember to ask him about the wedding cake."

"What about cars, Dad?" Alice asked.

"Dominic will call here with his father and Lady Monica. They will travel on together. One car will collect Matthew Dunn and his wife and then call here to collect Barry and Jen. A third car will collect Leah, Jessica, Bill and me and take us to Sally's house where the fourth car will be waiting for Sally and me. Alice will join Bill and Leah."

"That all sounds rather complicated," Leah said. "Are you sure it will work?"

"It will be fine," he assured her. "As long as Dominic gives the drivers the correct instructions."

"Thank goodness I already have an outfit which will do for the wedding," Alice said. "We shall go shopping on Saturday for Bill's suit and a new dress for Jessica."

"I'm glad I've done all my shopping," Leah said. "I'm looking forward to a relaxing weekend."

"So am I," Adam said firmly. "I'm ready for a break after the pressures of the last week."

"Dinner will be ready in ten minutes," Alice said. "I'll call Jessica."

Leah got up to lay the table and Adam lay full length on the settee. When Jessica came in, he was half asleep.

"Grandad," she said. "I've never met a Sir or a Lady. What are they like?"

"They are just like normal people," he said, smiling at her. "I haven't met Lady Monica but Sally says she is charming and friendly. Sir Humphrey is Dominic's father and I'm sure you will like him. He can be a lot of fun."

"Dinner's ready!" called Alice as they went into the dining room.

They spent a quiet evening talking among themselves.

"I suppose I'd better go up and pack my case ready for tomorrow," said Adam. "I'll be home by one o'clock."

"I'll put the lights out," Leah said. "I'll do my packing in the morning."

Chapter Thirteen

Adam was at work promptly the next day. He had an early appointment with the florist and ordered the flowers for the wedding. By the time Sally arrived, he had already taken another look at the list of furniture and had made one or two changes. He gave the revised list to Sally and she printed it out. Then he phoned the company and placed the order. It would be delivered in the next week, just before the computer people arrived. He checked with Sally that there were no other appointments in the diary then he went to find Barry. He made sure that everything was running smoothly and returned to his office. He called Sally in and told her that he would be leaving soon.

"Make sure you take a taxi to the station and leave in plenty of time," he said. "I'll see you on Monday. Have a good weekend."

Sally kissed him.

"I hope you and Leah have a relaxing time. You can certainly do with a break."

As he drove home, Adam began to think about the coming weekend. He was really looking forward to their time together and determined that it would be as perfect as he could make it. Alice and Jessica were not at home but Leah was just finishing her packing.

"You're home early," she said as he kissed her.

"I thought we would try and get there in the daylight," he said. "I'm ready to go when you are."

"I'm about ready. I'll leave a note for Alice to say we have left and the address and phone number of the hotel."

Adam put the cases in the car while Leah wrote the note.

They were soon on their way and although it was a Friday afternoon, the traffic was light. They found the hotel without any trouble and booked into their room. Everything was beautifully presented and there was a mini-fridge with a selection of drinks.

"This is very nice," he said. "I'm going to enjoy a life of luxury." He turned to Leah. "Thank you for a wonderful Christmas present," and he took her in his arms.

Then they unpacked the cases and then went down to the lounge for afternoon tea. After tea, they went to explore the rest of the hotel.

"I shall look forward to the spa room and a nice relaxing massage," she said.

"I think I'll join you. It will be good to get rid of some of the tensions of the last few months."

They went back upstairs and Adam lay on the bed and closed his eyes. Before long he was fast asleep.

There was a brochure on the coffee table detailing the local attractions, including a map of the nearby village. Leah studied the map and noted the position of the little church and the village shop. It also showed Kitson Hall which was situated on the edge of the village. She was looking forward to seeing it. She stood up and checked her watch, deciding to have a shower and get ready for dinner before waking her sleeping husband. An hour later she was ready and she gently shook him.

"Wake up," she said firmly. "It's time for dinner."

Adam slowly opened his eyes. He put up his arms to pull Leah on to the bed with him but she didn't move.

"No," she said. "You must get up. I'm all ready."

He sat up and looked at her.

"You look beautiful," he said as he got to his feet and kissed her.

He had a quick shower and they were soon going down to the dining room. Their dinner was delicious and they moved to the lounge for coffee. Soon they heard music coming from the dining room and they went back to find that the tables had been cleared from the centre of the floor and a space made for dancing. Adam ordered a bottle of wine and they sat and enjoyed the music and an occasional dance together.

"This brings back memories," he whispered as he held her close.

The evening passed quickly and by eleven o'clock they were both ready for bed. Upstairs, Leah looked at the bed which was king size.

"I could easily get lost in that bed," she said.

"Don't worry. You won't get far. I'll be holding you."

The bed was very comfortable and Adam turned towards Leah. He put his arms around her and kissed her.

"There," he said. "Do you feel safe now?"

"Not really," she said. "I don't know what you are going to do next."

Adam held her closer and kissed her again.

"Is that better?" he asked.

"Oh yes," she sighed, "much better."

Her hands went up to the back of his neck and he shivered slightly. They clung together as if pulled by some magnetic force that was irresistible. They were still in each other's arms when they woke in the morning.

Leah woke first and she got out of bed and opened the curtains. It was a cold, frosty morning and she quickly returned to the bed. She was quite cold as she cuddled up to Adam.

"You have cold feet and cold hands," he muttered.

"It's a cold day outside," she answered.

He opened his eyes and stared at her.

"You haven't been outside?" he asked incredulously.

"No, of course, I haven't," she laughed. "It was enough just to look out of the window."

"What shall we do today?" he said, wide awake now.

"I should like to go and look at the nearby village. It will be good to have some idea of what it will be like next Saturday."

"We'll do that this morning and we'll book a spa session for this afternoon," he said.

They quickly got dressed and went downstairs. After breakfast, they asked the receptionist for directions to the village and were soon on their way. They drove slowly as they came to the houses and stopped outside the village shop.

"Sally said that if we wanted any information, Mrs Watson, the village shopkeeper was the best person to ask," Adam said as they got out of the car.

They went into the shop and a cheery old lady greeted them.

"Good morning," she said with a smile. "We don't get many visitors to the village at this time of year. How can I help you?"

"You must be Mrs Watson," Adam said holding out his hand. "My name is Adam Richards and this is my wife Leah," and they shook hands. "We are friends of Mr West who recently bought Kitson Hall."

"You are most welcome," she said, clapping her hands. "Can I offer you a cup of tea?"

"That would be very nice," Leah said. "It is very cold outside."

"Come through into the parlour. It is warm in there." And she lifted up the counter to let them through.

Mrs Watson busied herself making the tea and all the time she talked about how pleased everyone was that the young master was coming back to the Hall and how excited the village was about the wedding.

"You know the villagers are planning a celebration?" she said happily. "They want it to be a special day too."

Adam looked at Leah and then at Mrs Watson.

"How are they thinking of celebrating it?" Leah asked. "Or is it a secret?"

"We want it to be a surprise for the happy couple," was the reply, "but if you can keep a secret, I'll tell you."

"We can keep a secret. I give you my word," said Adam.

Mrs Watson handed them their tea.

"That's good enough for me," she said and hesitated for a moment. "We plan to decorate the church with holly and mistletoe from the garden at Kitson Hall. We will also put a floral display inside."

"What a lovely idea," Leah exclaimed but Mrs Watson hadn't finished.

"The church is very small and I understand that it will be a simple ceremony with very few guests, so some of the ladies have formed a small choir to sing during the service. They will also make special green arches which the children will hold above the path from the church to the road."

"It sounds wonderfully romantic," Adam said. "We will certainly keep it a secret. We would like to visit the church. Do you think that might be possible?"

"It's only five minutes' walk from here and I have a key," she said. "You are welcome to borrow it."

Just then the shop bell rang and Mrs Watson hurried to answer it. It was not long before she was back, followed by a man with a golden Labrador.

"This is Bert," Mrs Watson said as she introduced them.

"And this is Pepper," Adam said as he stroked the dog. "Mr West has told me how you both keep a watchful eye on Kitson Hall."

"Pleased to meet you," said Bert. "I do look in on it most days and come the Spring, we shall have some working parties up there to start to put the garden in order."

"We should like to have a look at the place while we are in the area," Adam said. "Will that be possible?"

"The driveway is overgrown but you can still get a car along it," Bert answered. "It is not looking at its best but I'm sure you will appreciate how it will be when it is restored."

"I'm sure we shall meet again," Adam said. "Now we are going to look at the church."

They all shook hands and Adam took the key from Mrs Watson.

"We shall be about an hour," he said. "Then we will return the key."

Adam and Leah walked out of the shop and into the cold morning air.

"I hope it won't be as cold next Saturday," Leah said. "We shall need our thermal underwear."

They carefully walked up the slippery path to the church and Adam unlocked the door. Inside, it felt cold with bare stone walls. He shivered.

"I hope they have some form of heating."

"It will look more inviting when it has been decorated," Leah said. "It is very small."

There was a table at the front and a lectern to one side. The wooden pews looked most uncomfortable.

"I hope it's a short service," Adam said as he sat on one of the pews.

"They will have to sign the register in here," she said. "There is no other room."

"I've seen enough," he said. "Let's get back to the car."

As they went down the path, they stopped and looked back. A pale sun had broken through the clouds and it highlighted the stone arch over the door.

"It is a good background for the photographs," said Leah as they walked on down the path.

They returned the key to Mrs Watson and thanked her for her hospitality, then they drove slowly through the village. There was a traditional English pub on one side and a fish and chip shop opposite it. They drove along the road for half a mile until they saw the entrance to Kitson Hall on the right. They went along the driveway and stopped in front of the house. They sat in the car and gazed at it for a few minutes. It was a magnificent sight even in its present state. The watery sun glowed on the pale stone façade and the perfect symmetry had an imposing door at its centre.

They got out of the car to have a closer look. The windows were dirty and ragged curtains hung inside but they could just see the magnificent stone fireplace in the drawing-room. They walked around to the back and saw the lawn which was totally overgrown and the small cottage in the garden. As they walked back, they stood in front of the house and looked at the rose garden which still had one or two blooms on it. They went down the path to the clearing and sat on the seat, looking out over the sea.

"It is a beautiful spot," she said, "but what a lot of work."

"Dominic has the means to achieve it," he said. "It is going to cost millions."

They returned to the car and drove back to the hotel. They were glad to get back in the warm and they went straight to the bar.

"Two coffees and two large brandies," Adam ordered as they went to sit near the roaring fire.

They stayed there for the next hour talking about the events of the morning. They moved to the dining room for a light lunch and then went upstairs and lay on the bed. At three o'clock they went down to the spa room and each had a relaxing massage, followed by a dip in the jacuzzi. Adam felt all his worries and pressures melting away and for the first time in his life, he was as light as a feather.

"I feel as if I could float away on a cloud," he said as they went back upstairs.

"That's good," she said firmly. "I'm glad it has worked for you."

They dressed for dinner and enjoyed another gourmet meal after which they sat in the lounge. There were a few other guests there and they spent a pleasant evening chatting with them. They were not late going to bed and both had a good night's sleep. On Sunday they went for a walk in the grounds and after lunch, they were on their way back home.

When they arrived, they found Alice at home with Bill and Jessica. They were playing a game on the dining room table but as soon as she saw them Jessica rushed upstairs. When she came down, she was wearing her new dress with a short jacket; she had new shoes as well and light tights.

"Do you like it?" she asked breathlessly as she twirled around.

"It's fabulous," Adam said. "You look like a lady."

Jessica went up to him and gave him a kiss then she turned to Leah.

"What do you think grandma?" she asked.

"I think you look quite grown up," Leah said.

"I'm glad you like it," said Jessica, giving her a kiss.

"Now go upstairs and hang it up," said Alice and Jessica left the room.

"Did you have a good weekend?"

"We had a lovely relaxing time," replied Adam. "We had tea at the village shop, visited the church and went to see Kitson Hall."

"What was the hotel like, Leah?" asked Bill.

"It was great," she said. "The bed was comfortable and the food was good. We both relaxed in a spa room and there was a real roaring fire in the lounge."

"It sounds wonderful," sighed Alice. "We had a busy time shopping but at least Bill bought his new suit and a shirt and tie."

Adam looked at Bill with sympathy.

"Not my favourite occupation," Bill said. "I'd have much preferred to watch the rugby on the television."

Adam patted him on the back.

"You're lucky," he said. "I've still got to face that one."

Alice went off to make a cup of tea and Leah went upstairs to unpack the cases. The two men sat in the lounge and Adam told Bill about Kitson Hall.

"It is an enormous project," Adam said. "It will take at least two years and about five million pounds."

"Where are they going to live in the meantime?"

"I'm not sure," Adam replied, "but I think Dominic intends to buy a house near Oxford."

"I suppose when money is no object you can get things done quickly," said Bill. "I don't expect he has ever had to save up for anything in his life."

"Money can be an advantage," Adam said wisely, "but it can have its downside. It can devalue the very things which create a happy and fulfilled life. Anything worth having is worth striving for."

Alice came in with the tea and they sat around chatting until Bill said:

"I'd better get back to my place and start to think about work."

"We have a busy week ahead," said Adam. "I'm hoping that the electricians finish and some furniture should be delivered before the end of the week. We shall also have to arrange for the carpet to be fitted."

"I'll see you tomorrow," Bill said as he left.

"It's time for your shower, Jessica," Alice said, "and a good night's sleep."

They went upstairs and Leah moved on to the sofa next to Adam.

"It was a lovely weekend," he said. "We must do it more often."

"That would be nice," she said contently as he put his arm around her. "But now we have to concentrate on the week ahead. I have the catering manager coming to see me tomorrow and then I shall have a better idea of what needs to be done."

"I hope it won't make too much extra work for you," he said in a concerned voice.

"Don't worry," she said quickly. "Alice and I will deal with it and Jen will help too."

Adam was silent for a few minutes.

"We mustn't tell anyone about the villagers' plans. They want it to be a complete surprise."

"I shan't even mention it to Alice," she said quietly.

"And I shan't tell Sally," Adam added. "Let's have an early night. There is a busy week in front of us."

He locked up and put out the lights and soon they were tucked up in bed and fast asleep.

Chapter Fourteen

The next morning Adam was up early. He had a shower and was at work by nine o'clock. He went straight up to see Mr Carter and found him deep in conversation with the electricians.

"How is the work progressing?" Adam asked.

"We are getting on very well," replied Mr Carter, "but the electrician says that they can do the basic installation but they need to know where the computers are going in order to put in the special sockets."

"I'll speak to the technical department this morning," said Adam. "And I'll get them to send someone along as soon as possible. I'm also going to get the carpets fitted soon, hopefully before the furniture arrives."

"We will get the floors swept and clear away the rubbish," said Mr Carter. "The lift people will be here next week."

"What about the heating system?" Adam asked.

"It would be difficult to connect it to the current system. So, it is going to have to be individual heaters in each office and a larger heater in the reception area."

"I would value the electrician's advice on the most economical way of doing that. Can you ask him to come and see me at eleven o'clock?" Adam said.

He went down to his office and noticed that Sally wasn't in yet. He spoke to Julie.

"It looks like Sally is going to be late," he said. "Can you manage?"

"Yes, I can manage Mr Richards."

"Can you get the technical department on the phone please Julie?" he asked as he went into his office.

He sat at his desk and almost immediately the phone rang.

"Adam, I am sorry I shall be late," said Sally. "I'm on my way back from London and the traffic is heavy."

"Don't worry," he said. "Julie is here and she can manage."

"I shall have to go home first because I have so many parcels. I may not be in until midday."

"I'll see you later," Adam said and he put the phone down.

Once again it rang and this time it was the technical people. Adam had a long discussion with them and they agreed to send a computer expert the next day. He left the office and went to find Barry who was in the main area.

"Bill is using my office for a client," he explained so Adam took him back with him to his room.

He told Barry about the way the work was progressing upstairs and then about his weekend away and his visit to Kitson Hall. Barry was very interested to hear about the hotel.

"I have a feeling that Leah will be talking to Jen," he said, "and she will fancy a weekend away."

"It would do you the world of good. It was really relaxing," Adam said.

"Sally is late today. That is most unlike her."

"She spent the weekend in London, shopping," Adam said. "She will be here by midday. Julie is quite capable of looking after the office. Have you found anyone to help Laura?"

"One of the girls in the main office is very interested," Barry said. "We'll see how she fits in."

"Kenny Rogers will be starting next Monday," Adam said, "but we still need at least two extra members of staff. I suggest you place an advert in the company magazine."

"I'll do that today," he said as he left the room.

Adam continued to work at his desk until there was a knock at the door and the electrician came in. They had a long discussion about the heaters and other installations and it was twelve o'clock before they finished.

He decided it was time for lunch and put on his coat. He left the office and on his way to the Bistro, he noticed a gents' outfitters shop. It reminded him that he needed a new suit and he decided to go into it on his way back. He enjoyed the bowl of hot soup with a roll which

Bridget brought him and the warmth of the café made him sleepy. He roused himself and walked back towards work. He went into the outfitter's shop to look around. There was plenty of choice but he knew exactly what he wanted, as he spoke to the assistant who came up to help him. He chose a dark grey worsted suit of the finest quality, knowing that it would be the most appropriate for all the special occasions which were coming soon. He added two new shirts and a tie to the order and felt very pleased that he had completed the purchase so quickly.

When he arrived back at the office, he was pleased to see that Sally was there. He called her in and asked Julie to fetch two cups of coffee. She looked tired and Adam was rather concerned.

"It has been a busy weekend," she sighed. "I was whisked from shop to shop and on Sunday we went to the bank."

Adam looked at her in surprise.

"Banks don't normally open on Sundays."

"We were the only people there with the bank manager," Sally said faintly. "Dominic wanted to look at his grandmother's jewel collection. He wanted me to choose something to wear for the wedding."

"Something old, I suppose," Adam muttered.

"There was so much to choose from that I was quite overwhelmed. In the end, I chose a diamond brooch. Even Dominic was amazed at the amount of her jewellery. He had never looked at it before."

"He obviously had never told his first wife about it?"

"I didn't ask him. I was too exhausted by everything."

"Did you have a successful shopping trip?" he asked.

She thought for a moment.

"Yes, I did," she said at last. "Money was no object and Dominic insisted on paying for it all. But I put my foot down about my wedding outfit. I sent him off while I chose it and paid for it myself."

"I'm pleased to hear that," he said firmly. "It is important that you stand up for yourself and that he considers your feelings."

She looked at the large carrier bag which was leaning against the wall behind Adam's desk.

"It looks like you've been shopping as well," she said with a smile.

"I had my orders," Adam laughed. "I was told I had to have a new suit to escort you down the aisle. It will also be handy for all the other formal events."

"I'd better do some work," Sally said as she stood up.

"Julie is coping very well. I suggest you take the rest of the day off," Adam said, "and have an early night."

"Dominic never seems to run out of energy but I'm not used to living such a hectic life."

"This is an exceptionally busy time, Sally. Things will settle down in time. Leah is seeing the catering people this morning. Give me time to check with Barry and then I will take you home. We can call Leah and find out about the catering arrangements."

Adam went to find Barry and Sally went to check with Julie that there were no problems. Thirty minutes later they were on their way. Adam had phoned Leah to make sure that she was at home and when they arrived, she welcomed them with a cup of tea.

"I had a very interesting morning," she said. "The catering chap had a good look around and decided where the furniture needed to be moved. The bar will be in the conservatory and the food will be laid out in the dining room. There will be two waiters, one for the drinks and one for the food. In the kitchen, there will be two people dealing with dirty dishes and they will provide all the cutlery, plates, glasses and serving dishes. They will be here by nine o'clock on Saturday morning."

"What about the wedding cake?" asked Sally.

"They have been told to provide a two-tier cake."

"That all seems very satisfactory," said Adam. "It looks like we shall be living upstairs on Saturday."

"Are you sure you are happy with the arrangements?" Sally asked anxiously.

"I'm quite happy to hand my kitchen over to someone else for the day," Leah said firmly.

Sally went up to her and kissed her.

"I can't thank you both enough," she said in a voice that was filled with emotion. "I couldn't have faced this alone."

"Let me take you home," Adam said. "You've had a busy time and you need a good rest."

Sally said goodbye to Leah and Adam drove her home. On the way back, he stopped off at his apartment. The heating was on low and the place felt warm and comfortable. He'd almost forgotten how peaceful it could be. He checked the windows and doors and then drove home. Leah admired his new suit and they settled down for a quiet evening.

"I must phone Peter this evening," she said. "It is quite a while since I spoke to him."

"It will be difficult to see him this Sunday," said Adam, thoughtfully.

"The catering chap said that everything would be cleared up by twelve o'clock on Sunday. No doubt there will be food leftover. We could ask Peter to come a bit later than usual?"

"He may have other plans," he said. "See what he says."

Leah went into the dining room and came back with a piece of paper.

"This is the menu for Saturday," she said.

Adam read it and let out a cry of surprise.

"This is a veritable feast for fourteen people! We shall never eat all of this." The wine list was also included; "And that is a large amount of wine to go with it."

"No doubt the catering staff will be well fed and watered too," she said. "Dominic has booked rooms at the Premier Inn for them."

"He seems to have thought of everything. The only thing I shall remind him of is the photographer."

"Apparently there are two photographers, one at the church and one here," she said.

"I just hope the weather is fine and it doesn't snow," Adam said finally.

Leah went to phone Peter and Adam rested his head on the back of the settee and closed his eyes. Ten minutes later Leah returned.

"Peter said that he would like to see us on Sunday. He didn't seem very happy. I don't know what has been going on. It will just be himself and the children and they will arrive at about one o'clock."

"It will be good to catch up with him," Adam said. "We haven't really kept in touch since Christmas."

"I'm going to make a cup of tea and then have an early night."

"I think I'll join you," he said, as he closed his eyes again and thought about the busy week ahead.

The next morning, Sally was in at her usual time.

"I had a lovely quiet evening," she said. "Just one phone call and a good night's sleep."

"I'm glad to hear it," said Adam. "We shouldn't be too busy in the office this week and you need to try and relax a bit before Saturday."

"We are going back to my house after the reception. We are going to visit my mother on Sunday morning so I shall have to do my usual shopping earlier this week. Dominic is coming down on Wednesday so I might try and do it then. He can help with carrying it."

Adam had a sudden thought.

"Did he ever ask his mother to the wedding?"

"Yes, he mentioned it to her but she wasn't interested. She said that she had made other arrangements for that day. I think he was very relieved."

"I can understand that, but at least he asked her," he said.

They settled down to work and the morning passed quickly. Adam met the computer rep in the afternoon and they discussed the positioning of the various machines with the electrician. Adam was pleased that the office was running smoothly and that the building work was on schedule. He insisted that Sally should not come in to work on Friday and in the morning, he met the manager who would be looking after the branch on Saturday. He introduced him to the staff and they were all happy with the arrangement.

On Thursday afternoon, the whole office assembled to present Sally with a beautiful crystal flower vase and a large bouquet of flowers. Once again, Adam took her home and she cried nearly all the way.

"I shall miss you all," she wept.

Adam smiled at her.

"You won't have time to miss us," he laughed. "Dominic will keep you busy. You know how much energy he has."

"I shall be back at work next week."

"Let's wait and see," he said wisely.

Alice and Leah cleaned the house from top to bottom on Friday. They packed away all the ornaments and photographs and cleared all the surfaces ready for the caterers. They were all worn out by Friday evening and everyone went to bed early.

Chapter Fifteen

Saturday morning was crisp and frosty. Leah was glad to put the heating on. Everyone was up early and finished breakfast by eight-thirty. At nine o'clock, the first of the catering staff arrived and immediately began moving the furniture. A bar was set up in the conservatory and three small tables and chairs provided extra seating. Tables were put up in the utility area and plates and dishes were stacked on them.

Leah had taken a kettle and coffee upstairs so that they could have a drink together with a tin of biscuits. By nine-thirty the food had all arrived and the champagne was on ice. At ten o'clock there was a knock on the door and Adam went to open it. A man stood there holding a beautiful posy of pink rosebuds and coming up the path was a lady carrying a large box of buttonholes and sprays. Adam took them into the lounge and called for Alice.

"Bill can take you to Sally's house now," he said. "Take Sally's flowers with you and don't forget that she must leave for the church at eleven-thirty. I'll be there by eleven fifteen with Bill, Jessica and Leah."

Alice made sure that she had everything she needed for the ceremony and Bill drove her to Sally's house. Sally was very pleased to see Alice.

"I've been like a headless chicken this morning," she said impatiently.

"Let's sit down and have a cup of coffee," Alice said as she led Sally into the lounge. "It has been pretty busy at home too."

Sally sat down with a sigh while Alice made the coffee. They sat and relaxed for a few minutes.

"I suppose I'd better go and have a shower and get dressed," she said.

Alice looked at her with surprise.

"You don't sound very enthusiastic!"

"It's last-minute nerves," said Sally. "Life is a bit of a blur at the moment."

"A few deep breaths will cure that," Alice said firmly. "Would you like me to come upstairs with you?"

"Yes, please. I shall need zipping up."

Sally went to have her shower and Alice tidied up the kitchen.

"I'm ready!" Sally called.

Alice went up to the bedroom. A beautiful deep cream dress and matching coat lay on the bed and Alice helped Sally put it on. It fitted her perfectly and Alice fastened the pearls around Sally's neck and admired the diamond bracelet which had belonged to Lady Kitson.

"You look stunning," she said as Sally put a large cream hat on her head. The hat was decorated with a pink rose attached to one side of the brim.

"I need a drink," Sally said. "Let's open a bottle."

They found a bottle of wine and each had a glass.

"Here's to a happy day and a long life together," Alice said as she raised her glass.

There was a knock at the door and Alice went to open it. A man stood there in a chauffeur's uniform.

"The car has arrived Madam," he said. "We are due to leave in ten minutes."

"We must wait for the other car," Alice said. "It should be here any time now."

"I will wait in the car," said the chauffeur and touched his hat.

Alice went indoors and found Sally pacing up and down in the lounge. She poured another glass of wine for each of them and made Sally sit on the settee. They chatted to each other until there was another knock on the door and this time Adam was standing there.

"Time for you to go," he said to Alice as she said goodbye to Sally.

Alice went out to the car and it drove off.

"You look magnificent, Sally," he said, putting an arm around her and kissing her.

"I'm shaking like a leaf," she said as she finished her glass of wine.

Adam smiled at her.

"You'll be just fine," he said firmly. "Now have you got everything you need? It's time to go."

Sally picked up her bouquet of roses and her clutch bag. She put the keys to the house in her bag and then went out to the car. They were soon on their way and she began to relax as the car purred along.

"Did you see Dominic this morning?" she asked. "Was he alright?"

"He was fine," Adam said a little untruthfully. "I gave him a brandy and that steadied his nerves."

She gave him a quick look.

"In other words, he was as nervous as I am?"

"You know how uptight he gets when he has to sign his name," Adam laughed. "He was most worried that Sir Humphrey would drop the ring."

"I hope they haven't been drinking too much."

"I know they each had a snifter in their pockets," he said. "But they were both quite sober. Lady Monica was keeping an eye on them."

"She is very nice," Sally said. "I'm glad Sir Humphrey has a lady friend."

It was quite warm in the car and Sally's eyes began to close, but Adam wouldn't let her go to sleep.

"You don't want to arrive with your hat over your eyes, do you?" he said sternly.

They sped along the country roads and Adam pointed out the hotel where he and Leah had stayed.

"Not far now," he said, "about ten minutes' drive."

As they came into the village, Adam told the driver to slow down. He wanted to be sure that everyone else had arrived first. The car stopped at the front gate and Adam got out. He saw Bert standing there and asked him. He said that the guests were already in the church and that the vicar was waiting in the porch. Adam looked at his watch. It was twelve fifty-five. He signalled to the chauffeur to open the door for Sally. There was a small crowd at the gate and they clapped and cheered as she walked up the path on Adam's arm.

They were met at the door by the vicar and as he led them into the church, the congregation of villagers sang the first verse of 'Morning Has Broken.' They walked up the aisle and joined Dominic at the front of the church. The marriage ceremony was soon complete and after a short address from the vicar, it was time to sign the register. Adam and Sir Humphrey also signed and then it was time to leave.

The congregation sang the second verse of the hymn as the couple walked down the aisle. They paused in the porch, waiting for their guests to join them, then they posed for the photographer. Dominic turned to thank the vicar and gave a cheque for ten thousand pounds towards the restoration work for the roof. They walked down the path which was lined by cheering villagers. Bert and Pepper were waiting at the gate and Dominic stopped to speak with him. He took another cheque out of his pocket and gave it to Bert. This one was for twenty-five thousand pounds for work to start on the gardens, plus the instruction that everyone should have a free drink in the village pub and a fish and chip supper from the local shop. Dominic then spoke to the driver and told him to drive up the road to Kitson Hall. All the other guests piled into cars to take them back to Swanton. Adam and Leah joined Sir Humphrey and Lady Monica. Bill, Alice and Jessica were in the second car and Barry and Jen with Matthew Dunn and his wife were in the third car.

Sally and Dominic sat in their car and looked at Kitson Hall.

"I'd like to look at it in the fresh air," Sally said quietly.

They left the car and stood on the gravel drive looking at the house. The sun was glinting on the frosty trees and it was very cold. Sally touched the bracelet which she was wearing and immediately she felt a warm glow inside her.

"Grandmother is very happy," she said.

Dominic looked at her in surprise.

"How do you know that?"

"The bracelet told me," Sally answered.

Dominic put his arm around her and kissed her.

"You really are one of the family now," he said softly as he led her back to the car.

When they arrived back at Adam's house, the party had already started. Sir Humphrey had insisted on opening the champagne and when Sally and Dominic eventually arrived, he said:

"Tut, tut, my boy. Where have you been? You are missing valuable drinking time."

163

"I'm sure you have made up for our absence, father," Dominic said with a laugh.

They greeted the other guests and Sally said:

"I am quite hungry," as she went into the dining room.

The wine waiter was hovering with a tray full of champagne and Dominic took a glass. He drank it in one gulp and immediately took another.

"That's better," he said. "I really needed that."

Lady Monica was deep in conversation with Jessica, telling her stories of when she was young. Alice was talking to Matthew Dunn about the divorce and Sir Humphrey was chatting to Adam. There was a great deal of lively conversation, fuelled by the champagne. Leah and Jen were in the dining room with Sally.

"How are you feeling?" Leah asked.

"I'm feeling fine now," she said, "but I was like a jelly this morning. I'm so relieved that it all went smoothly."

"We still have the speeches to come," warned Jen. "That may cause a few surprises."

"I am immune to surprises," Sally said. "I've given up on being surprised. I've decided to go with the flow."

"Good luck to you," Leah laughed. "Don't expect a man to change just because he is your husband. It is a habit of a lifetime, believe me. It sounds as if the speeches are about to start. We had better go back in."

Everyone assembled in the lounge.

"Charge your glasses, ladies and gentlemen," Sir Humphrey said, "and prepare yourselves for some words of wisdom."

All the glasses were filled and Sir Humphrey stood up rather unsteadily. He held on to the back of a chair with one hand and held his glass in the other. Sally looked at him in concern.

"Is he alright?" she whispered to Dominic. "I hope he won't fall over."

"He'll be fine. I'm more worried about what he is going to say."

They watched as Lady Monica went up to Sir Humphrey.

"Now Humpy," she said. "No rude jokes or pointed remarks."

Sir Humphrey put his arm around her and sweetly said:

"Of course not, my dear," and he kissed her on the cheek.

Lady Monica sighed and raised her eyebrows, then she went and stood by Leah. Sir Humphrey puffed out his cheeks and started his speech.

"Since I am the best man at this celebration," he began looking around for applause which duly came, "it is my privilege to speak first. I want to thank you all for coming today and special thanks to Adam and Leah for welcoming us into their home. Thank you," and he went to sit down.

Dominic was laughing and Sally looked rather confused. Lady Monica went up to Sir Humphrey.

"I think you have forgotten something, Humpy," she said quite sternly. He kissed her on the other cheek.

"Did I forget to do that?" he said with a frown. "How very remiss of me."

"Humpy!" Lady Monica said crossly. "Pull yourself together and do your duty."

Everyone was quietly laughing at what was happening and Dominic stepped forward and said in as serious a voice as possible,

"A toast everyone, to my forgetful, elderly father."

Everyone raised their glasses and repeated the words. Sir Humphrey reacted immediately.

"Less of the old, my boy, of course, I'm not forgetful. I remember your wedding very clearly. It was brass monkey weather in that church. Cold enough to freeze the brain. Only just beginning to thaw out. Now, where was I?"

He emptied his glass and the wine waiter quickly refilled it. He looked around the room until he saw Dominic standing with his arm around Sally. He tottered unsteadily towards them and kissed Sally on both cheeks.

"My brand-new daughter-in-law," he said happily. "Welcome to the family, my dear," and he put both arms around her.

Sally just stood there while Dominic gently pulled his father away from her.

"Hands off my wife," he said firmly.

Sir Humphrey stepped back and Sally looked pleadingly at Adam. He took Sir Humphrey by the arm and led him back to his chair. Then he turned to the others.

"Earlier today, I gave Sally away to Dominic but that does not mean that I have abandoned her, in fact, I would not have given her to anyone except him. I know how much they love each other and I have watched that love grow over the past six months. I wish them every happiness in their lives together and I ask you to join me in a toast to Dominic and Sally."

They all raised their glasses to drink the toast after which Dominic spoke.

"On behalf of my wife and myself, I want to thank you for being with us today to celebrate our marriage," he said with his arm around Sally. "Let us drink a toast to a happy and successful future for each one of us."

They all raised their glasses and drank the toast. Then they settled down in the comfortable seats and resumed their conversations. Dominic went to get something to eat and Sally sat down by Lady Monica.

"I'm so sorry for Sir Humphrey's behaviour today, Sally," she said. "He really has drunk too much champagne. He needs a strong coffee to sober him up."

She signalled to the wine waiter and asked him to bring a strong cup of coffee with two sugars for Sir Humphrey.

"Don't worry, Lady Monica," said Sally, patting her hand. "I think the pent-up emotion of the day finally overcame him. He will be full of apologies tomorrow."

"There have been a lot of tensions over the past few weeks," Lady Monica said. "He is in the middle of his own divorce and that is not straightforward. He is selling the house and the contents and that is creating problems and he hasn't decided where he wants to live when it is all settled."

"We have been so busy with our own arrangements that we haven't given him the time he needed."

"Don't be too upset," said Lady Monica. "I know you have been busy and I have kept a close watch on him. Tomorrow he will be full of apologies."

"You are very good to him. Dominic and I are really grateful."

Sally moved on to have a long conversation with Matthew Dunn and his wife and Lady Monica moved closer to Leah.

"You have a charming Granddaughter, "she said and Leah told her a little bit of Jessica's history.

"We all have our problems," Lady Monica said. "My eldest boy was killed in the war and my youngest has a big problem with drink and drugs. I have a daughter but she lives in Canada and I haven't seen her for ten years. I have invited Humphrey to come and live in my house but he hasn't made up his mind."

"Sometimes problems sort themselves out, given time," said Leah. "I think we shall have another wedding in a few weeks when Bill and Alice tie the knot. They will make the perfect family with Jessica. It will give us great pleasure when that happens. Sally and Dominic have a lot of decisions, the first one being where are they are going to live before Kitson Hall is ready."

"I understand that they intend to buy a house in this area and I guess Dominic will have to spend some nights in London," Lady Monica said thoughtfully.

"Sally wants to continue working. She really enjoys her job Adam tells me and he would have a problem replacing her."

"Might be a little difficult for her, being the wife of the Managing Director?" Lady Monica asked.

"I don't think so. It is a very happy office and Sally has been there so long that she wouldn't dream of taking advantage."

The evening passed quickly and soon it was time to cut the cake. More champagne was served and everyone was beginning to feel the effect of it. Sally was getting sleepy and Dominic decided it was time to take her home. One of the chauffeurs was waiting outside to go back to London so his first trip was to go to Sally's house.

"We'll call by in the morning to pick up some cake to take to mother," Sally said as she kissed Leah goodbye.

Dominic went up to his father.

"I'll phone you in the morning. You should be sober by then. Mind you behave at Lady Monica's house."

He kissed his father goodbye and shook hands with Adam.

"Thank you to you and Leah for making the day go smoothly. I'll see you tomorrow."

The guests stood at the door to wave the happy couple off then they went back inside. Matthew and his wife prepared to return home and Lady Monica said goodbye to Jessica and each of the guests. Sir Humphrey was given a strong cup of coffee to help him wake up and by the time the car returned they were ready to leave. Most of the catering staff also left, taking all the clean china with them. The two members of staff who were left cleared the kitchen and covered the food on the table. They promised to be back at nine o'clock the next morning to finish clearing up. Adam and Leah collapsed on to the settee.

"What a day," he said. "I'm exhausted."

"I think we all are," Barry gasped. "I've never drunk so much champagne."

"We have drunk plenty of beer in our time," Bill said, "but I've never had so much of the bubbly. I just want to go to sleep."

"I think we all need a strong cup of coffee," Leah decided and she went into the kitchen.

Jessica was half asleep in the chair.

"I think she is ready for bed," Alice said and she took Jessica upstairs.

"I'll go and help Leah," Jen said as she left the three men in the lounge.

"Dominic was quite subdued today," Bill said.

"I think he was very nervous," said Adam. "He always gets uptight when he needs to sign his name."

"And yet he is such a successful businessman."

"Dominic has been brought up in the business world. His

understanding of personal relationships is very limited. I wouldn't be surprised if what has happened today is only just creeping into his conscious mind."

"I prefer to get a grip on life as it happens," Bill said thoughtfully.

"Most people like to do that but Dominic is unusual in many ways. He is having to learn how to behave like most people. Sally has quite a problem to face."

Meanwhile, Sally was actually fast asleep on her own settee. When they had returned to the house, Dominic had helped her into the lounge where she straightaway lay down on the settee. Dominic went upstairs to get her dressing gown and he managed to remove her wedding outfit before wrapping the gown around her, realising she had drunk too much champagne. Quite a homecoming, he chuckled. He made himself a cup of coffee and sat down in the armchair. He looked at Sally sleeping peacefully and it suddenly dawned on him that he was now a married man.

He knew all his responsibilities had changed this day. He had to consider his wife, not just himself. He thought about all the frantic activity which had taken place over the past six months and he suddenly felt very weary. He couldn't remember the last time he had been able to truly relax. And yet right now he knew he was at peace with the world. He put his head back and closed his eyes. In his mind, he relived the events of the day. He tried to remember every small detail but he soon realised that everything had happened so fast and yet so smoothly; a wonderful day spent with friends. There had been no airs or graces, no need for social niceties or pretensions, just normal people. He was beginning to understand what Sally had meant when she said about being a 'proper person' as opposed to just a businessman.

Sally was beginning to stir on the settee and Dominic moved over and knelt by her side. He kissed her on the forehead.

"Wake up, Sleeping Beauty."

She opened her eyes and looked at him.

"How long have I been asleep?" she mumbled.

"Sixty long minutes," Dominic said with a smile. "Quite an unusual way to start our married life."

169

She sat up and looked at him.

"I'm so sorry," she cried. "It was all of the champagne."

He put his arms around her.

"It's alright my love," he whispered. "We can soon put it right."

Sally tried to stand up but her legs were too wobbly.

"I'll make you a nice cup of tea. You stay where you are."

He went into the kitchen and Sally tried to remember everything until the speeches but after that, it was all a bit hazy. She decided she should really stay off the champagne or one day she might do something really embarrassing.

He came back with the tea and Sally's hand was shaking as she drank it.

"I'll be alright in a minute," she said. "I wasn't drunk, just sleepy. It has been a busy time."

"I know it has been busy for both of us. We both deserve a rest."

"We have to find somewhere to live," she said. "That is our next big task."

"That shouldn't be too difficult. We just need to decide on the location."

"Our friends all live in Swanton," she said. "Perhaps we should look there. I'll get a property paper next week."

Dominic was thoughtful for a few minutes.

"We shall need a place with an annexe or separate accommodation for Gretchen and George. They will be coming back soon."

"I'll see what's available," she said.

They stayed in the lounge, chatting about the day's events until they both started to yawn.

"Time for bed. I'll put the lights out," he said and he helped Sally up the stairs.

He soon followed her and they lay side by side under the duvet.

"I do love you very much, Dominic."

He put his arms around her.

"I love you more than I can say."

"Show me how much you love me," she whispered as Dominic kissed her passionately.

His hands caressed her body and they were soon lost in their own private world. They slept soundly until the morning.

They had decided to visit Mary, Sally's mother, on Sunday morning but when they got up Sally said:

"Where is your car?"

He was confused and looked out of the kitchen window.

"It's still at Adam's house," he said. "I'll have to phone Adam and ask him to come and pick us up."

He dialled Adam's number and Leah answered,

"He is still in bed," she said, "not fully recovered from the celebrations, but Bill is up and quite sober. He can be with you in twenty minutes."

"That is fine. We will be ready."

They collected together the things they needed to take like the sherry and Sally's bouquet.

"We'll take a good size piece of the cake," Sally said, "and maybe a small selection of any food that is left over."

Bill arrived promptly and soon they were back at Adam's house. He had just got up and was drinking a strong coffee. Leah helped Sally to put the cake in a box and Dominic had a short conversation with Adam.

"Have you spoken to your father today?" Adam asked.

"Not yet, I'm sure he is being well looked after."

"We have the grandchildren coming at lunchtime," said Adam. "I think I need a cold shower to wake me up."

The two men from the catering company were busy tidying up and putting furniture in its proper place.

"We'll transfer the food to your plates and leave it on the dining room table. The unopened bottles can go in the utility area," said one of them.

By midday, everything was cleared away and Leah could reclaim her kitchen. After the catering men had left, she made a cup of tea and they sat in the lounge.

"I never thought I would be pleased to get into my own kitchen," she said in wonder. "At least I shan't need to do any cooking today."

"I was looking forward to a full roast dinner," Adam teased her.

"Don't be mean, Dad," Alice chided him. "Mum has had withdrawal symptoms."

Just at that moment, there was a loud knock on the front door and Jessica went to open it. Two little people rushed past her.

"Granny Leah, Granny Leah!" Benjie shouted and Lucy ran straight to Adam, jumping up into his arms nearly knocking him backwards.

Peter came up the path after them and kissed Leah.

"I'm sorry," he said. "They have been so excited."

Leah looked at him and smiled.

"It's alright," she said. "It is just that we are all a bit fragile after yesterday." She looked more closely at him and said in a concerned voice, "You look very tired. Is everything alright?"

"There have been a few problems," he admitted. "I'll tell you later."

Jessica took Benjie and Lucy into the conservatory to find their toys and Alice went to make Peter a cup of tea. Adam introduced Bill and the two men were soon discussing a recent rugby match. Benjie came looking for Leah in the kitchen.

"I'm starving," he said. "What's for lunch?"

"It is something special today," Leah told him as she uncovered the food on the dining table.

Benjie's eyes opened wide as he saw the variety of miniature delights in front of him.

"Can I choose?" he said breathlessly.

Leah gave him a plate.

"You can choose three things and when you have eaten those you can choose three more," she said.

He took his plate into the conservatory and it wasn't long before Lucy came to make her choice. Jessica joined them and they had a picnic in the playroom. They used the tea set which had been one of Lucy's Christmas presents and Leah gave them a jug of orange squash to pour into the tiny cups.

In the lounge, Adam was telling Peter about the wedding and Peter was very impressed.

"You will have something to live up to, Bill," he said.

Bill laughed.

"Dominic doesn't understand what a simple occasion means but he will find out when he comes to our wedding."

"I'm looking forward to meeting this Dominic," Peter laughed. "He sounds quite a character."

"Come and get something to eat, Peter," Leah called and he went into the dining room.

"Some spread," he said admiringly.

"This is about half of what was on the table yesterday," Leah said, "and the champagne flowed like water. Now tell me how you've been?"

"Things are not good between us. Janet and I are drifting further apart. We are only together because of the children but in reality, we live separate lives."

"Is either of you seeing someone else?" Leah asked bluntly.

"I'm not but I am not sure about Janet."

"Is it affecting the children at all?"

"She still looks after the children very well. I know she still loves them but she doesn't love me." He was silent for a moment then he said: "We don't love each other anymore."

"Is there anything we can do to help?"

"Not really, Mum. Whatever happens to me, the children's welfare will always come first."

Leah put her arms around him.

"If you ever need help, promise me you will ask for it?"

"I promise," he replied, sincerely.

Lucy was getting tired and she went to sit by Adam on the settee. She had a picture book with her.

"I'm going to tell you a story," she announced. "It's about a tiger who came to tea at my house."

She curled up next to Adam and started the story but before long she had fallen asleep. Adam closed his eyes and they lay there together.

"What a picture," Alice said, and she took a photograph on her Polaroid camera.

"I'd better get my things together and make a move," said Bill, standing up. "It's back to work tomorrow."

Alice followed Bill out of the room. Peter sat down and looked at his father. He wondered how he had come to have such an influential friend as Dominic. He realised that he didn't really know his father at all but there was definitely something special about him. He decided he'd like to get to know him better. Then Peter rested his head on the back of the settee and closed his eyes. He felt an atmosphere of peace and contentment in the house and couldn't help comparing it with his own home. He must have dropped asleep because he was woken by Benjie tugging at his arm.

"I need a wee," Benjie said.

Peter got wearily to his feet.

"You don't need me to come with you," he said. "You know where the loo is."

"I can't find the light," Benjie said.

"It's nearly time to go home," Peter said. "Please tidy up the conservatory. I'm sure Jessica will help you."

He tapped Adam gently on the arm.

"Time for us to go, Dad," he said, quietly.

"I wasn't asleep," Adam said indignantly. "I just had my eyes closed."

"You were dead to the world," Peter laughed. "You will probably want to sleep all day tomorrow too."

"I shall be fine by tomorrow. I've got a busy week ahead of me."

Peter managed to put Lucy's coat on her and he carried her out to the car. Leah helped Benjie into his coat and kissed him goodbye. Then she kissed Peter and said:

"Don't forget."

"I won't forget," he promised.

"I'd like to meet up for a meal and a chat, Dad," he said as he shook hands with Adam. "Let me know if you can manage it?"

"I'll make time for it," Adam said.

Peter waved goodbye as he drove away.

"There's trouble brewing in that household," Leah said sadly. "I worry about the children."

"Peter is a sensible man. He will make sure they are properly cared for," said Adam.

They spent the rest of the evening relaxing in the lounge before having an early night.

Chapter Sixteen

The next day was the beginning of a new term. Jessica was up early, dressed in her new school uniform. Alice went to the school with her and met the class teacher. She promised to make sure that Jessica had a happy day and took her in to meet her classmates. Jessica was a sociable girl and found them easy to talk to. The day passed swiftly and at home time she walked back to the house with another girl who lived in the same road. Alice was very relieved that Jessica seemed happy and hoped that she would soon make some friends.

It was also the first day of school for Leah. There had been so much activity during the holidays that they had passed quickly. Leah was not looking forward to getting back into the routine.

Alice was waiting to hear if she had been successful in her application for a job at the library. She decided to start looking through one of the boxes which belonged to Dominic. She found the two boxes which had been left in the utility area and took them into the conservatory. They were quite heavy and one of them made a loud rattling noise. She opened that box and was astounded to find it full of napkins and cutlery. She took out one of the spoons and examined the marks on it. She recognised the markings which told her that it was solid silver. Each piece had a crest on it and was exactly the same design. Alice looked at them in wonder and thought about what to do with them. They were obviously family heirlooms that should stay in the family. She decided to tell Sally about them and let her decide where they should go. The napkins were made of linen and Alice arranged them on top of the cutlery and put the box to one side.

The second box was not quite so heavy and she carefully opened it. There were more linen napkins and underneath them, there were small silver dishes and condiment sets. Another box for Sally to look at, she decided. The other boxes were down at the apartment and she decided she had to get her Dad to fetch them. She made herself a cup of tea and sat in the kitchen. She thought about all the things which had happened since Christmas and suddenly remembered about the car. She found the relevant paperwork to register it in her name. Then she phoned an insurance company and paid the insurance on her credit card. She was ready to go out in it for the first time.

She decided to drive to Jen's house. It was such a long time since she had driven a car that she felt quite nervous. She spent some time familiarising herself with the controls and the different knobs on the dashboard before driving off. It was an easy car to drive and she soon got used to it. When she arrived at the house, she found Jen in the utility room loading the washing machine. They soon moved into the kitchen with a cup of coffee and had a good chat.

"I'm trying to persuade Barry to have a weekend at the same hotel as Leah but it is hard going. He says he is much too busy at work."

"I'm sure they could manage without him for a couple of days," Alice said. "Why don't you have a word with Dad and then book the weekend anyway?"

"I'm not sure Barry would like that," Jen said. "He would probably refuse to come."

"I'd come with you in that case," Alice told her.

Jen laughed.

"I might just do that," she said as Alice went back to her car.

On Monday morning, Adam was up early. He had a shower and was in his office by nine o'clock. He went straight up to see Mr Carter and found him talking to the electricians.

"They will finish the first phase of the job today," he said. "And return when the computers have arrived."

"Those should be here by the end of the week," Adam said. "I'm hoping that the carpet will be laid tomorrow and the furniture should arrive on Thursday."

"We'll leave everything as tidy as possible this evening," said Mr Carter. "I shall wait to hear from you that it has all gone according to plan."

"I'll keep you informed," said Adam and went downstairs to his office.

He noticed that Kenny Rogers had arrived and Bill was directing him to one of the tills. Adam went over to speak with Bill.

"Jenny usually works this till," Bill said, "but Barry has asked her to help Laura out this week so I thought it would be good experience for

Kenny."

"Quite right," Adam said with a smile. "Keep up the pressure."

He went into his own office and noticed that Sally was not at her desk. Julie knocked on his door and came in.

"Sally rang to say that she would be in late this morning," she said.

"I'm surprised she is coming in at all," Adam said.

He sent Julie for a cup of coffee but before she returned there was a knock at the door and Dominic came bursting in.

"Good morning, Adam," he said cheerfully. "My wife insisted I brought her in to you even though I told her that she was now endowed with all my worldly goods."

Adam laughed.

"I don't think she wants all your worldly goods," he said. "She'll have her hands full with you."

"Well, I can't stop long because I need to check on my old father. It appears that he has slept for most of Sunday so I am told. I thought I would have a quick look upstairs so I can report back to him."

"I'll take you up there," Adam said. "We're getting on very well."

Dominic was most impressed by the progress which had been made.

"When do you expect it to be finished?" he asked. "We must arrange a grand opening."

"If all goes according to plan, it should be ready in three weeks."

"I'll bear that in mind," Dominic said. "This coming Friday is the reception for the present Board and their wives and the following week the new Board will meet. Sally will have to come to London on Friday morning."

"I've already told her that there will be times when she won't be in to work," Adam said. "It's not a problem."

"Well, I must love and leave her until Friday," Dominic said as he stood up. "I must put on my business hat. Sally is going to start looking for a house in Oxfordshire."

"At least she is now mobile," Adam said. "Alice has licensed her car

178

today but I don't suppose Sally has had time to do it?

"I must remind her," Dominic said. "Mind you look after her while I'm away."

"I'll do my best," Adam promised as he said goodbye to Dominic.

A few minutes later, Sally came into his office.

"I really wasn't expecting you in."

"I needed a bit of normality after the weekend," she said. "I didn't want to mope about the house."

"How did you find your mother?"

"She was very well and her tongue was as sharp as ever. You know she calls Dominic, Nick? Well after he presented her with a bottle of sherry, she was all over him. She wasn't interested in any of my details of the wedding but she hung onto his every word. I was reduced to making tea and putting my flowers in water. I was even reminded to wash up the cups and put them away."

She was almost in tears by the time she finished the story. Adam put his arms around her.

"Never mind," he said. "You did your duty and that is all that matters. Now get yourself a coffee and find out how Mr Rogers is getting on."

Sally left the room and ten minutes later she reported back. She was laughing.

"Mr Rogers is doing very well. He has only made three mistakes so far. He is so nervous that Bill has to stand next to him for the simplest transaction."

"Excellent!" said Adam, clapping his hands. "We'll make a man of him yet. By the way, Alice registered her car today and insured it. I don't suppose you have had time to do the same?"

"No, I haven't done anything about it. I had almost forgotten that it was in the garage."

"Why don't you look up some insurance companies this morning? You can take time out when you please now that you are part of the governing company."

"I don't want any special favours when I am at work," she said firmly.

"I'll do it when I have a few spare minutes."

The phone started ringing.

"Your daughter wishes to speak to you," said Julie.

"Put her through. Hello, Alice, is everything okay?"

"Yes, it's fine Dad. I just need some advice," and she told him about the boxes of silver and cutlery. "I really need Sally to look at them."

"Sally is right here," he said. "You can ask her yourself."

Alice and Sally had a long conversation and Sally promised to tell Dominic about them.

"There are eighteen more boxes to go through," Adam said. "I wonder what other treasures Alice will find."

The phone rang again.

"The carpet people want to speak to you," Julie said.

"Put them through," he said.

They explained that there was a slight delay and they wouldn't be arriving until early afternoon. They would unload the van and lay the carpet on Tuesday.

"I would like to start planning some visits to different Branch Offices," said Adam. "And I need to find out what is happening about the Birmingham office. Can you get the admin department on the phone?"

They worked until lunchtime when Adam went out to the main office. It was very busy and he looked around for Kenny Rogers but he was nowhere to be seen. He went up to Bill and asked where he was.

"He's on his lunch break," Bill said wearily. "At least I can now do something else. I have had to hold his hand for most of the morning."

"Keep him busy," Adam said. "He will soon get used to it."

After lunch everything in the office was quiet and at four o'clock Adam said:

"I've had enough for today. Get your coat and I'll take you home. You can have a look at those boxes on the way."

They arrived home at about the same time as Leah. Alice made them all a cup of tea before showing Sally the contents of the boxes.

"These have the Kitson Crest on them," Sally said. "They will have to go back to Kitson Hall eventually but I don't know where they will go in the meantime."

"They should go into secure storage with the rest of the furniture," Adam said, "but they can stay here until you get your own home. I'll put them under the stairs. You haven't seen my apartment, have you? I'll show it to you on the way to your house and I can pick up some more boxes for Alice."

He drove down to his apartment and showed it to Sally. She was most impressed and looked forward to enjoying sitting by the river in the summer. The first thing she did when she arrived home was to register and insure her car. She had no intention of driving to work but it would certainly be useful for shopping and visiting her mother.

Adam returned home and unloaded the boxes. They had a quiet evening and an early night.

The rest of the week passed smoothly and the carpet was laid in the new offices. Some furniture arrived on Wednesday and the computers were delivered on Thursday. Friday was a quiet day and Adam was pleased with what had been achieved during the week. Sally went to London on Friday morning and was met at the station by one of the chauffeurs who took her to Head Office. She had a property paper in her bag and she had made a note of two possible houses. One was a newly built, five-bedroom house and annexe situated in one of the villages. The other was a similar-sized house at "The Birches" in Swanton. Dominic was waiting for her in his office and greeted her with a kiss.

"I've missed you," he said as he put his arms around her.

"I've missed you too," she said. "We have a lot of catching up to do."

"I have one more meeting," he said, "then we will go back to the flat."

He called his secretary and told her to take Sally to the visitors' lounge and make her a cup of coffee. She led Sally along to a plush lounge with a bar and a coffee machine.

"You can have something stronger if you like?" Miss Jennings said with a smile.

"No thank you," Sally said quickly, "a coffee will be just fine. Won't you join me?"

"I'll take an early coffee break," Miss Jennings said and the two women talked about their respective jobs.

"I have spoken to you on the phone," Sally said, "and it is nice to meet you in person."

"My feelings exactly," Miss Jennings said, "but please call me Rosie. That is my name."

"I don't suppose it would be right for you to call me Sally. I shall have to get used to being Mrs West," Sally said rather sadly.

"When we heard that Mr West was getting married again, we were all a little anxious because his first wife was so bossy and demanding, but I can see that you are much more down to earth and pleasant," Rosie said.

"This is all new to me," said Sally. "I have so much to learn."

"I know we will all help as much as possible," Rosie said. "So, don't be afraid to ask." They chatted for a while longer until Rosie said: "I'd better get back to work. Will you be alright here by yourself? I'm sure Mr West won't be long."

"I'll be fine. I know how to work the coffee machine."

Rosie went back to the office and it was not long until Dominic came along. He kissed Sally.

"Time to go, my love."

They left the building. It was only a short walk to the flat and Dominic carried the suitcase. Inside the flat, they sat and caught up with each other's news.

"How is Sir Humphrey?" she asked.

"He has been staying at Lady Monica's but I did see him at the club last night."

"Is he alright?" Sally asked anxiously.

"Lady Monica said that he took two or three days to get over the weekend and he doesn't realise that he is getting older and can't party like he used to. But he seemed alright last evening and he is looking forward to seeing you this evening."

"Will Lady Monica be there?" Sally asked.

"Not this evening. I think Mother will be coming with Father because she still has shares in the company. It will be a very different occasion from what she normally attends. I don't know how she will react."

"It should be a very interesting evening," Sally said. "I must remember to stay off the champagne."

"We'll bring a bottle back with us," he said. "You can get used to it in the safety of the flat. The dinner is in the dining hall at Head Office so we shan't have far to walk. Let's have a rest on the bed."

They lay there holding hands and talking about the future. Eventually, they both went to sleep. Two hours later, he woke up and gently shook Sally.

"Wake up," he said. "It's time to get ready."

They both got dressed and Dominic zipped up Sally's evening dress.

"I shall enjoy unzipping it tonight," he said.

Sally wore his grandmother's necklace and diamond bracelet.

"You look fabulous!" he said as he kissed her.

They arrived at Head Office in plenty of time and Dominic explained how they would meet the guests. Sally was very nervous. She knew that everyone would be looking at Dominic's new wife.

"Don't worry," he said. "Most of the retiring members are elderly and they will be very courteous to you. Their wives are elderly too and I don't know many of them but I'm sure they will be pleasant and well-mannered. The only problem might be Mother but Father has promised me that he will keep her under control."

As the guests began to arrive, Sally stood next to Dominic and shook hands with them. Each one was announced by the toastmaster and most of them had titles. The men were all very attentive to Sally but the ladies took more notice of Dominic. Sir Humphrey had arrived early but there was no sign of Lady Melissa until the last minute. She swept in like a galleon in full sail and just gave a slight nod to Dominic and Sally before she took her seat at the top table.

She was seated at the end of the line between Sir Humphrey and one of the most senior Board Members. She was not at all happy with her position and complained loudly to Sir Humphrey. Sally was next to Dominic on the top table and on her other side was Sir John Dunn, Matthew Dunn's father. She enjoyed his conversation and found his wife charming. At the end of dinner, Dominic made a short speech. He was introduced by the toastmaster and at the end of it, they all drank a toast to the success of the company. Sir John Dunn answered on behalf of the Trustees and it ended with a toast to Dominic and his new wife, Sally.

After that, the men retired to the smoking-room and the ladies to the visitors' lounge. Sally chatted with the other wives but Melissa made a point of ignoring her. This did not bother Sally but it did not go unnoticed by the others. They made sure Sally always had someone to talk to her but finally one of them broke ranks.

"What do you think of your new daughter-in-law, Melissa?"

"I'm sure she is very nice," Melissa said stiffly.

"Then why don't you speak to her?"

"I'm sure we have nothing in common," came the haughty reply. "Please excuse me," and she left the room. Almost immediately the atmosphere changed as everyone breathed a sigh of relief.

Melissa left the room in a very angry state. She knew that she had been upstaged by the comments and she was furious. She returned to the dining hall and asked one of the staff to fetch Sir Humphrey from the smoking room. When he came, she berated him so loudly that all the staff temporarily left the room. Sir Humphrey just stood there and when she had finished shouting, he calmly said:

"I'll call you a taxi."

He accompanied her to the main door and hailed a cab. He waved goodbye and returned to the smoking-room. The evening was coming to an end as the guests started to leave. When the last one had gone Dominic, Sally and Sir Humphrey went back to the flat, taking a bottle of champagne with them. They sat and chatted until Sally's eyes began to close. She excused herself and went to bed.

"What happened with Mother?" Dominic asked.

Sir Humphrey told him and added:

"I'm seeing Sir John early next week to discuss the divorce options."

"What have you in mind?"

"I'll let her have the house and most of the furniture but there are some pieces which belong to my family. They will have to go into storage for now. They might be useful to you when you move into Kitson Manor."

"We have to find somewhere to live for the next three years," Dominic said. "We may be able to store them for you. But where are you going to live?"

"I think I might take up Lady Monica's offer," said Sir Humphrey. "We can keep each other company in our dotage."

"I think that would be a good idea. You can keep each other company."

"I shall be glad when it is all settled," Sir Humphrey said. "The whole thing is very distasteful."

"I know what you mean but the result will be worth it."

"Yes, I know," Sir Humphrey replied in a tired voice. "I'm feeling very tired. I think I'll go to bed."

Dominic took him into the second bedroom and said goodnight. Then he went in to Sally but she was fast asleep. He returned to the lounge and poured the last of the champagne into his glass. He sat down and began to think about the evening's events. The dinner had been successful and the speeches had gone well. Then he thought of his mother's behaviour and the effect that it had on his father. He could see that he was beginning to feel the strain and he was determined to be ready to help him through this divorce business. It was a good decision to live with Lady Monica, she would look after his father. He made up his mind to talk to Sally about it.

The next morning, they had a leisurely breakfast before Sir Humphrey went off to talk to Lady Monica. Dominic and Sally decided to go sightseeing in London and they all agreed to meet up in the evening for dinner at the Grosvenor Hotel. Dominic and Sally returned home on Sunday morning and on the way, they took a look at the two houses which Sally had highlighted. They preferred the new-build and made an appointment with the estate agent to view it during the week.

Chapter 17

On Monday morning, Adam had an early phone call from Matthew Dunn.

"I've just received the details to complete Alice's divorce. She will need to sign the final document and have it witnessed. I'll fax it through to you."

"That is a good start to the week," Adam said. "I'll get her to do it this evening. I'll ask Sally to witness it."

"Everything should be settled by the end of the week," Matthew said confidently.

"Thank goodness for that," Adam said. "Now she can start to look ahead."

Sally was late coming in. As she rushed into Adam's office she said:

"Dominic will insist on bringing me, even though he knows what the traffic is like especially on a Monday morning."

"You must not worry about it," Adam said. "Julie is always here to cover for you. In any case, I'll take you home this afternoon because I'd like you to witness Alice's divorce papers."

The carpet fitters had finished upstairs and Adam went up to look at it. He was pleased with the result and called Barry to see it.

"Some of the furniture will be arriving tomorrow and the computers on Thursday," he said.

"It's quite exciting to see all our ideas come to life, isn't it?" Barry said with enthusiasm.

"Yes, it is. We shall soon have to start thinking about the grand opening but let's get this week over first. I shan't be in on Friday. Leah and I are going to London for the dinner for the new Board of Directors. Sally will be away too."

"That should be an interesting evening. Are you going to make it a weekend away?"

"I have booked in at the Grosvenor Hotel for two nights. It is all expenses paid so we might as well take advantage of it. We may take in a show on Saturday."

"I remember you saying that you thought London was a dreadful place," said Barry.

"I wouldn't choose to go there but it seems to be part of the job. I'd far rather spend the time at home."

"Jen wants to have a weekend away at the same hotel as you and Leah. We haven't fixed a date yet."

"It would do you both good. I know that we thoroughly enjoyed it."

There was a knock at the door and Sally came in.

"I have Dominic on the phone. He'd like to speak with you," she said.

Barry left the room and Adam picked up the phone.

"Good morning, Dominic. What can I do for you?"

"Father would like to come and see how the building work is progressing. Would tomorrow be convenient?"

"We are having the furniture delivered tomorrow, Thursday would be better."

"I'll speak to Father and confirm later. I've booked you in to the Grosvenor for two nights and booked Mr and Mrs Carr in as well. I'll arrange for a car to meet you at the station. Perhaps Sally will travel up with you?"

"That is possible," said Adam. "I'll speak to her about it."

"Father is beginning to get anxious about his retirement party in two weeks," Dominic said in a worried voice. "See if you can chat about it when you see him. I know he values your opinions."

"I'll do that if the opportunity arises," said Adam.

After the phone call, he sat back in his chair and thought about Dominic's request. He felt a twinge of a knot inside him. Why did Dominic think he, Adam, could influence Sir Humphrey? He knew nothing about politics or how the government functioned. He didn't even know the exact position Sir Humphrey held or the role he played in Parliament. He called Bill into his office and told him what had been said.

"This is in strictest confidence," Adam said. "No one else knows, not even Leah."

He felt a little better after sharing it with Bill and waited for his reaction. Bill thought about it for a moment.

"Dominic obviously trusts you completely and he values your opinions. Your background is more varied than his and you have a much deeper understanding of human nature and how people interact with each other. You have a certain kind of respect from the lowest to the highest."

Adam could not believe what he was hearing. "

"But I am just an ordinary person," he spluttered, "just like thousands of others."

"You are actually one in a million," Bill said firmly. "You are universally popular and as far as I am concerned it is an honour to have such a close connection with you."

"You were supposed to make me feel better," Adam grumbled. "But now I don't know how I feel," and he sighed deeply.

"You wanted my opinion and I'm sorry if it upset you but I had to be honest."

"Yes, thank you, Bill. I need to think about what you have said."

Bill left the room and returned to the main office. Adam stayed in his chair. He couldn't comprehend all that Bill had said. As far as he was concerned, he had lived his life to the best of his ability. He thought about Mr Carr's premonitions and the comments which Barry had made in the past. Now Bill was saying the same things. There must be some truth in it. He felt churned up inside and couldn't concentrate on anything. He called Sally in and told her what had happened.

"Has the fax come through from Matthew Dunn?" he asked her.

"I'll go and check," she replied.

Soon she was back with a piece of paper in her hand.

"It has just come in," she said as she gave it to him.

"I'm going to phone Alice to make sure she is at home and then I shall ask her to come into the office so that we can get it signed and returned."

He spoke to Alice and she agreed to come into Oxford immediately. She arrived an hour later and the document was signed and sent back to the lawyer. Bill took an early lunch break and he and Alice went out to celebrate with a coffee.

"When Alice returns, Sally, I shall be ready to leave," he said. "I'll take both of you home."

He had already decided that he was going to his apartment by the river. He needed time by himself when he could try to make sense of his life. He told Barry that he was leaving the office and would see him the next day and by mid-afternoon, he was in his apartment. He knew exactly what to do.

He opened the curtains and collected the duvet and the pillows from the bedroom and laid them on the lounge floor. He had remembered to buy some milk and he switched the kettle on to make a cup of tea. It was very quiet in the apartment as he lay down on the duvet. He stared up at the ceiling and tried to remember what Bill had said to him but his mind kept wandering back to his time up North. It was almost as if he had to punish himself for his success. He had forgotten the hard times and had taken the good times for granted. He closed his eyes and tried to visualise his life without Leah and his good friends like Bill and Barry, but he couldn't do it. He couldn't understand how much his life had changed over the past nine months. He hadn't changed; he was still the same person but something had changed inside him.

He suddenly realised that being back with Leah was now the most important thing in his life, not work, not even friends, Leah was his one true love. He felt he was nothing without her. He relaxed a little and moved his head on the pillow. He was beginning to feel a little more settled. He stretched out his legs and breathed deeply. Perhaps he shouldn't try to understand it, just accept it, but he wished Bill hadn't told him. However, on the other hand, it had helped him to understand why he became so suspicious when those things kept happening. All he craved was a quiet life but it looked as if that was not his destiny. Good things could happen as well as bad things; he had to try harder to accept what each day brought.

By now he was feeling much calmer and he closed his eyes. He slept for two hours and when he woke, it was dark outside. He switched on the light and closed the curtains. He tidied up the lounge and washed his face in the bathroom. He made sure that he had locked the door and then drove home.

Leah was waiting for him.

"Where have you been?" she asked anxiously. "We were worried about you."

"I spent some time at my apartment," he said. "I needed to think."

Leah did not question him anymore and she kissed him on the forehead.

"We've saved your dinner," she said. "Come and eat it."

They had a quiet evening and went upstairs early. When they were in bed, Leah said:

"Something is troubling you. Are you going to tell me what it is?"

He turned towards her and put his arms around her.

"Something was troubling me but it is alright now," he said as he kissed her.

Chapter Seventeen

The next day the furniture arrived for the new offices and they really began to take shape. Sir Humphrey had postponed his visit until the next day so Adam and Sally started to carry the area folders up to the office. He placed James Brown's antique desk in the centre of the room. It was very dusty and Adam asked Julie to go out and buy some polish and plenty of dusters.

"We must see about employing a cleaner," he told Sally.

When Julie returned, Adam rolled up his sleeves and set to work polishing the desk. First, he took out all the drawers to make sure they were empty. He realised that they had forgotten to order wastepaper baskets and told Sally to make a note. The desk was covered in years of dirt and grime and Adam worked hard on it for most of the morning. After his lunch break, he called Barry and Bill into his office and told them about Sir Humphrey's imminent visit.

"It will be very low-key," he said. "He is really coming to look at the upstairs offices."

The next day, the computer technicians arrived and began to install the new terminals in the main office. At eleven o'clock, a large black car drew up outside with a police motorcycle escort in front of it. Sir Humphrey and another man stepped out and the car drove off. Sally had been waiting for their arrival and she welcomed them at the door. Sir Humphrey kissed her and introduced her to the other gentleman. Then she took them into Adam's office.

"I'd like you to meet the Right Honourable David East," said Sir Humphrey. "He is the Education Minister and he is very interested in your idea of introducing young adults into the Building Society."

They shook hands and Adam offered them both coffee. They accepted and Sally went off to make it. When she returned, the three men were deep in conversation. She served the coffee and then left the room.

"Sally is my new daughter-in-law," said Sir Humphrey. "She is also Adam's secretary."

"A charming lady," said David East.

"Yes," said Sir Humphrey. "Dominic chose well."

They finished their coffee and went upstairs with Adam. He showed them the different offices and spent some time in the small lecture theatre.

"This room has a dual purpose," he explained. "It will be a conference room for area managers but also a lecture room for students. I have a staff member who will be responsible for the educational side but I shall also use outside lecturers for different aspects of the business."

David East was most impressed by Adam's enthusiasm and asked a lot of questions.

"It is an excellent use of the space you had and a new and interesting approach to introducing the work ethic to sixteen-year-old students," he said.

They went back to Adam's office and Sir Humphrey went in to speak with Sally. David East and Adam continued their conversation in Adam's office.

"We work as a team in this office. Would you like to have a closer look at what we do?"

"I would like that. It is possible to learn so much from other people."

"I will ask my manager to show you around. He has co-operated with me on the planning upstairs."

He rang through to Sally and asked her to send for Barry to escort David East around the building. Sir Humphrey returned to Adam's office and they sat and talked.

"I'm not looking forward to my retirement," he said. "I shan't know what to do all day."

"You will have plenty to do with sorting out your divorce," Adam said. "There will be many decisions to be made."

"I've already made the biggest decision," Sir Humphrey said firmly. "The rest are only minor things."

"They are far from minor," Adam said firmly. "You have to make sure that the final result is fair for you and your wife."

"I don't mean to be rude but I just want to see the back of her. I'm tired of having to be responsible for her outbursts and vitriol."

"You have a good lawyer in Matthew Dunn and you would be well advised to listen to what he proposes."

"It's not all about my wife, Adam. I am also concerned about who is going to do my job in the government."

"I'm afraid I can't help you there; I don't even know what your job is."

"I am the personal adviser to the Prime Minister but very few people know my position, so please don't tell anyone."

Adam was astounded by what he heard and looked at Sur Humphrey in amazement.

"Who else knows this? he asked.

"Dominic and Lady Monica and most of the Cabinet, but not Melissa. Dominic would be the obvious choice but he is not at all interested."

"There must be Junior Ministers who could take over?"

"There are plenty of those but not one I would recommend. They have all been cosying up to me since my retirement became public and they will all be at the retirement party. I will introduce some of them to you. I would value your opinion."

"I'll do what I can to help you, Sir Humphrey but really I have no interest in politics."

"My job is more personal than politics. It is helping the PM to stay grounded in real terms, in the midst of all the intrigue at Westminster."

There was a knock at the door and Barry came in with David East.

"Thank you, Barry," said Adam, as David and Barry shook hands.

Barry left and David East said:

"You run a very smooth outfit here. Everyone is happy and they all work well together."

"Thank you," said Adam. "It is important to me that everyone feels comfortable."

Sally came into the office.

"Your car is here, Sir Humphrey."

"Thank you, Sally," he said and turned to Adam. "I shall look forward to seeing you on Friday week but I'll be in touch before that. Please give my regards to Leah and thank you for your hospitality today." He kissed Sally and left through the main door.

Adam went back into his office in a bit of a daze. He asked Sally to get him a cup of coffee and sat back in his chair. When Sally returned, she took one look at him.

"Are you alright?" she asked, anxiously.

"I think so."

She closed the door and sat down opposite him.

"You have had a shock," she said. "I've seen that look before."

"Yes, I think I have," Adam replied, "but I can't explain it to you."

"You need to go home and recover," Sally said firmly. "You have a busy weekend ahead."

"We will meet you at the station tomorrow morning," he said. "You must take a taxi from your house. Alice will bring Leah and me. Once we get to London, we will be met by a company car."

"I'll see that everything is locked up this evening," she said.

Adam picked up his briefcase and went to find Barry.

"I'll see you on Monday morning," he said as he left.

He didn't drive straight home but went to his apartment. It felt warm and he made a cup of tea. He fetched the pillows from the bedroom and sat on the floor leaning against the settee. He thought about the events of the morning and the information which he had been given. He wondered why Sir Humphrey had trusted him with it. A heavy feeling of responsibility came over him when he realised that he couldn't even tell Leah. Then it occurred to him that he could actually talk about it with Dominic and he felt relieved. But there was something else bothering him. Why did Sir Humphrey value his opinion? He knew nothing about any of the men Sir Humphrey wanted to introduce to him, but perhaps that was a good thing. He had no pre-conceived opinions so he could be completely honest.

Adam was beginning to understand his problems and he felt more settled in his mind. His thoughts turned to the weekend ahead and he decided to concentrate on that. He was quite looking forward to it since he already knew most of his fellow guests. He and Leah would have some precious time to spend together and that was a bonus. He cleared up the room and left the apartment. He drove home and parked his car on the grass, then he went in to find Leah. She had just come home from the hairdresser and was making a cup of tea. They sat on the settee side by side and talked about their day.

"We must pack our cases this evening," she said. "It is an early start tomorrow. Bill will take us in on his way to work."

"I hope my dress suit doesn't smell of mothballs," he said.

"I've had it out of the wardrobe and it smells okay. I just hope that it still fits you."

"I am still my lean, animal self."

"Of course, you are but you might not be able to do up the buttons," she said, tapping him around the waist.

"You have been feeding me too well," he grumbled. "But I'm not complaining," and he kissed her.

After they had eaten, they went upstairs to pack their cases. They double-checked that they had included everything they would need. Adam had a shower and Leah had a nice bubbly bath. They slept well and were up early the next morning. Bill collected them as arranged and there were no delays on their journey to the station. Sally was already there and they waited on the platform. The train journey was uneventful and they were soon at Paddington station. They were met by a chauffeur-driven car; Adam and Leah were taken to the Grosvenor Hotel and Sally on to Head Office. They were shown to their suite and the luggage was left by a uniformed page boy.

"This is pure luxury," Leah said as she looked around.

Adam had gone exploring the bedroom and he stood in the doorway with a grin on his face.

"You haven't seen it all yet," he said. "Come and look here."

Leah went into the bedroom and saw the two bathrooms.

"One for each of us," she gasped.

Adam came up behind her and put his arms around her waist.

"This is going to be a fun weekend," he said happily. "With lots of new experiences."

"I could do with a coffee," Leah said as she went towards the kitchen.

"You don't have to make it," Adam said quickly. "I'll order room service."

He rang down to reception and before long a waiter appeared with a pot of coffee and a plate of biscuits. They unpacked their cases and then went downstairs to the main lounge. They sat down and looked around. Various couples were chatting and some people were thumbing through the daily papers but the whole atmosphere was calm and peaceful. It was nearly lunchtime when another uniformed page boy approached with a note from Dominic, who had phoned through to reception.

"Sally and I are coming to lunch at one o'clock. I'm hoping you will join us?"

"Please tell Mr West, we'd be delighted to see him at one o'clock," said Adam.

They relaxed in the lounge for the next hour until Sally and Dominic arrived. They had a light lunch and then Dominic went off to speak to the manager about the dinner that evening. After lunch, Leah and Adam decided to go for a walk and Sally and Dominic went to his flat.

Later that evening, they dressed for dinner and went down to the bar. Some of the other guests were already there and Adam looked around for Mr and Mrs Carr. He found them deep in conversation with Sir Humphrey and Lady Monica. He introduced them to Leah and they were soon chatting amongst themselves. Dominic and Sally arrived and they all went into the small function room which had been prepared for them. Everyone was served with wine and then the starters arrived. Adam found himself sitting next to one of the two Directors who were still on the Board. He was Sir John Hastie, a friend of Sir Humphrey.

"Humphrey is very complimentary about what you are doing in the Oxford office. Tell me about it?"

Adam explained what he was aiming to do.

"It sounds most interesting. I hope I shall have the opportunity to visit it."

"We shall have the Grand Opening in three weeks and I shall be inviting all the Directors. I hope to see you there," said Adam.

After the main meal, the champagne was served. Dominic welcomed the new Board of Directors and a toast was drunk. The champagne flowed freely as the ladies retired to the lounge. Sally made sure that they all had drinks but she did not drink any more champagne. As the evening drew to a close the guests gradually dispersed until only three couples were left. Sally, Leah and Lady Monica sat in the lounge drinking wine while Dominic, Adam and Sir Humphrey sat at the bar drinking champagne. They could hear music coming from the dining room and Dominic and Adam went to find their partners while Sir Humphrey sat with Lady Monica.

"Well," she said. "What a pleasant evening. So different from last week."

"Yes, it was a very good dinner. I think the Company will move forward with this new Board."

"It is good to have some younger members," Lady Monica said. "Have you said anything to Adam?"

"I planted a seed in his mind yesterday but I haven't spoken about it since then," Sir Humphrey said. "I'll leave it now until after my retirement party."

"I'm ready to leave when you are," Lady Monica said.

"We'll go as soon as they come back."

They had to wait quite a while but eventually, Adam and Dominic returned with Leah and Sally.

"What it is to be young," sighed Lady Monica.

They said their goodbyes and Sir Humphrey helped her into a taxi. Dominic and Sally were only five minutes away from the flat and they decided to walk. Adam and Leah went upstairs to their suite and sat down on the settee. There was half a bottle of champagne in an ice bucket on the coffee table and Adam poured two glasses.

"Let's drink to ourselves," he said. "You are my wife and I love you now and always."

Leah clinked her glass with him.

"You are my husband and I love you more than words can say."

Adam set their glasses down and put his arms around her.

"Let's go to bed," he whispered as he led her into the bedroom.

The bed was comfortable and they both slept well. On Saturday morning after a good breakfast, they went on a sight-seeing tour of London. They had coffee at Fortnum and Masons and lunch at Covent Garden. By the middle of the afternoon, they were both tired and they took a cab back to the hotel. They both lay on the bed and went to sleep. Adam was woken by the sound of the phone ringing and answered it quickly.

"We will be with you in fifteen minutes," said Dominic. "We are running a bit late."

"We'll meet you in the bar," Adam said and woke Leah.

They hastily dressed for dinner and were downstairs just before Dominic and Sally arrived. They had a drink before going in to dinner. Dominic wanted to order champagne.

"I would much rather have wine," said Sally, looking at Leah.

"So, would I," she said.

Dominic turned to Adam.

"It's your decision. What will it be?"

"I think I would prefer wine this evening," he replied.

So, the wine was ordered. They had a delicious meal and afterwards, they retired to the lounge. The ladies went to the powder room and Adam and Dominic were left alone. Adam took the opportunity to speak with Dominic about Sir Humphrey's unusual request.

"I don't understand why he wants my opinion," Adam said.

Dominic thought for a moment.

"I know that the question of his successor has been troubling him. He was hoping that I would step into his shoes but I have enough to do running the company and overseeing the project at Kitson Hall."

"He told me what the job entails," Adam said, "but swore me to secrecy about it. I can't even discuss it with Leah."

"His job is confidential. He probably knows more of the country's secrets than anyone else. He has served six different Prime Ministers irrespective of their politics. It is a very personal post and needs someone neutral and trustworthy."

"There must be somebody in the government who fits those criteria?"

Dominic laughed.

"There is no-one in Westminster who fits that description. That's why Father is concerned. It is going to have to be an outsider, someone who is not tainted by the intrigues of government."

Adam could see Sally and Leah coming back so he did not pursue the subject. They spent a pleasant evening until Leah started to yawn.

"I'm sorry," she said. "The London air has finally caught up with me. I'm ready for bed."

"It's getting late," Dominic said. "We are meeting Father for lunch tomorrow before I take Sally home."

"We will get a taxi to take us to the station," Adam said. "Bill will meet us in Oxford."

They said goodnight and Adam and Leah went upstairs. They each had a shower and were soon fast asleep in bed.

The next morning after breakfast, they packed their cases and took a cab to Paddington station. They did not have to wait long for a train and Adam phoned Bill to tell him their arrival time. When they reached Oxford, Bill and Jessica were there to meet them. They were glad to get home and to be in a familiar environment.

Chapter Eighteen

The next week passed quickly. More furniture was delivered and the computers installed. Sally and Adam carried the rest of the folders up to the new offices. They ordered the chairs and desks for the lecture theatre and a large screen was installed at the front. The reception desk at the top of the stairs had its own internal telephone system. Adam felt that it was time to set the date for the Grand Opening. He decided on the second Thursday in February, but before that, he had to go to Sir Humphrey's retirement party. He was becoming more and more nervous about it.

Leah knew he was feeling stressed but didn't know why he felt that way. As the time drew nearer, she tried to ask him what was bothering him but he wouldn't tell her. Sir Humphrey had booked them in at the Grosvenor for two nights and had explained the security procedures they would have to go through. They travelled up to London and booked in at the hotel. They had arranged to go to the Houses of Parliament with Dominic and Sally. At six-thirty an official car drew up outside. Dominic and Sally were already in the car and Adam and Leah joined them. They were all quite nervous. The car swept through London and in through the main entrance. They passed through the first security check and the car stopped in front of the door. As they got out, a uniformed officer came up to them.

"Please follow me," he said. "I will escort you to the reception."

First of all, he took them to the table where they had to show their passports and were given official badges.

"You must wear these badges at all times," the officer said, "and you must return them when you leave the building."

They followed him along the corridor until they came to a great oak door. Two policemen were standing outside it and once again their identities were checked.

"It is easier to get into my bank than to get in here," Dominic muttered.

The door was opened and they saw a great medieval hall in front of them. It was full of people, mainly men in dark suits. Sir Humphrey saw them come in and came over to greet them.

"Welcome, welcome!" he said. "I have been waiting for you." He turned to Dominic and said quietly: "I must warn you. Your mother is here with her new man. I have Lady Monica with me."

Dominic resolved to stay away as far as possible from Melissa. Sir Humphrey was ushering them into the hall towards a small group of men who were standing at the far end. As Adam came closer, one of the men seemed vaguely familiar and Adam recognised him as the Prime Minister. Sir Humphrey introduced Dominic and Sally and then he turned to Adam:

"This is Adam Richards and his wife Leah." Adam was lost for words but Sir Humphrey said, "I'll take Leah to see Lady Monica while you two get acquainted."

Dominic and Sally went with him and Sally looked back anxiously at Adam. She tugged on Dominic's arm.

"What's going on?" she asked urgently. "Will Adam be alright?"

"He'll be fine," Dominic assured her as he looked at Leah who seemed to be in a daze. "You get Leah to sit down and I'll find some drinks."

They sat by Lady Monica who put an arm around Leah.

"Don't worry. Adam will be alright. He is quite capable of looking after himself."

Leah looked at her with wide eyes.

"No wonder he has been stressed for the past week. He must have known about this but couldn't say anything."

Dominic came back with the glasses of wine for the ladies and almost immediately went away again as he recognised some old friends. Sally was still worried about Adam and kept glancing over towards him but he appeared to be having a good conversation with a group of men.

The three ladies were chatting among themselves when suddenly a booming voice said:

"Lady Monica. How nice to see you."

"Good evening, Melissa," Lady Monica said calmly. "I think you already know Sally who is Dominic's wife and this is Adam Richard's wife, Leah."

Melissa acknowledged Sally with a nod and briefly shook hands with Leah.

"Have you seen Susanna?" she asked Lady Monica. "I understand that she was coming with her new partner. The boys should be here too. After all, they are Humphrey's grandsons."

"I haven't seen them," Lady Monica said and out of the corner of her eye, she saw Dominic coming towards them. "Perhaps you should phone her and ask where she is."

"I'll do that," Melissa said as she hurried off in the opposite direction from Dominic. He looked at Sally as he came up.

"Is everything alright?" he asked.

"Yes, it's fine," Sally answered. She was relieved to see Adam coming towards them with Sir Humphrey.

"It is time for some refreshment I think," he said as he helped Lady Monica to her feet.

There was a long buffet table down one side of the hall. It was laid with all sorts of nibbles and canapes. They helped themselves and then sat down at one of the small tables which were dotted about the hall.

"Nearly time for the inevitable speeches," Sir Humphrey said. "You'll have to excuse me." He went to find the toastmaster.

Dominic made sure that everyone, except Sally, had a glass of champagne. The great oak door opened and Susanna and her partner came in followed by her two sons. She marched up to Sir Humphrey and greeted him in a loud voice. Then she stood back as the two boys shook hands with their grandfather. Sally looked around for Melissa and saw that she was looking daggers at Susanna for upstaging her in this way.

Dominic went over to his father and Sally turned to Leah and Lady Monica.

"I don't believe those two boys are Dominic's sons," she said bluntly.

"Why do you say that? Leah asked.

#

"They don't look a bit like Dominic. One has ginger hair and the

202

other is fair and look at them. They don't seem to have an ounce of self-confidence. They are totally under their mother's thumb."

Leah and Lady Monica studied the boys more closely.

"I can see what you mean," Lady Monica said. "They are more like the man she is with now."

"Exactly," Sally said but at that moment the toast master's voice was heard announcing the speeches.

Several toasts were drunk and then the Prime Minister and his entourage left the hall. Sir Humphrey came over to the table.

"Thank goodness that is over," he said. "Now I can enjoy myself." He took a glass of champagne from a passing waiter. "Come with me," he said to Adam. "I want you to meet a couple of people."

Adam followed Sir Humphrey and he was introduced to several men who were obviously junior ministers looking for promotion. Adam chatted to them but found them quite boring. He met one or two of the secretaries who were female and he found them much more interesting to talk to. The evening passed quickly and when it was over, he realised that he had actually met a large number of influential men and he had felt quite comfortable talking to them.

Before they parted, an arrangement was made for dinner on Friday evening at the hotel where no doubt they would hold a post-mortem on the evening's events. When Adam and Leah were back in their suite at the hotel Leah said:

"It's called networking isn't it?"

"What are you talking about?" he asked.

"The way you worked through so many conversations this evening. You hardly stopped talking."

Adam looked at her.

"I must admit that I enjoyed the evening. I met some interesting people but most of them were quite boring. There wasn't one I would have employed in my office."

"Sir Humphrey kept you pretty busy. I didn't see much of you."

"I'm sorry if I seemed to ignore you," he said, putting his arms around her.

"It's alright, I had an interesting evening too," and she told him what Sally had said. "Did you notice Dominic's sons?"

"Not really," he replied. "I noticed that he hardly spoke to them but I didn't look closely at them."

"I think Sally's right and he should have a DNA test to prove it one way or the other."

"That is their decision," he said firmly. "My decision is that it is time for bed."

They both slept soundly and had a leisurely breakfast. They decided to go for a walk in the local park during the morning and then they had a light lunch. They had a rest in their room in the afternoon then changed for dinner and went down to the lounge. It was not long before the other two couples arrived and the champagne began to flow. The conversation turned to the events of the previous evening.

"I feel that I can really proceed with the divorce now," Sir Humphrey said. "I am no longer employed by the government and there are no more formal occasions when Melissa will be expected to be present."

"I can take back control of the company so that will allow you the time to sort out the details," Dominic said. "I hope you will talk to your old friend Sir John about it."

"You were very busy working the room, Adam?" said Sir Humphrey.

"I really don't know how that happened," Adam said. "One conversation merged into another and I certainly can't remember any particular one."

"So, what was your overall impression?" Sir Humphrey asked.

Adam hesitated before he answered. Eventually, he said:

"I found them all boring. I wouldn't employ any of them in my office."

Sir Humphrey laughed aloud, the others said nothing.

"My feeling exactly," he said. "I just needed to confirm it."

"I'm sorry if I upset you," Adam said, "but I had to be honest."

Sir Humphrey raised his glass.

"A toast," he said, "to the most honest man in the room." He looked closely at Adam. "Now give me another honest answer. How would you feel if I offered you the job?"

"I would think you were joking," Adam said immediately.

Sir Humphrey stood and went up to Adam.

"I am not joking, Adam Richards, I am offering you the post of Personal Advisor to the Prime Minister of this country."

Adam just sat on his chair with his mouth open.

"You don't have to give me an answer now," Sir Humphrey said. "Take a few days to think about it before you accept. Now let us have a good dinner and more champagne."

The rest of the evening passed in a daze as far as Adam was concerned. Leah and Sally were both in shock too; only Lady Monica remained composed.

Dominic was also very surprised. Sally looked at him.

"Did you know about this?" she asked.

Sir Humphrey interrupted her.

"I discussed it with Lady Monica, no-one else. I couldn't say anything until the PM had actually met Adam. That couldn't happen until last evening and he was happy to go along with my recommendation."

That evening, when they were back in their room Leah and Adam sat on the settee holding hands.

"I must be dreaming," he said faintly.

"I think we are both in some kind of parallel universe," she said. "Nothing is real."

"I can't do two jobs and I don't want to leave the Building Society."

"You need to find out more about what this PM's job is exactly," she said firmly. "You didn't even know such a post existed."

"That's true but I do know that I was right about one thing."

"What is that?" she said looking at him.

"I knew that there was some mystery in the air and that there was a hidden agenda. My gut feeling was right." He put his arm around Leah. "I'm sorry if I have seemed a bit distant for the past two weeks. So many unusual things have happened that I found it difficult to concentrate and I haven't been able to share it with you."

"I have known that something was bothering you and I have tried to support you as best I could."

"You have been very patient and I hope there are no more secrets I need to keep from you. I promise I will explain it tomorrow. I'm too exhausted tonight."

They went to bed and were soon fast asleep.

Adam woke up quite early on Saturday morning. He got out of bed and dressed quickly. Then he made himself a cup of tea and sat in the lounge. He thought about the proposal which Sir Humphrey had made. He had known instinctively that something was brewing but he had never, in his wildest dreams imagined what it turned out to be.

He thought he was no-one special. Why did others think he was some kind of superman? He knew nothing about politics or the way that Parliament works. He didn't know any politicians; he was a complete outsider. He sat there thinking about the situation which faced him. Sir Humphrey is a clever old fox, he thought. He must have had this well-planned and it all fell into place. He convinced himself not to be rushed into any decisions; he would find out more details about the job first. He heard Leah calling his name and went into the bedroom.

"I was wondering where you were," she said. "I missed you."

He kissed her.

"I wasn't far away," he said. "I was just having a quiet think."

"You are going to have to do more than just think. You need to find out some facts."

"Yes, I know. I must talk to Sir Humphrey."

They went downstairs for breakfast and afterwards, they packed their cases ready to leave. They were about to call a taxi when the phone in their room rang.

"I'm glad I caught you," Dominic said. "We would like you and Leah to come round for coffee before you leave. We are only five minutes' walk away."

"Thank you for the invitation. We would be delighted to come,"

Adam said. "We will be there in fifteen minutes."

He arranged to leave the suitcases at reception and they walked along the road to Dominic's flat. Sally welcomed them at the door and took them into the main lounge. Dominic was waiting there and greeted them warmly.

"Come with me," Sally said to Leah and led her out into the kitchen.

She made two cups of coffee and took them into the lounge. Dominic and Adam were deep in conversation and after leaving them their coffees, Sally went back to join Leah in the kitchen.

"My father's announcement last evening was as much a surprise to me as it was to you," said Dominic. "I knew he was planning something but he didn't even drop a hint. What are you going to do?"

"I need a lot more information," Adam said, "and first of all I want to know how it would affect my present job?"

"Your present job is quite safe," Dominic said firmly. "I have absolutely no intention of any changes in that department. It really depends on whether you feel that you could manage both jobs. You would have total freedom to decide how you do that."

"I need a lot more details from Sir Humphrey before I make any sort of decision," Adam said, "and I should want to meet the Prime Minister on a more formal footing than last night."

"I'll speak to father and arrange for you to come up to London for a meeting. It might mean that you will have to go to Chequers in order to meet the PM."

"I really don't understand why it has been offered to me in the first place. I have no strong political views and I have no ambition in that direction. I am more than happy in my present position and I just want to develop my plan for it. I've got my life back on course and my family to think about."

"You have just outlined the very reasons why my father thinks the job would suit you. You are very much your own man and confident in your own views without being boring or overbearing. You can always be relied upon to steady the ship," said Dominic.

Adam looked at him.

"Everyone seems to be telling me who I am or what I am capable of.

I am losing track of the way I see myself. I am being overtaken by the speed of change and I don't like it. I need Leah and the stability of my own family in order to function properly." His voice was cracking with emotion.

Dominic became concerned.

"You have unconsciously dealt with some enormous pressures over the past years," he said. "You must allow other people to help you. Bill seems to be a very useful young man. Give him more responsibility like the development of the educational aspect of your new office. I would also suggest that you have regular meetings of the office managers on a rota basis. It would mean that you could meet them all without visiting every office in your area."

"I'll think about what you have said. It looks as if I am going to have to re-evaluate my lifestyle but I am telling you now, Leah and my family will always come first."

Sally and Leah came back into the lounge. Adam stood up and put his arms around Leah.

"Time to go home, my love," he said. "We must go back and sign out of the hotel."

They said goodbye to Dominic and Sally and walked back to the hotel. The doorman hailed a cab for them and they were soon at Paddington station. The train left ten minutes later and within an hour they were back in Oxford. Bill and Jessica met them at the station and before long they were back at home.

Adam was glad to be back in familiar surroundings and the quietness of the house. He unpacked his case and had a shower. He was looking forward to a relaxing weekend. Leah too felt exhausted both mentally and physically. Alice could see that they were both very tired and she didn't ask too many questions about their trip to London. On Saturday afternoon, Bill took Jessica to the swimming pool at the local leisure centre so Adam and Leah were able to have a sleep. They all sat in the lounge in the evening and Alice and Bill listened while Adam told them all about their visit except for the reference to the Prime Minister.

On Sunday, Adam and Leah went to his apartment. They were still recovering from what had been discussed in London and needed some time alone. It was warm and cosy as Adam pulled back the curtains.

"I really must get some decent settees," he said. "This leather one is driving me crazy. I'll be glad to give it away."

"We can go and have a look in the shop this afternoon," Leah suggested. "You never have much time to go shopping."

"We'll see. I can't make any decisions today."

He fetched the pillows and the duvet from the bedroom and they sat on the floor drinking their tea.

"This is what I do when I feel stressed," he said. "It always manages to make me relax."

"It is very peaceful. I can understand why you do it. Have you thought any more about Sir Humphrey's offer?"

"There's not much point in thinking about it until I have more details. I'm waiting to hear from Sir Humphrey. I still don't know why he chose me."

"Other people see attributes in you which you don't see in yourself," she said. "You have a straightforward attitude to life. You can go straight to the heart of the problem and clearly see an answer."

"I am becoming more and more confused about myself. I seem to have strayed off the rails and don't know how to get back on. I have always dreamt of a quiet life with you but I am constantly being bombarded with change."

Leah was quiet for a while.

"You have a secure life with me and the family," she said. "You know we are always there waiting for you to come home. But you need more than that in your life. You actually enjoy a challenge and new experiences don't frighten you at all."

He looked at her in surprise.

"You are the one with a special gift. You always know the right thing to say in any situation. You are the most astute person I have ever known. I am so lucky that you are my wife."

He put his arms around her. They lay there on the floor wrapped in a long embrace.

"I feel better already," he said at last. "I might even enjoy a visit to the furniture shop."

They tidied up the lounge and went shopping. Adam chose two settees and a comfortable armchair.

"Now all I need is for Alice to buy a house and relieve me of this cream monstrosity. I must speak to her about it."

"I'm sure she's thinking about it," Leah said. "Don't put pressure on her."

That evening as they sat in the lounge, Bill spoke to Adam and Leah.

"Alice and I would like to get married soon," he said. "We would like to buy a house. Alice will use some of her divorce settlement as the deposit and I will take out a mortgage. We would like it to be arranged before the lease is up on my rented property."

"You have got it all worked out," Adam said. "Of course, you have our blessing. I can't wait to see the back of that cream sofa."

"Dad," Alice said with feeling. "Is that why you are pleased with our news?"

"No, of course not," he said hurriedly and he went and kissed her. "I'm delighted for both of you. Have you told Jessica yet?"

Alice nodded her head.

"Yes, we told her yesterday and she is so excited."

"We only want a quiet wedding with our friends," Bill said, "plus my mum and brother."

"You can have the reception here," said Leah. "No doubt Dominic will provide the champagne. Let me know when you have chosen a day?"

"How about Saturday week?" Bill said with a grin. "We already know how to organize a quick wedding."

"That's too quick for me," Adam said. "I need Bill at work. I've got plans," he added mysteriously.

"I'd better go back to my place and start thinking about the new week," Bill said as he stood up.

"I need to speak to you tomorrow," Adam said. "Come to my office at eleven o'clock with two cups of coffee."

Bill said goodbye to Leah and Adam and then Alice accompanied him to the door.

When they were in bed that night, Adam said to Leah:

"Do you remember that on my fiftieth birthday Dominic gave us a plane ticket for a holiday in Spain, all expenses paid?"

"Yes, I remember that," she replied, "but I can't remember the actual dates."

"I think it was around Easter time. I must check it and tell Alice. We don't want it to clash with wedding plans."

"I hope Alice will invite Peter and his family. She probably should ask Harriet and Thomas but I doubt if they would come."

"It's going to mean extra work for you once again," he said. "Perhaps we should go to a local hotel?"

"Let's wait and see what Alice would prefer. I'm happy to go along with her choice," Leah said.

Chapter Nineteen

Adam was up early on Monday morning and he was in his office by nine o'clock. Sally was late coming in and Dominic came with her. He was in a hurry as usual but he did go upstairs to see how near it was to completion. He went back to Adam's office.

"We must start to think about the opening ceremony," he said. "Invitations will have to be sent out."

"I'll think about it this week," Adam said. "I'll talk to you about it on Wednesday or Thursday."

"We went to look at a house yesterday," Dominic suddenly said. "It was very nice. A definite possibility. Sally will tell you all about it. I'll speak to father today and I'll be in touch," and with that, he was gone.

Adam called Sally in. She looked rather tired.

"Are you alright?" he asked.

"It's Dominic," she said wearily. "He has boundless energy and I can't always keep up with him."

"Well, you have a couple of days on your own now to recover."

"I'm not sure about that," she sighed. "We saw a house yesterday in one of the local villages. He liked it very much and if he had his way we would move in next week. He really has no idea of the many logistics which are involved."

Adam looked at her.

"What is more to the point is did you like it?"

"Yes, I liked it. It is a newbuild, five bedrooms and an annexe for Gretchen and George. Total cost one and a half million pounds; although Dominic thinks his lawyers will be able to reduce that."

"What are you going to do with your house?"

"I haven't even thought about it. I'll probably let it and the income will help with my mother's costs."

"You need to take your time before making any decisions," he said. "Now I want to order the seating for the lecture room so let's go upstairs."

Sally collected her notebook and the furniture catalogues and followed Adam. Most of the computers had been installed and the heating radiators were in place. They went into the lecture room which was still quite empty.

"We need a large screen at the front behind the desk and a projector at the back of the room."

Sally made a note of that.

"What about curtains or blinds?" she asked.

"I think we will have blinds at the windows rather than curtains. Now about the seating, chairs or benches?"

"I like chairs best," she replied. "They are more comfortable and they can be stacked if necessary."

"I think you are right, Sally. They are more versatile than benches. We will have good quality upholstered chairs and a nice leather chair for behind the desk."

They went into the reception area and looked at the space.

"A desk is going to look rather lost in all that empty space," he said. "I think we will have something like a semi-circular counter. It will look more impressive as you come up the stairs."

They went back to Adam's office and finalised the order which Sally sent to the suppliers.

"I must give my desk another polish," he said. "It is beginning to look really good."

"I'll have a go at it and Julie can too. Have you got a date for the opening?"

"It will be during the last week of February but I have yet to confirm which day," he replied. "I shall have to consult Dominic."

There was a knock at the door and Bill came in with the coffee. Sally left the room and Bill sat opposite Adam.

"What I am going to tell you is totally confidential. You will be one of only six people who know about it," Adam said and proceeded to tell Bill about what had been proposed in London. Bill just sat there with his mouth open. Adam sat back and waited for Bill's reaction. It was several minutes before Bill could speak.

"Whatever did you say?" he spluttered.

"I said I needed to think about it," Adam replied calmly.

"And have you thought about it?"

"There's not much point until I have more facts to help me," Adam said. "But the reason I am telling you is that it may affect you too."

"How can that be?" Bill asked in amazement.

"You will have to take full responsibility for the educational development and sometimes you might have to deputise for me in the position of area manager."

"But what about Barry? He is senior to me."

"It is vital that Barry concentrates on the core business of this office. It will be a flagship office and must be run accordingly. We will find him another assistant manager. In due course, you will be promoted to educational manager but I think you can begin to think seriously about how to organise it. The opening ceremony will be during the last week in February and I would hope to get your thoughts about it during the next week."

"I'll do that," said Bill as he stood up.

"Just one other thing," Adam said. "Leah and I will be going on holiday around Easter time."

"We will make sure the wedding takes place before that. It will probably be sometime in March. We want to buy a house before my rental agreement runs out."

"Let Barry deal with your mortgage," Adam said.

"We have to wait and see exactly how much Alice will get before I think about a mortgage," Bill said, "but I'll tell Barry what I intend to do."

Bill left the office and Adam stayed in his chair. He began to think about arrangements for the opening ceremony and he called Sally. She came in with her notepad and diary but before they could begin, Julie rang through to Adam.

214

"Mr West wishes to speak to you."

Adam took the call.

"I've spoken to Father and he will come to Oxford tomorrow to talk. Is that convenient?"

"Yes, I can manage that," Adam said.

"He also said that you should keep next Saturday free. He will explain more tomorrow."

"Very well."

"I need to speak to Sally," Dominic said urgently.

"She is right here," and he passed the phone to her.

"I've heard from the estate agents that the vendors will consider a lower offer. What do you think?" Dominic asked.

"I think I would like to have a second viewing," Sally said firmly and Adam smiled to himself.

"I'll arrange it for next weekend," Dominic said with a touch of annoyance. "I'll ring you this evening," and he put the phone down.

Adam looked at Sally.

"He likes his own way you know."

"He may like it but he can't always have it," she said with determination. "He has no conception of money values and it won't hurt him to stew for a few days."

"So, you are going to say yes to the house eventually?"

"When I'm ready," she said shortly. "Now what did you want to see me about?"

"I wanted to talk about a date for the grand opening and who should be on the guest list."

"What date do you have in mind?"

"I was thinking about Thursday, February 23rd but it depends if that is suitable for Dominic?"

"I'll ring his secretary and see if he has anything booked for that day," said Sally and left the room.

Adam sat back and thought about tomorrow's visit. More intrigues, he thought and wondered what was going to happen on Saturday.

Sally came back from her office.

"Dominic has nothing booked in for that date," she said. "So, you can go ahead and suggest it to him."

"Can you let me have the details of all the other area managers? I want to know how many there are and how long they have held that position?"

He closed up the file on his desk and put it in his briefcase.

"I've had enough for one day," he said. "I've got a wedding to think about."

"Who's wedding are you thinking about?" asked Sally in surprise.

"Alice and Bill. They announced it last night."

"Have they fixed a date?"

"Not yet but sometime in March has been suggested."

"It sounds as if the next couple of months are going to be very busy," she said.

"They certainly are and that is why I am going home early, to get some extra rest," he said in a serious voice.

Sally looked at him.

"That is the worst excuse I have ever heard for skiving off early," she laughed.

"I'm trying to keep my sanity, Sally but it is not easy with all the intrigues which are taking place," and he told her about Sir Humphrey's visit the next day.

"Well, you should get a better picture of what the new job is all about."

"You speak as if I have already accepted it and that is not the case," he said firmly. "I can still say no."

Sally said no more and returned to her office. Adam put his coat on and went to find Barry before leaving work. When he arrived home, he found Alice busy in the conservatory. She was opening another of Dominic's boxes. This one contained some beautiful damask tablecloths and napkins. The bottom of the box was lined with silver coasters and napkin rings. Alice could imagine a large dining table at Kitson Hall covered with one of these cloths and laid with the silver cutlery. She opened another box and this one contained sewing needles and cottons, silver thimbles and scissors and other bits and pieces for daily use. When Adam came in, she stopped what she was doing and went to make them a cup of tea.

"How much money do you think I will get from my divorce, Dad?"

"I've no idea," he replied. "I don't know the value of the house. You could phone Matthew Dunn and ask for a rough estimate but don't forget he will be taking his fees out of the total sum."

"I'll phone him tomorrow morning," she said. "You are home early today. Are you alright?"

"I'm fine. I'm going to my apartment for a couple of hours; I need to think."

Adam left the house and ten minutes later he was at the apartment. He had remembered to buy some milk so he made himself a cup of tea. He arranged the pillows as usual and lay down on the floor. He thought about Sir Humphrey's visit and considered what questions he would like to ask. He wondered why he needed to be available on Saturday but try as he might, he could find no answers. In the end, he gave up and closed his eyes. It was dark outside when he woke up so he put the light on and closed the curtains. He replaced the pillows and washed up his cup then he went out to his car. He drove home and spent a quiet evening with Leah.

He went to work the next morning wondering what the day would bring. He told Barry and Bill that Sir Humphrey would be arriving during the morning and he went into his office. He called Sally.

"Have we got any decent biscuits?"

"I'm sure we could manage," she smiled, "but I'll go and buy some more."

She could sense how nervous Adam was and did her best to calm him down.

"Sir Humphrey is only going to explain things to you. He is not going to interrogate you," she said.

"I know that," he sighed, "but I have no idea of what he is going to say and I feel totally unprepared for any further shocks or surprises."

"I'll send Julie for the biscuits," Sally said, "and we will start thinking about the grand opening. That should keep your mind occupied."

She gave Adam a list of area managers which he had asked for and went to speak to Julie. When she returned, Adam was studying the list.

"There are not many," he said. "One in Wales and one for Eastern England. One for the North and one for the London area. My area seems to be the largest. I think there needs to be an overhaul of the whole country. Some of the area managers have been in their jobs for quite some time; it will be interesting to meet them."

"Are you going to invite them to the opening?" Sally asked.

"Yes, I shall invite them. I shall invite the other Board Members and their wives. I'm also thinking of inviting the headteachers of local schools to introduce them to our idea of an insight into the workings of the company through seminars."

"How will you organize the opening?"

"We'll use the lecture room. We can assemble in there and I will give a welcoming speech followed by a speech from Dominic. I don't know that anyone else will want to speak."

"What about food and drink?" she asked.

"We'll have a selection of buffet food and get a catering company in to deal with that. A local wine company can provide the drinks. I'll have to check with Dominic if he wants champagne or just wine."

"You seem to have it all planned out. Now you just need to confirm the date."

"Can you contact Dominic and do that?" he asked.

Just at that moment, the phone rang.

"Sir Humphrey has just arrived," said Barry. "And he has someone else with him."

"Thank you," said Adam said and stood up.

There was a knock at the door and Sir Humphrey walked in. He shook hands with Adam and kissed Sally. Then he turned to the man who was standing behind him and said:

"I'm not in the habit of kissing secretaries but this one happens to be my daughter-in-law."

The other man laughed and stepped forward. Sir Humphrey introduced him to Adam.

"This is Sir Charles Blaine, the Prime Minister's Private Secretary," he said and the two men shook hands. Then Sir Humphrey turned to Sally. "And this is my daughter-in-law Sally," he said and Sir Charles shook Sally's hand.

"Would you like coffee first?" Adam asked.

"That is a good idea," Sir Humphrey said. "Sally makes excellent coffee."

She blushed a little and left the room.

"I understand that you have an interesting project here?" said Sir Charles. "I would like to see what you are doing."

"I would be delighted to show you," Adam said. "It is nearly completed."

"Why don't you go now and I'll wait here for the coffee," said Sir Humphrey.

Adam took Sir Charles upstairs and explained his plans. Sir Charles was very impressed.

"This could be the start of a change in the way we view vocational training," he said with interest.

They went back to the office and found Sally pouring the coffee, after which she left the room. The three men sat in the office for the next hour talking about the responsibilities of Adam's new job. Finally, Sir Humphrey said:

"Have you any further questions, Adam?"

"I don't think so. You have given me a great deal to think about." Sir Humphrey rose to leave and Adam continued: "There is one thing I'd like to know. Why did you tell me to keep the weekend free?"

"I'll be in touch with you tomorrow," Sir Charles assured him as they shook hands.

Adam accompanied them to the door where a police escort was waiting. They said their goodbyes and Adam returned to his office. His head was spinning with a myriad of thoughts. Sally came in to collect the coffee cups and found him sitting in his chair gazing up at the ceiling.

"Are you alright?" she said anxiously.

"Yes, I'm alright. I've had too much information. I can't take it all in."

"Well, I will tell you one more thing, then you can go home. Dominic says that February 23rd is okay for the grand opening. Now be careful how you go when you drive home."

He cleared his desk and picked up his briefcase.

"I'll see you tomorrow," he said. "Tell Barry I want to see him in the morning."

He called into M&S to get some sandwiches for his lunch and some milk for his cup of tea. Then he drove straight to his apartment. He laid out his duvet and his pillows and opened the curtains. He sat in the kitchen to eat his sandwiches and drink his tea, then he lay down on his pillows. His mind went blank and he closed his eyes. He slept for the next hour and woke feeling refreshed and ready to think about what he had heard earlier. He now knew a lot more about what the job entailed and how much of his time it would involve. It meant many more visits to London and possible travels abroad. Adam had to consider the impact which it would have on his present job but more importantly, on Leah and the family. He decided that he would discuss everything with Leah.

That evening, Alice drove over to see Bill and when Jessica was in bed, Adam told Leah about his day.

"There was such a lot of information but I remember the important bits. It will mean spending more time in London and doing more travelling," he said. "How do you feel about that?"

"I shall miss you but I can put up with that if you are happy in your job," she replied.

"The job itself seems reasonable but it is all the bowing and scraping that I don't like. You know I can't stand that."

"Unfortunately, you can't avoid it, Adam, as you climb up the social ladder."

He was horrified.

"I don't want to climb anywhere," he said angrily. "I just want to be myself."

"I don't think that is your destiny," she said calmly. "I think you are destined for higher things so you might just as well embrace it. You are going to have to wear two hats. You can still be yourself when you are at home or with friends but at other times you will be the perfect businessman. If Dominic can manage it, I'm sure you can."

"Do you know that when I first met Barry, he told me that Mr Carr had told him that I was destined for higher things? Bill said the same. I thought it was rubbish but perhaps he was right. I can't accept a job just because of someone's comments."

Leah looked at him closely.

"You have been blessed with an unusual talent. It would be a shame not to use it."

He looked at her with wide eyes then he put his arms around her.

"If anyone has an unusual talent, it's you," he said. "You always say and do the right thing," and then he kissed her.

Chapter Twenty

When Adam arrived at work the next morning, he found three police cars parked outside and several police officers inside the building. He hurried over to Barry who was looking rather bewildered.

"What's going on?" he asked.

"I'm not sure. The Inspector in charge is over there talking to Bill," Barry said.

Adam went over to Bill who was pleased to see him. He introduced the Inspector and Adam immediately took him to his office.

"What is this all about?" he demanded.

"We had a message at eight-thirty this morning to say that an important visitor was arriving at this office at eleven o'clock and that we should do a security check," said the Inspector.

"This is all news to me," Adam said angrily. "Why wasn't I given notice of it?"

"We didn't know until this morning," the Inspector said calmly, "Perhaps a message has come through to you? I must see that everything is safe," and he left the office.

Adam called Sally and asked her if she knew what was happening.

"I've spoken with Dominic and he did not know about it but he thinks it may be the Prime Minister, since security is involved."

"Surely somebody would tell me?" Adam said crossly as his phone rang.

Julie's voice came through:

"Sir Charles Blaine wishes to speak with you."

"Put him through."

"Good morning, Mr Richards. I'm sorry about such short notice but the PM wants to visit you and this morning is the only free time available."

"He is very welcome," Adam said, "but the place is swarming with

222

police and we do have a business to run."

"It will be a low-key visit. He is coming to meet you and of course, he is very interested in what you have planned."

"I will alert the other managers," Adam said, "but I shan't name the visitor. I hope the police will be discrete and not intimidate our customers?"

"We will be with you at eleven o'clock," Sir Charles said and he put the phone down.

Adam told Sally to call Barry and Bill and when they arrived, he told them what was going to happen.

"I have a client at eleven o'clock," Barry said. "So Bill will have to deal with any problems."

"I'll manage," said Bill. "At least I met Sir Charles Blaine yesterday. Is Sir Humphrey coming?"

"I don't think so," replied Adam. "His name has not been mentioned."

Barry and Bill went back to the main office where the police were still in attendance. Barry went up to the Inspector.

"Have you nearly finished? The customers are getting a bit anxious."

"We have finished the security check of the building but we shall have two policemen on the door from ten forty-five to do personal checks. There will also be a police motorbike escort outside."

"Bill, you will have to keep a watch on the door," said Barry. "Make sure reception phones through to Adam as soon as the car arrives."

Back in his office, Adam called Sally in.

"You had better prepare for coffee," he said, "I shall certainly need one even if the PM doesn't."

Eleven o'clock was fast approaching. Adam cleared his desk except for the plans for the extension and the folder with the details. At exactly eleven o'clock a message came through:

"The car has arrived."

Adam quickly left his office and went to the front door. The policemen were standing to attention as two men walked through. Adam recognized Sir Charles Blaine and he assumed the other man was the Prime Minister. They were accompanied by two security men who followed them in. Adam stepped forward and shook hands with Sir Charles who then quickly introduced him to the Prime Minister. He led the way back to his office and the three men sat around the desk.

"Would you like coffee before we start? Adam said. "My secretary will make it."

He called Sally and asked her to bring some coffee. When she returned, Sir Charles stood up.

"It's Sally isn't it, Humpy's daughter-in-law? I can give you a kiss since he is not here to see me do it."

He introduced Sally to the PM who shook her hand. She poured the coffee and then left the room. After a few minutes Sir Charles stood up and said to the PM: "If you would excuse me, I'd like to have another look upstairs."

The PM nodded his head.

"Sally is next door," said Adam. "She will get one of the managers to show you around."

Sir Charles left them and Adam and the PM continued their conversation.

Sally took Sir Charles to meet Bill who took him upstairs to look at the new offices. He explained about the educational aspects of the development and Sir Charles listened carefully.

"This might be a blueprint example for other companies," he said thoughtfully. "Whose idea was it originally?"

"I don't know for certain," Bill said, "but I'm pretty sure it was Adam's idea."

An hour later, the PM was ready to leave and Adam went to the main entrance with him.

"I will phone you this afternoon," said Sir Charles to Adam as he left.

The car and its escort drove off and the police presence melted away. Adam went back to his office and called Sally in.

"I need a strong cup of coffee and some sandwiches," he said urgently.

"I'll send Julie for some sandwiches and I'll make the coffee. I won't be long."

Adam didn't move out of his chair and when she came back, he said:

"I shall have to stay here until Sir Charles has phoned. After lunch, we may as well start designing the opening invitations."

"I'll go and see if Julie is back," Sally said and she left the room.

She soon returned with his sandwiches and then went back to her office.

Adam sat in his chair for the next hour trying to come to terms with what he had been told that morning. He had enjoyed his conversation with the PM and had not felt intimidated by him. There were many views and values which they had agreed on but there were also one or two disagreements. Sally came in later with her notebook and diary. They were just making a note of the area manager's homes and addresses when the phone rang.

"Mr West wishes to speak to you," Julie said.

"Hello Dominic," Adam said, "How are you?"

"I'm fine but more to the point, how are you?"

"Bursting with information! Life is too fast."

"You'll be fine after a good night's rest," said Dominic. "How did you get on with the PM?"

"We got on well. We had a good discussion."

"And have you made a decision?"

"I'll do that at the beginning of next week. I'm waiting on a phone call from Sir Charles Blaine."

"Can I speak with Sally?" asked Dominic.

"She is standing right here," Adam said and passed her the phone.

Dominic and Sally had a chat and then she put the phone down.

"He has arranged a second viewing on the house for Saturday morning. He is already discussing a reduction in the price."

"You will have to start thinking about your house," Adam said. "Are you going to sell it or rent it out?"

"I'll probably rent it out and the income will go towards mother's costs," Sally said.

The phone rang again.

"Sir Charles wishes to speak with you," said Julie.

"Good afternoon," said Adam.

"Hello, Adam. The PM has instructed me to invite you and your wife to Chequers this weekend. A car will collect you at four o'clock on Friday and will return you at four o'clock on Sunday. I trust this is convenient for you?"

"Yes, we can manage that."

"It will be an informal weekend with no official functions and no other guests," said Sir Charles. "There will be plenty to keep you occupied," and he ended the call.

Adam looked at Sally.

"Why do I feel that I am being pressured into taking the job?"

"I can understand why you think that. No-one actually says it but they use very subtle strategies to steer you towards it."

"I don't know what Leah will say when I tell her where we are going on Friday," he said in a worried voice.

"Leah will do everything possible to support you," Sally assured him. "She is the absolute model of a loyal wife."

"I'd better go home and warn her. We will prepare the invitations tomorrow."

He had to concentrate hard on the drive home, so many thoughts were whirling in his head. Alice was at home and she was looking through another of the boxes. It was full of writing paper, notebooks, pens and pencils.

"This is all private correspondence, Dad," she said. "I must give it straight to Dominic."

"Did you speak to Matthew Dunn?"

"Yes, I did. He couldn't give me a final figure but he reckoned it would be over five hundred thousand pounds."

"That is a lot of money," Adam said seriously. "You must take your time to decide what you are going to do with it."

"I am hoping you will give me some advice?"

"Of course, I will help you when the time comes. I'm going to the apartment. Do you want me to take some boxes back and bring some more home?"

"I think the boxes of cutlery will be safer here under our stairs but you could bring a couple more boxes back."

Adam drove to the apartment and made himself a cup of tea. He arranged his pillow as usual and thought about the latest call. Everything seemed unreal. He could not believe the invitation he had received. His life was upside down. Why couldn't they leave him alone? He really didn't want the hassle; he was so tired of it. He stretched out on the floor with his head on the pillows and he was soon fast asleep. When he woke up two hours later, he felt much calmer. He sat up and stretched. He knew exactly what he was going to do. He was going home to talk to Leah. He replaced the pillows and tidied up the kitchen. Then he put three more boxes in the boot of his car and drove home.

Leah was in the kitchen preparing the evening meal. Adam kissed her.

"I need to talk to you this evening."

She looked surprised.

"It sounds urgent."

"It is urgent," he said. "It affects both of us."

After they had eaten, they all sat in the lounge while Jessica did her homework. Adam was reminded that he had promised to buy her a desk for her bedroom. Jessica went upstairs to bed and Alice went with her.

"What is it?" Leah asked. "What is so urgent?"

"We are going away at the weekend. We are going to Chequers to spend two nights there with the Prime Minister and his wife."

"It this one of your awful surprises?" she gasped.

"It certainly is a surprise but it is not a joke."

"When did you find out about it?"

"This afternoon. We shall be picked up at 4 pm on Friday and returned at 4 pm on Sunday."

"Picked up like a parcel," she muttered. "What if we had our own arrangements for the weekend?"

"I don't know how we would get out of it," he said, feeling a little worried about her reaction. "It is almost like a Royal command."

"Will there be other people there?"

"No, I understand that we are the only guests. It is just a friendly weekend."

He was pleased that Leah was beginning to calm down and relax.

"This is all to do with this job you have been offered," she said. "It looks as if it is going to involve me as well."

"I expect there will be occasions when you would be expected to attend but they wouldn't happen very often."

Leah looked straight at Adam.

"I get the feeling that you have decided to accept the offer," she said. "Have you made up your mind?"

"The more I think about it the more interesting it becomes. It is a unique opportunity and I feel honoured that is has come my way."

"Aren't you bit afraid of the responsibility that comes with it?"

"I am a bit apprehensive but I think I know how to keep a level head and the worst thing that can happen is that I either resign or get fired," he said. "I shall wait until after the weekend to definitely accept the post."

"Well, at least I don't have to buy any new dresses," she said thankfully. "But I shall have to get a new suitcase soon."

"The PM is easy to talk to and I'm sure his wife is equally charming. It might be a very pleasant weekend," he said. "We shall obviously have to tell Alice and Bill but no-one else. I shall tell Sally and she can pass it on to Dominic."

#

"It worries me a bit that our lives are being ordered about by other people and outside influences."

"It won't always be like this," he said soothingly, "Life will return to

228

normal and we shall adapt to it." He put his arms around Leah and kissed her. "Let's do something normal now. Let's go to bed."

Chapter Twenty-One

When Adam arrived at work the next morning there was a large furniture van parked outside the office. Chairs were being unloaded and taken upstairs. The reception desk was being assembled and the large screen fixed at the front of the lecture room. The whole place was beginning to take shape. Adam's chair for his office had arrived and the desks and chairs in the smaller offices were in place. He called Sally in.

"This afternoon we will go upstairs and see what smaller items we still need, like lamps and waste-paper baskets. We might also need some folding tables for extra display space. This morning I want to get the invitations designed; can you start thinking about that? Now I need to speak with Bill."

Sally called Bill and he came to the office. Adam told him about the weekend and Bill was astounded.

"Have you made a decision?" he asked. "Things seem to be moving pretty quickly."

"Not until after the weekend," Adam said. "There are one or two other things to clarify first."

After Bill had left the office, Adam called Sally.

"I need to speak with Dominic," he said. "See if you can get him on the phone."

Sally came in a few minutes later.

"He isn't in the office right now," she said. "He will ring you when he returns."

"Have you any ideas for the invites?" Adam asked.

She opened her notebook and showed Adam some sketches she had made. Adam examined them and finally, he pointed to one.

"I like this one. What do you think?"

"I like that one too," she said. "It could be printed on white card with a gold edging. I think that would look quite important."

"We'll decide on that one. You'd better get one hundred printed.

Better too many than too few. I'll move into the upstairs office on Monday and you can move the same day. That will give Barry and Laura time to move into this office by the end of the week. Bill will have Barry's old office but later he may have to move into the other upstairs office."

"I shall need some help to take all these upstairs," she said.

"Ask Barry to make Kenny Rogers available on Monday. Running up and down the stairs will keep him fit."

The phone rang.

"Mr West wishes to speak to you," said Julie.

Sally left the room and Adam picked up the phone.

"Hello Dominic, thanks for ringing back."

"I've been talking to Father. Mother is being difficult."

"I'm sure Sir Humphrey will be getting good advice from Matthew, he just has to stay firm," Adam said.

"That's the trouble, he is too soft-hearted. Anyway, what can I do for you, Adam?"

"I haven't made my decision yet. There are a couple of points I must clarify. Firstly, will it affect my present job in an adverse way?"

"It will make no difference to your current employment other than there will be times when you won't be in the office," Dominic said.

"That is my second point. I should like to appoint a deputy to take responsibility for the area office when I am not here."

"That sounds a good idea. Have you anyone in mind?"

"Yes, I would like to offer it to Bill. He could work closely with me, although it would be on an unofficial basis. He wouldn't have the title of deputy area manager though that is what he would be."

"I am sure that can be arranged," said Dominic. "Bill is a very able young man, but how will Barry feel?"

"Barry will have the main office to look after and that will be a full-time occupation but I'll talk to him. We shall be sending out the invitations to the grand opening soon. Can you let me have a list of the people you would like to invite?"

"I'll let Sally have it in the next day or two. I understand you will be away at the weekend?"

"News travels fast," Adam said shortly. "I'll make my decision after the weekend."

"I'm coming down tomorrow. I'd like to see the final result."

"It's not quite finished," Adam reminded him, "but you are welcome to come."

He put the phone down and called Sally. He took the furniture catalogue out of his drawer and went upstairs. They looked carefully in every office to see what else was needed for the workspace. They ended up with quite a long list of smaller items.

"You can order these from the supplier and I want to add one other item which is a small desk for Jessica."

They went back downstairs and Adam went to speak to Bill.

"I want to see you at ten o'clock tomorrow morning in my office."

Adam cleared his desk and said goodbye to Sally. On his way out he spoke to Barry.

"Come to my office at nine-thirty tomorrow morning. I need to talk to you about the grand opening."

As he started to drive home, he had a sudden urge to stop at his favourite pub. Bob gave him a warm welcome and poured him a drink. Adam ordered cod and chips and sat at the bar chatting to Bob.

"I may have some visitors who will need rooms in two weeks' time," Adam said. "How are you fixed?"

"We are quiet at present. I'm sure we shall be able to accommodate you."

Adam took his fish and chips to a table near the fire and enjoyed his meal. Then he drove home to find Leah in the lounge with her feet up.

"I've had a very long day at school," she said. "Several of the staff are off sick with a flu bug and I had to cover their lessons."

Adam kissed her.

"Perhaps you should think about giving up school and concentrating on your home tuition?"

"Yes, perhaps I should," she said. "School was once very important to me but now my life is full of other distractions and it is wearing me out."

"Give it some thought. You could give in your notice at half term."

"I'll think about it," Leah promised.

Adam was pleased with what he had achieved that day and he told Leah about it.

"I should like you to be there at the grand opening," he said. "I expect Lady Monica will come. I must invite Jen as well."

"When is it?"

"February 23rd."

"That is in half term week so I won't have to ask for the time off," she said.

Alice came into the lounge and sat down.

"I heard from the library today," she said. "They have offered me a part-time job starting next Monday."

"That's good news," Adam said. "Now that Jessica is settled in school you can begin to look at your own future."

"Bill and I were talking about a date for the wedding and we would like it to be towards the end of March."

"That should be alright," Adam said. "Hopefully life will be a bit quieter by then." He looked at Alice and then he said: "Your mother and I will be away this weekend. If I tell you where we are going you must keep it a secret."

"I won't tell anyone, "Alice said.

"We are going to spend the weekend at Chequers with the Prime Minister and his wife."

Alice was speechless.

"Is this a joke?" she stammered.

"It's not a joke," he said calmly, "but it is a secret."

Alice still could not believe it.

"But why?" was all she could say.

"Because I have been offered a job by the Prime Minister and he wants to talk about it."

"Does Bill know about this, Dad?"

"I shall tell him tomorrow, but I know he can keep a secret."

Alice still couldn't believe it and she looked at Leah.

"What do you think about it, Mum?"

"It is hard to believe but it is true. It is another of your father's surprises but the biggest one yet."

"He can't go much higher than the Prime Minister," Alice said. "The next step up would be the Queen."

"It is as much a surprise to me as it is to you," Adam said seriously. "I'm not sure how it will end."

"Do you mean you haven't accepted the job?" Alice asked in amazement.

"I'll decide after the weekend."

Alice went back to the kitchen to finish cooking their evening meal and Adam and Leah relaxed in the lounge.

"I must buy a decent suitcase," Leah sighed. "I'll see what I can find tomorrow."

On Wednesday morning, Barry went to Adam's office at half-past nine. Adam told him the date of the grand opening and asked him to invite Jen. Then he told him about his job offer from the PM. Barry was astounded. He looked at Adam and said:

"Mr Carr was right, wasn't he?"

"It looks like it," Adam admitted. "I hope he won't be making any further predictions."

"How will it fit in with your present job?"

"That is what I wanted to talk to you about, Barry. There will be times when I shan't be here and I am thinking to ask Bill to cover the area manager's job together with Sally. You will be in complete charge of the office and we will appoint a new assistant manager. I need to know from

234

you how Kenny Rogers is getting on."

"He is slowly learning the ropes but he lacks enthusiasm. I don't think he is ready for responsibility."

"There is one lady in the main office who has caught my eye," Adam said. "I think her name is Christine. I think we should consider her for the job."

"She works hard and is very sociable," Barry said. "I'll speak to her."

"I shall be moving into my new office on Monday so you can start to move in here on Tuesday. Bill can have your office for now but in time he will have the other upstairs office. Get Kenny to help Laura with moving the files etc."

Barry left the office and Adam called Sally in.

"I expect you have heard where Leah and I are going at the weekend?" he said.

"No, I haven't heard anything. Where are you going?"

"We are spending the weekend at Chequers with the Prime Minister and his wife."

Sally was speechless.

"Have you accepted the job then?" she stammered.

"Not yet. I'll decide after the weekend. I shall be leaving at lunchtime on Friday."

"How does Leah feel?"

"She is okay now she has got over the shock. We are the only guests so it will be very informal."

"How will you manage the two jobs?"

"I have asked Bill to stand in for me if I'm away and I'll appoint a new assistant for Barry. He will be kept busy being in charge of the Branch."

"Everything is happening so quickly."

"Yes, but it is all under control," Adam said firmly. "When will the invitations be ready?"

"They will be here tomorrow."

"Good," said Adam. "Let's make a list of people to invite. I'm just about to speak with Bill so we'll do it in an hour's time."

Sally left and five minutes later Bill arrived. He sat down opposite Adam and waited for him to speak.

"I think I have told you that I have been offered a job by the PM. Leah and I are going to stay at Chequers this weekend and I shall make my decision after that. If I do decide to accept it, I would like you to deputize for me as the area manager with help from Sally. Barry will have full control of the main office and I will appoint another assistant manager to help him."

"I can't believe that you are going to spend the weekend with the Prime Minister. You must feel very honoured."

"Yes, I suppose we do. I have told Alice and Barry and like them, you must keep the secret."

"Even if you haven't made up your mind about the job, you have obviously thought about the implications of it. I would be very willing to do what you suggest at the same time as working out the educational programme."

"That's good," Adam said gratefully. "I'm glad that is all in place. Now, have you chosen a date for the wedding?"

"We were thinking about Saturday 23rd March. That is two weeks before Easter."

"That is fine as far as I know but you need to check it out with Leah."

"We will do that this evening," Bill said. "It will be at the registry office and only a few guests. We thought we would have the reception at a local hotel where my family could stay as well."

"That is a good idea but you will have to book it up soon. Easter is a popular time for weddings."

"We'll make a decision this evening," said Bill.

He returned to the main office and Adam called Sally. She came in with a pile of invitations and her notebook.

"Let's check the list," Adam said. "We had better ask Dominic whom he would like to invite. Can you get him on the phone?"

Sally went back to her office and Adam studied the list on the desk.

He read the names of the Board members and the area managers and realised they should invite some local people as well. His phone rang.

"Dominic is on the phone," said Sally.

"Good morning, Dominic."

"I'll be down tomorrow morning," he said. "And I'll bring a list with me."

Sally returned and sat down with her notebook.

"I want you to take note of the names of the school headteachers in the Oxford area," Adam said. "If we invite them to the opening, they will be fully aware of what we will be offering them. I suppose we could even rent out the room to other employers when we are not using it."

They worked on the list all morning and by lunchtime it was complete.

"You can start writing out the invitations this afternoon," he said, "but we won't post any of them until Monday. Next, we must work out the programme for the day and the catering arrangements."

"We are going to be busy for the next two weeks," Sally said. "Thank goodness I don't have to go up to London. We shall be looking at a house so Dominic will have to come down here."

"I shall have a better idea of my commitments after this weekend," Adam said. "I don't want to go to London either."

She left the office and Adam started to think about the programme for the opening. He called Bill to come and see him. It was half an hour before he arrived and he looked a bit flustered.

"I'm sorry to be late," he gasped. "Two of the machines have gone wrong this morning. When can we expect out new computers?"

"I'll get on to the engineers," said Adam. "I'll try to get a definite date from them. I wanted to ask you to prepare a short introduction for our educational aspect which you can announce on the opening day."

"I can do that," Bill said. "I'll show you what I am going to say."

At that moment, Julie popped her head around the door.

"Sorry to interrupt," she said. "Bill, Alice is on the phone for you."

Adam indicated he should go and take the call. He left the room and when he returned, he was smiling.

"Alice has had a letter from the lawyer and he says the final figure will be five hundred and sixty thousand pounds. Now we can start looking for a house."

"She is going to have to work out how best to invest the money," Adam said seriously.

"Yes, we have a lot of thinking to do. The first thing is to find out from Barry the amount of mortgage I can take out."

Bill left the office and Adam sat back in his chair. He reminded himself to take one day at a time as he thought of all the things which needed his attention. There was a knock at the door and Barry came in.

"A van load of assorted goods has just arrived. I've told them to take it all upstairs."

"The small desk needs to come in here," Adam said. "That is for Jessica."

Barry went off to organize that and Adam called Sally.

"We had better go and see what has arrived upstairs," he said.

They left the office and went up to the first floor. There were boxes and packages all over the place, including files and other stationery items, folding tables and display boards.

"We will have to store the stationary in the staff room for now," Adam said, "but we can put the other things in their proper places."

They spent the next couple of hours clearing up and when they had finished the whole place looked clean and business-like.

"When we get the files moved up it will really feel like our new office," Adam said with feeling.

Sally spent the rest of the day sorting out the names of the local headteachers and by the end of the afternoon, she showed it to Adam.

"We'll wait until after Dominic has been tomorrow," he said, "then we will finalise the list."

He was tired when he went home that day and he looked forward to a quiet evening with Leah. Alice drove over to see Bill and once Jessica was in bed, they had the lounge to themselves. Adam told Leah what Bill had said about the wedding and she agreed with his suggestions.

"It will make it easier for me at home," she said, "and we can always invite people back here after the reception."

They talked about possible arrangements until it was time to go to bed. Before they went to sleep, they heard Alice come home.

"I hope they made some decisions," Adam said sleepily but Leah didn't answer. She was fast asleep.

The next day it was very busy in the office. Sally wanted to get all the files upstairs and she persuaded Barry to let her borrow Kenny Rogers. He spent the morning carrying files up to the new offices.

"This will keep you fit," Adam laughed as he passed him on the stairs.

Adam's office was soon cleared and Sally's was finished by lunchtime. Their new offices looked very smart.

"It just needs a large vase of flowers on the reception desk to make it feel really welcoming," said Sally.

In the afternoon, Barry moved into Adam's old office and Laura would be taking Sally's place. Kenny carried Barry's books and files into his new office but they left Laura's until the next morning. It was another busy day and Adam was glad to get home. In the evening Alice spoke to him and Leah,

"We have decided on a date," she said. "Tomorrow I will confirm it with the registrar and book the hotel. It will only be about sixteen guests and we shall have a buffet lunch. Jessica will be my bridesmaid and Bill's brother will be best man. I am going to start looking for houses so that hopefully we will have a place by the time his rental runs out."

"That all sounds straightforward," Leah said. "Let's hope it all goes smoothly."

That night when they were in bed, Adam said:

"Alice will be quite well off. I hope she will invest it wisely."

"You will be able to advise her, won't you?"

"Yes, I could do that but she may need some professional advice."

"I'm sure she will be sensible," Leah said as she turned over to go to sleep.

"I hope she will," he replied, closing his eyes.

The next morning Adam went straight up to his new office. Sally was already in, tidying up her new room and she had brought in some flowers and a vase for the reception desk. Adam sat in his chair and looked around. He had a great feeling of satisfaction that everything had gone smoothly. His phone rang.

"Dominic will be here at about eleven o'clock," said Sally.

Adam went to check that everything was in order. The chairs were set out in the lecture room and the front desk was in place. The stationery was stacked in the staff room. The toilets were in working order and the only thing missing was the lift at the rear for disabled access. Dominic arrived promptly and went straight upstairs. He was most impressed by what he found.

"It is looking great," he said. "You have done a superb job of it, congratulations. You must be proud of what you have achieved."

"It has been a team effort," Adam said, "and I am very pleased that it has turned out so well."

He showed Dominic the list of names that he and Sally had drawn up.

"Have you any names to add to the list?" he asked.

Dominic looked at the list he had brought and then at Adam's.

"It looks pretty comprehensive to me," he said. "There may be one or two late additions but otherwise you have included everyone I had in mind. I think it was a masterstroke to invite the headmasters."

"Sally can start filling out the invitations and we will send them out on Monday," said Adam.

"I need to speak with Sally," Dominic said. "Is she in her office?"

"She is next door. I'll send Julie for some coffee."

Dominic went to find Sally and Julie went for the coffee.

Dominic kissed Sally.

"I've got some good news. I completed the purchase of Kitson Manor this morning so now we can start on the renovations."

"How long is it going to take?"

"About three years and at least three million pounds."

"How are you going to pay for it?" she asked in wonder.

"I have sold the country house I had in Ireland and the farm which I owned in Yorkshire and I intend to sell one of my London houses. That should cover the cost."

"What about the house we hope to buy in this area?"

"I've already got that covered," he said. "We'll have another look at it on Saturday and then decide. I will come down tomorrow and pick you up from work."

He kissed Sally goodbye and shook hands with Adam.

"I hope you have an enjoyable weekend," he said as he left.

Adam busied himself sorting out his files and other papers and Julie made a master copy of the list of guests for the opening. Adam reminded her that he wouldn't be in the office the next day. In mid-afternoon, he tidied up his desk and decided to go home. He said goodbye to Sally and went to tell Bill and Barry that he would see them on Monday. He drove straight home and parked his car on the grass. Alice was in the kitchen preparing the evening meal.

"Where's Jessica?" he asked.

"She's gone to a friend's house, Dad. She will be back for tea."

"She has settled into her new school very nicely."

"She is a sociable girl now that her confidence is returning," Alice said. "She will be okay. Her friends go to a badminton club on a Saturday morning and I think she might start going too. Now I shall have the money to buy anything she needs for her sport. It is a good feeling."

"You are both in a good place," he said, kissing her. "The past is behind you."

"I've booked the registrar for the wedding," she said, "and I've booked a local hotel for the reception and two rooms for Bill's family. I was lucky because they were their last two rooms available for that weekend."

"I want to get this weekend over before I start to think about anything else but at least you and Bill can begin to make some firm plans."

He went into the lounge and found Leah asleep in her chair. He took off his shoes and lay full length on the settee. He closed his eyes and was soon asleep.

The front door shut with a bang and that made them both wake up. The tea was ready and Jessica was very excited.

"I'd like to go with Penny to badminton on Saturday. Can I go, Mum?" she asked.

"Yes, of course, you can," Alice said. "I've got my old badminton racquet upstairs. You can have that to start with. I played a lot of badminton and I was very good at it, wasn't I, Mum?"

"You certainly were," Leah said. "You cost me a pretty penny in kit and racquets and petrol, but it was worth it."

After tea, they sat in the lounge and talked about Alice's news.

"Can I be your bridesmaid?" Jessica asked.

"I wouldn't want anyone else," she said putting her arms around Jessica.

"I'm so happy," Jessica said with tears in her eyes. "We shall be a proper family."

"Yes, you will," said Adam, "and who knows, one day you might have another brother or sister."

"Dad!" Alice exclaimed. "What will you say next?"

Adam just laughed and touched his nose. They relaxed for the rest of the evening and went to bed early.

Chapter Twenty-Two

On Friday morning they didn't get up in a hurry. They had a leisurely breakfast and started to pack their cases. Then they each had a shower and by lunchtime, they were ready to go to meet the Prime Minister. The car arrived at precisely four o'clock and by six o'clock they were at Chequers. Dinner was served at seven and so began their weekend. On Saturday the PM's wife took Leah into the local town to have coffee and cake. In the afternoon they went to a Women's Institute meeting where they had a practical demonstration on making marmalade. While they were out the two men had long conversations. They found that they had many things in common and a mutual respect. They had dinner together on Saturday evening and Leah and Adam felt quite relaxed. On Sunday morning they all went for a walk in a nearby wood and after lunch, they packed their cases. At four o'clock the car arrived and their visit was over.

When they arrived home, they found Bill there with Alice and Jessica. They were pleased to be home and talked about their weekend without mentioning where they had been. When Jessica was in bed and Alice was upstairs Adam spoke more openly to Bill.

"We got on really well with the PM and his wife. They were really nice people with no airs and graces. They were most welcoming."

"So, have you made a decision?" Bill asked innocently.

"I think I have but I need to talk to Leah first."

Alice came back into the room.

"Jessica is hooked on badminton," she said. "She wants all the gear and apparently the instructor said that she has natural ability and was most impressed."

"Like mother, like daughter," said Leah. "You'll soon be ferrying her around every weekend."

"I shall go up with her next Saturday to see how good she really is," said Alice.

After the weekend, Adam went to work on Monday morning feeling very happy. He had talked to Leah the previous evening and she had confirmed his decision to accept the job. Sitting in his new office he phoned Sir Charles Blaine to tell him that he would accept the post of Personal Advisor to the Prime Minister. Once he had done this, he felt the weight lifted from his shoulders and he visibly relaxed. He called Sally and told her about the phone call. She was very pleased that he had agreed to it and kissed him on both cheeks.

"How was your weekend?" he asked her.

"We had a second viewing of the house and we both liked it so Dominic has made an offer. We should get a response in the next day or two."

"No doubt you will be pleased to get settled somewhere together. There is no chain so the vendors might well accept an offer."

"Yes, I think Dominic will be glad to have a proper home again," she said, "and to have his own furniture around him."

"How did you get on with the invitations last Friday?"

"I have to finish them this morning, then they will be ready for your signature."

"I'll get on with signing the ones which are ready," he said. "I'd like to get them posted today."

Sally brought the pile of envelopes to Adam and went back to her office to complete the rest. He was kept busy all morning and by lunchtime, they were all ready to be posted. The invitations had specified eleven o'clock until two o'clock so Adam began to work out the details of the day. Guests would arrive and refreshments would be available including wine, coffee and various nibbles. At twelve o'clock he would make a welcoming speech and at twelve-thirty Bill would explain the education side. For the last hour, more refreshments would be available and there would be time for questions. The programme of events would be displayed on the screen and on the reception desk.

He showed the plan to Sally and she was in favour of it.

"Now we have to book the caterers," she said. "I'll see who is available locally." She contacted several local companies but they couldn't provide what was needed. "I'll speak with Dominic," she said. "Maybe we can get the company caterers to do something like they did for our wedding."

"That covers most things," Adam said. "Now we just have to wait for the replies."

He decided to go downstairs to see how Barry was getting on with his move. He found his old office in a mess with books and papers on every surface. He went to speak to Laura who was looking flushed and worried.

"All of Mr Wilson's files and books have been moved but he hasn't had time to sort them out. He has had two clients this morning and Mr Birch has been busy sorting out the computers," she said breathlessly.

"The new computers should be here next week," said Adam. "The old ones are wearing out. Tell Mr Wilson to come and see me when he is free and you must get a junior from the main office to help you out."

He went into the main office to speak to Bill and then back upstairs. Sally came into the main office.

"I've spoken to Dominic," she said, "and he will arrange for the catering department to deal with the refreshments. They will send someone down to find out exactly what you require."

"Thank you very much," Adam said. "That will be most helpful."

There was a knock at the door and Barry walked in.

"You wanted to see me?" he said.

"Yes," replied Adam. "You seem to be overstretched at the moment and I wondered if there is anything I can do to help?"

"All my files and books were moved last Friday but I have been too busy to sort them out. I have clients every morning and have to spend time with Laura in the afternoons. Bill has a full-time job looking after the computers so he can't help much."

"Would you like me to see your morning clients?" asked Adam. "Then you can spend some time sorting out your new office. There is one more thing, Laura must have some help. She is getting stressed out and we must do something about it."

"I'll see if there is anyone in the main office who would like to help her out. You said something about another assistant manager for when Bill goes upstairs," Barry said. "Have you thought any more about that?"

"I'd like to speak to one of the ladies. I think her name is Christine."

"Shall I tell her you want to see her?"

"Yes please," said Adam. "As soon as possible."

"If I could have a couple of free mornings, I could get my office sorted out," Barry said, "and then I could help Laura with her move."

"That can be arranged," Adam said and Barry left the room feeling a lot better.

Ten minutes later there was another knock on the door and Christine came in. They talked about the possible promotion and she was very interested. Adam told her to come back the next day with her decision. He then told Sally that he would be helping Barry out for the next two days and suggested that Julie might be able to help Laura out at the same time.

The following morning Christine went to Adam and told him that she would accept the assistant manager's post under Barry. Adam was pleased and he called Barry who was happy with the arrangement.

"I put a notice up about the assistant secretary's job," said Barry. "And one of the girls has shown an interest. I will interview her this afternoon and perhaps you could see her tomorrow. It will mean that we shall need two new cashiers."

"That shouldn't be a problem. Just put a notice up in the main office," Adam said as he prepared to interview Barry's clients.

Barry went into his new office and looked around. It was much bigger than his old office and he was looking forward to working there. He took off his coat and started to sort out his books and files. By lunchtime, he had cleared his desk and filled his wastepaper basket. In the afternoon he started to move some of Laura's files and called Kenny Rogers to help him. He had a chat with Beth who was interested in the secretarial job and arranged for her interview with Adam.

Adam was relieved that the staffing problems were being resolved. He knew that a happy staff was needed in order to run an efficient office. He looked at the books all neatly arranged in his new office and he thought of all the files stacked up in Sally's room. He decided he had to get to grips with the area manager's responsibilities, which he hadn't given much thought to lately.

When he arrived home that evening, he found the conservatory floor covered in empty boxes. Piles of linen were everywhere and Alice was sitting in the middle of it.

"Dominic has enough table linen here to furnish a marquee," she said. "I must let Sally see it and sell any pieces she does not want. Can you bring her here tomorrow evening, Dad?"

"I'll ask her in the morning, Alice."

"I spoke to Matthew Dunn today," she said. "He has a large bank transfer ready for me and he wants to know where he should send it. I said I would ask you."

"If you send it to your bank account you need to warn your bank manager first, otherwise it might create a problem for him. You could put it in a Building Society account with us. It would be solely in your name and we would know the origin of it."

"I think I'd rather do that," she said. "There would be two of you there keeping an eye on it."

"You wouldn't keep it there for too long," he said. "When you have paid your share of a house then you must look to invest the rest in the best possible way."

"I shall get an allowance for Jessica until she leaves school and that will go a long way towards uniform and sports equipment and I shall be earning something as well. I think we shall be comfortably off."

"Where are you going to look for a house?"

"We are looking in this area," Alice said. "A house like this would suit us very nicely."

"It is certainly convenient for the schools and the town," Adam said, "but they don't come on the market very often. Let us hope that you are lucky."

That evening Alice drove to Bill's house and Leah put Jessica to bed.

"Grandma," she said. "Will mummy invite Jonathan to her wedding?"

"She will probably invite him but I'm not sure that he would come. Do you miss him?"

"I do sometimes," Jessica admitted, "but I wouldn't want to go back there."

"I doubt that he would recognise you. You are now quite grown up. I'm sure you will see him again one day."

"My friend Penny has a brother and they get on okay."

"When I was a little girl, I had no brothers or sisters but I had some really good friends," said Leah. "I'm sure you will do the same."

Leah went back downstairs to Adam and told him what Jessica had said.

"I wonder if Alice misses Jonathan?" he said. "She has never mentioned his name."

"I'm sure she misses him but she is concentrating on her new life," she said.

They settled down for a relaxed evening and early to bed.

The rest of the week passed quickly. Laura moved into her new office and Barry sorted out his room. Everyone was very busy and at the weekend Adam's new settees were delivered. The lounge in his apartment was over-crowded with furniture but he hoped it would not be long before he could get rid of the cream leather sofas.

At work, the guestlist for the opening was beginning to take shape and Adam was kept busy arranging accommodation for some of them. There was a good response from local schools and from the area managers.

"We shall need some name badges," Adam said and Julie went to buy them.

The catering department was providing the food and drink and a couple of technicians were going to be present to explain the new computer system. Adam alerted the rest of the staff as to what was going to happen on the day.

Thursday 23rd February was fast approaching but during that week, Adam had to go to London for the initial introduction to his new job. He met the Prime Minister and the rest of the Cabinet in Downing Street and spent two days familiarising himself with security and other procedures.

He was back in his office on Wednesday morning and checked all the final details with Sally. Then he sat at his desk to write his speech. He thought back to when he had first come to Oxford and to the initial discussion with Barry about what should be done with the upstairs space. He thought about meeting Leah again and how fortunate he was that she had been so forgiving. He thought about his own personal journey during the past seven months and the changes he had experienced in his life. He suddenly realised that he was no longer frightened of change but was ready to embrace whatever came his way. That thought lifted his spirits and he had no trouble writing his speech.

On the day of the opening, Adam was early to work. The catering staff arrived at eight-thirty and unloaded their equipment and the food. Adam went to check that all was in order then he went into the main office to reassure the staff. He alerted the reception desk and chose two staff members to direct the guests upstairs. At twelve o'clock the guests began to arrive and soon there was quite a crowd. Adam was looking out for Sir Humphrey and Lady Monica when Dominic arrived. He went straight up to find Sally and hustled her into her office.

"I've got some good news," he said cheerfully. "They have accepted my offer on the house and it should be completed next week."

Sally was overjoyed and kissed him.

"A home of our own," she said. "I can't wait."

They went out into the main area and Dominic went up to Adam and shook his hand.

"Congratulations! You've done an excellent job here."

"Thank you, Dominic but I am waiting for Sir Humphrey to come before I make my speech."

Dominic looked at his watch.

"He should be here any time now. Sir Charles had a meeting this morning but that was due to finish at eleven. Father is coming with him."

"I didn't know that Sir Charles was coming."

"It was a last-minute decision," Dominic said. "Actually, the PM wanted to come but he was delayed so he has sent Sir Charles instead."

Just then Adam heard a voice coming up the stairs.

"Take it slowly, my dear. Nearly at the top."

Sally stepped forward towards the stairs.

"Lady Monica," she said. "How nice to see you. Take my arm and I'll find you a chair."

"Thank you, my dear," Lady Monica said as she puffed her way to a chair. "These two gentlemen are too busy chatting."

Sir Humphrey kissed Sally and Sir Charles kissed her hand, then they went to find Adam who was talking to Dominic.

"We were wondering where you were, father."

"Traffic, roadworks, accidents. It all conspired against us this morning," said Sir Charles.

"Help yourself to refreshments," Adam said. "I shall be doing my welcoming speech in ten minutes. I'm still waiting for Leah. She said she would try to be here by one o'clock."

Sally took Lady Monica into the lecture room and sat her down. She put a reserved notice on the seats either side of her, one for Leah and one for herself. It was not long before Leah came. She greeted Lady Monica.

"I had to go into school this morning and then I had trouble parking in Oxford. I thought I was going to be late."

"You have made it in time," Lady Monica consoled her. "Adam is about to make his speech."

The room was rapidly filling up and people were standing at the back. Adam stood up and the room fell silent. He spoke for about twenty minutes and then invited questions. Finally, he introduced Bill who spoke about the educational aspects of the new venture. There were more questions and then the speeches were over. Adam had prepared some leaflets which set out the general aims with a telephone number to call and he left them on the front desk. He noticed that many of the school representatives took one. The guests began to drift away and Sally took Leah and Lady Monica into her office. She brought them a cup of tea and went to see if Adam needed her. She found him in his office talking to Sir Humphrey and Sir Charles. Dominic was in the main room chatting with the area managers. Sally went back to her office and sat down.

"The last few days have been hectic," she said, "but I think it has passed off very well."

"I thought it was very well organised," Lady Monica said and turning to Leah she added, "Your husband is a very capable man. He will be a great asset to the PM."

Adam rang through on Sally's intercom.

"Will you go and tell the caterers to take the rest of the food down to the staff room?"

Sally excused herself and went to find the man in charge then she returned to her office. She told them about the new house and Leah told Sally about all the linen which Alice had found. Lady Monica was most interested.

"You must keep all of it, Sally," she said. "You never know when you might need it at Kitson Hall."

"At least we shall have somewhere to store it," Sally said. "We shall have more than enough bedrooms in the new house."

The door opened and Sir Humphrey came in.

"A most successful day," he said cheerfully. "I've met lots of very interesting people."

"I've enjoyed it too," said Lady Monica. "It's nice to see Leah and Sally again. We must visit Dominic's new house soon."

"Yes, of course, we will do that. We'll bring the champagne the minute he takes up residence. Now it is time for us to leave. The car will be here in ten minutes and you have to negotiate the stairs."

"Don't worry, I will come with you," Sally said as she helped Lady Monica to her feet.

Adam came in to say goodbye and Sally helped Lady Monica down the stairs.

"Movement on the divorce front," Sir Humphrey said to Dominic. "I'll speak to you tomorrow." He kissed Leah and then he was gone.

"I'd like to take Sally home now," Dominic said. "Is that okay?"

"Yes, that's fine. We'll clear up the mess tomorrow," Adam said. "It's been a busy day but a successful one."

"The feedback will be interesting," said Dominic, thoughtfully. "I think it will be quite positive."

Sally went to get her coat and Dominic kissed Leah and shook hands with Adam. When they had gone Leah said:

"Are you pleased with the result of all your hard work?"

"I am delighted," Adam said as he kissed her. "Now let us go home and I'll take you out for a celebratory dinner."

They left the office and drove their cars home. Then Adam took Leah to his favourite pub and they had fish and chips with a bottle of wine. Several of the area managers were also staying at the pub and they all had a drink together.

"Are you sure you are fit to drive home?" Leah asked.

"I only had two glasses of wine," Adam said. "The rest was water."

He drove home carefully and they went into the house. Alice and Bill were there and Alice was holding a white envelope.

"This says that five hundred and sixty thousand pounds has been deposited in a Building Society account for me."

"You are a rich woman," Adam said. "I shall know where to go when I am short of a penny."

"I must admit that it rather frightens me," Alice said. "It is so much."

"When you have decided what to do with it, you will feel much better," said Bill.

"Well, it is safe for now," Adam said, "and it is helping to pay my salary and Bill's."

"I shall start looking for a house tomorrow," Alice decided. "It is only a month till the wedding and buying a house usually takes at least six weeks."

She went out to make a cup of tea.

"The staff didn't take long to finish off the food which was left over," said Bill. "I think they really enjoyed it."

"I'm glad about that," Adam said. "It made them feel part of the celebrations."

"It was a good day, Adam. And I had a lot of enquiries about the educational possibilities."

"We must not forget that it was primarily organised for the area managers. It sounds as if I shall have to book it in when I want to use it," Adam joked.

"It has been a long day," Bill said. "It is time I went back to my place."

Adam and Leah drank their tea.

"I'm ready for bed too," said Adam. "Let's have an early night."

They went upstairs and were soon cuddled up under the duvet. Adam put his arms around Leah and pulled her close.

"A perfect end to a perfect day," he said as he kissed her.

Chapter Twenty-Three

There was a cold north wind blowing as Adam walked from the car park to his office. He was the General Manager of the largest Building Society in Oxford and he was glad to walk through the main door into the warmth of his office. He said good morning to the staff who were already in their places and went upstairs. He looked around him with satisfaction. The new office had been opened two weeks ago and already there was a buzz of activity. He knew that today was going to be very busy and he went straight in to his secretary. He expected to see Sally but it was Julie, her assistant, who greeted him.

"Sally is caught in traffic," she said, "She will be a little late."

"You must go and check that everything is ready for the meeting," he said, "and then take your place at the reception desk. I will answer any phone calls."

Adam had organised a seminar for the local managers to discuss company policy and to share ideas for forward planning. It was the first meeting in the new lecture room and he wanted it to go smoothly. He called Bill who was the education manager and the general assistant. Bill came into the office carrying two cups of coffee and an impressive-looking file.

"What have you got there?" Adam asked.

Bill smiled at him.

"It contains my important information," he said. "It is the status symbol of my new position."

"That's a good start," said Adam, laughing. "We must see if we can fill it up without delay. Now is everything ready for the meeting?"

"Yes, it's all arranged. I'll get one of the girls from downstairs to serve the coffee if Sally doesn't arrive in time."

Just then a very breathless Sally appeared in the doorway.

"I'm so sorry," she gasped. "Dominic always insists on bringing me in to work on a Monday morning even though I remind him about the traffic."

"Don't worry, Sally. It's all under control," said Adam.

"I'll go and start the coffee machine," she said. "The first guests should be arriving soon," and she hurried away.

"Before anyone leaves at the end of the meeting, I would like you to give a brief description of what we are proposing to do for local secondary schools. We could also include training courses for assistant managers," said Adam.

"I'll go downstairs and see if Barry needs any help and wait for Julie to let me know when you are ready," Bill said as he left the office.

The managers were beginning to arrive. Adam greeted each one and Sally served them coffee and biscuits. Soon the room was full and Adam addressed the meeting. There was time for a discussion and a question-and-answer session. Before it closed, Bill explained about the education programme and this led to more questions. By lunchtime, everyone had left and Adam was able to reflect on a very successful seminar. He called Sally into his office.

"Everything went very smoothly, Sally. I'm really pleased with the result."

"It all depends on careful planning," she said. "And that is something that you are very good at."

She sat down on a chair and sighed.

"You look tired," he said. "Did you have a busy weekend?"

"Dominic has completed the purchase of Kitson Manor and he was planning the renovations for most of the weekend. We went and had a more detailed look at the house we are buying in the next village and thinking about furniture and I have to decide what to do with my house. My brain is tired of making decisions."

"I think you should concentrate on the new house," said Adam. "Dominic will appoint a project manager to oversee the work at Kitson Manor and you can't have much input into that. When you have moved into your new house then you can decide what to do about your present house."

"It is going to be an organisational nightmare," Sally sighed, "All Dominic's furniture will be coming out of storage and I have no idea what he has. Thank goodness we shall have spare rooms where we can store some of the larger items. The only definite thing that we shall need will be a new bed."

"A very important piece of furniture," Adam said with a twinkle in his eye.

"I think you are right. Dominic will be kept busy at Kitson Manor and I shall be busy sorting out the new house. I may have to take some time off."

"You know you can have whatever time off you need. I can't refuse a request from the wife of the Managing Director. In any case, Julie is now quite able to take your place when necessary."

"The new intercom system is working well," she said as a message came through from the office next door.

"Sir Charles Blaine wishes to speak with you."

"Put him through," Adam said as Sally left his office.

"Good morning Adam, I trust you are well?"

"Yes, thank you, Sir Charles. We have just finished our first manager's seminar and it all went smoothly. I am pleased with the result."

"That is encouraging. I need to arrange for you to come to the PM's office for your security briefing. Would this Thursday and Friday be convenient for you?"

"Yes, I could manage that."

"Good," said Sir Charles. "It will be in the PM's office and will start at 11 am. Let me know what time your train arrives and I will arrange for a car to meet you at the station."

"Thank you. I assume I can arrange my own accommodation for the night?"

"Yes, you can do that, all expenses paid of course but we shall need to know where you are staying in order to collect you on Friday morning."

"I'll confirm the time of my arrival tomorrow."

"I'll phone your secretary," said Sir Charles.

Adam sat back in his chair and closed his eyes. This promised to be an interesting experience, he thought as he rang for Sally to come into his office. She came in with her notebook and diary.

"I shall be out of the office on Thursday and Friday," he said and told her where he was going. "This is absolutely confidential. Don't even tell Barry or Bill where I shall be. Just say I have some business in London."

"Where will you be staying?"

"I thought I would book into the Grosvenor," he replied. "I've been there before and it will feel familiar."

"I'm sure Sir Humphrey will have dinner with you on Thursday evening if you would like him to. You would be able to talk to him about the events of the day."

"That is an excellent idea," he said. "Sir Humphrey is the only person I could talk to. I need to talk to you about my work here but first of all, I think it is coffee time."

Sally went off to get the coffee and Adam tried to collect his thoughts. He knew he would have to learn how to switch between the two jobs. Sally came back into the room.

"It is still my intention to visit all the offices in my area," Adam said. "But it is going to need some careful planning. I want you to divide the area into sections with three or four offices within a reasonable distance of one another. Then I can make maximum use of my time when I am in each section."

"I'll start by looking at the number of offices in each county then I'll divide it up from there."

"That's a good idea," he said, "See if you can get a blown-up picture of the area to go on the wall then we can work out the actual distances between each office."

"It will mean an overnight stay for some of the visits. How do you feel about that?"

"I shan't mind that. I have a feeling that there will be overnight stays in London too."

"Who will be in charge here?"

"I shall leave Bill as my temporary manager and he will work with you. Barry can spare him now that he has a new assistant manager and I am always there on the other end of a phone if necessary."

"When do you hope to start these visits?"

"I think I will wait until the spring for the longer trips, Sally. But I could be getting on with the more local ones. In any case, I should know more about my commitments after this Friday."

"I'll go and see if I can find a suitable map to enlarge," she said, "It should be a very interesting exercise."

As she left the office, almost immediately his phone rang.

"Mr West wishes to speak with you," said Julie.

"Put him through. Good morning, Dominic. How are you today?"

"I've just arrived at the office to a mountain of paperwork," Dominic said grumpily.

"It makes you appreciate the value of a good secretary," Adam said soothingly.

"I've got a good secretary," he said shortly. "I've also got the Monday blues."

"Cheer up, half your paperwork is probably junk mail."

"I expect you are right," Dominic said a little more cheerfully. "I have a message here from Father. He wants me to have lunch with him at the club. He says it is important."

"Well, that is something to look forward to. A good lunch and a fine bottle of wine will soon make you feel better."

"It is the important bit that bothers me. I think it may have something to do with the divorce."

"I've no doubt there are going to be problems with it," Adam said, "but you have to deal with each one as it comes. It is no good anticipating anything."

"I know how difficult Mother can be. I just hope that Father is strong enough to stand up to her. Anyway, I'm really ringing to let you know that my furniture will be arriving at the new house next Tuesday. I shall have to be there because some of the larger pieces will have to stay in storage until Kitson Manor is completed. Sally will have to be there but do you think you could be there too? I could do with some moral support."

Dominic was sounding a bit desperate and Adam assured him that it could be arranged.

"That's a big relief," he said. "Now can I speak with Sally?"

"I'll put you through," Adam said as he pressed the intercom.

Dominic had a short conversation with his wife and when it was over, she came into Adam's office.

"He really must calm down," she said, "or he will make himself ill."

"What are you going to do about your house?" asked Adam.

"I'm not going to rush into doing anything. We shall still need somewhere to live until we have finished the new house properly. I have to be at the new house on Monday to receive the keys from the estate agents, so I am going to have to take next Monday and Tuesday off. Is that okay?"

"Yes of course it is," he said quickly. "It looks as if I shall be there with you on Tuesday."

He told her what Dominic had asked him.

"I shall have to buy a kettle and some mugs," she said. "It looks as if my coffee-making skills will be needed. I must remember to do that at the weekend."

I'm sure Alice will come over to help you if you would like her to? Dominic's surprise Christmas presents are going to be very useful. Now let us get down to some work. Have you found a map?"

"Not yet. I may have to photocopy each section and then fit them together on the wall."

"That will be an interesting exercise," he said thoughtfully. "Make sure each section is on the same scale."

Sally went back to her office and Adam decided to stretch his legs. It was nearly his lunch break and he went downstairs to speak with Barry. He couldn't find him in the main office and he went to find Laura, Barry's secretary. It was strange to be going into his old office but he was pleased to see that Laura had settled in very nicely.

"You seem to have everything under control," he said to her with a smile.

"It is so nice to have more space," she replied. "Everything has its proper place and it makes such a difference."

"Where is Mr Wilson?"

"He is with a client. Shall I tell him that you want to see him?"

"I'm just going out for lunch," he said. "I'll see him when I get back," and he left the room.

On his way out he saw Bill and asked him to come to his office at two o'clock.

He walked out into the street and immediately turned the collar up on his overcoat. A cold wind was blowing a few snowflakes around and the sky was dark and menacing. Adam hurried up to the warmth of his favourite bistro and ordered a bowl of soup. Bridget, the waitress, brought it with her usual smile.

"You look very happy, "Adam said to her. "What have you been up to?"

"My boyfriend is coming from Holland on Saturday," she said, "and he will be staying with me for three days. I am really looking forward to it."

"It looks as if he is bringing some Dutch snow with him," Adam laughed as he took the bowl from her hands.

The soup was delicious and it quickly warmed him up. As he left the bistro to return to the office, he had a thought. He went into W.H Smiths, found the travel maps and chose one which said South West of England. It was exactly what he needed. He then looked for the West Country version and when he looked at them together it showed him all the details he needed. He bought the maps and hurried back to his office. He called Sally and showed them to her. She was delighted.

"I've been looking all over the place and couldn't find anything suitable," she said. "These are ideal. Let's study them and find the best way to display them. We'll pin them on the wall tomorrow."

`Adam and Sally spent the next day fixing the maps to the wall. They studied them carefully and Sally produced some large-headed colourful pins which they used to indicate the position of the various offices. It looked very impressive and gave a clear picture of the distances between towns.

"This is going to be very useful," Adam said. "It will mean that I can plan my visits very clearly. Next week we will look at those offices which are nearest to Oxford."

Sally was looking closely at the maps.

"There are so many places that I have never visited. We think nothing of flying abroad for a holiday when there must be dozens of beautiful places right here."

"I've never been to Devon or Cornwall," he said. "There might be an opportunity to take Leah with me and we can have a short break."

"I'm sure she would love that. I might even suggest a weekend away to Dominic. I know he is going to get rather over-stressed."

"I need to talk to Bill about my being away from the office on Thursday and Friday. Ask him to come to see me as soon as he is free?"

Sally left to find Bill and Adam began to think about his visit to London. When she returned, he asked her to phone the Grosvenor and book him in for the Thursday night. Then he spoke to Dominic on the phone. He told him where he would be and asked if he thought Sir Humphrey would have dinner with him that evening.

"I'm sure he would be delighted to," Dominic said. "Have you got his telephone number?"

"No, I haven't," Adam replied. "I'm not sure how to contact him."

"I'll give you his number," Dominic said. "It is the phone he takes his private calls on."

"Thank you," Adam said as Dominic dictated the number. "I will ring him straight away."

He finished talking to Dominic and then dialled Sir Humphrey's number. They had a short conversation and arranged to meet on Thursday evening.

There was a knock on the door and Bill came into the office.

"You wanted to see me?" he said.

"Yes, Bill. I need to talk about Thursday and Friday. I am leaving you in charge of this office, together with Sally. I have to go to London on other business and while I am away you can have use of this office. I'll give you a number where you can contact me at the hotel, in case of any emergencies but I really don't anticipate any problems. I shall be in on Monday but on Tuesday I have promised Dominic to be at his new house when his furniture arrives. Sally won't be here on Monday or Tuesday so you will be on your own. Julie is quite competent so she will help you out. How do you feel about what I have told you?"

"I am ready to take the responsibility that you are offering as long as you feel sure that I can handle it," Bill replied seriously.

"I am sure you can handle it. So that is put in place and I have every confidence in leaving you in charge. Now, there is something else I want to ask you, how are the wedding plans going and have you found a house?"

"The date is fixed for the Saturday before Easter weekend and the hotel is booked for the reception. My family are booked into the same hotel so now it is just sorting out the guest list. That shouldn't take long since it is mainly Alice's family and a few mutual friends. I think Alice wants to talk to you and Leah about it."

"We will have a discussion one evening soon," Adam said. "Have you found a house yet?"

"We want to be sure to be in the right catchment area for Jessica's next school so we are looking in the area where you live but there are not many houses on the market. We have registered with a local estate agent and we are in a good position because it won't take long to arrange a mortgage and Alice can put down a substantial deposit."

"I hope it won't be too long before you find somewhere," Adam said thoughtfully. "I know Alice's money is earning interest but it could be put to a far better use."

"I'm sure something will turn up," Bill said cheerfully.

Adam was deep in thought but eventually, he said:

"You can always move into the apartment as a temporary measure or you could rent Sally's house for a while?"

"I hope we shall find something soon but thank you for your offer," Bill said. "We weren't planning on a honeymoon so perhaps we could just use the apartment after the wedding. I shall have to remember to give notice on my present house and decide what to do about my furniture."

262

"That will probably have to go into storage until you have found a house. My furniture is in storage too so hopefully, you will be able to furnish your house without having to buy anything."

"That will be very helpful. Weddings can be expensive however simple you try and keep them."

"I'm sure to see you at the weekend and we'll talk about it then. After all, Alice is my daughter," he said as he stood up. "Now I must go and have a word with Barry before I leave the office."

Bill returned to the main office and Adam went to find Barry. He checked with him that everything was running smoothly and told him that he would be back on Monday morning. Then he said goodbye to Sally and collected his briefcase. Outside it was cold and nearly dark and he was glad to be going home.

The house was warm and welcoming even though there was no-one at home. Adam stretched out on the settee and was soon fast asleep. He was woken by the sound of Jessica's voice as she came into the lounge with a friend.

"Hello grandad," Jessica said. "You're home early. This is my friend Poppy. We are going to do our homework upstairs," and they left the room.

Adam was just about to stand up when the door opened again and Alice and Leah came into the lounge.

"You are home early this evening, Dad. It is nice and warm in here."

Leah bent down and kissed him.

"Are you alright?" she asked anxiously. "It's not like you to leave work early."

"I'm fine. I couldn't settle to do anything in the office so I thought I might as well come home. I suppose I couldn't stop thinking about the next two days. By the way, Alice, will you take me to the station in the morning? I want to catch the 8.40 am train."

"Yes of course I will. I just hope we don't have too much snow."

Adam spent a quiet evening at home and went to bed early. He was feeling rather apprehensive about the next two days and woke early on Thursday morning. By eight o'clock he was packed and ready to leave.

Chapter Twenty-Four

The journey to the station was uneventful and the train arrived on time. Adam found a seat and opened the newspaper which he had bought. He had never been really interested in politics although he had always carefully studied the financial markets. When he arrived in London, he was met by a chauffeur who drove him to the PM's office, where he was met by Sir Charles Blaine.

"Most of the day will be taken up with your security briefing," Sir Charles said, "but the PM would like you to have a light lunch with him at one o'clock. Tomorrow you will sit with him at various committee meetings as an observer."

Adam was whisked away by one of the security staff and his initiation into the world of politics began. By the end of the day, he was exhausted and glad to be taken back to his hotel. He went straight up to his room and lay on the bed, his head spinning from all the information he had been given. He closed his eyes and wished he was under his own double duvet. He had to phone Leah, he thought as he fell asleep.

Two hours later, he woke with a start and saw it was dark outside. He looked at his watch, nearly seven o'clock; he suddenly remembered he had to meet Sir Humphrey. He had a quick wash and went downstairs to the dining room. Relieved to find that his guest had not yet arrived, he went to the bar for a drink to steady his nerves. Shortly after, Sir Humphrey joined him. They chatted briefly before moving to their table. Adam ordered the wine and they were soon enjoying their meal. Inevitably the conversation turned to the events of the day.

"How was your first day in your new job?" Sir Humphrey asked in an innocent voice.

Adam looked at him and smiled.

"I felt like Daniel in the den of lions," he said. "By the end of the day, my head was spinning."

Sir Humphrey laughed out loud.

"I remember my first day," he chuckled. "At the end of it, all I wanted to do was to resign there and then. But Melissa wouldn't let me. That is the kindest bit of advice she ever gave me."

"It is a completely different world to mine," said Adam. "There is a strict hierarchy and no-one steps outside their allotted place."

"That is true, Adam. You must remember that you are entering at the higher level. You have not had the experience of rising through the lower ranks and you must be careful not to upset the protocol. There will be many people whose job it is to serve you and you must accept your superior position. There are not many men who will have more influence on the PM than you."

Adam looked at him in dismay.

"I had no idea that the responsibility was so great. I'm not sure that I can handle it."

"My advice to you," Sir Humphrey said firmly, "is to do what is asked of you to start with and not to get involved in anything outside your remit. Then as you become more confident, you can gradually increase your input."

"I'll remember that, Sir Humphrey. How is Dominic? I haven't spoken to him lately."

He thought for a moment.

"He is very busy with the plans for Kitson Manor as well as his normal work and I must admit that I feel rather guilty."

Adam looked at him in surprise.

"I don't understand. Why do you feel guilty?"

"There are problems with my divorce and I had a long chat with him about it on Monday. I feel I may have added to his worries," Sir Humphrey sighed and poured himself another glass of wine. "Melissa is demanding more than her fair share and I am not prepared to give it to her."

"Surely that is a problem for the solicitors to sort out? Adam said in surprise. "I understand she won't be on her own when the divorce goes through so it isn't as if she will have to support herself."

"I am giving her the house as the main part of the divorce settlement but she insists that she wants the contents as well and I will not agree to that. I inherited some of the furniture from my parents and it is quite valuable. There are also some other bits and pieces which belong to my family and which I want to pass on to Dominic. They will fit nicely in

Kitson Manor. Thank goodness she doesn't know about the family jewels locked away in the bank vault."

Adam looked at him in astonishment.

"Are you saying that you have kept that a secret all your married life?"

"Somehow the opportunity never arose," Sir Humphrey said in an innocent voice and with a twinkle in his eye. "One day Sally will have a diamond ring on every finger if she so wishes."

Adam laughed out loud.

"I really can't imagine that," he chuckled. "Maybe she will have a pet pig with a diamond ring in its nose," and the two men spluttered into their drinks.

When they had recovered their composure, Adam ordered another bottle of wine and they retired to the lounge.

"Have you decided where you are going to live?" Adam asked.

"I have accepted Lady Monica's kind offer. As soon as the furniture problem is sorted out, I shall move in with her. She has a very large house and I think she will be pleased to have some company. I shall keep my apartment at the club so that I have a base in the city. I shall have more time to help Dominic with the running of the business while he is busy with Kitson Manor."

"I assume he will appoint a manager to oversee the whole project? It is a big undertaking."

"We already have architects and other specialists working for the company so presumably he will use them." Sir Humphrey said. "I know he has been down several times already. He is also in the process of selling some of the country properties which he inherited."

"His furniture is being delivered to his new home on Tuesday and I have promised to be there to help him. I'm sure Sally will sort things out and I think Alice is going to help her."

"It will be good for him to have a proper home again, Adam. He hasn't had a stable home life for many years. I wonder if Gretchen and George will be coming back soon?"

"There is an annexe at the new house ready for them but I haven't heard Dominic mention their names. It would certainly be helpful to

Sally if they were there."

Sir Humphrey gave a loud sigh.

"I shall be glad when everything is sorted out and this divorce is behind me. I'm looking forward to a more peaceful life with Lady Monica."

"You two will get on very well together," said Adam, smiling. "She will keep a beady eye on you and you will enjoy her company."

"You have another busy day tomorrow," Sir Humphrey said as he stood up. "You will find it most interesting at your first Cabinet meeting. There will probably be one or two surprises too."

"Life is full of surprises at present," he said drily. "I shan't be sorry to get back to Leah. She is very good at putting things into perspective."

The two men shook hands and Sir Humphrey left but Adam stayed in the lounge. He poured himself another glass of wine and sat back in his chair. So much had happened during the day that he felt exhausted and yet his mind was full of so many different thoughts. There was one particular question that troubled him: how had he managed to find himself in the situation which now faced him? Twelve months ago, he had been a normal building society manager. Six months ago, his life had changed dramatically and now he found himself talking with government officials and millionaires. He was totally unable to understand how he had arrived in this position. He remembered Mr Carr's prediction that he was destined for higher things. He remembered Barry's and Bill's comments about him but how could they foresee things about him when he was not aware of them himself?

He felt very confused so he drank up his wine and went up to his room, deciding he needed to hear a bit of common sense. When he phoned Leah, it was comforting to hear her voice and they had a long conversation. At the end of it, he felt much calmer and he looked forward to a good night's sleep.

He rose early the next morning ready for the day ahead. After breakfast, an official car arrived and took him to the PM's private office. He was introduced to the other members of the Cabinet and given a seat immediately behind the Prime Minister. He listened carefully to the discussions but did not say anything. At the end of the meeting, the PM asked him to accompany him to his private office. They sat and talked for the next hour then the PM said:

"Attending the Cabinet meeting every Friday is an important part of your job because it will be followed by our private discussion on the Cabinet conclusions. I shall want to hear your thoughts on the decisions which have to be made."

"Am I allowed to make notes during Cabinet?" Adam asked.

"Yes, anything you write down will obviously be confidential; it will be for our information only. I shall expect you to be here every Thursday and Friday but if any problems arise, then it might involve extra days. Are you happy with that arrangement?"

"Yes, that is fine," Adam answered. "It means that I can plan my other duties for the beginning of the week."

"Good, that is settled then. Now you need to talk to my private secretary who will provide you with the notebooks etc. which you will need and also explain how to claim your expenses. I shall look forward to seeing you next week unless there is a crisis in the meantime."

Adam left the Prime Minister and went to the office of the Private Secretary. He spent an hour trying to familiarise himself with the different procedures then he left Downing Street and returned to his hotel. He collected his luggage and took a taxi to the station. He was soon on his way back to Oxford, glad to be going home and looking forward to a relaxing weekend before the busy time of next week.

There was no-one at home when he arrived back so he kicked off his shoes and lay full length on the settee. He was soon fast asleep. He didn't hear Leah come in and it was only when she kissed him on the cheek that he realised she was there.

"You're back early," she said. "I wasn't expecting you until later."

"Too many new experiences. My brain couldn't take any more."

"I'll make you a nice cup of tea," she said soothingly, "then you can tell me what you have been doing for the past two days," and she went off to the kitchen.

Adam sat up and stretched. He reached down for his shoes and then stood up. He realised he had been living in a different universe for the past two days and really didn't know what he had done there. He sat down again. Leah came in with the tea and sat beside him.

"You are tired," she said.

"I'm mentally exhausted," he sighed. "I shall never get used to all the pressures and protocol."

"It is going to take time. You are expecting too much too soon."

"I had a good chat with Sir Humphrey at dinner last evening and he said the same thing. But it does worry me that I might get something wrong."

"You will get more confident," she assured him. "But to begin with it is best to keep a low profile and just observe what is happening around you."

Adam put his arms around Leah and kissed her.

"You are so calm and sensible," he said. "Of course, I will follow your advice," and he hugged her.

That evening, as they sat in the lounge with Alice and Bill, the conversation turned to possible guests at the wedding.

"There will only be my mother and brother on my side," Bill said, "but obviously I'd like Barry and Jen to be there too."

"I should like to make sure Jonathan has an invitation but I doubt that he would want to come," Alice said, "and we must let Harriet and Thomas know. Then there is Peter and his family and Sally and Dominic. That makes fifteen adults plus Benjie and Lucy. Jessica will be my bridesmaid and I don't know who Bill will have as his best man."

"I'm going to ask Barry," Bill said. "I have known him for a long time."

"That all sounds fine," Adam said. "I shall pay for the reception and fifteen sounds about right."

"Thank you, Dad," Alice said as she kissed him. "I certainly have no doubts that it will be a happy occasion."

"Have you found a house yet, Bill?" asked Adam.

"We are looking at one on Saturday," he said. "It is around the corner from here and in the right school catchment area for Jessica. It looks quite promising."

"Well, you won't have to buy any furniture to start with. There's all my furniture in store and you have some of your own. You will be able to replace it gradually," said Adam.

"We shall probably end up with two of everything," Bill laughed. "I hope we don't get another toaster as a wedding present."

That night, when they were in bed, Adam looked at Leah and said:

"I wasn't here for Alice's first wedding. You paid for it all."

"I paid for the food at the reception but William's father paid for all the drink. And there was plenty of that!" she added with feeling.

"How many guests were there?"

"About sixty at the reception and about a hundred in the evening," she replied. "I shudder when I remember it."

"Was it really that bad?" Adam asked anxiously.

"I suppose it was fun at the time. It is the result of it that really upsets me."

"This one will be different," Adam said confidently. "Bill is a good man, kind and gentle. They will be very happy and who knows, Jessica might have a brother or sister."

"I'm sure you are right but I hadn't thought about the brother or sister possibility. It would be nice to have a baby in the house," she said dreamily.

"You are a big softie," Adam said as he kissed her goodnight.

Adam was glad to have a quiet and relaxed weekend. Their only visitors were Peter and his children who came to lunch on Sunday. Benjie and Lucy were as noisy as always but Peter was surprisingly quiet. Leah was worried about him and spoke to Adam.

"There is something wrong," she said. "See if you can have a chat with Peter?"

The opportunity came after lunch. Jessica played with Benjie and Lucy in the conservatory while Leah did the washing up in the kitchen. Adam and Peter were in the lounge.

"We haven't seen you for a while," Adam said. "How have you been keeping?"

"I'm sorry we have not been down but we have had a few problems,"

Peter answered. "We are probably going to get divorced."

"I had no idea things were that serious," said Adam, his voice full of concern. "What about the children?"

"They will live with Janet but of course, I shall continue to see them. We shall have to sell the house and Janet will buy her own place."

"But what will you do?" Adam asked anxiously.

"I shall probably rent a small two-bedroomed place so that the children can stay with me sometimes."

"Is there anyone else involved?"

"I believe there is another man and I understand that Benjie and Lucy have already met him," Peter said wearily.

"I'm so sorry that it has come to this. I do hope that we shall still keep in contact with you and the children."

"Of course, you will," Peter said quickly. "Mum would be devastated if she couldn't see her grandchildren and I think you would miss them too."

"I certainly would," Adam said with a smile, "but if there is anything we can do to help, you only have to ask."

"Thank you," Peter said sincerely. "I just hope that it won't upset the children too much."

At that moment Lucy came running in with a book.

"Jessica and Benjie are playing a game so I have come to read you a story," she said as she cuddled up to Adam.

"I'll go and help mother," Peter said. "I've heard Lucy's stories before," and he went into the kitchen to find Leah.

The afternoon went quickly and soon it was time for Peter and the children to leave. Adam carried Lucy out to the car and Leah kissed them all.

"Please keep in touch, Peter and let us know if we can help in any way?"

She waved them goodbye and went back into the house.

That evening Adam and Leah expressed their concern about Peter's situation and resolved to support him in every possible way.

Chapter Twenty-Five

Adam had a good night's sleep and on Monday morning he went into work feeling quite relaxed. He was relieved to find that there were no problems. He could see that Barry was becoming a very competent manager and Bill doing very well as his deputy when he had to be away.

He remembered that Sally was collecting the keys to her new house and he missed having her to chat with. He called Julie into his office and asked if there had been any messages. She explained what had been happening whilst he was away and Adam was surprised how busy Bill had been. It would appear that there was quite a demand for the lecture room, not only from schools but also from various organisations in the city.

"I'll just go and find Mr Birch, Julie. He can fill me in on all the details."

Before he went downstairs, Adam had a good look around the new offices and the lecture room. He felt very satisfied that all his plans had come to fruition. He was pleased to see that the disabled lift was in working order and everything looked clean and tidy. He found Bill in Barry's office and the three men had a discussion about the progress which had been made. Laura brought their coffee and the conversation turned to the subject of Bill's wedding.

"I shall have a field day as best man," Barry said with a laugh. "I have so many stories I can tell about Bill from our University days."

"I was young and carefree in those days," Bill said sounding a little worried. "Just remember that I am a respectable businessman now."

Adam stood up and laughed.

"I wasn't that young at University but I remember the things that the younger students got up to. I'm sure we shall hear some very interesting information. Now I must go and do some work." He went towards the door and stopped. "Don't forget that I shan't be here tomorrow," he said. "I'm helping Dominic at his new house."

He went upstairs and called Julie into his office.

"I think you should speak with Mr Wilson about training one of our junior staff as a receptionist up here. Sally won't always be available and you will have to take on her responsibilities."

"I will do that tomorrow," Julie said. "She could also support Mr Birch as an assistant secretary when he is so busy."

"That is a good idea, Julie. It is important to build up a skill foundation that involves different people. Now I want to try and pinpoint the rest of the office sites on this map."

She fetched the folder and they were busy for the rest of the morning. Adam went out for his usual lunch and when he returned to the office, he found Sally there. She looked exhausted and there was a pile of bags full of shopping on the floor.

"I have been stocking up for tomorrow," she said wearily. "I just wanted to make sure that we had tea and refreshments for everyone. I borrowed a trolley from M&S to get it all here to the office but I don't know how I am going to get it home."

Adam looked at her in surprise.

"Didn't you bring the car to Oxford?"

"No, I came on the bus," Sally said. "I know how difficult it can be for parking. I didn't realise how many bags I would have."

He looked at her and laughed.

"There is a straightforward solution," he said. "Get a taxi."

"That never occurred to me," she said, staring back at him. "I've always thought of taxis as an expensive option. Now I suppose I can afford one."

"Well, it won't break the bank, Sally," he said with a grin. "You can take a taxi straight to your new house. Now Julie will get you a nice cup of coffee while you have a rest."

They sat and chatted about the arrangements for the next day.

"I really must go," she said, standing up. "I've collected the keys to the new house and I'll take a taxi to drop off all these parcels before I get him to take me to my house. I have no doubt Dominic will be phoning me this evening. He is already in a bit of a panic about tomorrow. Thank goodness Gretchen and George will be back the next day and they will help me sort it out."

"I will come over in the morning and bring Alice with me," he said. "What time are you expecting the removals' men?"

"They said it will be any time after 9 am. I shall have to be up early," she sighed. "Dominic is staying at my place tonight so there is no risk of him being caught in traffic in the morning."

Adam called Julie and told her to order a taxi for Sally and they helped to carry the bags down to the main entrance. When it arrived, they loaded it up and said goodbye to Sally.

Julie turned to Adam and said:

"I don't envy her what she has to face tomorrow. It's bad enough moving from one house to another but when your furniture has been in store you can't even remember what you have."

"Sally has a bigger problem," he said. "She hasn't even seen most of the furniture which is coming and some of it will have to stay in storage. It is going to take some time to sort it all out."

Julie went back to the office and Adam went to find Barry and Bill. They were busy in the main office but Bill came over to speak to him.

"Is everything okay?" he asked. "Sally looked flustered."

"She is worried about tomorrow," Adam said. "Dominic is already in a panic."

"Is there anything I can do to help?"

"You can look after things here in your usual efficient way," Adam replied. "That is the best help you can give at present."

"I'll do that. The lecture room bookings are keeping me busy."

"I've told Julie to get another member of staff to train as a receptionist and part-time secretary for you, Bill, so that should make things a bit easier,"

"That will be a great help. Thank you."

Adam went off to see Barry and then he returned to his office. It was the middle of the afternoon and he cleared his desk.

"I'm leaving the office, Julie but I will be in as usual on Wednesday morning."

He collected his briefcase and went out of the main entrance. There was a cold North wind blowing and he turned up his collar. He hurried towards the car park and was soon on his way home.

The next morning, he woke to find a covering of snow on the ground.

"We are going to have a difficult time unloading the van," he said to Leah. "I'll call at the supermarket and get some salt in case there is ice on the ground."

After breakfast, Adam and Alice were soon on their way to meet Sally. When they arrived at the new house, they found the vans already there. The men were having a cup of tea in the kitchen before starting to unload. Dominic was talking to the man in charge. He was telling him that the first furniture to come off the van had to go into the annexe because it belonged to George and Gretchen. That was quickly accomplished and they started to unload the furniture for the main house. There were a great many boxes but fortunately, they were all labelled with the contents. The bedroom and bathroom furniture came next and Sally made sure that the beds were put in the correct rooms. The first van was now empty except for a very large wardrobe. The foreman looked at Dominic and then at the wardrobe. He had noticed that every bedroom had built-in wardrobes.

"Where do you want this one?" he asked.

"I don't want it at all," Dominic replied with feeling. "You can take it back to storage."

The foreman looked relieved. It would have taken six men to get it out of the van!

Alice had been busy in the kitchen making sandwiches and cups of tea. The removal men had found some chairs in the second van so they were able to sit down and rest. Adam and Dominic sat on the chairs with their tea.

"I could do with something a bit stronger," sighed Dominic. "There is still a whole van load of stuff to unload."

They heard the sound of a car coming up the drive.

"I'm not expecting any visitors," he said as he stood up and went to the window. "I don't believe it," he said in a surprised voice. "It's Father."

Adam joined him at the window just in time to see Sir Humphrey getting out of the car carrying a very large bottle of champagne. He came up to the front door which Adam opened. He slapped Dominic on the back and shook hands with Adam.

"Couldn't let today pass without a celebration. I've come to christen your new house. Now, where is your good wife? Which way will I find some glasses or shall we take it in turns to drink it out of the bottle?" he grinned.

Dominic at last found his voice.

"What are you doing here father? You are supposed to be looking after the business?"

"Rosie is quite capable of looking after the business for an afternoon and I thought I could be more help here," Sir Humphrey promptly replied.

"We are only half unloaded," Dominic tried to explain. "We can't stop to drink champagne."

"It won't take long," Sir Humphrey said cheerfully. "A couple of glasses will lift your spirits and renew your energy. Now let's find your wife. No doubt she will be in the kitchen."

Sir Humphrey led the way into the kitchen and the others followed him. They found Sally and Alice washing up the dirty dishes from lunchtime. Sir Humphrey went up and kissed them both.

"These ladies need a treat," he said loudly. "Now find some glasses."

Sally looked at Alice and laughed.

"We haven't any glasses," she said. "Only mugs."

"Then mugs it will have to be," Sir Humphrey said with enthusiasm. "This will be a first for me. I've drunk champagne out of many different containers but never out of a mug."

As he spoke the cork popped out of the bottle and Sally quickly handed him a mug. When everyone had a drink Sir Humphrey proposed a toast.

"To Dominic and Sally's new home. May everyone who lives in it be happy and prosperous."

He refilled the mugs until the bottle was empty. The party was going well until there was a knock at the kitchen door. The foreman was standing there wondering what all the noise was about.

"We've finished unloading the van," he said. "All except for a very large sideboard. Where do you want us to put it?"

Dominic looked at Sally.

"We will come and look at it," he said. "Perhaps it will have to go back to into storage with the other large pieces of furniture."

They went out of the kitchen and Sir Humphrey gave a loud sigh.

"I shall be moving in with Lady Monica soon and I shall have a house full of furniture to dispose of. There are many antique and hereditary pieces which I would like Dominic to have but I'm not sure he is going to have room for them."

"They will probably suit Kitson Manor more than this house," Adam said. "They will have to go into storage until the manor is restored."

Suddenly the phone started to ring. Sir Humphrey was nearest and he picked it up. The irate voice of Lady Monica could be heard by everyone.

"Where are you Humpy? I've been trying to reach you all day. You haven't forgotten that you are expected for dinner tonight? Sir Charles and his wife will be here."

"Calm yourself old gal," Sir Humphrey said sweetly. "Of course, I haven't forgotten. I'm on my way now. Lady Monica knows that I wouldn't forget about dinner," he said to the others. "I'll be there in plenty of time."

Adam looked at him and laughed.

"You will soon get used to being told what to do."

"I'm a free spirit," Sir Humphrey insisted. "At least I shall be when this divorce is settled. Now I must find Dominic and Sally but I shall come again next week and hope to see the new house in all its glory."

He shook hands with Adam and left the kitchen.

"I had better finish the washing up," Alice said. "I think we have done enough for one day."

Adam went to look for Dominic and found him talking to the foreman.

"Everything's unloaded," he said wearily, "but there is one more van

278

load tomorrow full of boxes and small pieces of furniture so it shouldn't take long to empty it. George and Gretchen will be arriving and I will bring them down in the afternoon."

"I'll come over in the morning to help Sally," Alice said. "We can at least get their rooms a bit tidier."

"I think we have done enough for one day. I don't know how to thank you," Dominic said sincerely.

"It will take you a while to get straight," Adam said, "but at least you have Sally's house which is neat and tidy."

Adam and Alice prepared to leave and Dominic and Sally were left in the house alone. They were standing in a room full of odd pieces of furniture and boxes of all shapes and sizes. Sally looked at Dominic and burst into tears. Immediately he put his arms around her and held her close. He waited until her sobs had subsided then he wiped away her tears.

"It has been a very stressful day," he said. "I've never worked so hard in all my life. Let's lock up and go back to our cosy little nest. I think we'll have fish and chips for supper."

Sally managed a little smile.

"Just like the first time," she said.

Dominic kissed her.

"Not quite," he said, softly. "It could be even better than the first time."

They switched off the lights and locked the doors, then they drove back to Sally's house.

"I need a shower before I have my supper," Dominic said as he went straight upstairs.

Sally put the kettle on and made a cup of tea. She sank down on the settee and took off her shoes. She put her tea on the coffee table but before she could drink it, she was fast asleep. She woke an hour later to the smell of fish and chips and suddenly she felt very hungry. Dominic came in with two separate packages and they ate them out of the paper. When the last bit was eaten Sally stood up.

"I feel much better," she said and went into the kitchen to wash her hands.

"One more van to unload tomorrow," Dominic said as he followed her. "Then we can take our time sorting things out. George and Gretchen will arrive tomorrow so we must make an effort to tidy up their rooms."

"I don't think I shall be returning to work this week. I must speak with Adam about it," Sally said.

"I must get back to London on Thursday. Goodness knows what father has been doing in the office."

"I think I've had enough of today," Sally decided. "Let's go to bed."

Sally had a quick shower and when they were both in bed she said:

"I shall miss my cosy little room. The bedroom in the new home is three times this size."

"You will get used to it," he said, smiling. "And it will be just as cosy to us as this one has been." He leaned over to kiss her. "I love you more than anything in the world," he said softly as he drew her closer to him.

"Oh Dominic, I love you too, more than I can say," she said as her hands caressed his face and she kissed him back.

They drifted into their own little world and did not notice the snow which was silently falling outside.

Adam woke up to a white world too.

"It's going to be a nightmare driving into work," he said to Leah.

"Do you have to go?" she asked anxiously.

"I can't expect the rest of the staff to make the effort and not go in myself," he replied. "But I don't think it would be a good idea for Alice to drive in this weather. Sally will have to manage on her own today."

He went to the shed to find a shovel and some old bits of carpet which he put in the boot of his car.

"Just in case," he said to Leah as he kissed her goodbye.

He drove carefully into work and arrived at the office quite early. He found a few of the staff had managed to come in but it was obvious that they would be short-staffed.

"I don't think we will have many customers today," he said to Barry. "We could probably close early this afternoon."

He went up to his office and was pleased to find that Julie was there.

"I think a nice hot cup of coffee is the best way to start today," he told her and she went off to make it.

At that moment the phone rang and Adam heard Bill's voice.

"My car won't start. I think it is frozen up," he said in a worried tone. "I shall have to catch the bus and I don't know what time I shall be in."

"Don't worry," Adam said. "We are not going to be busy. Why don't you just have a day at home? We have enough staff for today."

"Are you sure that is alright?" Bill asked anxiously. "I could do with a bit of a rest after all the activity of the past few weeks."

"Make yourself a cup of tea, Bill, curl up on the settee and go to sleep. That's what I would do."

"I think I'll follow your advice," he replied. "Tell Barry that I'll see him tomorrow."

Adam and Julie spent the morning studying the map on the wall and working out the distances between the various offices. At lunchtime, Adam walked up to his favourite bistro and had a bowl of soup. The office was very quiet all day and by three o'clock it was beginning to get dark outside. Adam gave the order to close the tills and by four o'clock they had all left.

Adam was glad to get home and find Leah already there. He parked the car on the grass and went indoors. He remembered that he had to order a taxi to take him to the station in the morning and he went into the lounge. Leah had made a cup of tea and they sat there talking about their day.

"I wonder how Dominic and Sally managed today?" he said and picked up the phone. "I'll try them at the new house first."

Sally answered, sounding very tired.

"We are just about to leave. We have been here since nine o'clock this morning and I am worn out. We can't move for boxes but at least we have managed to sort out George and Gretchen's rooms."

Adam chatted to her for a few minutes then he put the phone down and turned to Leah.

"I must keep in touch with Sally," he said. "She sounded quite stressed. It will be good when Gretchen and George are there to keep her company." He sat down next to Leah and put an arm around her. "I shall be away for the next two days," he said in a voice full of concern. "Will you be alright?"

"I'll be fine," Leah answered. "If we have any more snow then I shan't drive into school."

"I hope the trains are running on time. I expect London will be a really slushy place. I'm not looking forward to my trip. I think I'll order that taxi now and allow myself a bit of extra time."

Leah stood up and went into the kitchen to start preparing the dinner. Adam made his phone call then he took off his shoes and stretched out on the settee. Before long he was fast asleep and didn't wake up until dinner was on the table. After they had eaten, they all sat in the lounge with their coffee.

"I don't like the snow," said Jessica. "I hope it soon disappears. I'm going to bed early."

She stood up and went upstairs to her bedroom. Alice was surprised at Jessica's comment and followed her up the stairs. She found her lying on her bed with tears streaming down her cheeks. Alice gently wiped away her tears.

"What is it?" she asked, quietly. "What don't you like about the snow?"

Jessica hesitated for a few minutes.

"It snowed last year and I couldn't go to school. I had to stay in my room all day because Jonathon's friends came round and they were having snowball fights. They called me names because I wouldn't go out and join them and they kept throwing snowballs at my bedroom window and I thought they would break it and Dad would have said it was my fault and he would have been mad with me."

Alice put her arms around her.

"That is all in the past now. Don't worry about it. No-one is going to throw snowballs at you. If the snow is still there in the morning then you can stay at home with me."

"The boys were throwing snowballs at playtime this morning," Jessica said. "So, I went and hid in the cloakroom."

"It won't hurt to have a couple of days off school," Alice said. "You've still got those workbooks which grandma brought home for you. Now go and wash your face and you will feel better. I'll tuck you up in bed with your teddy and you will soon be fast asleep."

Alice went back downstairs and told her mother and father what had happened.

"I wonder how many more bad memories are locked away in her mind? We must be careful to be aware of any signs of worry," said Adam, thoughtfully. "I'm not going to be late to bed tonight, Leah. I shall have to be up early in the morning."

"Bed will be the warmest place," she replied as she stood up. "I think I'll join you."

Chapter Twenty-Six

When Adam woke the next morning, he was pleased to see that it hadn't snowed during the night.

"The main roads will be quite clear," he said to Leah, "but the side roads are still very icy. Do be careful if you decide to go to school."

He went off to the station and was relieved to find that the trains were running normally. He was soon in London and reporting in at the PM's office. He had a busy day of meetings and was glad to get back to his room at the hotel. He knew that Dominic would be in Oxford after meeting Gretchen and George at the airport and he didn't think that Sir Humphrey would want to venture out on such a cold night, so he had dinner alone in the restaurant. He sat in the lounge reading a newspaper until his eyes were getting heavy and he went to his room. The first thing he did was to phone Leah. They had a long conversation and Adam was pleased to hear that everyone was fine. He opened his briefcase and took out some papers to check over but he found it hard to concentrate and soon gave up trying, deciding to just watch the news headlines then go to bed.

The next day was very busy again and he was glad to be finished by mid-afternoon. He collected his luggage from the hotel and was soon on his way back to Oxford. He was relieved to get home to a nice warm house as he stretched out on the settee. That evening he caught up with the family news and in particular, the arrangements for Alice's wedding.

"It's all under control, Dad," she said. "And the best bit of news is that our offer has been accepted on the house around the corner."

Adam stood up and kissed her.

"That really is good news," he said, clapping his hands. "When will it be available?"

"The completion date is two weeks after the wedding. Bill had already given notice on his house but he has managed to extend it by two weeks so we shan't have to worry about what to do with the furniture. Now we have to decide where we are going to live for those two weeks."

"Why don't you spend your honeymoon in a modern apartment with a view of the river?" Adam said in a casual way.

Alice looked at him in surprise.

"That would indeed be a luxury," she started to say but she stopped when she saw that Adam was laughing. "Do you mean that we could use your apartment?"

"That is exactly what I mean," he said with a smile. "I'm sure you would be most comfortable and you can stay there for as long as you need it. Jessica can stay with us but you can see her at any time."

"Thank you, Dad, it is a most generous offer," Alice said sincerely. "I'll talk to Bill about it."

"Your mother and I will be going to Spain during the Easter holidays. Dominic has arranged for us to have a holiday in his Spanish villa so you can both stay here with Jessica while we are away."

"We are hoping to have a proper holiday later in the year. Bill has no intention of taking time off work."

"That is good," Adam replied. "Barry will need him in the office while I am away."

"Everything is in place for the wedding. I need to take Jessica shopping this weekend to buy her a new dress."

"Thank goodness I shan't need to go shopping," he said. "I've already got a nearly new suit. Will you need to go shopping, Leah?"

"Jen and I are going next week. I'm going to buy a new hat. I don't need you to come with me."

"I'm pleased to hear that," Adam said with a sigh of relief. "Shopping is my least favourite occupation."

Alice filled them in with more details of the wedding and the evening passed quickly.

"I'm looking forward to a quiet weekend," Adam said. "I intend to sleep for most of it."

"I don't think Peter will be bringing the children down," Leah said. "It is best for them to stay at home in the warm during this cold weather." She turned to Alice. "I know you have invited them all to the wedding but I can't help wondering if Janet will find an excuse not to come."

"It won't matter if she stays away," said Adam. "The children are all well behaved and we can help to look after them. Have you heard back from Thomas and Harriet?"

"Thomas has decided not to come but Harriet is trying to book a flight. She will know for sure by next Saturday," replied Alice. "That will be just a week before the wedding. It will be nice to see her."

Adam stood up and yawned.

"I've had a very busy week," he said, "especially with the snowy conditions. I'm going to have an early night and probably a late morning."

He kissed them both and left the room.

"I will make a cup of tea, Mum," said Alice. "Then it will be my bedtime. I do hope that the weather will improve."

When she came back with the tea, she sat on the settee by Leah.

"Dad seemed to be very tired this evening," she said. "I hope he is alright."

"He is a very busy man. He is holding down two responsible jobs and still finds time to help Dominic with his move. We must make sure that he has time to relax when he is at home. I'm glad the wedding plans are going so well," she said as she stood up. "I'm sure it will be a very happy day. I'm going to leave you to put the lights out tonight. I'm going to bed."

She kissed Alice and went upstairs.

Adam had a quiet couple of days at home and by Monday morning he was feeling much better. He was pleased to find Sally at work and called her into his office.

"How was your weekend?" he asked her.

"Busy, very busy but thank goodness Gretchen and George are back and they have been a great help. We have managed to sort out the lounge and the kitchen but we still have to do the dining room. We are using one of the bedrooms as a storeroom for all the boxes and we have been thinking about the extra pieces of furniture which we shall need."

"Have you sorted out the bedrooms yet? Have you actually slept in your new house?"

Sally laughed.

"We haven't found the sheets and duvet yet, so we have been returning to my house each evening. Gretchen is going to look for them today. It has made such a difference having two pairs of extra hands and George has been carrying all the boxes upstairs."

"I'm so glad you have some extra help," he said. "You really needed it and it will be a relief to Dominic too. I'm sure he is looking forward to coming home to a tidy house so then he can concentrate on other things."

They settled down to work and soon had two visits sorted out for the following week. Adam was hoping for a few quiet days in the run-up to Alice's wedding. He was relieved that Bill and Alice had organised it by themselves and that he only had a minor role to play. He was woken from his daydream by a knock on his office door. It was Bill with two cups of coffee. Bill sat down and they began to discuss the business of the day.

"We have had a lot of interest in booking the lecture room for various events," Bill said. "I was wondering if you might need it at any time?"

Adam shook his head.

"I haven't anything planned," he replied, "unless you have something in mind?"

"I would like to organise the first of our own educational seminars and I thought you might like to be there as well?"

"Yes, I would like to be there," Adam said with enthusiasm. "When have you in mind?"

"I thought early in the summer term, possibly mid-May?"

"That will be fine, Bill. Just make sure it takes place at the beginning of the week. Now tell me, is everything ready for Saturday? Is there anything I can do to help?"

"Everything is ready," Bill said with a smile. "All you have to do is deliver my bride to me."

"I can do that. I'm first-rate at delivering brides," Adam said with a laugh. "We are expecting everyone to come back to our house after the reception and we shall continue the celebrations into the evening."

"I shall need to get my mother and brother back to the hotel," Bill said looking worried.

"I'll call a taxi when they are ready to go," Adam said. "I doubt if any of the guests will be fit to drive them."

They continued to chat until Adam's phone rang. Bill left the office.

"Mr West wishes to speak with you," Julie said.

"Put him through," Adam said at once.

"Just a quick call, Adam, to say that I will provide the champagne for the evening party and I was wondering what Bill and Alice would like as a wedding present?"

"Thank you for the champagne, Dominic. Have you spoken to Sally about the present? She will have some suggestions I'm sure."

"I'll ask her this evening and let you know tomorrow. We are both looking forward to it. I'll see you on Saturday."

Adam looked in his diary and found no appointments for that afternoon so he called Sally into his office.

"I want to arrange two visits to fairly local offices for early next week," he said. "Can you check with them this afternoon so that the visits can be put in the diary?"

Sally went off to make the phone calls and Adam's thoughts turned to the arrangements for the wedding. It was only four days away and he had to check with Leah this evening, in case there was anything he had forgotten. Sally knocked on the door and came in with the diary.

"I've booked you in for two visits each morning," she said.

"That's fine," he replied. "I'll just check that everything is Ok in the main office then I shall be leaving. I have some shopping which I need to do."

He was soon on his way home and the house was quiet when he arrived. He took off his shoes and lay on the settee. It was very peaceful and he soon drifted off to sleep.

The rest of the week passed quickly and Friday evening soon came around. Leah did the last-minute shopping and Adam made sure that the drinks were organised. On Saturday morning everyone was up early. After breakfast, they made sure that the furniture was in place and Leah laid out the nibbles and the party food on the dining room table. The flowers were delivered as arranged and soon it was time for everyone to get dressed. Leah wore the outfit which she had worn to Sally's wedding and Adam wore his best suit with a pale grey tie. Jessica looked quite grown up in a light brown dress with a matching jacket. She was very excited and couldn't sit still. Alice came down wearing a cream silk dress with a matching coat. Her shoes and handbag were light brown and she had a single rose in her hair.

"Do I look alright?" she asked anxiously.

Adam went to her and put his arms around her.

"You look fabulous!" he said. "I shall be a very proud father."

"I'm really nervous," she said. "I'm shaking all over."

"You'll be fine," Adam assured her. "It is time to go."

The drive to the registry office only took five minutes. Adam parked the car in the car park and Alice was relieved to see that Bill's car was already there. They went up the stairs and stopped outside an ornate door. Leah opened the door and went in. The other guests were already there and they stood up as Leah entered. The music changed to the Wedding March and Alice walked down the aisle followed by Jessica. Adam held on to her tightly until she was standing by Bill. The registrar began the ceremony and soon it was all over. They signed the register together with Adam and Bill's mother and then they greeted their guests. Bill and Alice drove to the reception in Bill's car. His mother and brother went with Barry and Jen. Jessica went with Sally and Dominic and Peter drove Janet, Lucy and Benji in his car. Adam and Leah went alone.

The hotel was about a fifteen-minute drive away and everyone arrived safely. The meal was delicious with just a couple of glasses of wine because of the drive back to Adam's house.

"Bill," said Adam. "How would you feel about waiting until we are back home before having the speeches? The champagne is already on ice."

"I think that is a good idea. No doubt it will loosen a few tongues," he said with a laugh.

He went off to speak to Barry who then announced the slight change of plan to the guests. Adam went off to pay the bill and soon it was time to leave.

When everyone had returned to the house, Adam opened the

champagne and the party really began. After half an hour, Barry tapped his glass and announced the speeches. They all gathered in the lounge.

"Charge your glasses," said Barry. "This may take some time."

Adam made sure that everyone had a full glass and Barry stood up. He started by saying:

"It is my duty as best man to propose a toast to the bridesmaid. So, I want you all to raise your glasses to Jessica, who has discharged her duties so well."

Everyone looked at Jessica. She blushed and Alice put an arm around her.

"It is also my duty," continued Barry, "to propose a toast to the bride and groom but before I do that, I want to be sure that you all know Bill as well as I do. Our friendship goes back a long way to our time at University."

He proceeded to tell them some of the antics they got up to whilst they were there. Bill sat there looking more and more embarrassed until finally Barry exhausted his supply of jokes and turned to the more serious business of proposing a toast to the bride and groom. They all raised their glasses and then Bill stood up.

"I'm not going to deny anything that Barry has said about me but I am going to make the excuse that I was young and fancy-free. I would also like to remind Barry that he was a willing accomplice on many of the occasions which he has so graphically described. I must now turn to more important matters and say thank you to everyone for sharing in our happy day. On behalf of my wife and myself, I should like to propose a toast to everyone in this room for being here at our celebration. But I particularly want to thank Adam and Leah for welcoming us into their home this evening. Let us all raise our glasses."

They all drank a toast and Adam made sure that the glasses were refilled. Leah handed around the nibbles and soon the hum of conversation filled the room. Bill and Alice mingled with their guests until Alice went upstairs to change out of her wedding dress. Sally went to help her.

"Where are you going tonight?" she asked.

"Dad has given us the key to his apartment," Alice replied. "So, we are not going far. Bill wants us to see his mother and brother before they leave tomorrow morning. We hope to stay in the apartment until the house sale is completed then we shall be able to arrange for the furniture to be delivered and we can move in."

"I hope it all goes smoothly for you," Sally said. "We are hoping to move into our new house next week. It is nearly sorted out then I'll be able to relieve you of all those boxes."

They went back downstairs and Alice and Bill said goodbye to their guests. Finally, Alice turned to Jessica.

"I'll be waiting here for you when you get home from school on Monday," she said. "Grandma and Grandad will look after you. Don't forget I love you very much."

Jessica's eyes filled with tears as she hugged her mother. Bill came over and put his arms around both of them.

"Don't worry," he whispered to Jessica. "I'll look after her."

They left in Bill's car and ten minutes later they were in the apartment. Bill took Alice in his arms.

"Alone at last," he said, softly. "I've been wanting to do this all day."

He kissed her tenderly; Alice responded and they stood locked together in their love.

Meanwhile, back at the house, the party continued until Bill's mother spoke to Adam.

"I think we should be returning to the hotel," she said. "We have a long drive tomorrow and we need a good night's sleep."

"I will call you a taxi," he said and picked up his phone.

The taxi arrived ten minutes later and they all said goodbye to Bill's mother and brother. They both thanked Adam and Leah for their hospitality and for a very happy day before they left.

Jessica was half asleep on the settee and Leah went to her.

"Time for bed, Jessica. It has been a very busy day."

They went upstairs together and soon Jessica was tucked up in bed. She put her arms around Leah's neck.

"I know Bill will look after Mummy. Soon we will be a proper family."

Leah hugged her and kissed her goodnight. She went back downstairs with tears in her eyes. Adam saw her and went over to her.

"Are you alright?" he asked urgently.

Leah nodded her head.

"I was just remembering how Alice and Jessica came to us and thank you, God, for this happy day."

"It has been a very happy day," he said. "I shall miss Alice and Jessica not being here when I come home."

"I shall miss them too," Leah said sadly. "It means that I shall have to do all the cooking."

Adam laughed.

"Perhaps I have undiscovered skills which will help you out. We are going to have to get used to being self-sufficient."

Before long, Jen and Barry decided it was time to go home and soon after Dominic and Sally left too. Adam and Leah looked at the empty glasses and half-eaten bowls of nibbles.

"We will clear it up tomorrow," Adam decided. "I am ready for bed."

"I feel emotionally exhausted," Leah said with a sigh.

"So, do I," Adam said quietly. "We both need a good night's sleep."

He turned towards Leah and kissed her then lay back on the pillow and was soon fast asleep. Leah stayed awake going over the events of the day in her mind. She suddenly realised that it would be just the two of them in future. They would have to adapt to being on their own again. She began to wonder how they would manage. The thought worried her and she had a restless night.

Chapter Twenty-Seven

Adam and Leah gradually became used to having the house to themselves but Leah especially missed Alice. They had shared the housework and the cooking and Leah found it hard to do everything. It was not long before she resigned her teaching post and concentrated on her home tuition pupils. She felt a lot more relaxed being in control of her own timetable and she had more energy to support her husband.

Adam continued to be very busy at both his jobs. He held regular meetings with all the managers in his area and the venue was always in high demand for the use of other local businesses. Bill was kept busy with organising seminars for young graduates and Adam found that he was relying on him more and more. He had already made up his mind that Bill would succeed him as area manager. He was beginning to get tired and had a couple of health scares.

Leah begged him to see a doctor but Adam refused.

"I'm not ill," he said firmly. "I'm just tired."

He carried on working until one day he collapsed in the office with chest pains. He was taken to hospital and Leah hurried to his side. After two days he was allowed home but the doctors explained that what had happened had been a warning and that he must change his lifestyle. He resigned his position as advisor to the Prime Minister and received a knighthood in recognition of his years of loyal service.

Adam spoke to Dominic about the appointment of Bill as area manager and he immediately agreed to it. Adam gradually passed all his responsibilities in the building society to Bill. He was confident that Bill would keep up the high standards that he had maintained throughout his working life.

Adam's condition gradually deteriorated but Leah still insisted on looking after him by herself. Finally, Alice and Bill decided to move in with Leah to give her some support.

Adam was getting weaker and Leah spent all the day at his bedside. Bill and Alice stood at the bottom of the bed but they could only watch and wait. Adam's breathing was becoming shallow but he managed to call out:

"Leah," he gasped. "Don't leave me."

Leah squeezed his hand.

"Don't worry my love," she said softly. "I'll never leave you. I'm coming with you."

She stood up and walked around the bed. Alice and Bill stepped back to let her pass but she never even saw them. She slipped under the double duvet beside Adam and held his hand. He gave a final sigh and stopped breathing. Leah heard that sigh and she knew that her task was over. A great feeling of peace engulfed her and she felt as if her heart would burst with love. She saw, in her mind's eye, the two of them walking along the road which led to that golden city up on the hill and she knew that everything was alright. She gave a sigh and went into an everlasting sleep.

Alice and Bill were still standing at the foot of the bed. Bill put his arm around Alice.

"Together in life, together in death," he said softly as they left the room. They stopped in the doorway and looked back.

"Together forever," Bill said as they went downstairs.

Epilogue

Adam made a great success of both his jobs and was highly esteemed by his colleagues. Leah resigned her teaching post and was kept busy with her home tuition and Adam's social responsibilities.

Alice and Bill bought a house and eventually had a son of their own. Jessica did very well at school and excelled at all sports.

Dominic and Sally moved into Kitson Manor after living in their first home for three years. They too had a son and the two boys became inseparable friends. But that is another story.

Available worldwide from Amazon and all good bookstores

Michael Terence
Publishing

www.mtp.agency

www.facebook.com/mtp.agency

@mtp_agency

Lightning Source UK Ltd.
Milton Keynes UK
UKHW010638270521
384471UK00001B/28